Wolf Magick

Secret Mysteries of Draakensky

Paula Cappa

PUBLISHED BY CRYSTAL LAKE PUBLISHING
WHERE STORIES COME ALIVE!

Crystal Lake Publishing
www.CrystalLakePub.com

Join the Crystal Lake community today on our newsletter and Patreon!
https://linktr.ee/CrystalLakePublishing

Download our latest catalog here.
https://geni.us/CLPCatalog

ISBN: 978-1-968532-57-4

Cover art:
Joanna Halerz—jo.widomska@gmail.com

Layout:
Lori Michelle—www.theauthorsalley.com

Wolf Magick, Secret Mysteries of Draakensky is a stand-alone novel, the second in an epic storytelling that began with *Draakensky, A Supernatural Tale of Magick and Romance.*

Follow us on Amazon:

WELCOME

TO ANOTHER

CRYSTAL LAKE PUBLISHING
CREATION

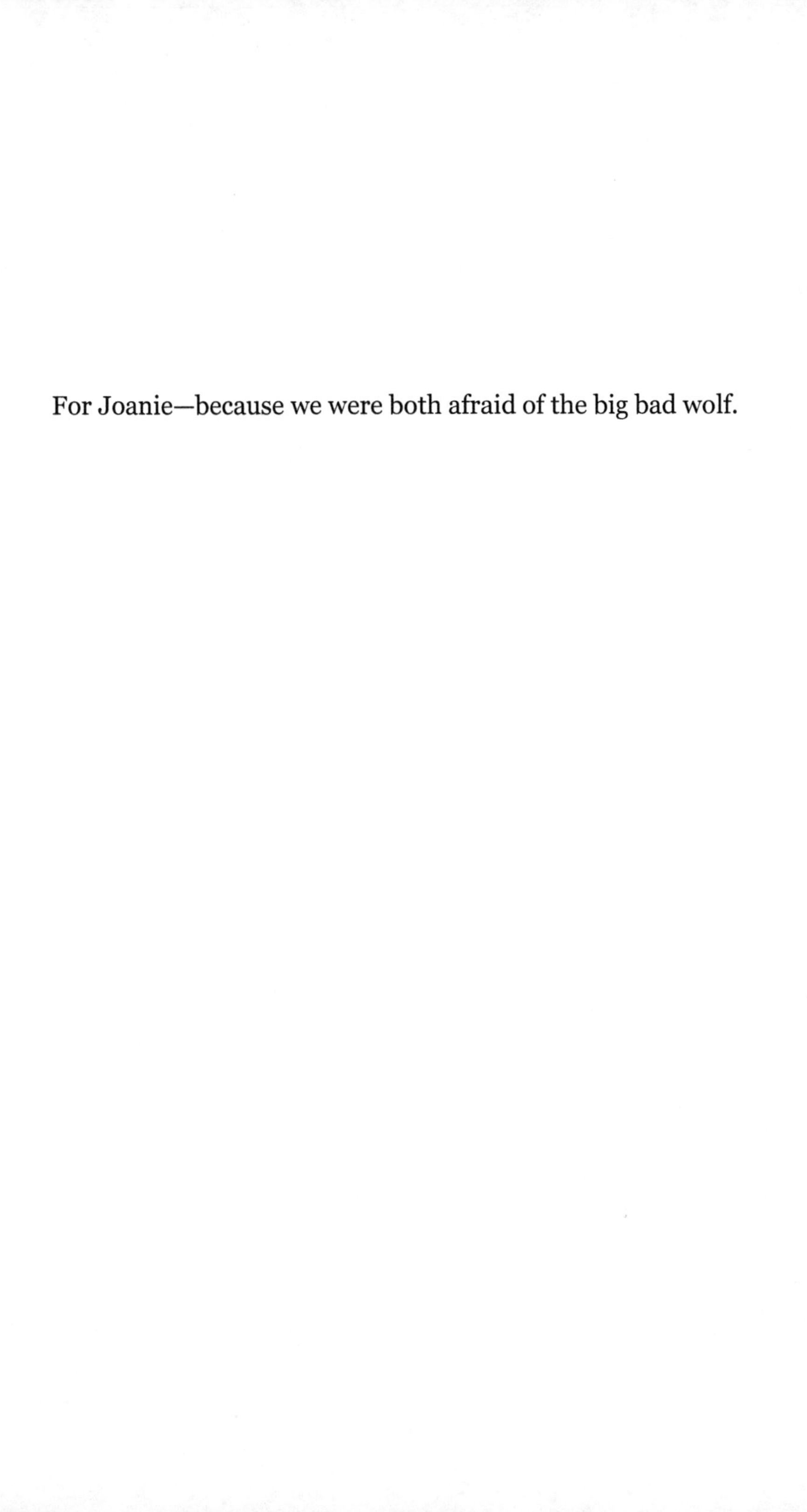

For Joanie—because we were both afraid of the big bad wolf.

Table of Contents

Book II

Book I

"There is in each person, in every animal, bird, and plant,
a star which mirrors, or matches, or is in some sense
the same as a star in the heavens."
—Attributed to Paracelsus

Prologue

The Realm Walker

Inside the peace of the wild forest, the sky tore open the darkness. Earth drew her magick across the northeast landscape while the man slept in his chair in a wood-smoked cabin.

He woke to wolf howls. Their voices grew thick with melancholy calls: the Lord of the Wolf accepted the summons without question.

Under flash of red and scent of blood, the wolf lord listened to the howls fade into a lone cry. Within seconds, he called up his enchantment. His body drummed stinging rhythms into his skull. His bones stretched. His muscles beat out aching pulses. Hair sprouted into fur. Hands and feet shifted to form clawed paws, and the jaw vibrated until it became a snout.

The Lord of the Wolf was no savage werewolf. Powers hid behind his glittering eyes. He was no moon stalker nor the clever figment from the imagination. This man triggered his highest skill to *image forth* himself into a fully blasted male gray wolf, a warrior with a staggering prowl.

Skilled in the art of wolf magick, he expanded his

consciousness. The wolf lord's heart raced within a triple-spiraled web of light swirling around him. That meant his heart had endured the transformation and the enchanted power that would seal him outside of Earth's realm.

Ready for the journey, he surged into the magickal mist that would transport him to the northwestern Alaskan landscape. Five red-throated loons escorted him to the breakout region.

His reliable travelers with their swift wings leveled the winds, their beaks directing. Soon the wolf lord rocketed across the freezing Adirondack Mountains at a dizzying speed. In hyper-time, he blurred over massive tracks of Canadian forests and rivers of the Alaskan north, zooming above rocky terrains, over tundra with the scent of black spruce.

He made one final leap beyond the glaciers, landing on a crooked hump, its sides breaking with snow under a starry dome. Beneath the trees, a lone she-wolf lay shivering, her tongue draped over her teeth, each breath scarce. She bled out, her belly wounds convulsing, staining the snow brown and red.

Such a young beauty, in silver and gray fur, stunning bronze on the face, like the essence of a blossom now withering. He could not save this one, not even with his magick as Lord of the Wolf, not even with his wolf heart as Finnwolf.

Sniffing the air, he caught the scent of musk, earthy loam, and blood from the bullet wounds that had torn her abdomen. Wolf hunters and their magnum rifles. The hunter had shot her twice. Yet this brave female, cunning and devious, refused to be taken and had fled to this copse to die in peace among the trees.

Several yards off, a shadow wolf patrolled.

The ghostly creature waited in secret silence. He hackled his back, fur spiking. Watchful, the shadow wolf stalked, primed to snatch the life force when the she-wolf's soul lingered in the body at the last exhale.

White triangles shone on both sides of his black head—the mark of the Ripper. This was the alpha male of his pack. He swung around, solid as iron, and snapped his jaws.

Finnwolf snapped back. He growled a warning. Standing his ground, the wolf lord paused, giving the shadow wolf opportunity to retreat, to honor Providence, a gesture that often failed. The Ripper, a defiant, ferocious shadow wolf with bone-socketed eyes and fanged jowls, stomped the ground.

Circling each other, Finnwolf's eyes blazed golden while the Ripper's flamed crimson inside black sockets. Above, nighthawks sent their caws in harsh notes. Stars observed in a sturdy silence; the constellations brightened their light.

The Ripper growled, thrashing his head—soul hungry. He surged up like a blackened, twisted propeller, leaping straight for Finnwolf's neck.

Finnwolf shot higher into the air, his claws hooked out. He came down, charging his highest wolf magick into a mesmerizing net of whistling arrows. The bolts rocketed into the Ripper's massive chest.

The shadow wolf spun into blackish streaks that buzzed loudly across the snow. Evergreens shivered in the wind. Nighthawks gathered the streaks on their wings and flew above the treetops.

Starlight drew the Ripper up, rolling his shadow spirit back to the pits and tunnels of Black Wolf Realm.

No seals or barriers held strong enough to confine shadow wolves for long or subvert the pods of the past. In magick, nothing can be destroyed, only transferred, honoring ancestral Providence.

How many times had Finnwolf sent the savage Ripper and his

relentless pack of shadow wolves back to their lost realm? A wearisome number. A wearisome fate for each one of them. As Finnwolf, he executed their *return to the realm,* which remained his task by oath and old bones.

These shadow wolves with their unquenchable hunger owed their souls to darkness. Soul-eaters, they were, hunting nourishment to infuse their shadows with a living essence—*Anam* it was named, "soul," *life's vigor* in the Gaelic sense. Absorbing the blood of a newly dead wolf fed their withering wolf souls.

With the Ripper gone, the nighthawks soared back to their nests.

Finnwolf hurried to the she-wolf. The wolf lord lowered his legs, stretched out, and warmed her body with his chest. Her heart's weakened taps dragged her out of earthly time. He spun a thick web to bind their space together, then chanted his power-song in soft notes, sending her the meaning of each howl.

The wilderness summoned me to you. I am Finnwolf, the realm walker. My path is safe with light of blue. I carry you because I am Guardian. Rest yourself in my command.

Her tail raised slightly, a gesture of trust. At her last breath, she released the aroma of fragrant perfume, revealing she had spent many summers running meadows of violet lupine flowers. Her exhale released a moan, her plaintive goodbye to Mother Earth. She let go, eyes fully open.

If not for Finnwolf, she would have died abandoned, shivering in pain, nose pressed in snow, her soul in peril of being consumed by the wolves of Black Wolf Realm. Finnwolf carried her sparkling light wrapped around his chest like a banner—his heartbeat keeping her safe. He drank in the stars, the threshold guardians guiding him through the veil to the roiling sea. There he searched for Manannán mac Lir, Celtic son of the sea, with his magickal white steed to lead the way across to the Otherworld. Lady of the Stars presented her lights positioned between the constellations Cepheus and Draco.

Knowing the cosmic geography ahead, the slender borders between worlds and secret portals, Finnwolf gathered his strength, his head near bursting with the Lady's starlight. He traveled south toward the realms. He used his best skills through the shrouded winding tunnels lined with fanged serpents and lurking beasts ready to strike from their blackened pits.

Souls were the same in all living creatures, man or beast. All wolves deserved safe travel to the Otherworld's starry wolf realms, lest they become lost between the realms or in parallel chasms, or worse—consumed by the shadow wolves of Black Wolf Realm.

Finnwolf skirted the tunnel's gaps where he knew the writhing serpents hid. He leaped the chasms like the champion he was, claws firmly gripping the edges and safely skidding as if he had wings.

The wolf lord's blue path opened, rolling them toward Star Wolf Realm. Upon reaching the raftered gate, though he did not observe it, Finnwolf knew the she-wolf would now manifest herself into her otherness form and gallop away to her family of wolves. She would rub wolf heads and prance in the fields of purple and white lupine. She would belong to her pack again and be fearlessly free.

He turned away as was his pledge, his heart aching to join her in the brilliant Star Wolf Realm, to race the green terrain with her, to sleep with furry wolf-bellies at his side and savor their loyal affections.

As he departed, he named the she-wolf Lupine, after the

sweetness of her breath. He burned the image of her in his memory. *Lupine, we will meet again. By the stars, I swear. Everything in nature holds us together.*

Finnwolf returned faithfully to his earthly abode, to linear time, the red-throated loons guiding him safely back over the Adirondacks. In his wolf magick, he belonged to what ends; he belonged to what begins. Here, as always, the Lord of the Wolf downshifted his body back into the Celtic man he was in linear time, living in the countryside of Lewisboro, New York.

Shaking the stardust from his blond hair, the arc of night upon his back, he entered his cabin surrounded by tree spirits, rock, cold moss and mud, and the peace of wild forest.

His oak horsehead wand leaned against the brick fireplace; his Mask of the Red Mouth hung on a timber. He dropped into his high-backed chair, a three-headed wolf sculpture—one head at the crown of the chair, twin wolves carved into the arms.

The Lord of the Wolf grasped his hands on the arms, caressing the wolf heads beneath each palm. On the mantel, a clock's visible coils, springs, wheels, and pendulum rocked fate forward. For this mage, time moved beyond linear. A braid of past, present, and future time with secret doors begged to be opened. Which keys would he need? What knowledge was he missing? Searching for that knowledge became an ever-present quest.

Exhausted from the journey, blue eyes fixed on the balls of ash in the cold hearth, throat swelling with the sweet taste of lupine, the man Matthew Liam Sexton burst into an unspeakable release of tears.

Chapter One

Shadow Wolves

In his green barn house in Bedford, New York, surrounded by pine and hemlocks, Marc Sexton swore to cast off all shadows. Not just the shadows of day or night; Marc swore to cast off his lurking fear of shadow wolves.

Their spectral shapes hovered on the bedroom wall—which woke him at random, triggered by what, he could only guess. He renounced the blackened forms flaunting their brute ears that loomed so high their shadowy heads stretched onto the ceiling.

The voice of his father, Matthew Liam Sexton, surfaced—deep, smooth, captivating. *Your wolf magick lives inside your soul, Marc. If you wish to perform your own wolf magick, my boy, you'll have to swear off all thoughts of the mere supernatural. Our wolf magick is far greater.*

"I don't wish it," Marc had recalled answering Da, a quaver holding each word.

Even though it had been many years since that conversation when he was ten years old, the words still haunted Marc at age thirty-nine. The stinging disappointment on his father's face at the rejection of wolf magick, the way he ran his fingers through his blond hair as if to deny the answer—and the pain saturating his blue eyes—never could Marc wipe that crushing moment from his memory.

The specters on the wall foretold the monstrous shadow wolves were stalking closer than ever before. Marc moved to the bedroom window: on the pond and surrounding woods, a calm moon rested over the twenty beauties in his ogham tree grove. Tree spirits soothed and shed goodness, his magickal beings of green kin—oak and ash, willow, pine, birch. Apple and hazel. Hawthorn and blackthorn. Rowan, alder, and holly, all waiting for his greeting every day. And his splendid owls, thirty-nine of them, visited the tree grove regularly in spectacular flocks.

Moonlight shimmered on the pond's smooth surface. Were those loons flying over the water, red throats blazing? Five of them faithfully returned to his pond every April, but he had yet to see them, and it would be May 1st tomorrow. Beltaine, the Celtic magickal festival of fire.

At sunset on Beltaine, Marc would build a bonfire of rowan and oak in his stone fire pit by the pond to welcome summer. To celebrate sun and stars. To celebrate the woman he loved, Charlotte Knight, and give her a taste of the Celtic tradition. Champagne, roasted salmon, Green Man salad, and brown bread baked with the family's world-famous Sexton Irish Whiskey.

He had commissioned Alice Eve, his *floral maestro*, to make a wildflower head-wreath for Charlotte to wear—kept cool in the fridge. The engagement ring, a generous emerald-cut sapphire, blue as the deep sky, was kept safe in his dresser drawer. Would she be dazzled by it? Fall into his arms? He could hardly wait to slip it on her finger.

Thundering broke his reverie. He recognized the drumbeats

penetrating his head, enchantment suddenly upon him. Feeling feverish, body aching, limbs tightening and expanding, Marc fought it off. He willed the drumbeats away, dreading the summons.

Determined will is the beginning of all magickal operations. How often had he recalled Paracelsus's quote at moments like this?

Falling into bed, fingers surrounding the silver wolf pendant at his neck, he drew up his highest will for protection. A clawing wind burst through the open windows. He rose to shut them as screech owls broke out their warnings. Blinded briefly by moonlight, he glanced to the far side of his property.

A pack of humped shadow wolves emerged, skulking between the trees. Sturdy, like bone and flesh, legs muscular as lions, they bore a swinging weight, stomping across the lawn. At least a dozen wolf eyes shone with vapory fire, fearless and unfettered, these snarling hunters, the Ripper pack of Black Wolf Realm.

His father had warned him: *Beware of shadowing*—words said on the day the man died.

The largest wolf came forward, black head flaring white triangles on both sides—the Ripper, the pack's alpha male.

Marc's body responded automatically with sharp energy accelerating down his spine. Drumming broke deeper into his forehead. The triple-spiral web spun light over him, urging his body into a power shift. He beat back the urge to surrender. He would *not* surrender to the summons.

Wherever his mind went, his magickal energy would flow. Again, Marc held his silver wolf pendant. He would not look upon these wolves. He would not speak aloud the name of the alpha wolf of Black Wolf Realm—no switch-words to trigger their power.

"You will not hunt me."

Drumbeats echoed up from his gut, surging his body, racing his heart to power up the shift. Refusing to look at the triple spiral tightening around him, he heightened his will, speaking his incantations and reversals against the transformation. The wolf pendant grew hot on his neck.

Marc raised two fists above his chest, invoking the words that his grandmother Mamó had taught him to resist the shift into Finnwolf. *Fist your hands, cross them upon your chest like an X. Use all your strength and speak the incantations. Image forth your star magick.*

Moving toward the bedroom door, Marc placed each foot down firmly. With each footing, he connected to his willful heart. Repeating the incantations, crossing the carpet, beating his wrists on his chest, he projected his life force to abort the transformation.

At the door the triple spiral ruptured. The elements coalesced, then dissipated with a dull ringing.

The enchantment broken, he crossed into the hallway. Marc climbed the stairs to the third-story attic of his renovated barn. On the landing, before the door, at the bookcase stuffed with his father's books, he withdrew Da's navy blue volume—Yeats's *Collected Poetry*. He opened to "When You Are Old" and withdrew the key. With a *snap*, he opened the lock to his secret chamber, then returned the key to Yeats.

When he pushed open the door, darkness flowed out. Marc paused, as he usually did before stepping in. He knew he didn't possess the high magickal skills of his father. Nature magick was more Marc's talent, and celestial magick, certainly—his star magick remained the sacred gift from the water goddess Vivienne, never to be misused or abused. And he'd be nowhere without his father's advice on intellectual magick:

The present time must spread out and disappear, like a ripple behind a duck as it floats away. The past must unwind and coil into a drumming energy field.

Marc entered stepping softly. Outside, shadow wolves howled their songs from his ogham tree grove. Savage and demanding. Stomping the earth. Black Wolf Realm on the hunt.

His body clenched. *Da, what battle is this now? Please answer.*

Silence.

He listened deeper. The consistent pattern of that silence, Da's tumultuous silence, clung to him. "Answer. Where are you? Give me something Da, some sign!"

Three words surfaced, the same three words that had been haunting him for weeks.

Sharpen your sword.

Chapter Two

White Spring Phantoms

Charlotte Knight buckled herself into the seat belt, the two-hour United Airlines flight from Chicago on its descent to Westchester County Airport, New York. Returning to Bedford after twelve days of packing up her apartment, she was returning to Marc Sexton with her whole life packed up in cartons shipped off to Draakensky Windmill Estate.

She would not miss city life; Chicago blew gritty winds with a crushing populace. After selling off most of her furnishings and housewares from her telephone-booth-sized kitchen to the new tenant, she had happily closed the door and departed.

Yet, her childhood years living in Long Grove with Aunt Loretta would remain her dearest of memories, as would her *Be Joyful* years with Sister James as her guardian at St. Sophia's convent. One thing was certain—after the convent closed, those dreaded foster care years during her teens would be easier to forget now. *Break free of the old fences*, Sister James had said at their bittersweet goodbye.

The jet plane hit the runway exactly on time, landing smooth as a loon on a still lake. During the drive out of the airport—Marc had insisted on treating her to the Bedford Car Service—she enjoyed the vibrancy of May 1st's green landscapes. When the driver turned onto Route 172 and sped past the familiar yellow barns and horse paddocks, a glossy black stallion behind a white fence stood in the sun-filled morning. His gigantic dark eyes faced her, the head enlarged as if wearing a mask of bones, showing off wickedness. She blinked away the thought.

She was done with wickedness. Done with ghost-witches. Done with the ghost-witch of Hanover Hill in Chicago who had haunted her childhood. And done with the ghost-witch Heida Mead on Draakensky Windmill Estate.

Charlotte mentally ripped off the horse's mask. She imagined flinging open the gate. The brave stallion leaped up with excitement, running off with the sun slicking his back, tail flying, belonging to the clear wilderness again. Resting her head back, she decided: now she would belong to Marc's wilderness.

A horn blast brought her musings to a halt and back to the direction ahead. Someone had cut the driver off, but now they were speeding away again, only to come to a slower pace. The tedious traffic made Charlotte impatient to see Marc.

She craved to be in his arms again with his luscious kisses, listen to his smooth voice call her *m'lady* like she was a goddess. She hungered to sit at The Grackle Bar and Grill again, Marc at the helm, mixing her a sassy drink, sporting his infectious smile.

Charlotte loved the engaging and heady conversations with the Bedford clientele and Marc's friends at his restaurant. He was a master at bar chat and a thrilling storyteller, attending to the customers on his line with finesse and panache, all the while shaking up exotic cocktails without losing a beat of the narratives.

Marc would be working now. Should she surprise him early?

Leaning toward the front seat, she asked the driver, "Do you know The Grackle Bar and Grill? In Bedford Village?"

"Sure do. You mean the bar with the stuffed birds on the chandeliers? Marc Sexton's place, right? You want that address?"

"Yes, that's the one."

Marc wasn't expecting her flight to land until five PM; she'd managed to catch an earlier standby flight. At this hour, he would be busy attending the lunch crowd service. A surprise might be too intrusive.

"Probably best not to pop in at the moment. Go on as planned to Mianus River Road."

Charlotte settled back in her seat. She would shower and change, then drive to The Grackle around three-ish when the restaurant had a lull.

Within minutes, the driver was turning at the black iron gates, into the long driveway to Draakensky Windmill. As soon as they arrived, Charlotte slid out of the car, feet back on the good earth of Bedford. The driver lined up her luggage at the doorway to Jaa Morland's windmill. The sails turned gracefully against a Dutch-blue sky. Draakensky's *blauw*, Jaa would have pronounced the color, describing the sky crowning her esteemed family estate.

But it wasn't Jaa's windmill anymore. Jaa's untimely death on Draakensky had changed everything. And her sister Heida Mead's death on Yew Crag in the Mianus River hung with menacing memories. Draakensky's *bird sisters*—as the two women were known, Jaa and Heida—served as a reminder that Charlotte knew little about the trials of sisterhood.

As the driver pulled away, rattling the gravel, she snatched the key from her handbag. Charlotte held the doorknob for a moment, her fingers stiffening. Hearing the drifting air gather around her, she became aware that she was breathing in shallow breaths. The sun cast a pale light where the door's address plate read CHARLOTTE KNIGHT. Draakensky Windmill Estate's new owner and landlord, Alice Eve, had already embossed it in brass.

This windmill would be Charlotte's new home. And hadn't she agreed to this with Alice? Both of them pleased and excited to sign the rental lease?

Yet, she was about to set her foot at the door of Jaa's death. What secrets were left inside these walls? Could she live in a home that housed Jaa's powerful wind magick? Or live on the same land where Heida had unleashed her witchcraft across all of Draakensky?

Charlotte could not bring herself to enter Jaa's windmill. Tossing her handbag down, Charlotte headed for the river path. *Listen,* she told herself, shifting her weight from one boot to the other on the stony path. *Dive in.* Jaa might have said these exact words to her. She forged ahead to the Mianus River.

Dozens of pines soared, all columned into a chamber. Black poplars edged the riverbank. Bramble bushes spread a nourishing green, and an intoxicating whiff of fern-scented air heightened all her senses. Birdsong! The notes floated, bright voices punctuating the air. How polished the forest appeared, dripping in giant leaves and budding wildflowers—hot pinks and white yarrow. Lilac bushes bloomed in a stretch of purple blaze along the paths, their perfume drawing her to touch the petals.

Like music, the river's spirited splashes and resonant echoes swept her up—the deepest pockets of water trembling its river magick, calling out her name.

"Here I am, Draakensky," she answered. Enchanting Draakensky never failed; she had dearly missed its splendor. The river waves cheered her, tiny ancient faces bubbling on the surface. At the bridge spanning across to Yew Crag on the opposite side, she halted. Jaa's warning surfaced: *Beware of hiking the crag. If you hike to the horseshoe ravine, turn back immediately, for you have entered the crag at its most dangerous and isolated backside.*

She had often wanted to hike deeper into the crag. If she crossed the bridge, it would be the third time on Yew Crag—the first time, she had met the ghost-witch of Heida beneath the giant yew tree, the second, she had met the ghost of René.

Bursts of mist shot up as she followed the Mianus River's tumultuous churning to the bank's edge, keeping her attention on the white glossy rapids and the steep waterfalls' beating percussion.

River's teeth are sharp, she heard inside her head—Thomas Harrogate's words. A dead man's presence still holding to Draakensky. Or still occupying a corner of her mind? Not until she walked farther downriver, when she approached the plateau of calmer waters, did she relax.

A great white swan floated across the surface, wings a-flurry, fluting the air in a welcome. The swan remained a gift from the Lady of the Lake, the water goddess, Vivienne of Avalon. If not for Marc, her smart young Merlin, Charlotte would have never discovered Vivienne's magick to become a daughter of Avalon. And found her own magick within her artwork. What inner voyages would Marc carry her through next? What secret gates would he open for her this time?

The swan melted into the sunlight, and Charlotte moved slowly along the riverbank. A mess of May violets like tiny lanterns sprouted in a sunny patch. She felt a smile emerge and then suddenly froze. Beyond the violets, a baby fox curved around a small rock—its body shrunken, legs stiff, baby paws clinging.

Poor thing was dead. But the animal had retained its fur like the shining silver of a sword. What an extraordinary sketch this would make. The lost beauty of a babe.

On the tail, she spied a thin streak of dark yellow fur. "Werner's King Yellow, Number 67. That's how I'd color that streak," she said aloud.

She would bring the fox back to Draakensky for a proper burial. Lifting the animal, she carried it like a baby in her arms. There wasn't a spot of blood anywhere. Its face was sad, lids closed. Had it died in its sleep?

The lilacs hushed as she passed them. She pet the baby fox, soft as silky flour. Charlotte hugged the cold animal to her chest. Three words entered her mind. *Carry me home.*

When she approached the windmill, the sails spun like a clock speeding up time. She entered the stone-walled garden and sat on the white bench. This had been Heida's garden. And what a spring garden it was, groomed with dozens of colorful tulips standing sharp, not a weed to be found—evidence of Alice Eve's talents preserving Draakensky's legacy.

She laid the silver fox on the earth. As if by decree, she pulled out her sketch pad and quickly drew a rendering. She streaked yellow on the thin tail. Her quick sketch would never compare to Carlos Salazar's famous silver fox, but it would serve for the moment.

From the shed, she found a shovel and dug a hole in the corner of the garden, beneath the dogwood tree whose buds were ready to bloom. From behind her, Heida's salt-box-style cottage grabbed her peripheral vision.

Shabby, peeling paint, every window had been boarded up with white wood in semicircle shapes as if nameless tombstones, suggesting that what was buried there deserved no memory. The climbing ivy hung loose now, some leaves going brown. Even in the cheerful daylight, the structure boasted a grimace ominously bearing down on her. She shook off the mocking feeling.

The fox lay at her feet. "I suppose I should name you. How about Aesop? For all the foxes in Aesop's fables." With trowel in hand, on her knees, she created a loose bed of soil. Gently, she placed the body into the grave, tears rising as she covered Aesop with soil. She marked it with a rock, aiming its point at the sky.

As she leaned back, brushing the dirt from her hands, a shadow zoomed over her shoulders. A long-keeled grackle with a green iridescent head perched on the bench, then swept up and landed on the windmill roof. Marc's grackle. Here at Draakensky again.

Charlotte knew Draakensky to be a force of nature. River magick permeated the land with its flowing awareness. Yew tree magick ruled its wisdom over rock and earth, becoming dark green phantoms when the sun hid behind clouds. Draakensky owls, ever watchful, hid in the trees, their feathers designed to fly silently and pull the darkness around them. Owl magick. Was Camaroon nearby? Was that murderous owl still present on Draakensky?

Charlotte had her own magick now, summoned by pen and paper—and her deep, deliberate passion.

Her wristwatch chimed the half hour. 1:30 PM. She walked to the front door bearing her name in bold letters. She turned her gaze sweeping Draakensky—the sun flashing over a far elm tree, lighting the river footpaths, bathing the vacant green lawn. Staring at spaces, at the empty air, she swallowed a thick gulp. *No one is here.*

All dead, they were, Draakensky's residents. Jaa. Heida. Thomas Harrogate. "Except for me . . ."

Charlotte slipped the key into the lock of Draakensky Windmill. The door swung open, a hand perhaps pulling it from the inside. As she stepped over the threshold, a flit of sunlight followed her in. *Carry me home.*

Chapter Three

May Thunder

At *The Grackle Bar* and Grill in Bedford Village, Marc's office desk clock pinged 1:30, the glass case revealing its mechanisms of wheels and weights. His grandmother Mamó's clock. Even the copper sun-face plaque hanging on the wall—Celestial Sun Father—had belonged to Mamó. Time certainly can steal the years but not the memories.

Charlotte's flight was due at five PM; counting down the hours made him edgy and impatient. His office door opened. *What now?*

Petrovna poked her head in with a fearful expression. "Police are here, Marc," she said, her Russian accent slurring the words.

Marc bolted from his chair. "Is it Officer Davin? What's happened?"

"I don't know your locals here. He's asking Liz questions at the bar. Ohhh!" Petrovna leaned back. "Here he is. Excuse me," she added politely to the officer, who now stood in the doorway.

"Hey, Marc."

He breathed a sigh of relief at seeing Jimmy in his blue uniform. "Petrovna, this is Chief Jimmy Cruz. A good friend. Hi Jim. Meet our kitchen manager, Petrovna."

They exchanged pleasantries, and she bowed out politely. Marc sat down, feeling suddenly exhausted with a headache and rumbling stomach. Jimmy rested his hand on his holster, a gesture Marc knew meant he had official business.

"We got a call about a break-in, Marc. Last night, at Betty's Place. The shop's back window was broken. Minor vandalism inside. A few antiques are missing. Did you see or hear anything suspicious going on next door after eight o'clock?"

"You're kidding. A robbery? I was off last night. Is Betty okay?"

"She's fine. The security alarm failed. She's going through a nasty divorce. Might be her ex making trouble. Do you know her ex, Josh Summers?"

"No. I didn't even know Betty remarried."

"Rebound after Winston died. What happened to your trash dumpsters out back? Did someone ransack them? Litter is strewn on the gravel."

Marc hadn't noticed when he arrived. "Raccoons sometimes get in if the lids aren't closed securely. Is that relevant?"

"Everything is relevant at this point. Betty said you share your recycling dumpster with her. True?"

"I let her dump her cardboard and plastics."

Jimmy laughed. "Still the boy scout helping out the elderly?"

"I guess. Betty's a sweet gal," he said with admiration. "She compensates by making a yearly donation to the Homestead Foundation, and that pleases me more."

Jimmy checked his watch. "Do you mind if I question your staff and inspect the parking lot? And I'll need to check your video surveillance."

"Sure, no problem. Petrovna can help you with all that." He texted her a message instructing her to cooperate with the chief.

"She's doing the orders in the back office." Marc rubbed the back of his neck and winced with pain.

"You okay, Marc?"

"Had a bad night. Couldn't sleep."

Jimmy boasted a sudden grin, eyebrows raised. "Tonight's the night, right?"

Marc swallowed hard. "Yeah, yeah. Ring night. This is it."

"I see terror all over you. Afraid Charlotte is going to say no?"

Was he afraid Charlotte would say no? He felt himself go blank, his focus glued on Jimmy's deep Spanish black eyes, the spiffy short beard, all that Castilian bravado.

"Is she expecting a ring?" Jimmy asked, pulling Marc's attention back.

"We've not discussed a ring. I mean, I have told her I want her to marry me."

"And her response was?"

"She said she would always love me," he confessed.

Jimmy rocked back on his heels and wore a smart expression. "You know, they don't call it wedlock for nothing. There's a serious gap between a yes and a no answer to a marriage proposal. There's maybe, I'm not sure, it's too soon, I'm not ready, you're not ready, your family is wacky."

Marc swiveled in his chair, tapping his thumb on the arm. "You proposed to Rosie at six months. She didn't say any of those things. She said yes."

"Yeah, well . . . Rosie insisted I resembled the actor Antonio Banderas, and I made good use of that by charming the hell out of her."

"You look nothing like Banderas."

"I didn't argue the point. Are you confident in a yes tonight?"

Charlotte wanted him. Loved him. He knew that. "Halfway there," he lifted his voice for confidence.

In the hallway, Marc heard rapid footsteps clicking down the tiles until they came to a stop outside his office door. A double knock, pause, double knock again. He recognized that staccato rap from when he was a boy.

No, it can't be. Not today.

"Anybody home?" The door opened, and Kelsey Sexton stood in the doorway, dressed in a peach-colored pantsuit, white silk scarf flowing at the neck, her strawberry-tinted waves scattered thinly across her forehead.

"Mom?"

"Surprise attack," she beamed, full of glee, suitcase dropping to the floor. "Hello, hello. Jimmy!"

"Kelsey. I haven't seen you for ages." Jimmy hugged her. "You are beautiful as ever. How are you?"

"Aww, Jimmy, always the sweetheart. Your family well? Rosie and the boys?"

"We are, thank you."

Marc was on his feet, unsteady with the shock of his mother in his office on a Wednesday afternoon and with no warning. "I had no idea you were flying over today."

"Hello, my darling." Her hug and cheek kiss had a brisk touch, different from her usual embrace. "You know me. Living the spontaneous life now that I'm retired." She took a seat in the armchair near the door, inspecting the office wall to wall.

"Well," Jimmy gave a mock salute. "Duty calls, if you'll excuse me. Catch you later, Marc. Nice seeing you again, Kelsey." And with a thumbs up behind Kelsey's back, he exited, closing the door behind him.

"Marc, you redecorated again. Stylish copper tones. New wallpaper?"

"Just a spruce up. Are you okay?" he asked, hearing the trepidation in his voice.

"Of course. Auntie Bree sends her love. I tried to talk her into coming with me, but she really couldn't handle the eight-hour flight from Dublin. Now, tell me how the Afternoon Irish Teas are going for the Homestead Foundation. I noticed the last report showed good numbers."

What was this now? They had spoken about the financials a week ago. "April teas went well. We may do it again in September. Chef Charlie deserves a good deal of credit. We're still working for that Michelin star rating. Can I get you something?"

"No thanks, I'm fine. A Michelin star. That would be outstanding." She locked her vision on him, giving him that cool glaze that never failed to hold him still, even as a man.

"Mom, you might have let me know you were coming. I wasn't expecting you until August. How long are you staying?"

"As long as it takes."

He remained calm, even with that deadpan expression she gave him, which wasn't easy after a sleepless night and his stomach out of sorts. "As long as what takes?"

"I came to meet her."

His gut tightened. Kelsey Sexton, still the smart beauty, approaching sixty-seven, pretty as a thin bell, was tempered with a spine of steel. And that spine kept all three of her children straight and true. But he was used to her dropping little bombs into his lap. He thought it best to say nothing and let her have at him.

"Why didn't you tell me you're engaged, Marc? I had to find out from your sister."

"I'm not engaged yet. Sheila shouldn't have told you my plans." He regretted blurting the news to his sister. Sheila had been so thrilled with the prospect of having a sister-in-law that she immediately insisted on getting Charlotte's phone number so they could chat it up together—a call that lasted nearly two hours. Sheila the Talking Wall, Marc used to tease her.

"Don't blame Sheila. I tricked her into telling me. Why is this a secret?"

"I've not given Charlotte a ring. There's no announcement. Please don't tell me you flew eight hours here because of this?"

"No ring yet, well, that's something," she softened her tone. He saw a blink of relief. "When can I meet her?"

"She's out of town." A sudden dread gripped him. He had put this off for a reason. Strategic pacing was imperative. Marrying out of the Irish tribe was practically a crime in the Sexton family. And he was the first offender.

"Marc, I think it would be healthy for you to come home to Dublin with me. Take a break from all this. Spend time with your aunts. Mamó's house in County Cork needs you for the renovations. Might be good for you to walk the land of your ancestors. Come home, Marc."

Come home? "My home is here, you know that," he said firmly. "I saw my aunts at Christmas. Mamó's renovations can wait."

"Can they? You are the trusted owner of your grandmother's home now." She straightened her shoulders and smoothed her jacket.

"I take that position seriously. The house is safe."

"Is it?" she said slowly as if to gather strength. "I ran into Shannon a few weeks ago. She asked about you. Shannon is a treasure. She's planning a trip to the States soon. Did you know that?"

"Shall we have lunch? We opened the patio this week. Just in time for Beltaine."

"How nice. I saw the ribbons streaming from the ceiling in the dining room when I walked in," she purred. "Silver apples on the bar are a nice touch. Now, did Shannon tell you she's coming to New York next month for a pediatric medical convention? She's presenting as a guest speaker. There's serious talk that she might relocate her practice here."

"Mom, I told Shannon at Mamó's funeral last year that I have no romantic intentions with her. We are not in love. Leave it there, please." He stood up. "Let's have lunch."

Marc led his mother to the patio, where the red azaleas bloomed along the back border. Kelsey chose the farthest table from the patio entrance—a table for four centered with white geraniums—and settled in with the menu. They sat across from each other in a private alcove of potted lemon trees, boxwoods, and bay laurels.

"I'll have the artichoke risotto," she told the waitress, absorbing the patio setting. "You've added a grapevine arbor. Lovely."

"Alice Eve's design. It was her idea to make private dining alcoves." Marc gave a nod to the waitress. "Thank you, Dara. I'll have the same. And a bottle of the Sauvignon Blanc special. You know the label?"

"Of course," Dara answered and scooted away.

"You'll have the same?" his mom repeated, surprise painting her face.

"Why not? Chef Charlie's risotto is the best. His Chinese-Italian distinctions create magnificent cuisine."

She ran her fingers through her hair and curled a shoulder. "You've not ordered the same dish as me since you were fourteen years old. Remember when you used to do that?"

He had forgotten that trick he played whenever his mom disapproved of his behavior, which happened frequently during his boyhood rebellions. Ordering the same meal pleased her. Was he instinctively trying to please her?

She tapped her forefinger on the table before one of the empty chairs. "Might we have another place setting, please?"

Marc moved to the server table to fetch the setting. It was a Sexton tradition to keep a place at the table for the deceased, even though it had been nearly two decades after his father's death. He positioned the plate in front of the empty chair, fork and knife aligned, stemware at the right, white napkin folded on the left. *What's this?* A bluish stain on the napkin corner; he made a mental note for Petrovna to check the linen service. What if a Michelin inspector saw that stain? He flipped it to the clean side.

The patio remained quiet. Kelsey continued to peruse the menu for dessert options, no doubt. His phone blinked, and he answered the text quickly. When he raised his head, she was staring straight at him, her dark green eyes like goldstone, evergreen crystals flecked with copper.

"Well," she finally said. "What is this girl's name, for heaven's sake?"

"Charlotte Knight."

"Knight? English then?"

He didn't disagree. Nor would he mention the mix of her Italian heritage. But he had to give his mother something to chew on. "Her father was Charles Knight. From London. Charlotte has a European mixed lineage."

She bit her lip. "Any Irish mixed into Charlotte's lineage?"

He shifted in his chair. "I couldn't say. Both parents died. Her aunt raised her."

"How old is she?"

"Thirty-four."

"She's a bit young for your thirty-nine."

"Same age as Shannon and you don't think she's a bit young for my thirty-nine."

"I think Shannon is perfect for you."

"Perfection might be overrated," he answered politely.

Dara returned, placed down the plates of risotto. She poured the wine slowly. "Will there be anything else I can get you?"

"Thank you, Dara. No."

Marc downed several gulps of the white wine, grateful for Dara's timing.

"Marc." His mother leaned forward, waiting until Dara exited. "Does Charlotte know who you are?"

Marc dug into the rice. Artichoke hearts, black olives, pine nuts, Parmesan. He savored each bite. "Leave this to me. Charlotte knows enough for now."

"You've not told her," she stated with a disapproving note. "She has no idea of your capabilities?"

"Please, Mom," he hushed. "I know how to handle this."

"However you handle it, it won't go well for her. It didn't for me when I found out your father was—"

"Stop."

His mother sat back in her chair. "Marc, this girl doesn't have a single cell of Irish blood in her, does she? How will she ever accept what you are?"

If he had to walk through hell, he knew he would have to do it as if he owned the place. "What if I told you Charlotte is pregnant?"

She went white as the geraniums on the table. "She is?"

"No. She is not. But that's what this is about, isn't it? The Sexton heir? My child, who will inherit the Finnwolf gift?"

"You know perfectly well we have a family duty to protect the gift. That's a quote from Mamó. If you marry this girl, you risk weakening the powers of your heir, corrupting the gift, and the entire Sexton legacy could be betrayed. What would Mamó say about your marrying an outsider and risking the Finnwolf bloodline?"

He didn't mention that Mamó had sent him a dream from the Otherworld. He had found himself at her home in County Cork. Mamó had invited Charlotte to enter her red door at the front of the house, and he interpreted that dream as her approval. "I'm not worried about Mamó. She understands the circumstances."

"I doubt that. More importantly, what would your father say?" She lifted her fork and began eating.

With only the two of them on the patio, the minutes dragged by. Marc pushed salad around his plate. Only the piped-in piano music broke the awkward distance. The tinkling notes brought up a flash of his mother playing their upright in their Lewisboro farmhouse, her singing to him, joy on every trill in her voice.

"I wouldn't know what Da would say," Marc offered, "since there's been zero communication with him from the Otherworld."

"Yes, I've been meaning to speak to you again about that. I know, the *same old* is here again. It's just that Matthew's silence . . . all these years."

Here it comes again. Those same words he's heard like an echo. *Where is he?* "Mom, you've asked me this dozens of times. My answer is no different." He placed his fork down as if that could change the subject.

"Is he lost somewhere? Trapped? You must have some idea. The way he died—that must mean something."

He repeated the same answers because she apparently needed to hear it again and again. The medical cause on the death certificate never satisfied his mother. Or him. For the sake of family, he had to maintain some rationalization for everyone. "He died of a cardiac arrest. He was overweight. He sometimes drank too much. The stress of shifting, stress of his Otherworld journeys. We know all this."

But his father's death was a funeral knell constantly ringing in his head, asking the same questions. *Where is Da? Is he lost? Trapped? Caught between realms?*

"We know all this," she imitated his inflection. "The Otherworld has its risks. The dark powers. We know that too. You know the realms."

"I don't know them. I cannot go on a realm journey and find him."

Marc knew deep realms existed but had no knowledge of their access or exit portals. He knew his father had been on a dangerous trance journey the day he died. He knew the man explored time loops. He reminded her: "The geography of the Otherworld is a mystery to me. I'm not a realm walker. I don't know the portals."

"You have the gift. You have the knowledge."

"Da wasn't the only realm walker. He said there were other Sextons who journeyed the realms. Other cousins."

"Matthew didn't know that for sure," she insisted. "As far as we know, your father was the only living Sexton realm walker. Lord of the Wolf," she whispered, but the desperation of her voice still hit. "And now you may be the only living Sexton who has the gift—possibly the last Sexton if your child doesn't carry the legacy. Or, if you fail to have a child."

He poured more wine into both their glasses. Kelsey's hand shook when she lifted her glass.

"The Silver Brotherhood and the Sisterhood must be maintained," she declared.

"Clearly, I'm not a member of the Brotherhood."

"You are son of Finnwolf. Your DNA. You know perfectly well that your blood carries the Sexton magick. Blood pledges have been made."

"Not by me, they haven't."

Her expression tightened as if she might go mad. "The Sextons have had an unbroken succession of realm walkers."

"The gift has skipped a generation here or there. It's skipped William and Sheila."

"It has not skipped you." She reached across the table and touched his hand. "What are you doing with your life? Your gift? Marrying an unsuitable spouse? Please, do not challenge the patriarchy. Do not challenge the legacy you were born to fulfill," her voice trembled. "Marc, you cannot marry this girl."

Chapter Four

Hearing the Silence

Charlotte drove her bright yellow Fiat into Bedford Village. She had chosen a new dress with embroidered swirls, ankle-length, which flared out in shades of aquamarine, an expensive fashion indulgence during her final days in Chicago. With all Marc's talk about celebrating Beltaine, she decided to dress up, and adding this early arrival made it all the more enticing. If he was tied up with business, she'd wait at the bar and chat it up with Jackson, the manager, who was always friendly. Maybe even Sir Duncan, the Earl of Kent, would be sitting at the bar, Sexton and soda in hand, with his inexhaustible *joie de vivre*.

She swerved into a parking space at The Grackle's back lot, gave a quick toss of her brown waves loose over her shoulders, and hopped out of the car. As she passed the restaurant's patio, she noticed umbrella tables. Admiring the garden décor and flowery tablecloths, she found her way to the gated opening on the side, figuring she'd sneak in the back entrance and go straight to Marc's office unannounced. He often worked at his desk around three-ish. As she entered the patio, she heard his sexy baritone voice.

Seeing no other patrons around, she ventured forth in his direction.

"Bradley, I don't have those numbers with me right now. Can I call you back later? I don't expect it to be a problem," he said, all business.

Bradley? Isn't that his accountant? She peeked through the ivy trellis. He sat alone, expression serious beneath his strong brow, his blond wavy hair freshly cut. She loved that black-and-white pin-striped shirt he often wore. *Sinfully sexy*, Sister James might have said and added her amusing warning, *Be careful, you lucky girl.*

Stepping quietly, she edged her way toward the bank of potted trees and came around to the opening. There she stood, waiting for him to lift his head and see her.

He clicked off, laid the phone down, and blinked up. "Charlotte!"

Before she knew it, she was in his arms, lost in a kiss so fervent she went delightfully dizzy. "No matter where I go, I'm always coming back to you," she said and drank in all six feet of him, and the awesome spread of his shoulders. Clinging to their embrace, running her fingers along his blond temples, she added, "I got an early flight back. You like surprises, right?"

A bit stunned, he murmured, "Yeah," then took a breath. "Of all days. Great Scott, Charlotte!" He hugged her again, teasing her with kisses.

"Good thing we're alone out here. May I sit? I'm dying for a—" She halted, lifting a white scarf off the back of the chair, taking in the two luncheon plates, wine bottle, and a napkin with lipstick stains on it. She pinned him with her stare.

"My mother flew into town today. Speaking of surprises."

She slapped her hand to her mouth. "Kelsey Sexton? She's here?"

"In the ladies' room. We just finished lunch." He took her into his arms again. "Let's run away, you and me," he crooned into her ear. "Rome? Paris?"

"Well, this is cozy." Charlotte heard behind her. Marc instinctively released her.

"You must be Charlotte. Lovely to meet you."

Kelsey came forward and shook her hand—refined, calm, and in total control. "Will you join us for dessert and tea? How perfect that you are here today. Please, sit down."

The anxiety grew endless for Marc as Kelsey foiled her disapproval with a series of polite questions about Charlotte's family and Midwestern childhood. He sensed Charlotte was uncomfortable, especially speaking about her teen years in foster homes. Mostly though, her answers were well composed and steady. He introduced the subject of Charlotte's upcoming art exhibit of the illustrations of Rilke's poetry at Van Cleeves Gallery in New York City—which appeared to genuinely impress Kelsey.

"Rilke was a marvelous poet, of course," Kelsey threw in, "but we favor Yeats. My husband adored Yeats. Our favorite was 'When You Are Old' . . . '*full of sleep . . . of their shadows deep.*' "

Charlotte chimed in. "I love Yeats too. His mysticism never fails. Quite hypnotic verses. We studied his poems at the convent. I still have a battered copy of *The Wind Among the Weeds.*"

"The convent? A Catholic convent?" Kelsey's chin clamped.

Marc noticed Charlotte's chin braced too. "Well, ahh," she

stumbled, "after my Aunt Loretta died, before I went into foster care, I lived with the nuns at St. Sophia's Convent for a few years under the supervision of Sister James. Yeats wasn't Catholic, but Sister James adored him. We memorized a good number of his poetry together."

Marc changed the subject again. He thought he'd go mad redirecting the topics over their spice cake and bourbon-flavored tea, his mother rerouting the topics back to Ireland, and the Sexton ancestry. "My Marc is a prince," Kelsey said one too many times.

"I am far from a prince," he quipped back with a last gulp of tea. "We have rain clouds up there. Shall we go in? And anyway, there are far better things than princes."

"Is there? I guess that would be kings." His mom made a click of her tongue. "Charlotte, in our family we have a tradition of First Kiss stories. Do you know Yeats's line about the first kiss? 'Ephemera. *How far away the stars seem, and how far is our first kiss.*' "

"I don't think I know that one."

"Owen and Mamó's first kiss was on her front porch. Her name was Branwen, but she's Mamó to us. Matthew kissed me while we were dancing at a wedding. Tell me about Marc's first kiss."

Charlotte's jaw dropped.

A low note pinged in Marc's head. The gravity here was absolutely real. Marc poured more tea into Charlotte's cup. She pressed her knee against his.

"Our first kiss was marvelous," Charlotte brightened. "We were in Marc's jeep. Lots of starlight. Johnny Mathis singing 'Autumn Leaves.' A perfect moment." She landed each word with a little punch. "In the history of kisses, this was one of the best."

Undaunted, Kelsey tilted her head, her expression full of

mischief. “And then what happened?” She lifted a plate of almond cookies in an offering to Charlotte, who declined with an engaging shake of her pretty hair.

“And then, Marc kissed me again . . . and again,” Charlotte added, sitting up brilliantly like a gemstone in a high setting.

Marc couldn’t have been more proud. “Okay, that’s enough snooping.”

“Did Marc tell you, Charlotte, that we Sextons have ancient Celtic ancestry?”

“Mom, let’s not do—”

“The Sextons are descendants of King Cormac mac Art, as are thousands of other people in Ireland, the Maguire clan being most famous. The Sextons have well-researched family records from the 1700s, maps from the scriptoriums and—”

“I believe it’s raining,” Marc interrupted. “Shall we go inside?”

“It is not raining.” Kelsey lifted her left shoulder, her emblem gesture, which he knew to mean, *Fine, see it your way, but it’s not accurate.*

“We’re going inside anyway.” He stood. “Dara? You can clear away.”

Within minutes back in his office, he sent Charlotte to the barn house with the promise that he’d be there in an hour. His mother mingled with the staff members from her old days running the bar and grill, fawned her kudos on Chef Charlie, and came back into Marc’s office to say goodbye. She closed the door behind her and sat down.

He perched on the edge of his desk. “Are you staying with Cousin Diana tonight?”

“She’s on her way now to get me. We’re traveling to Concord on Friday to see Sheila. I haven’t decided when I’m returning to

Dublin. I might fly to L.A. to visit William." She cleared her throat, and her face grew serious. "I see you and Charlotte are important to each other."

That hung out there for more than a beat.

"And I see that you are highly attracted to her. She seems an intelligent and talented young woman. An artist, how quaint. Pretty gray eyes. Undeniably adorable."

Important to each other? Adorable? Charlotte's beauty could rival a goddess. I would lay down my life for her. Marc knew not to respond with such words. Instead, he quietly declared, "Charlotte is far more than that."

"I'm worried about you." Her intensity made him uncomfortable. "It's time. Someone has to sit in your father's chair."

He turned his attention out the window as a black crow hung in the air on a slow descent.

"Marc," she pleaded.

From his desk pitcher, he poured himself a glass of water. The liquid sloshed against the glass, beads of water clinging to the sides, ice cubes floating. He saw himself as a solid cube submerged beneath all the others. No space. No air. No way to surface to the top.

"Your father taught you well, didn't he? How to lock up all the secrets inside you. I spent years suffocating under your father's silence about his magick. His secret journeys. His private quests. I can still hear his silence. As his wife, I accepted his secrets and honored his mission for the good of all. But, I cannot accept your silence."

He drank the water down in gulps.

"What are you doing with your magick, Marc?" Her voice skidded high with emotion.

"I serve another." He would give her that much, but he would never break the seal. He could never reveal how he serves the goddess Vivienne by initiating daughters into Avalon's magick through the ritual passages. He would never reveal anything about the paths of ecstasy or his star magick.

"And how does that serve your father's legacy?"

"It doesn't. I don't have Da's wolf heart, nor his high wolf magick."

She rose and reached to his open collar. She lifted the chain. "What if you *are* the last Finnwolf? You still wear a silver wolf head. Is wolf magick *not* your destiny?"

He tucked the silver pendant back under his shirt.

"The Silver Brotherhood—these old ones, Marc—will not suffer a betrayal of the Sexton legacy. They have risked too much to let you damage their lineage or your heir."

He sat down, Mamó's glass clock ticking time forward. Time breathed inside those old mechanisms. Did he want his child to carry the Sexton gift and walk the realms in Matthew's footprints between worlds as Finnwolf? *What would Da say?* He'd probably say what he often said in his inimitable voice: *Everything is speaking to you. I swear by the stars, my boy. Listen!*

"Good night, Mom. Call me when you are safely back in Dublin," he said with a gentleness that surprised him.

At the doorway, luggage in her hand, she paused. One more turn back. She blew him a kiss. "My darling boy, I fear for you. And for Charlotte. The Old Fathers will never permit this marriage."

Marc's gut knotted as she closed the door behind her.

A loud rumble came down from outside his window. Drumming? No. The sky galloping. Mighty howls of a pack of wolves broke over him.

He stroked his silver wolf pendant. *Resist.*

Chapter Five

The Dreaming Dead

"Diana!" Kelsey waved her arms to the gray sedan circling Bedford Village Green. In a second, Diana pulled up in front of The Grackle. Kelsey stashed her luggage in the trunk and jumped in.

"Good timing," Diana said. "Wait till you see the new sunporch. They delivered the furniture this morning."

Kelsey failed to draw excitement about the sunporch. Renovating the aging Victorian house with Diana had been a pleasant priority for Kelsey's retirement years between Dublin and New York. Now though, she could think of nothing but Marc.

Diana chatted about the renovations for the entire forty-minute drive to Sleepy Hollow. She swerved up the driveway and halted. "The view at sunset will knock you out. You okay? You've not uttered a sound the whole ride."

"Things didn't go well with Marc." Kelsey threw open the car door and went straight to the sunporch, nodded approval, and settled on the floral chaise lounge that provided a wide vista of the woodsy acre.

"You need a stiff *gintastic*, dear cousin." Diana swiped back her pixie black hair that took years off her sixth decade. "Be right back." She dashed off to the kitchen.

Diana never failed to raise Kelsey's spirits with her cheery disposition—and a gin and tonic. Hedge crickets chirped, reminding Kelsey of the glades of Ireland. Loneliness had a way of stalking her since living with her sister, Bree, these last three years and helping her run their Dublin Bed & Breakfast. As busy as it was, she'd find herself staring out the window for Matthew to come walking up the hill.

"So, what happened?" Diana asked, handing over the tall cocktail gushing with limes. She sat in the vintage white fan-backed wicker chair that made her appear regal.

"Let's just say we didn't agree on anything. He has no romantic interest in Shannon."

"Ohh, sorry, Kel. If Marc's engaged, there's no point in your expectations for Shannon. Were you able to bring up the subject of Matthew? Did Marc have anything new to add?"

"No, he did not. Maybe another time when we're not at odds."

Kelsey didn't want to say too much. Diana had been a reliable cousin and respected the Otherworld Celtic beliefs that their deceased loved ones only changed worlds. But Diana didn't know the full Sexton family history. These secrets became phantoms over the years, holding Kelsey's heart like a ransom.

"Kelsey, are you still doing dream work to contact Matthew?"

"I gave up. I'm not very good at dream time traveling or contacting the mythical lineages. I don't get anything from Mamó either, and you'd think she would be there for me. She was in the old days."

Diana cranked open a window. "I know less about these things than you do. Sometimes I think dead people are the lucky ones.

Maybe you're feeling displaced and it's causing you to block. Retirement has its liabilities. You don't run the bar anymore. Your farmhouse in Lewisboro is gone. Your children are moving on with their lives. If Matthew is not communicating with you or with Marc, maybe this is more complicated than you think."

"Or . . . Matthew is unable to communicate with me." Kelsey slugged the gin.

"Why would he be unable to communicate?" Diana offered with an air of sympathy.

Kelsey's gut clenched. "What if . . . he's not in the Otherworld?"

Diana hardly blinked. "Unlikely, isn't it? And anyway, aren't there other possibilities? What about reincarnation?"

Kelsey often held the other possibilities in her mind. "I'm worried about the lost realms or even the forbidden realms. The Underworld. The House of the Dark One."

Diana grimaced. "Ohh, gosh." After an uncomfortable pause, she perked up. "Hey, Kel, let's have dinner. I made a mushroom quiche. I'll bring you a plate." She scooted out to the kitchen.

The sun reddened in the approaching twilight. Creaks filtered in from the kitchen's old wooden plank floor as Diana pattered back and forth and clinked silverware. Kelsey admitted to feeling fragmented about her life, and with the travel fatigue bearing down on her, she had a burning desire to scream bloody hell.

She thought back to when Matthew had told her about the Sexton legacy and who he really was. Lord of the Wolf. A shapeshifter. A multidimensional cellular transformation into wolf anatomy, a terrifying body of claws and fangs.

Matthew had opened his soul to her and revealed his gift of metamorphosis. No matter how much he pleaded, no matter the promises and reassurances, no matter how much she dearly loved this brilliant and affectionate man, the shock—the appalling fear of this man becoming wolf—made her feel as if she had been dumped alone into the middle of a dark storming sea swallowing her up. Lord of the Wolf. She practically died at the thought of Finnwolf. Crushed, she'd run straight away for months, refusing to see or speak to him.

If it hadn't been for Matthew's mother, for Mamó's guidance and reassurances about Celtic honor, Kelsey might never have agreed to give Matthew another chance to talk it through. Matthew's sincerity, his tenderness, and his deep love softened her fears. And Mamó's timely invitation for her to serve Matthew and the Sexton mission reeled her into shore. Kelsey landed safely in Mamó's wise arms, rescued from the storm.

Kelsey became a trustee of the Sexton legacy, a member of the Sisterhood who agreed to serve Matthew by honoring his quest, supporting his Finnwolf mission, and providing him with an heir to the Sexton gift with her pure Irish blood, guaranteeing the highest quality offspring.

Diana returned with plates of cheesy quiche piled high with sweet green peas. "In honor of Beltaine," she said with a flamboyant sweep of her arms.

"You did that just like a ballerina, Di."

"Ha. More like Thumbelina. I'm such a klutz."

They ate quietly for a moment. Kelsey put her plate down. "I have to tell you something, after all these years. Because you've been so generous to me."

"Oh goody, is it juicy? Are you having an affair?"

"God, no. Do you know why I married Matthew?"

"You two were crazy in love. Everybody could see that. Why, was there another reason?"

Kelsey felt herself go a bit teary. "Matthew's mother had a dream about me. The Old Fathers told her that Matthew was to marry a lass named 'Kel with hair the color of strawberries and cream.' Mamó believed that when your name is spoken in a dream, it's a secret calling from the ancestors." Kelsey stopped there, keeping her vow to remain silent about Finnwolf and the Sexton realm walkers.

"Ohhh, so that's the reason you decided to use dream therapy to contact the Otherworld?"

"Dreams have power. All that unconscious wisdom comes through. The Celts have long revered dreams as intelligent. The ancestral dead and all that."

"Tell me more." Diana curled her shoulders.

"Well, Matthew and I had already met by then. We couldn't bear to be separated. But we had this . . . falling out. A few days later, Mamó came to see me. She told me about her dream. And other things. Celtic souls. Destiny. There was no resisting Branwen Sexton."

"Yes, Auntie Bran. So strong and brilliant. Marc's relationship with her was wonderfully close. I used to envy that. His mamó. Shall I put on coffee? This is a perfect night for storytelling. Be back with dessert."

Kelsey finished off the last of the gin. Diana's backyard hedges and trees swayed in slow motion, quelling her anxiety. Words from a Yeats poem popped into her mind. *The shaking of its leafy head . . . ravens of unresting thought.*

Unresting thoughts. She might have heard Matthew's voice in those words. How he loved to read poetry to her.

At the far end, beneath the leafy-headed trees, a stag poised near the ferns. He was a brown-spotted beauty with high antlers and fearless wide eyes. In a single buoyant leap, he vanished.

Gone. It didn't appear that Charlotte would be gone any time soon. What if the girl knew that Marc was the son of Finnwolf the Realm Walker? Would she leap away? If she knew the man she loved could shapeshift himself into a giant wolf with savage fangs and claws—she might bolt. How would she handle her husband who had powers to travel the realms of the Otherworld and return home? And one day, God forbid, he might never come home. One day, she might find him dead in his wolf chair, horrific with his eyes glimmering white inside his half-closed lids.

Biting into a lime slice, Kelsey tore off a huge chunk, delighting in its tart sweetness.

Chapter Six

Under the Oak

Entering Beltaine, Charlotte wore a thin wreath of white flowers on her head at Marc's request, strolling across his back lawn, the grass cool under her bare feet, her long dress kicking out with each step. They dined on buttery salmon, hot bread, and an orange pudding. The champagne created an irresistible effervescence in every word between them.

Celebrating the heathland, Marc had announced to her as they relaxed in Adirondack chairs, the fire pit burning between them at their backs, sending their silhouettes to the lawn. The tree grove and pond made an idyllic setting as they chatted about Charlotte's goodbyes to her Chicagoan life.

Charlotte felt certain their evening would conclude later with a lusty finale upstairs in Marc's bed. She played it coy, so he'd want her all the more.

Shadows loomed on the darkened pond. At the line of bushes near the water's edge, something lit. Little eyes. Charlotte counted five sets. They stared straight at her while the fire pit smoked gray puffs.

"Marc, what's in those bushes?"

Marc stretched up to see. "Ahhh, m'lady, those are my Beltaine witch-hares."

"Witches?"

"Every Beltaine, after dark, witches turn themselves into hares to hop the countryside. My little ghosties. Fear not, they are good witches who bring cheer."

"Really. Good witches."

"Absolutely. There's a gray hare with one black paw who comes every year. She's my darling with the biggest gray ears you've ever seen. I named her Jilly. A bit of a trickster, she is. A master at quick turns. Jilly can vanish at will. She usually brings a few hares from her drove. One year, she brought all white hares with blue eyes right out of a fairy tale. Last year, tan and brown. If we're lucky, we'll get to see the hares fly away." He raised his eyebrows playfully.

Placing her glass down, she added flirtatiously, "You, Mr. Sexton, are a wicked tease."

He ran his finger along her chin. "You know what, I could take you right here, right now, under the stars, on my blanket, surrounded by candles. What a night for outdoor lovemaking."

She thought about it. "Sex in your backyard?"

"I have ten acres. We can tumble wherever we want. Only the stars are watching." He reached over and kissed her hand.

"The stars. You mean Orion? You want The Hunter to be our voyeur? What a show-off." *That might be fun, though, to show off our lovemaking to the stars.*

"Orion isn't visible up there now."

"Who is visible?"

"Let's see," he observed. "Polaris, Big Dipper. Little Dipper. Draco the Dragon is showing strong."

"A dragon constellation?"

"The only one. Draco is between the dippers. See the North Star? It aligns with the tip of Draco's tail. From the North Star, track left. Follow the stars along the tail. Loop down, then go up, like the letter U, to the head. The dragon's head is an odd-shaped square of four stars. Near Vega."

She studied the sky for several minutes and found the tail, the dragon's hump, and the head. "That's remarkable. I've never heard of Draco."

"The Roman myths, maybe Greek myths too, tell the story of Minerva tossing the dragon into the sky. Minerva froze it there above the North Pole."

"Minerva? That's my mother's name."

"I know," Marc said.

"You do? I don't recall telling you her name. I'm not fond of revealing that my mother was named after a Roman goddess of war, wearing a helmet, a great owl on her shoulder."

"Maybe she wasn't."

"My mother was definitely named after the war goddess Minerva, according to Aunt Loretta."

"Maybe Minerva is a goddess of wisdom and not war. Minerva was known by the Celts long before the Romans made her into a facade. Minerva is thought to be a Celtic goddess, called Minerva Vitrix. Sul or Sulis was her Celtic name. Brave Minerva with a sharpened spear."

"How do you know that?"

"The Druids. They knew everything and passed their knowledge down."

She rubbed her arms. "Getting a bit cool."

"I'm happy to warm you up."

"Hmm. I think we'll be more comfortable in your bed, even though I love the circle of candles here."

"Nature's bedroom is calling us," he urged.

"Marc, I am not undressing in this chill. Maybe another time we can play Adam and Eve in the garden."

"Another time. Promise? For now, let's bid farewell to Beltaine."

He sat down on the ground at her feet, the firelight illuminating his face. "Cup your hands together." He showed her. "Pretend you're about to catch a falling star."

She followed his example, curious to play along. Beltaine had a dreamy aura with flowers scattered on the lawn and colorful streamers blowing in the trees. Beneath the tree grove, dozens of candles flickered, a feast of fire like she had never seen.

Marc placed his own cupped hands over hers. "Close your eyes. Make a wish."

Inhaling the smoky air filled with apple scents, she lowered her lids. The hares in the bushes made rustling sounds. Or was that the wind in the oak leaves? Logs in the fire pit crackled. Settling in, she quickly got the impression she was on a balcony, no rail, just a platform overhanging a great green sea of color. And then a quiet spinning sensation delighted her.

Make a wish, he said. If this is a dream with Marc, may I never wake up.

"Good night, spirits of Beltaine," Marc intoned. "May the splendor always be yours."

Charlotte opened her eyes. Her hands lit with a flock of white butterflies. They flitted about, tickling her fingertips. She couldn't move for fear they would vanish.

"How pretty! How did you do that?"

"Blow them gently back to the sky."

With her breath, she sent the lacy flyers up. She watched each one ascend until her cupped hands were empty. Except. A glittering ring hid in the crease beneath her thumb, silvery, a sapphire with facets that tinted the air blue.

"Charlotte, will you be my wife?"

"Ohh Marc . . ." Her throat swelled. It was no surprise that Marc loved her, yet this moment she hadn't expected. They had spoken of marriage but nothing specific.

"Come dream with me. Imagine the thrilling life we can have together."

To dream with this man would be a privilege. She hugged her fingers around the ring, this promise he was offering—a life together.

With the flush of the night fully upon them, his face absorbed the firelight, and all his goodness shone. Behind him, shadows suddenly rocked. One shadow leaped high. Another slinked down. Dark apparitions hovered at his shoulders. *A cape?* She stifled a shiver. The left shadows reshaped into stubs. The right shadows streamed into something leggy. More shadows, with hairy, pointed ears, hooded his head—all of it swelling and swaying, which Marc was not.

Marc raised his shoulders and brushed away the shadows as if they were dust. The darkness dissipated.

What kind of fierce shadows had drifted there—and then fled? Shadows of a wolf?

The bushes *swooshed*. A gray hare trotted forward. The eyes flicked like yellow marbles, long ears straight up in spindly cones—the jowly, black-footed Jilly holding herself far ahead of the others who huddled behind her. Jilly's split upper lip showed a flash of teeth.

Marc took both her hands into his, and she heard the words, "Charlotte, how brave can you be?"

Every muscle went rigid. "What? What did you say?"

He tipped his head. "I said, Charlotte, will you marry me?"

She had to breathe through her mouth for a second.

"You want this, don't you?" His face showed slight panic. "Please tell me you want this."

No other person had made her feel so cherished. She kissed him, holding the ring in one hand and caressing his cheek with the other. He was certain to hear her pulse racing with excitement. "I do want this. I love no other man but you."

A sudden coldness brushed her forehead, stinging the flesh like pinpricks. One of the shadows? She pulled back. Jilly and the four hares inched closer.

"Marc, do me a favor. Send those witch-hares away."

"What? What for?"

"Why are they here?"

"It's Beltaine. May Day is a night of magick. We call up all of Nature. We let the stars and flowers play with us." He touched the tiny blossoms wreathed on her head. "These hares are here to share in our magick."

Our magick. Marc had taught her everything she knew about magick. He once told her that he *lived magick* and considered magick to be the blood of the universe . . . *because the world is magick.*

"Send them away. You can do that, right? Use your magick to send the witch-hares away?"

"It's only Jilly and a drove of her shy companions. I love my Beltaine hares. They're harmless. I promise."

"I prefer you send them away." Her voice was harsher than she intended.

Marc raised his left palm to the starlight and mouthed silent words to the hares.

A moment passed before Marc turned to her, resolve on his face. "The hares declined my request to leave. I cannot send them away. I have no power to cross the will of Nature."

The hares retreated slowly back into the bushes. They held their position with steady eyes glowing through the branches.

The giant oak tree swayed—a heady scent of fresh earth and sweet ash wafted over them. "Charlotte, will you give me your hand in marriage? Beneath the stars, by their light, will you accept my promise?"

Charlotte inhaled a new breath. Points of starlight tipped the ogham tree grove's leaves. In the moving spaces between the trees, sending a clean breeze, she felt restored.

Charlotte lifted her hands and held the sapphire ring. "Yes! Make me your wife."

Under the oak and a whitened moon, Marc slipped the silvery sapphire across her flesh, his fingers thrilling her.

Around them, hooded shadows climbed up, veiled faces illuminating the firelight.

Chapter Seven

Lilies in the Fire

On Draakensky Windmill Estate, beneath the revolving murmurs of the sails turning the wind at the windows, Charlotte spent two days unpacking boxes and crates. She was eager to settle in and get back to her sketches and artwork. Distracted, she often found herself standing at the window, fondling the sapphire ring on her left finger, admiring the depth of the blue sparkle. She recalled Marc's lovemaking on Beltaine night and how he never failed to make her go wild. Moments with this man kept getting better.

Draakensky gushed with evergreen that drew her unceasingly. She breathed with Draakensky now, like a soft ballet of twirling inhales and pirouetting exhales. The abundant forest romanced her with its dappled light; the river's voice became a tune in her head. Everything pulsed at a higher speed.

Give me the wind, she said on her morning walks to the river, the windmill blades continuously spinning the sky.

Jaa Morland's homestead, akin to a mighty wind phantom, unraveled itself hour by hour. What had been a foreboding structure was now spruced up with fresh paint and new furnishings, thanks to Alice Eve. Thursday and Friday flew by with repeated disruptions. Jung May from Sterling Publishing had called about the Rilke poetry book featuring her sketches, nearly ready now for publication. The poems required another round of reviews—would she mind?—and also, could she meet with Frederik in New York as soon as possible?

The Van Cleeves Gallery in Manhattan left phone texts about mounting the show, which was now pushed ahead of schedule to open next Saturday. Director Geoffrey Brink called requesting portrait sketches for contrast to distinguish the unifying Rilke themes. Could she bring four new sketches with her on Thursday? Could she do a phone conference on Saturday evening to discuss her "Earl of England" portrait?

All this thwarted her attempts to set up her studio on the second floor. Her easels stood crippled in the corners, sketch pads and canvases tossed akimbo, boxes of her art supplies waiting in rows.

Weary on Saturday morning, she climbed the spiral staircase, determined to set up her studio by noon. With Marc having to work the bar full-time over the weekend, the clock ticked in her favor to indulge her entire weekend with sketching. And wouldn't it feel spectacular to do it in her spacious new studio, her first real studio?

When the front door knocker echoed, she sighed at the interruption, but a familiar voice called her name. Charlotte went running down the spiral staircase. Alice Eve stood at the front door, sporting oversized sunglasses, her curly black hair tied back loosely, arms stretched out. "Charlotte! You're here!"

If there was ever a friend who would walk beside her, it was Alice. After a long hug, Alice plunged in with bags and an abundant bunch of red Shirley Poppies with green basil, the minty fragrance making Charlotte swoon.

"Welcome back to Draakensky. I'm delivering a few more kitchen items that arrived late. I've been away at the flower show in Boston."

Charlotte stroked the yellow scarf draped on Alice's shoulders. "Pretty on you." The bright yellow brought back the image of Jaa's body splayed on the boardwalk by the river the night she and Marc had found her—no breath left in her body.

"Jaa's scarf. I wear it all the time now. She's still with me."

"And here in the windmill with me, too," Charlotte agreed. "Oh, these poppies are super."

"Jaa used to say she could hear the poppies creaking open. Flowers were such a presence for her." Alice sniffled. "So. What do you think of the makeover I've done here?"

"Magnificent. You bought all new furniture. I didn't expect that. I love the pale yellow on the walls. How did you get it done so quickly while I was away?"

"My brother is a house painter, and I insisted he bring his crew in. They did it in four days. The furniture arrived Monday. We put Jaa's things in storage. I can't go through it all now." She plopped down on the ice-blue sofa. "Kitchen's fully stocked with all new cookware and china. Did you see?"

"I did. The modern style is perfect. You have quite the decorator's flair." Charlotte joined her on the sofa. "I noticed Heida's cottage is boarded up."

"I've been meaning to explain about that. I need to demolish it. The structure is in terrible shape, and it's not worth the extensive renovation costs. I won't get to it until the fall. You okay with that?"

"Of course. Anything you need. I'm grateful to be here at all."

"And I'll keep up the gardens for you. Heida had lots of

perennials. It'll be easy." She pulled a small framed picture out of her satchel. "This is Jaa's."

Charlotte examined the image of a green dragon with blue wings and a long, curling tail. She knew immediately the painting was vintage.

"I found it when clearing out Heida's cottage. It's a copy of 'The Dragon,' 1460, Dutch, from the National Library of the Netherlands. Not a bad reproduction. The artist was a Morland cousin in Belgium."

Charlotte took the picture.

"I was going to keep it, but it belongs here at Draakensky. Maybe you can hang it somewhere?"

"Sure."

"The Morlands named the estate after this dragon. Did you know that? *Draak* means dragon in Dutch."

Charlotte shook her head.

"Jaa claimed to have seen wind dragons flying the sky when she was a child. So Joseph Morland built the windmill to honor them, or maybe appease them. Not sure which."

"Oh. Draakensky. Of course. I'll hang it in the kitchen. There's a spot near the back door, at the threshold."

"Perfect. Thank you." Alice surveyed the room with an approving expression until she landed on the vase of yellow lilies on the pedestal dining table.

"The lilies were a beautiful welcome when I walked in, Alice. Wilted now, but I did change the water."

"I arranged them on Sunday before I left. I'm surprised they lasted this long." She rose and fondled the dry petals. "You know," she said, her voice going meek, "Jaa favored yellow lilies. Every spring, I'd bring her a bunch. When they died, we'd burn them in the fireplace." Alice pulled out one of the Napoleon-style dining chairs, nearly falling into it. With her head down, hand over her mouth, she slid into tears.

"Oh, Alice." Charlotte went to her. "This must be heart-wrenching for you. To have me living here instead of Jaa."

"Whoever said loss gets easier with time was stupid. Don't mind me, I go gushy all the time. Jaa was my dearest friend, like a sister." Alice squeezed Charlotte's hand. "I love it that you're here."

"I know you do." One of the lilies dropped a browned petal. "Shall we burn the lilies in the fireplace? To nourish Jaa's memory?"

Alice's face lit up. "I would love that."

In the fireplace, the flames grew slowly as they sat crossed-legged on the floor at the hearth. "These are hybrids, not poisonous, so safe to burn." Alice sniffled again, putting her palm up for Charlotte to take. They held hands while the lilies fully ignited. Alice kept her chin down. She swiped away tears. "Beauty bright, wasn't she, our Jaa?"

"She was." Charlotte dabbed her own tears.

"Do you think Jaa is with Heida? Do you get any sense of the sisters being together in the afterlife? Because I don't." Alice shivered.

Charlotte knew Heida had a destiny that did not align with Jaa's wind magick or Jaa's distinguished character. Heida's witchcraft had triggered a dark path of desire and manipulation. Heida's destiny into Black Wolf Realm still made Charlotte cringe—a realm that Marc refused to speak about because of its danger.

Knowing Black Wolf Realm can draw its power down upon us, Marc had said, and denied any more discussions. So much in

Marc's life turned by invisible wheels and hidden knowledge. What dark paths lingered in his life? She wiped away another tear with her left hand.

"Charlotte!" Alice pointed to Charlotte's hand. "Is that what I think it is?"

"Marc popped the question."

"It's stunning. I've never seen an emerald-cut with so many sparkling facets. Oh, wait, I have a bottle of champagne in the trunk. We must have a toast, and you can tell me how he proposed."

"It's not even eleven AM."

"Live dangerously, girl." She raced out the door and back.

Sitting at the maple table, clinking their glasses, they feasted on chocolate wafers and chatted about Beltaine festivities. "One thing, though," Charlotte said, being in a confessional mood. "I don't think Marc's mom is too keen on me."

"Once she meets you, it'll be fine."

"We did meet. On Wednesday, when I arrived."

"I didn't know Kelsey was in town."

"Long story short, I got the clear sense from her that I'm not the woman she wants for her son, the prince."

"Kelsey will come around. And Marc, he knows how to calm a storm. It's his best strength."

"Maybe. Unless Kelsey Sexton is a hurricane."

"That's a possibility, I hate to say. I know her from when she managed the bar and from Bedford Business Association meetings. I recall Heida once called Kelsey a 'fiery Gael straight out of the Iron Age.' " Alice broke into a nervous laugh. "How long is Kelsey in town?"

"Marc didn't say. But I got a text from her around midnight

last night. Kelsey wants to meet for lunch sometime. Just the two of us to get to know each other. Alice, should I be worried?"

Alice pursed her lips in a silent whistle. "If Marc is the prince, then that makes Kelsey the queen. Definitely be worried."

Chapter Eight

A Jet of Blood

On Saturday morning, Marc woke later than usual. Feeling restored, in safe harbor—Charlotte had said yes—he had hoped for a quiet evening together to talk about marriage plans. She was inclined to wait, desiring the engagement reveries. He had another scenario planned.

Thursday and Friday had been grueling at The Grackle with two staffers off and his manager, Jackson, out sick. He would have to cover the gaps, regretting he couldn't take time to be with Charlotte. And with the Kentucky Derby horse race on Saturday—he never missed tending the bar on Derby Day—The Grackle would be packed with horse fans celebrating their equestrian love affair.

Bedford had long been known as the star equine mecca of the northeast, with stables and horse farms aplenty. On his morning runs, Marc would often cut over to Castleback Road to admire the thoroughbreds at Rackman Stables. Their beauty—their immeasurable grace and strength—often made him stop and admire. To borrow their wild freedom just for one day . . . an impossibility, yet who wouldn't crave such raw, vibrant power?

While coffee brewed in the kitchen, he quickly scanned text

messages, one from his mother sent at 12:10 AM. Another of Kelsey's midnight messages. She was Cinderella at the stroke of midnight—the fairy tale erupts into cold reality, then it's back to the cinders. Kelsey Sexton, the everlasting nocturnal, suffered midnight woes that never failed to drive her to the phone or email to fix things.

FORGIVE ME, BUT I BOOKED YOU A FLIGHT WITH ME TO DUBLIN ON WEDNESDAY. PLEASE COME FOR A FEW DAYS? WE MAY HAVE OUR DIFFERENCES, BUT FAMILY IS EVERYTHING. AUNTIE BREE WILL BE THRILLED TO SEE YOU. WILL YOU JOIN ME?

He responded: THANKS, MOM, BUT MAYBE ANOTHER TIME. CAN'T LEAVE THE BAR NEXT WEEK. HEALTH INSPECTOR'S DUE. AND I HAVE A JURY SUMMONS THE FOLLOWING TUESDAY. RAINCHECK?

He would wait for her to be back in Dublin before announcing the engagement was official with Charlotte. With a mug of steaming coffee, he stood at the kitchen window overlooking the backyard of his ogham tree grove, their trunks carved with the Celtic tree alphabet connecting tree knowledge to practical magick.

In the distance, a flash of white shot through the far woods. Sky Wolf. He sometimes saw her white brilliance at sunrise. Her magickal beauty stood poised among the forest trees, those amber eyes saying, *I am wolf.* This morning, she didn't howl her usual song for him. And she had no pack to sing with her. The lone wolf.

In a blink, she was gone.

On the lawn, the leftover Beltaine decorations were still scattered: candles, wilted flowers, ribbons, and the champagne bottle fallen near the fire pit. He had had the good sense to remove the dinner plates, but he forgot completely about the rest of it these past two days.

Marc strolled outside with a crate to collect the items. The pond water had turned dark under a passing cloud. His trees, which were normally bright green, wore a gloomy hue. No frogs jumping. No wind. After collecting everything, he walked to the edge of the pond to remove the ribbons tied to the tree trunks. One by one, he slipped them off, making his way around the twenty trees edging the pond. Near rocks bordering the weeping willow tree, he leaned around the thick trunk to untie its ribbon.

In the water, pointed gray ears and a jet of blood surfaced. Shocked, he hooked his neck over the rocky ledge. One slimy black paw floated up. *Jilly?*

His heart sank. "Oh my little Jilly. What's happened to you?" Crouching down, he swerved a stray willow branch to bring her closer to him. "Come on, babe. Come to me."

The water vibrated as he fished Jilly out. She had a wicked gash at the throat, streaming blood, whiskers matted to her head, gray fur clinging to her rib cage. His lovely Beltaine Jilly, ripped open by cruel fangs. At first, he thought it might have been a fox or coyote attack, but he'd not seen either on his land in the ten years he'd been living in the rebuilt barn. This was no fox attack.

He'd have to bury her. The thought of it made him flinch. He lifted her body to his lap, placed his hand over his heart, the other on Jilly's head, and sent her a blessing and gratitude for the joy she had brought him every Beltaine. The moment hung; he couldn't let her go. He scanned the pond and the lawn for the other hares. Had they flown away by their Beltaine magick? Why hadn't Jilly?

Bury her. Put her to rest.

His footsteps dragged in the grass as he walked to the driveway. In the garage, he fetched a shovel and found garden gloves. A bit of sun behind a cloud shot one ray out, a spear breaking through the blackthorn tree. The mother of the woods, the blackthorn was a warrior tree of the wise crone. That's where he'd bury Jilly, beneath the blackthorn.

The soft earth opened easily for him. He placed her body in it, her precious black paw stiff. Squinting, he made everything a blur. Still, he welled up as he covered her with dirt. Sitting beneath the blackthorn tree, musing, thoughts drifted to the pine, rowan, and birch. Air suddenly buzzed. He rose, his feet directing him to the rowan. There he touched the branches and the ogham letter *Luis* that he had carved into the trunk.

Below the rowan, in the wet mossy groundcover, he found a series of tracks. Massive prints led to the muddy edges around the pond—four symmetrical toes, the spread shockingly clear, X-shaped pads. Claw marks had sunk deep into the soil. Wolf prints. Too many to figure out how many wolves, but certainly more than one or two. And definitely not the small prints of Sky Wolf.

Something swam inside his head. Dank wolf breath filled his nostrils. Pain stabbed his chest like a chisel being speared into his heart, driven by invisible blows. Marc's head lifted submissively. His eyes automatically rolled to the sky, throat yielding, jaw dropping open against his will.

Dark, mangy humps spread across the grass. Shadow wolves.

Howl with us.

The thought streamed into his head.

Howl with us!

Marc's neck stretched back as a wail rolled up from his belly. A battle cry. A singular note inside his throat scratched to emerge.

He clamped his jaw. Rejecting the command, stifling the howl fighting to surface, he grasped the wolf pendant on his neck and drove his strength high, jamming silence into his throat—holding hard, holding his breath until his head throbbed.

The howl aborted. His throat softened. Battle won.

Marc walked away, inhaling his courage, exhaling his fear. In his hot panting, images of the bloody Jilly burned inside his mind. *Savages. Killing my Beltaine hare.* He punched open the back door to make his way to the attic.

Chapter Nine

Ancestral Magick

Sunday at two o'clock, Charlotte flung open the windmill door. Sir Duncan Hawkinge tilted his head regally with a bow, his time-weathered face and steel-gray hair distinguished. "Good afternoon, Miss Knight. At your service. I come at the petition of your newly betrothed."

"Sir Duncan, come in. Welcome to Draakensky."

He stepped inside, her first official guest, dressed in sharp white-and-navy Bristol fashion. Sir Duncan regarded the living room with astute observation. He turned to Charlotte as if called to arms. "Permit me to express my highest congratulations. What stunning news. All blessings be with you both." He pronounced exquisitely, accenting his vowels like a true Brit.

"Marc told you?"

"Did he ever. He rang me last night at one AM and said, 'Hey, what are you doing?' What in bloody hell did he think, I wasn't sleeping at one AM? Then he told me the cracking news. And, your troubles this week."

"Marc insisted on calling you. I'm on a deadline," she explained in an apologetic tone. "You're saving my life. I'm so grateful you're able to pose for me today. Your portrait is critical to my show. The Van Cleeves' director is thrilled to have it."

"The honor is all mine," Sir Duncan said. "I only have two hours to give you. I'm catching a flight to London tonight."

"Marc told me you have pressing business at Elysium Fields in Kent. I cannot thank you enough. Come upstairs. I have my studio all ready, and we can get to work. Can I get you something, a cold beverage or tea?"

"Not a thing. But I fancy seeing the sumptuous jewel Marc bragged about."

She lifted her hand.

"Ah! Smashing. Mr. Sexton does have brilliant taste." He placed a kiss on her forehead as he would a daughter.

Charlotte led him to her studio. Before Sir Duncan arrived, she had hurriedly completed the setup with her easels properly aligned beneath the natural window light, spotlights hung overhead, tripods positioned, pewter lamps casting the atmosphere in glare-free light. Round throw-carpets in sage-green patterns anchored the room, and a dozen misshapen pottery candlesticks on wall shelves added charm.

Even though the bookcases still had gaping spaces between her zig-zagging art books—*Fear & Art* facing out dead center, her visual reminder about taking risks in art—she was pleased her studio displayed balance and harmony. If nothing else, Charlotte felt confident her brand-new sanctuary held a professional posture.

"Do I have to sit and not speak for two hours for you to complete the sketch?" Sir Duncan asked.

"Not at all. It's helpful to chat while drawing." She pointed to a stuffed armchair, and he took a seat. "Geoffrey Brink at Van Cleeves loved the original sketch I did of you, but he requires the portrait to be larger. And, he wants higher drama in the narrative. More of a scene."

Geoffrey had made it abundantly clear during their phone conversation that the *Earl of England* portrait needed *more biography, more passion*, which meant Charlotte had to engage her subject at a deeper emotional level.

"So, we're going to start all over for a new theme," Charlotte said. "That okay?"

"Whatever you need. You are the genius, my dear."

She noticed him examining the framed oval mirror on the wall. "That came from my apartment in Chicago," she told him. "I inherited it from the previous tenant."

"The feminine carvings are curious. Heroic semi-nudes are always so scholarly. Classical Roman?"

"As far as I can tell." Charlotte took a moment to fix a proper angle. "Can you turn slightly and look over your shoulder a bit? Yeah, that's it. Your posture is so elegant."

"We Brits pride ourselves on an upright stance reflecting our upright state of mind." He flashed a noble smile.

She pulled her shoulders back, sucked in her stomach, and began her outline. His facial bone structure exhibited a high-toned surface with strong masculine fissures, reminding her of tower battlements. "I was thinking," she said, "of naming the portrait *Earl of England*. Or maybe *The Hawkinge*. Which would you prefer?"

"Neither one," he returned without hesitation, his jaw jutting out. "I'm flattered that this will be exhibited at Van Cleeves. However, Charlotte, you cannot name me as the subject or suggest any connection that this portrait is Sir Duncan Hawkinge of Elysium Fields."

She put her pencil down. "Sir Duncan, Geoffrey Brink was greatly impressed with you as the subject. You *are* an earl of Kent, England."

"I'm earl of nothing. That title is only a courtesy for my ownership as a territorial designation. I don't relish broadcasting my heritage." His brownish eyes grew darker. "Elysium Fields has a small castle of sorts, and a rather unsavory account as far back as the 1700s. To my utter lament, the Hawkinge ancestry has a way of perpetuating its ill repute even into this century."

"Can you lift your chin?" She began shading in the wedge of his jaw. "Unsavory, how?"

"Crimes of passion. Betrayed loyalties. Disingenuous valor. Think olden days. Swords and duels. Warring families and forbidden marriages. The lying scoundrels cheated at every turn."

"Ohhh, that's juicy. Sounds adventurous to me."

"If only it were that, it might be amusing. The women proved to be roving maidens, proud to be ladies of pleasure. The men: false at love and keen at hustling. I could tell you tales right out of a Sir Walter Scott novel."

"Delicious family dramas?"

"More bloody than I'd like to admit." He shifted his shoulders, as though shaking something off. "The Hawkinge men raided public houses across the county. They stabbed any poor soul who obstructed their path. Smugglers, they were—brandy and rum. The London Gazette documented all their crimes. Madmen and murderers, we Hawkinges were."

This was a dark side to the earl that Charlotte hadn't heard. "Murderers?"

"The Hawkinge gang, as they were known in the 1750s, hung their adversaries—local rivals and errant neighbors—in metal chains dangling inside stone wells. Imagine the horror. Two Hawkinges were executed for treason."

"Whoa." She nearly blurted out *how gruesome* but held her tongue.

"Several got away with their terrorism. Evil for evil." He spoke now in a hushed and uneasy voice. "In 1885, Theodore Hawkinge pushed his poor wife off the cliff on the back of the property. The cruel bastard. I swear they both haunt the timberland. One bad seed after one bad seed at Elysium Fields."

"I think of that era as full of honor and valiant champions. Elysium Fields is such a romantic name. Doesn't Elysium mean grace or heavenly?"

"The estate was anything but heavenly. Elysium Fields remains a place of isolation to this day. When I tell you the smoke from the chimneys is corrupt, I mean it literally. The sky practically falls with blackened flocks of wretched rooks—I am not exaggerating. They croak and squawk havoc all day, every day. What a revolting language. The land is uninhabitable. The castle is crumbling into a dungeon. Even I refuse to live there."

Charlotte pictured stalking angry rooks. Austere sun. Shadowy gulfs. "Rooks are common in England? Black crows, right?"

"Basically the same species. Elysium Fields has hundreds. A plague on the land. Full of malice, they are. I've given up trying to sell the estate. Months ago, I filed a petition to demolish the castle. As long as the rooks keep residence there, not a living soul will buy it."

"What keeps the rooks on your land?"

"The blasted force of evil."

Charlotte tore her vision off the page. "Say again?"

"Force of evil. I agree with Shakespeare that there is no hell, that all the devils are right here with us." He coughed, hunching his shoulders. "Do you want me to show my pearly whites? Or shall I remain serious?"

"Whatever is comfortable. What do you mean, because of the evil?"

"To breathe that air is to breathe the malice of years past. Science tells us we all breathe air that contains molecules of history, perhaps even ancient history. Perhaps the dinosaurs' air."

"Fascinating concept. So you suspect you're breathing the air of the wretched rooks?"

"Indubitably. And my wretched ancestors as well."

Charlotte continued to sketch, her hand making sharp, fast strokes.

Sir Duncan gazed out the window, watching the sails turn for a quiet moment. "Those revolving blades are quite mesmerizing. We have a number of windmills in England converted into houses. Ace idea. Living here must be like giving wind power to your dreams."

"I like that thought."

Sir Duncan appeared pensive, his lips sucked in. She hadn't known this gloomy side of him. With half the image sketched out, she focused on the forehead.

"I expect you'll be happy here, Charlotte. This structure has a sensible vibration."

"So far, I am happy here. The river is magnificent. Lots of footpaths through the woods. Quiet as a church most days. And so many old trees here to sketch." She began working on the eyes now—sad they were. Upon closer examination, she found dark spaces. Was there another world lost inside the brown shine?

For several minutes, she worked in a background of turrets and stone archways, unsure why those shapes came to her, but she trusted her creative process of discovering Sir Duncan's theme. "Do you need a break before I go on?"

He smiled, this time a bright one that shooed away the pervading chill of his words. He ran a hand through his gray hair. Charlotte fixated on the filigree-silver tone and made a mental note to highlight that in the sketch.

"I could use a stretch," he said.

"Hold it a second, let me get a photograph of your position to use as a reference."

Over a quick pot of tea and the final hour of Charlotte's sketching, the conversation drifted to Sir Duncan's flat in London, his nasty divorce, and his thirty-year-old daughter thriving in the London theatre. "Elinor plays queens and chameleons exceptionally well," he stated proudly.

"Maybe I'll meet Elinor someday." She walked him downstairs a few minutes past four o'clock.

He stood in the open doorway with an expression of gratitude. "What a quietly compelling afternoon, Charlotte. You are both a rare and remarkable lady." His grace swept her into an all-consuming glow.

"Sir Duncan, you are incredibly kind. It means a great deal coming from you. Thank you so much for sitting for me today. Will you be back in the States soon?"

"A few weeks."

"Good. I'll work on the finishing touches tonight, but I am happy with the results so far. Do you have a title for the portrait you think might be appropriate?"

Sir Duncan plucked at the cuff of his shirt and stood tall in his swank navy blazer. "The obvious, I think. *The Earl With No*

Name." With a smart wink, he walked through the garden, shut the gate behind him, and crunched over the gravel driveway, a wounded man on his way back to Elysium Fields.

Charlotte immediately headed to the studio while Sir Duncan prevailed in her mind. Sitting at the easel, she heard his words again: *Evil for evil . . . a plague . . . full of malice.*

As she stroked her pen, defining Sir Duncan's features, she found an unseen presence of dark plumage scattering from her ink across the background. A darkening sky. She struggled to get it right and nearly gave up.

At midnight, she decided she could do no more. Taking a step back, she scrutinized the drawing. Sir Duncan's face illuminated strength. *The Earl With No Name.* No, that title would not do. Not with this new narrative of rooks and bulging shadows. She'd have to find another title.

Charlotte closed the studio lights and descended the spiral stairs to the bedroom, swearing she could hear rooks squawking on the roof.

Interlude I

Draakensky

I am the forest dark. I am the forest light. I breathe as the earth breathes.

Yew Crag cracks and aches at my side in this sylvan landscape. My black poplars shake themselves over the Mianus River, their airy presence rushing like crosswinds. I have starlings huddled in my trees; they desire open pastures, which I do not have; the starlings reside here nonetheless—I'm not sure why.

Do you see my oak leaves are bigger than your hands? In autumn, the reds, oranges, and golds will leave you delightfully blind to be buried in color. At snow time, I boast a horizontal quiescence from my cold lips and order you away. Every spring, within the massive green, I ripen into an ancient pulsation from my winking cliffs to call wild geese who love to soar the canyons. Summertime, ahhh, summer is my fragrant goodnight wind, loading your head with dreamy space.

Can you hear Draakensky's heartbeat? Listen closely to its magick. It is alive just like any man or woman's heartbeat. Most visitors cannot hear it drumming inside my widened air. The daughter can hear it. The daughter of Avalon.

The daughter comes down the path at sunrise daily. She hears my chaunting wildflowers, especially the bloodroot and trout-lily melodies. I have swans too, their wings all clamorous, which she finds enchanting.

For now, I watch for the daughter, come spring or sorrow. Despite all my beauty, she will find a resonant gloom here within my gorges, ravines, and yew trees. The wooded groves beyond are as thick and shadowed as a jungle. My terrain holds darkness of weed and black briar, and something else. The daughter, she is here to discover this darkness. And she is present to know the heartbeat of Draakensky.

I breathe as the earth breathes. I am.

Chapter Ten

Wolf Kill

Wednesday, at The Grackle Bar & Grill, Marc poured ice water into a tumbler and chugged it. Sheets of rain beat the front windows.

The bar had been slow for lunch. Weather drove the restaurant business; some patrons didn't come out on a rainy day. On the bar top, he lit candles and poured a refill for his only customer at the corner stool. An older guy, flipping a red poker chip between his fingers while watching the national news on the TV screen.

Marc anticipated Charlotte's arrival at two o'clock, and although he had a hundred things to do in the office, this next half hour belonged to Charlotte. Not seeing her for several days had him unnerved. And now she would be gone for another twenty-four hours in New York City. They would at least have Friday night together before her art opening on Saturday at Van Cleeves.

The front door banged open, rain and wind pushing Charlotte through. Her tailored black-and-white lapelled jacket and pants struck him. All buttoned up, she was. Not her usual feminine artsy style. Even all those brown waves, she had them neatly tucked into a braided twist at the nape of her neck, like something out of a Victorian movie.

The poker-chip guy gave her a cheeky appraisal.

"My fiancé," Marc announced.

"Is she? Pretty lady."

"Hello there, Miss Knight." He declined to kiss her, not in front of staff and customers—no kissing on the job rule. Modeling proprietary standards had its frustrations.

Charlotte slid onto a stool at the center of the bar's L-shape. The Tiffany lamps overhead bathed her face in a pinkish glow. "You're looking swank in that V-neck sweater," she murmured with a wiggle of her fingers at him, the sapphire ring throwing shimmers. "I've missed you."

Swank. He loved when she said that. "May I serve you a glass of wine?"

"Half, please. Cabernet. I'm driving and this weather is dreadful."

"Rain is supposed to stop around six. You all ready?"

"I am. Car is loaded with my sketches for the gallery tomorrow. I'm meeting Jung May and Frederik for dinner at seven at Le Bilboquet."

"Very chic. So that's why the new fashion getup. Business elegant?"

"Well," she tipped in closer, "Jung said they have an offer they want to discuss. I need to make a sharp impression when I meet Frederik, president of Sterling Publishing. He's a Ph.D., multilingual, extremely analytical, and fastidious, according to Jung."

He streamed red wine into a goblet. "What kind of an offer?"

"Jung wouldn't say. A new project and highly confidential. Epic, she said. I'm practically dizzy with curiosity." She fidgeted with the cocktail napkin. "I rearranged the furniture in the living room this morning. Twice. And my studio is finally complete. Want to see it? Friday night? Will you come to Draakensky?"

"Nothing could keep me away."

"Not even your staff troubles? When is Jackson returning?"

"He's feeling better. I expect him Friday night. Poor guy had a wicked flu. I have two substitutes on for the weekend, so Saturday should be clear for me."

"And what about Kelsey? Did she go back to Dublin?"

"I don't know. Sheila said she was planning to visit William in L.A."

"So, she won't be coming back to Bedford?"

"Charlotte, my mother is a never-ending path of unpredictability."

Marc knew Charlotte was too bright not to sense the disapproval his mother had revealed during their meeting. Best not to discuss it at the moment. No point in rattling Charlotte. "You're going to knock 'em dead. Are you happy with the new illustrations for Van Cleeves?"

"For the most part. The portrait of Sir Duncan, I'm not so sure. The scene is authentic. I'm sure of that. But it has an . . . underbelly. Whether Geoffrey Brink will approve is a test I might fail."

Liz strolled behind the bar and gave Charlotte a polite wave hello with a pinched grin. "I heard the big news. Our Grackle grapevine. Congratulations, Charlotte."

Marc caught Liz batting her lashes at him. *Old flame alert. Ex marks the spot.* Liz was a skilled barkeep for his clientele, but toxic in a relationship.

"Thank you, Liz," Charlotte said, grace in her tone.

Liz turned sharply and began loading glasses on the shelf. He was sure Charlotte caught Liz's disingenuous tone, leaving them in an awkward silence.

When the TV news broke with a Special Report, the announcement broke the tension. A close-up of a wolf's face zoomed the screen. "When will Americans stop exterminating wolves?" the reporter, a woman clad in black attire, unleased in a harsh tone, framed by a stretch of Minnesota woods. "Hunters kill at least one thousand wolves every year. Many are breeding-aged females. Even though wolves were declared an endangered species by 1978, wolf hunting is still legal and thriving in Alaska, Idaho, Montana, and Wyoming."

Marc heard Charlotte gasp.

"In Minnesota, federal government agents kill wolves within the full force of the law, with taxpayer money, under the US Department of Agriculture, Wildlife Services. When ranchers lose cattle or other livestock to wolves, the agency kills the wolves responsible. Last year, federal agents killed nearly 150 wolves. Wolves are being hounded, snared, and crushed by hunters using cruel and archaic methods such as blind-and-bait tactics at wolf kill sites and electronic wolf calls to lure them into traps."

"Man is the true killer," Marc burst out. "Wolves hunt food for survival, not sport."

The report cut to a video of a hunter, rifle on his shoulder, lifting his kill, an exquisite gray wolf, head and chest bloodied, tongue hanging out in a horrific surrender. The man beamed victory as he pulled back the wolf's head to show off the jaws.

Marc squeezed his lids shut for a second, grabbed the remote, and flipped the channel to the weather station. He gave Charlotte a cue, pointing toward the back office. "I'm on break, Liz."

In the office, Charlotte perched against the desk. "That report was gruesome. Sickening. You okay, Marc? You don't look so good."

He needed to sit down. He didn't sit though. Instead, he stiffened his legs and grounded his feet against the carpet. Wolf kills and bounties had a dreadful history since the 1600s; he knew that. These days, man had stopped hunting whales and bison. They no longer killed herons or eagles. Even the redwoods were protected. But man could still legally slaughter wolves for sport and thrills.

"I'm fine," he said. "That video caught me off guard. Killing such a beautiful animal. Intolerable. Damn arrogance." Charlotte stood before him, so beautiful, her gentle face, the flushed cheeks. He stroked her cheek with the side of his pinky.

"I have to leave soon." She put down her wine glass and embraced him. "I want to kiss your anger away."

"I'm yours."

Her mouth came up to his. He slid his hands around her waist, holding her in both hands, clinging tighter. She kissed him gently, the shape of her lips fitting perfectly against his. Nothing tasted sweeter.

"How many times do you think we've kissed?" she said between gentle smacks on his jaw.

"Not enough."

Charlotte leaned back, her hand sweeping the sweater to his throat, where she fingered his silver chain. "This wolf pendant. There is something unusual in the wolf's expression that keeps catching my eye. I know you said you got it in Australia, but you didn't just walk into a shop and buy it, did you?"

"No."

"Did it come from some Aboriginal chief in the Outback who fashioned it after a real wolf?"

"There are no known wolf breeds in Australia. Don't you think you should get on the road soon? Rain will make for slow driving."

She released a little moan, examining the pendant. "The face is similar to Sky Wolf—the same regal expression I've seen on her when she trots through your tree grove. Who designed it?"

He shook his head. "Another time."

"This is about your magick, isn't it? All those secrets you keep."

He noted the probing hitch in her voice when she said *your magick.*

"Marc, if I am going to be your wife, you need to let me in. I want to know everything about you. About your magick. About Sky Wolf, and Australia, and why you wear a wolf on your chest every day."

There it was, her ever-present charming curiosity. Know everything? Sometimes he didn't know how long he could walk through his life holding so many heavy secrets. The task became a small war going on inside him, keeping the secret forces unspoken, guarding the occult darkness, the revulsions—the beastly risks—and at the same time, dying to unburden it all. *Remain cautious*, Da would be saying. *Revealing your magick will weaken it.* He needed his magick to be stronger than ever now.

"Let's talk about this Friday night." Charlotte placed more kisses on the cleft of his chin. "Please share your magick with me."

"You're working hard to reel me in here."

"Mmm. I'll see you Friday night. You can tell me your secrets then."

Marc knew the best way to keep secrets was to act as if there weren't any. But he had been ridiculously poor at that with Charlotte.

She left her kiss lingering on his lips and walked out the door.

Chapter Eleven

Witch-Hares

Friday night descended with cold darkness. In Draakensky Windmill, Charlotte struck a match to the kindling in the fireplace. Three rainy days had left the windmill damp and chilled. After the week of long hours at her easel and time in New York City—meetings with Jung May and Frederik, and Thursday with Geoffrey Brink mounting the art show—a good fire would be the ticket to burn off her stress.

"I can do that," Marc said from the sofa, as he kicked off his shoes.

"I've got it. Sit back and have your brandy." She poked the logs. Flames shot up. After straightening her embroidered sweater, she grabbed her brandy snifter and sat down next to Marc on the blue sofa. The ice-blue shade reminded her of the azure sky above Draakensky that greeted her each morning when she opened the kitchen door to Jaa's teeming verdant forest. Even the withered trees with their tangled, sloping limbs carried an invitation to walk their paths.

"Good night for a fire," Marc said, unbuttoning his vest and tossing his tie.

"Are you undressing?" she teased.

His laughter swooned her. "Maybe later. Do you want me to undress?"

"Actually, I was planning on sending you home early, so I could get a good night's sleep for tomorrow." She purposely used a business-like tone. Was that a frown he made, or was he teasing her now? "So what do you think of Alice's redecoration? I know Jaa preferred the Dutch blues, but I love the ice-blue and creamy yellow walls. Adds space and airiness, don't you think?"

He hesitated before answering; she couldn't tell what he was thinking. "Airy, yeah." She snuggled into his chest. He took her hand into his. "You feeling tension about the exhibit tomorrow?"

"Is it obvious? Art reviewers will be there. I've been called mediocre more than once. One good thing though, a well-known still-life artist, Philip John, has paintings in their upstairs gallery. His exhibit opened two weeks ago. He's known as a daring and defiant talent. I'm glad the focus won't be exclusively on me. Geoffrey Brink is expecting a big turnout."

"Did he approve of Sir Duncan's new portrait?"

"He had some hesitations. Called it distinctive, but he thought it might be too dark for the poetic context of the show. When I left, the illustration was still unframed in his office."

Marc flexed his fingers, his expression distracted. Only the fire's crackling broke the silence between them. All through dinner, his conversation had seemed preoccupied.

He squeezed her hand and fondled the sapphire ring. "Tell me what happened with the mysterious offer from Sterling Publishing. How did you get on with Frederik?"

Charlotte released a growly sigh. "It went okay, but I'm legally bound to confidentiality." She lingered, dying to tell. "If you swear to secrecy, I'll tell you some of it."

"I swear on my life. What are you now, a book ninja, spying on unscrupulous art publishers?"

That was the most amusing comment he'd made all night. "Not quite, although Frederik is obsessed that this project remains secret. Sterling acquired the rights to publish an encyclopedia of heroines and goddesses. It's a monumental textbook of historical feminine power, divine and earthly, taking the reader around the globe. From Abeona, the Roman goddess to Zipporah, the magickal wife of Moses." She made an excited squeal. "And they offered me a contract to illustrate the goddesses."

He put down his brandy. "Rock and roll! I am in awe. Are you thrilled?"

"Yes. If I weren't so terrified. I might have to hire models. And I will meet with the author soon. She's an anthropologist and has spent half her life researching and writing this book. Jung says it's a masterpiece."

"Zipporah, huh? Moses had a magickal wife. How about that. Why does Frederik insist on keeping the book confidential?"

"Industry competition. He fears another house will come out with something similar to steal his thunder. The money is quite good. I'll be working full-time for at least nine months, maybe more." She zipped her mouth. "The end for now."

Stretching back, she rested her head on Marc's shoulder. The firelight altered the room into a pastel ambiance. Melting into his arms, she couldn't resist. Sleep took her.

When Charlotte woke, the fire burned brightly, evidence that Marc had tossed on more logs. The dining table had been cleared, napkins left askew. In the kitchen, Marc had cleaned up her cooking mess she had left from the baked lasagna and her homemade peasant bread that he had devoured.

"Marc?"

"Upstairs," she heard from the spiral staircase.

When she reached the top step, she found him sitting at her easel, surveying her sketches. For someone who didn't know much about art, Marc had a laudable interest in her craft, repeatedly paging through her sketch pad with the highest admiration. Even her clunky thumbprint sketches that had earned the wastepaper basket, he thought worthy.

"Thanks for clearing the dishes. I was dreading it. What do you think of my studio?" she cheered.

He swiveled, facing her, pointing to the sketch propped on the easel. "What is this you've drawn?"

She hadn't told him about her latest exploration. "It's unfinished. I had this amazing encounter with hares. They came to me, Marc. Your Beltaine hares."

"Well that's unlikely. Where was this?"

"On Draakensky."

"When?"

His words carried an unusual angst. Why did he sound so worried? "I saw them on my walk, today, on the path to the river. I was startled at first, but there they were and—"

"Today?"

"This afternoon. I absolutely had to draw them. Jilly stood about three feet ahead and I thought, I must capture this for Marc. I went straight back to the studio and did a quick sketch from memory of Jilly and these four hares." His expression was more serious than she expected. Why wasn't he amused? "I had trouble though. I struggled to get them right on the page. It was almost a fight to get the form accurate."

"Why are they in that formation? Jilly at the lead—and the four others behind?"

"Because that's the way they sat on the footpath. Three hares in a line behind, one in front. Jilly up ahead of them. Blocking me, those little devils. I could have walked around Jilly, but not the other four. They were much larger than her."

He scrutinized the sketch far too long. She sat next to him on the stool and peeked around to his face. "What's wrong? I thought you would be pleased to have a sketch of Jilly and your Beltaine hares."

"That certainly is Jilly with the one black paw. You've captured her face wonderfully. But the other four are peculiar. Were they sitting up with their front paws raised like that?"

"They were. Not Jilly though. She's crouching down on her bottom."

"Charlotte, why are these four hares wearing black hooded capes?" Something in his tone hinted accusation.

An odd and uncomfortable feeling came over her. "Ohh yeah, that. I started drawing their heads and ears, and I'm not sure why, but the ears became hoods, and then the contours elongated into capes as I finished off. Do you like the yellow gemstones on the border?"

"Why did you draw them with no faces inside the hoods?"

"I did draw their faces, at first. Their features came out too horsey and angry. So, I erased them. I discovered the blank faces, the obscurity, became a subtext."

"What subtext is that?"

"Shadows highlighting the mystery. A clandestine ingredient. Sometimes that's the way a sketch develops. Allusions. Inferences. As my pencil moves, a picture comes forth and creates something that I didn't consciously intend. Art often creates its own story through the image. I think the hares dressed up with gemstones are kind of cute in their robes with their hidden faces. In art, we trust the creative process as it opens a higher narrative of imagination."

"A narrative from your imagination," he repeated, almost a criticism.

"Marc, the narrative becomes a rendering *of* imagination. Not a rendering *from*. Picasso believed a painting is not determined beforehand. The image follows the 'mobility of the artist's thought.' His words."

"Say again?"

"While the picture is being drawn or painted, the form changes as the artist explores and develops the images. It becomes a new vision. Think of it as a realm. All art, and literature too, has realms. Rilke knew about reaching into the imaginal realm to find the poem. I learned a lot from illustrating his poems."

He frowned as if trying to draw up patience. "What are they holding in their front paws?"

"Fire stones. Stones don't burn, of course, but these stones have tiny flames, and the hares are offering them to the viewer." Seeing his appalled expression, she added, "I'm sorry, I don't understand why you're upset. I was playing with ideas and dressing up the hares."

"Playing?"

"You sound angry."

"I'm not angry. I'm disturbed. I want to be clear, these four hares are not my Beltaine hares," he blurted out.

"Okay. Maybe I messed up. It's only my early drafts."

"You did more than mess up. My Beltaine hares are not black

for one thing. Beltaine hares are whimsical. Friendly. They bring good wishes."

"*You* told me your Beltaine hares were witch-hares. And that's how the narrative developed in my mind. As witch-hares holding fire stones. I dressed them up and made them cute. I was experimenting. It's nothing important."

"It is important, Charlotte, because . . . I found Jilly dead in the pond. On Saturday."

That news hit like a slap. "Good God, you can't mean it."

Marc rose, slamming his foot on the easel leg, nearly knocking it over.

"Dead? How?"

Putting his hand up, he moved to the armchair and dropped into it.

"Marc, tell me what happened. Please."

"Her throat was ripped open," he said, voice breaking.

Charlotte tried to remain calm. "By what? Another animal? A fox, maybe?"

"This was no small animal."

She sat down on the ottoman to be close to him. "I'm sorry. I know the hares were dear to you."

"Jilly was dear to me. My Beltaine beauty. Year after year, she came to my bonfire every May first." He shook his head. "And now I had to make Jilly's grave. I buried her beneath my blackthorn tree."

"I don't know what to say." She twisted her hands up. "I'm so sorry. Last Saturday? Wait a sec. If Jilly was dead last Saturday, then—?"

"That's right. You saw Jilly. Manifested alive. Today. On Draakensky."

"Six days after you buried her?"

"Something has connected here. This is the same as when your magick manifested the dead thirty-nine owls on my land. In March, you sketched the owls in your pad and manifested them back into my ogham tree grove, *alive,* and flying the sky."

"It's not the same." She caught her breath high in her chest. "In March, I had drawn the owls on the page *first*. From my own thoughts. From my desire to see them in the grove. Then after, they manifested inside the trees, alive, exactly as I had sketched them. But today, I drew Jilly in my pad after she was manifested."

"Did you?"

She recalled walking the footpath to the river, feeling impatient to sit on her favorite rock by the waterfall. Jilly had appeared first with her one black paw turned out. Four black hares had hopped out from behind a bush. One hare had black and brown fur. The four aligned in a triangle formation as if to say, *Look at us.* Charlotte had taken her time to observe their size and position—the lone one at the back was quite fat, her bottom wide like a sinking tugboat.

Instead of moving on to the river, Charlotte had hurried back to the windmill, to her studio, and quickly began a few studies in her sketch pad.

"Yes, I know I saw Jilly standing in front of the four hares. She wasn't really with them, though. I don't understand how I saw her manifested today on the path."

"You are a daughter of Avalon," he announced firmly. "Vivienne has given you the magick. Know this: those four hares are not my Beltaine witch-hares." A muscle rippled on his cheek like he was biting down on the words. "You saw something else on that path. Something menacing. Something dark."

Charlotte felt darkness rise inside her throat. *Witches?* She knew witches, the ghost-witch of Hanover Hill she had met in the abandoned lot near her Chicago neighborhood when she was a child. And Heida Mead's witchcraft, wielding owl magick that viciously targeted Marc and attacked Thomas Harrogate, and nearly sent Charlotte crashing down the Mianus River falls to her death. Jaa, on the other hand, was a wind-witch, practicing her own form of wind magick under the powerful Frau Holle, the wind being of Draakensky.

"Marc, what's happening? What power manifested Jilly and the four witch-hares on Draakensky?"

"I don't know. It's possible that your magick is redeveloping. Growing into what exactly, I'm unsure. Whatever it's becoming, we need to be cautious. We'd better bury that sketch of the hooded witch-hares." He went to the easel and snatched it.

"Why?"

"Because whatever these black witch-hares are, we don't want them returning. One thing is abundantly clear: they are not friendly. Do you have other sketches?"

"In the wastepaper basket."

After gathering them, he walked downstairs. In the kitchen, he placed each page ceremoniously into the sink and flooded them with hot water, chanting in whispers. She couldn't hear a single syllable clearly. He squeezed the mess into a flattened mound, his hands swelling up red. "Grab the fireplace shovel. Where does the sun come up here?"

"At the front, in the living room windows and then at the kitchen door."

They moved outside to the southern side of the windmill and walked several paces into the woods among moss and weeds. Marc dug a hole, dropped in the soaked mound, and covered it up. He pulled up a small cedar sapling and planted it in the soil. Cedars were thought to be cleansing; Charlotte knew that much.

"Marc, please tell me what you're thinking."

"Listen to me," Marc said, holding her shoulders, "you have an important day tomorrow. Let what happened here go. The witch-hare images you drew on Draakensky are buried now and returned to the earth. We trust Nature will attend to it. Focus on the present."

Back inside the house, Marc threw logs into the fireplace, and they sat on the floor, bright flames swirling with crackles.

"Marc, I'm sorry. When I draw, I charge the page with my intentions. I shouldn't have drawn the witch-hares. My God, why were those four witch-hares even on Draakensky?"

He placed a kiss on her forehead. "I think you know. This journey you're on draws compelling energy, and I think you know what it means."

She pulled back, swallowing hard. "What? What do I know?"

"These witch-hares came to you. Isn't that what you said? Ask yourself, why did you choose to live on Draakensky? Why did you insist on renting Jaa's windmill rather than find an apartment rental somewhere else? Why do you walk the paths through the woods and visit the river every day?"

"I love it here. This is my home now."

"I'm saying, Jaa is dead. Heida is dead. Now, Draakensky is alive through you." He squeezed both her hands inside his. "You, Charlotte, are Draakensky."

His words hurtled straight through her.

Chapter Twelve

Landscape of Morning

Dawn broke at the bedroom windows. Charlotte slept like a bride. Pure. Winsome. Gratified. Marc kissed her naked shoulder. Every caress, every touch from their lovemaking repeated in his mind. He had had plenty of sex with women in his thirty-nine years, but it was never just sex with Charlotte. The tides of her passion grew higher each time, her desires just a little untamed. They had slept, her thigh flung over his, tangled together.

Quietly he left the bed, zipped on a sweat suit and put on running shoes. When he exited the bathroom, she slit an eye open.

"Going for a quick run," he whispered and silently closed the door.

He drew up an image of his mom closing the bedroom door to his and William's bedroom, from his boyhood days in the Lewisboro farmhouse. Why think of this now? Maybe because his sister had texted that Kelsey was taking a flight out of Boston to Dublin at noon. What a relief she wasn't returning to Bedford. Still, he'd have to call her next week and inform his mother that the engagement was now official. Dreading it, he pushed open the windmill door and hit the ground running.

Marc loved first light, the sun kindling, pushing up a silver sky. Taking the back trail that wound through the forest, he was surprised the path had been freshly cleared of roots and debris. Alice must have hired a landscaper, knowing Charlotte would be walking the trails.

He trotted out, thinking of Jilly. Was Jilly a resident of Draakensky now? Would he find her on the path ahead? Or the four witch-hares following him, fire stones in their paws? What the hell was that about? Charlotte was deeper into her magickal realm than he had realized.

She didn't see it, but her magick was aligning with the forces of Nature, or possibly converging. Earth magick. Goddess magick. Why was he surprised? Earth was a feminine element in the universe. Earth gives birth to trees and nourishes the fruit of the land. Woman gives birth to new life and nourishes humanity.

With a full day ahead, he ran a mental list of the loose ends at the bar, calls and emails to return, and driving into Manhattan by four o'clock for Charlotte's opening. He knew so little about art. He increased his speed, his mind settling as he rounded bends and huffed up hills. On the path ahead, beyond a thicket of heavily leafed trees, he slowed down, taking in the view of the log cabin that backed up into the woods. He might have missed it for all the conifers surrounding the structure. Thomas Harrogate's cabin hid in a phalanx of thick green.

Harrogate's death on Yew Crag came flooding back. His body caged in yew tree branches on the river rock. Heida and her vicious owl magick the cause. Marc had never witnessed such vile witchcraft. Poor Jaa had been devastated.

After walking the gravel path to the cabin door, he peeked into the front windows. An empty L-shaped room, a ladder to a wide loft, a black iron wood-burning stove at the far end—it was similar to the one in his father's cabin in Lewisboro.

He tried the door. The knob released. Did Alice leave the cabin unsecured?

Inside, the cabin smelled of cleaning solution and cedar. Morning light gleamed on shellacked timber beams and polished floors in rich brown tones. The fieldstone fireplace held black irons and birch logs.

In the kitchen, a double-styled window shone, newly washed. Outside, the bushes spread thick with limbs touching the glass. Two bedrooms, facing east, held a flood of sunlight. What a treat to wake up to the sunrise streaming in. His bedroom in the renovated barn faced west.

He climbed the ladder to check out the loft. He found immaculate mahogany built-in bookcases, a skylight, and a cubby of bright windows for a reading corner.

Downstairs, the living room casement window overlooked the river, not more than forty feet away. Stunning. For a fleeting moment, he saw himself living there. How absurd. He loved his rustic green barn restored to perfection, his ten acres of privacy, and the clear sky above every night. Here, the trees towered over the roof. He'd never be able to stargaze. And he couldn't live without Orion, his ogham tree grove, and the pond.

"Well, what do you know," he said, his voice echoing. Hung on the back door was a straw-brimmed hat with a green band. His father had sometimes worn a similar garden hat.

The front door banged open behind him. He turned.

"Alice. Hi," he said, somewhat embarrassed. "I was on a run and found the door open. Sorry, I couldn't resist snooping. I didn't mean to barge—"

"Oh don't worry about it." She gave a polite laugh. "My fault for not locking up yesterday. How are you on this bright Saturday morning?"

"I'm well. You seem a little frazzled. Did I startle you?"

"Not really," she said, catching her breath. "I've got a possible renter coming to see the cabin, and I want to spruce it up." She placed a bucket of red flowers on the floor before the fireplace and another on the kitchen counter. "Flowers make even the dullest of rooms inviting."

"Who's the renter?"

"Financial analyst from the city. Wants a place for weekends over the summer."

"I didn't know you were advertising for renters."

"I'm not. This is through a friend of a friend. I'm not sure renting this place is going to work out." She rested her arm on the counter, hands jittery.

"Why shouldn't it work out?"

"Well, you know. The stories. Two unresolved deaths on Yew Crag are a big negative. Harrogate lived in this cabin. Heida owned it. People sense bad vibes." She whisked black strands from her forehead. "Is Charlotte excited about the opening today? I'm so disappointed I can't be there. My son is the lead in the school play tonight."

"Is he? What a thrill. Yeah, Charlotte's excited. She has an interview at Manhattan Art Life today, so she's taking a train in early. You know, the cabin looks smart. Great cleanup job. Whose hat is on the door?"

"I found it in Jaa's shed. Hats on a door are cozy. Do you think I should add a few flowers on the brim?"

"Probably not. It's a man's hat, isn't it?"

"Maybe." She grabbed a small flower from the bucket and placed it inside the green band, then tore it off. "You're right. It's a man's hat. Listen, I have one more small bag to get out of the car before the guy gets here so—"

"Sure. Go ahead. Good luck with the renter. I'm off to finish my run."

"Tell Charlotte I plan to get into the city in a couple of weeks and will stop by Van Cleeves. I'm so happy for her."

Marc left, closing the door behind him. Making his way to the alternate path along the river, he picked up his speed. The scent of balsams mixed with mud and algae from the river filled him. Breathing heavily, sweating in the rising heat, the sun a warm butter pat on his face, he enjoyed pounding out the tensions. Beyond a boulder to his left, a rabbit scampered. Not a rabbit. Silvery. With a long tail. A baby fox, tiny as a kitten.

He headed down another path. Approaching Yew Crag, at the bridge, he slowed his pace. Images of Heida Mead weighed him down. The dead Heida, cast into Black Wolf Realm. He hadn't thought much about Heida lately.

Beyond the arch of the footbridge, the old yew tree with its twisted trunk stood, evoking a green monster in a dark, shaggy jungle full of wind. Jaa came to mind, the magnificent wind sorcerer of Draakensky. Jaa knew Yew Crag as well as she knew her own soul, her last words to him—*I am the wind!*—as her yellow scarf waved bright like a beacon over the Mianus River.

A gust swirled, then slammed against his face. Jaa, the wind magickian. "You're still here, aren't you, Jaa? I suppose you'll never really be gone from Draakensky." A wedge of wind settled down on him.

No further thought was needed. He crossed over the bridge to

Jaa's Yew Crag, the river waves peaking into hands waving him on. River Magick. Automatically, he jogged to the giant yew.

There, on the flat river rock, raw and desolate, Heida Mead had met her death, creating a destiny that cast her into the realm between worlds. She had instinctively held on to her tempestuous nature, not unlike the defiant force of a wolf on the hunt. He often wondered if the shadow wolves hadn't lurked within her spirit. Celtic lore spoke of the hidden soul.

A crack sounded. Then another. Then a series of snaps. Heavy footsteps tramping twigs? He turned but saw nothing on the path, nothing across the river. Only a sky full of pine trees.

Until the pines swerved out wildly.

Each pine hooked its branches. Trunks twisted. Was he seeing this right? The river's white caps soared up in barrel rolls. Waves flipped, switching directions from south to north, making everything suddenly cartwheel on him.

The morning sky streaked down yellow in wind-milling circles. Astonished, his eyes burning and blurring, he fell back against a tree and stumbled to the ground. Flat on his back, he closed his eyes until the spinning surged into a slow churn. Waiting for his heart to calm, he counted down his breaths from ten to zero.

When he opened his eyelids, he met two shining eyes rimmed in yellow.

"Camaroon!" The hawk owl perched on his knee—ash-colored feathers, black and brown and white stripes. The red hues on the tail sharpened in the light. River, trees, and sky, all in their proper positions now, Marc sat up slowly.

Aurora bright, Camaroon tilted his head grandly.

"I've not seen you for weeks," Marc said, wanting to pet his feathers.

Camaroon blinked at him.

"I could have done with a less dramatic entrance."

His horny beak lifted. A couple of eerie hoots floated out.

"What? What do you want to say?"

Camaroon rustled his feathers, king supreme, flaunted his wide wings, and took flight. Marc rose on steady legs; he followed the bird's flight down the path, followed Camaroon's wings as they tipped across Yew Crag bridge to Draakensky Windmill. At the lawn, Camaroon zoomed to the garden to perch on the stone wall.

Owls are largely air. Jaa's words—her wind magick still present on Draakensky. *Of course it is. Magick never dies.* As the windmill blades turned, he had an urge to step back several feet.

Now he had a full perspective of Draakensky Windmill against the expanse of blue sky. Camaroon shot up and latched onto the roof's edge. A sudden pulsing crimson flushed his tail feathers—gesturing. A red flag?

Camaroon remained there, eyes like lanterns that see through darkness. Owls were the wise keepers of history. Protectors of the dead. Travelers between the realms of the unknown. Marc knew that from Da.

What darkness are you seeing here on Draakensky, Camaroon?

Chapter Thirteen

Lupus the Wolf

Charlotte sank deeply into the bathtub, soapy bubbles up to her neck. The day ahead in Manhattan required a serious soak. Splashes echoed. Steam lifted.

Marc would be back soon from his run. She had left the bathroom door ajar to hear when he returned. They hadn't had their talk on Friday night, witch-hares taking up all their time. Marc clearly didn't want to elaborate about the hares. Did he know something more than he had said? His secrets were heavy as rocks buried beneath the king's castle, and him the guard at the gateway. She'd find a way to pass through the gate.

"I am not Draakensky," she said, stretching up her leg and running the sea sponge over her calf. She inhaled the rose bath salts aroma, sinking deeper into the warmth, eyelids lowering.

"Very cozy," she heard Marc's voice.

Had she dropped off?

"May I join you, m'lady?"

"Mmmm, that would be splendiferous."

He stripped off his clothes and slid in behind her, cradling her hips between his legs, her back firmly against his chest. "This is paradise. Just what I need to escape."

"What are you escaping, Mr. Sexton?"

"Same old troubles, I guess."

Something in his voice sounded distraught, not his usual upbeat tone. "You okay?"

"Fine."

Resting together for several minutes, they didn't speak.

"I'm a bit sweaty," he offered, sloshing water.

"Sweat becomes you."

"Only you would say that."

She weaved her wet fingers through his. Charlotte loved his hands, the fleshy cushions, the warmth of the fingertips.

He placed his cheek against her head. "You smell delicious. All this steam. Here we are like Merlin and Vivienne in the warm mists of Avalon."

She sat up, curled her legs, and maneuvered a full turn to face him, splashing water over the rim. "An enticing thought, but I have to catch the 12:52 train to Grand Central."

"Okay."

"You'll be at the gallery by four o'clock?"

"I will."

"And how did you enjoy your run on Draakensky?"

"Very much. I took the southern path to the cabin. On the run back, I followed the river path. Guess what? I saw Camaroon."

"On Draakensky? Where?"

"Yew Crag. This was his territory, after all. The only reason he visited my property was because of Heida's spell-craft."

She held her tongue, not sure how to respond. Camaroon had been a vicious owl that attacked her and Thomas Harrogate.

"Hey, no reason to worry. Camaroon is safe. His spirit is healed now. He has absorbed the good light and is no longer under Heida's witchcraft. We can trust Camaroon's owl magick now."

"Is that so? And what about trusting your magick?"

He leaned in for a kiss, but the wolf pendant swung, and she reached for it, thwarting his kiss. The silver face reflected in the overhead spotlights. She examined the back and front. "Why is the wolf mounted on a shield?"

He shrugged.

"We didn't have our talk last night. About Australia."

"What do you want to know?" He soaked the sea sponge underwater and squeezed it out on her knees.

"How did you find this wolf pendant?"

"I didn't find it. It found me. I went to Australia after my father died. I was a mess. In shock. We were devastated. Sheila was thirteen and hysterical all the time. William was in high school and wouldn't speak to anyone, kept himself barricaded in his room. My mother was practically banging her head against the wall every day. Life hangs by a thread—death can strike anytime. In the summer, after my first year at college, Mamó convinced me to visit Australia."

"Why? What was in Australia?"

"It's not what was in Australia. It's what Australia was in. The Southern Hemisphere. Mamó insisted I needed to discover my magick. And I found it on Whitehaven Beach in Queensland." He played with the sea sponge, soaking it and ringing it out on her shoulders and arms. "There's a force in the universe, and Mamó directed me how to access that star magick."

His expression grew so serious that it almost frightened her.

"Finding one's magick is a risky adventure. I lived on the beach, south of the ecliptic plane. In a dark patch of sky, between the Scorpius and Centaurus constellations, is the star constellation Lupus. It belongs to the Hercules star family. Lupus is a full wolf formation, discovered by Ptolemy in the second century."

"Ptolemy? The astronomer?"

"That's the one. Mathematician and geographer too. He invented longitude and latitude. Ptolemy saw the four stars that make the wolf's curving body: Gamma Lupi, Delta Lupi, Beta Lupi, and Alpha Lupi. Two stars mark the front legs. The stars near Scorpius, near the pincers, form a triangle, and that's the head of Lupus the Wolf."

"Lupus the Wolf. And if I went to Australia, I could see this wolf in the night sky?"

"The stars are faint, but if you know what to look for, yes. The brightest star is named Alpha Lupi, a giant hot blue star. Mamó had given me instructions on how to locate it, the ritual, and the incantations. And how to draw down the star and accept its light energy into my body."

He cocked his head with an odd expression as if to say, *Am I shocking you?*

"Druids knew star power and lore," he went on, "and Mamó was a brilliant Lore Keeper. Wizards knew how to draw down star magick since medieval times."

"You're telling me you drew down a star?"

"I drew down Alpha Lupi's energy. This is not about drawing down power for myself. My Celtic ancestors knew stellar-based magick. Mamó had lore that the Lupus wolf represents a wolf killed by Centaurus."

Charlotte took the sea sponge from his hands and soaked it. All these names and stars and wolves reeled in her mind. *Drawing down stars!*

"I spent three days sleeping on the beach with no success in drawing down Alpha Lupi's energy. Until the fourth night. Starlight burst out, a thousand diamonds across the sky. A glittering shaft broke through. The light bolt hit me so hard, it knocked me out. Mamó didn't mention that part."

"Were you hurt?"

"The shock rocked me pretty bad. When I came to, I had this chain around my neck and the wolf head dangling. The metal left burn marks on my skin. I struggled to stand, dizzy as hell, couldn't catch my breath. And then I heard a single howling. A sweeping wolf song, breaking crescendos, so loud it pulsed the sky."

"Gosh, you're kidding."

"I'm not. The refrains penetrated my whole body until every part of me vibrated. I calmed myself. Circles brimmed over my head. A rush of energy spread out and merged me into the circles as bright as the sun."

Charlotte gasped, curling her toes in the water.

"And there she stood, a brilliant shining white wolf on the crest of a dune. Absolutely glorious. I don't think I was breathing. The depth of her eyes captured me. She locked me up deep into her. I loved every second of it."

Charlotte wanted to cry. "This changed you, didn't it?"

"Dramatically. Once you engage a wolf's eyes—I mean really connect into their light—that wolf takes you inside its spirit and holds you there."

The enchantment of his voice, low and tender, his soft accents, made a floating sensation between them. "Did you approach her?"

"I didn't dare. I did get close enough to see she had bits of silvery fur on her tail. She caught me staring and took off. Ran the beach, a speeding bullet, kicking up blue dust, sending her light sparkling across the sand. She performed like a white goddess."

Charlotte admired his flush of emotion, how he expanded with vivid intensity. She might have touched the glow between them. "Did you go after her?"

He was slow to answer. "I chased her down the shoreline. I never ran so fast in my life, this dazzling white wolf shooting tiny stars off her back that brushed my face as we ran the beach. The sun rose, and she was gone. She left her tracks in the wet sand, beautiful paw prints in a lacy pattern, until those prints stopped. I guess she leaped right back up to her star."

"How is it that Sky Wolf left prints in the sand? I mean, not being an actual physical wolf constructed of mass and weight?"

He grinned. "We never attempt to prove magick. This is not science."

Of course not. Charlotte held Sky Wolf in her mind. She imagined drawing the wolf into her sketch pad with stars dripping like marbled eyes and black lashes sweeping the sky.

"I'll never forget a single moment. I knew immediately that this wolf belonged with me."

"When did you find her again?"

"I didn't see her again until I purchased the barn and planted the ogham tree grove. *Mac Tire,* Charlotte. That's what we call a wolf in Ireland. And I named her Sky Wolf."

"Sky Wolf is your star wolf."

"Not mine. She's free. Sky Wolf belongs to the universe. She's a terrestrial being now. She chose to live here as an earthly wolf. If you cut her, she'll bleed. I don't know for sure, but I suppose she'll die someday like any earthly wolf. Although that would probably kill me. I can't bear the thought of losing her."

"Was she born into a litter like a normal wolf?"

"Not sure. She retains her magickal elements. No doubt about that. And she's very clear on how she uses her power."

"How long has she been here with you?"

"A few years. First time I saw her was winter—paw prints in the snow. She snapped up squirrels and ate them. She would sit in my tree grove. Most times she keeps me at a distance as any wild wolf would. Only once did she let me touch her. Sometimes I can't see her, but I hear her songs. Even though Sky Wolf is a full-blooded wild wolf who hunts, eats, and plays, she'll never lose her magick."

"And your magick? Is it from Sky Wolf?"

"Not entirely. When I came home, Mamó connected me to Vivienne. As water goddess, because Vivienne rules the wolf realms in the Otherworld, she granted me Sky Wolf that night on the beach. In gratitude, I serve Vivienne. I bring daughters to Avalon with my magick."

Recalling the night he gave her his magick in his bed, she said, "Like you brought me to Avalon?"

"Yes."

"How many women besides me have you brought as daughters?"

He shook his head.

Were there so many that he didn't want to tell her? And were they all sexual encounters like hers? He picked up the bar of soap and ran it across his chest, cupping water over his shoulders.

"There's always another secret buried inside you. What are you hiding? I'm worthy of keeping your confidences, Marc."

"You have no need to know, my lovely."

"I do need to know. How many others have you brought to Avalon? Five? Fifty? A hundred? Is it always a sexual passage?"

He held his lips together firmly. She practically could see his secrets—a nest of tiny birds filling his mouth that he refused to let fly out. She splashed him. "Tell me."

"I'll tell you this much. Erotic knowledge is empowering. There are different passages to empowerment and to becoming a daughter of Avalon. Is that enough now? Let's have breakfast."

"What kind of different passages?"

"You're going to drive me to my knees with this?"

"If that's what it takes. What kind of passages?"

He licked his lips thoughtfully. "Whatever passage is meaningful to the woman. Some prefer star magick or water magick, which is the magick of the sea. Earth magick employs trees or crystals. Moon magick. Sex magick. Mirror magick. You, Charlotte, were the twenty-fourth daughter of Avalon I brought to Vivienne. And I was proud to give you Avalon."

Twenty-fourth? "How many became daughters through your sex magick?"

"A selected few. Subject closed, please. Shall I brew us a fresh pot of coffee?"

"No coffee." He slid down lower into the water, the silvery wolf head shining at her. *Sky Wolf, drawn down from the star constellation Lupus in the Southern Hemisphere.*

She lifted the pendant; her fingertips fondled the rough-carved face of the wolf, and her pinky slid against the shield. Forcing more from him might be a mistake. Yet, she had Marc right there in her grasp. "Why is there a shield behind the wolf's head?"

"Shields are protection. A guardian. How about I scramble up a batch of eggs?"

"Why do you need a guardian?"

"Everybody has guardians. Don't Catholics have guardian

angels? Same thing. Would you prefer a cheese omelet?" He tossed the sponge at her chest.

"Wolves and angels are not at all the same thing. Why do you require a *wolf* guardian?"

He gave her a sideways glance. "It's nothing. Shields protect. Let's leave it at that."

"You're in danger, right?"

He shook his head as if to say no, but it was more like *no, I don't want to tell you.*

"It's because of Black Wolf Realm, isn't it?"

"There are boundaries here I'd prefer not to cross. Don't ask me, Charlotte," he said gently.

She tossed the sopping sponge at him. Another time on Draakensky he had told her not to ask about Black Wolf Realm as they had walked Yew Crag. *If I reveal that to you, or anyone, we would draw its power down upon us,* he had said. The words were not on his tongue then and were not now.

There was power in keeping secrets. Marc had that art mastered. Obedient to the creed, he was. What *would* he reveal? Because there was power in revelations too. What was this damn darkness he fiercely protected? "Marc, tell me why you need a wolf guardian."

"Charlotte, please. I told you about Sky Wolf. And the daughters I brought to Avalon. But I cannot speak of Black Wolf Realm. Relinquish control." His tone was harsher, his stare unrelenting.

The command sent her heart racing. "I might say the same to you. The threat *is* Black Wolf Realm. What danger are you in, Marc?"

His silence penetrated enough to make her want to slap him.

Was he protecting her? Or protecting Black Wolf Realm? She returned the same stare right back at him—the two of them, a standoff. She rose abruptly.

Splashing water everywhere, dripping naked before him, letting him scrutinize her curves, his eyes raised, hers lowered down on him, she lifted her leg out of the tub, half tempted to kick him. "Water's gone cold. You win. Keep your damn secrets."

Charlotte wrapped herself in the white bathrobe, then exited the room, throwing the door open to bang the wall behind her.

Chapter Fourteen

A Private Sky

Half an hour later, Marc rapped at the bedroom door that she had left half open. He knew he'd better smooth things over. "Am I banished?"

No answer.

"I brought you a hot breakfast. Cinnamon tea with cream." He waited for her to reply. "Charlotte?"

"Fine. Come in."

She sat at her dressing table in panties and bra, sweeping her eyelashes with mascara. Her sketch pad on the chest of drawers showed fat jack pines. *When did she draw this?* The thicket practically leaped off the page at him. He questioned why she drew the scene with falling autumn flakes instead of leaves.

He placed the plate down on her dressing table and sat on the bed. "Black lace undies. Very attractive." Ignoring him, she brushed color to her cheeks and ruffled out the shiny hair that curled down her shoulders like a queen's. "You know what, there are moments when you take my breath away." He ran his thumb along her arm.

"You know what, Marc?" she answered in a loud voice. "Your being cute isn't working."

"Oh. It isn't?" He handed her the mug of tea. "Okay, I'll move on. I was thinking, after the art show, we'd have dinner in the city. I made reservations at the Monk's Court on 53rd Street. It's a favorite of mine."

Charlotte snatched the plate of fried eggs and bit off a chunk of toast. "Why are you always feeding me?"

"It's what I do. I'm hospitality. Try the avocado and honey yogurt. It will soothe the beast."

"It will not. What's the Monk's Court, anyway? We're having dinner at a monastery now?"

"Monks in white robes will serve us French peasant cuisine, *moules marinières* in white wine sauce, lamb cassoulet with tarragon and white beans, bread made with cream, hot out of the oven."

"I dislike mussels, in white wine or otherwise."

He knew to try again. "Will dessert tempt you? Chocolate soufflé? Crème brûlée?"

"Ugh, how utterly ordinary. I will settle for nothing less than crêpes Suzette flambé."

She rose from the chair and wiggled into a silky slip, more black lace, and sat down on the chaise lounge to finish eating. He waited for her to throw another curve. She didn't.

"Okay, I get it. I apologize for being . . . obnoxious . . . and secretive . . . and—"

"And controlling and mistrustful and evasive."

"Yes, all those things. I'm sorry. Listen, the last thing I want to do is add to your stress today. Shall we discuss my behavior another time?"

She tossed a glance at the night table clock. "No. You have exactly five minutes to explain to me why you refuse to tell me the whole truth about your wolf guardian and why Black Wolf Realm must remain a secret between us."

She dipped her toast spear into the egg yolk and munched away, her steely grays on him the most determined he'd ever seen. How could he explain the hidden realms? Exposing the secret mysteries exposes the power—and risks vulnerability. Recalling his father's guidance on this, he offered what Matthew Sexton would have said.

"Charlotte, knowledge has eyes. And I don't want you to see this knowledge. What's more, I don't want this knowledge to see you."

She sipped her tea and huffed. "If there's danger here, I need to know what that danger is."

"Sometimes, the unknowable is a stronger place than knowledge. The unknowable can be a safe place. For you. For us. Can you appreciate that?"

Her face dropped, and he thought she might cry. "The unknowable? Really? My mother was the unknowable."

"What?"

"She died before I was two years old when her heart suddenly failed. I never *knew* her. Not a single memory. Not the sound of her voice or the touch of her hand. And my father . . . Charles Knight married my mom and went back to London the day after I was born. Never returned. Six years later he crashed his Cessna into the Atlantic. Another unknowable." She pushed the plate away. "I knew Aunt Loretta but then she died and took everything with her. And suddenly, I belonged to absolutely no one. Nowhere. There is nothing safe about living in the unknowable. Don't ask me to embrace uncertainty."

Marc stifled a cringe. He was aware that her childhood

abandonment was still a wound. *Be more careful.* "Is that why you became an artist? Drawing nature scenes so you could belong to the landscape, to everything that grows around you?" Her poker face told him she didn't appreciate that comment. "I'm sorry. That didn't come out right. I'm not playing with your head. I'm trying to understand, not trivialize. Your sketches of trees are magnificent. You are completely connected to nature. It's like you *are* a tree."

The way she glared, he thought she might throw her tea mug at him.

"Marc, do you have any idea what it feels like for a child to lose an entire family? Everything is detached. Displaced, belonging nowhere, belonging to no one. Your soul is starving. All you can think of is how hungry you are. Sometimes the only attachment you have is the very earth you stand on. So, yeah, trees and flowers and plants have been a sanctuary for me. I am always nourished by their companionship. The trees are rooted there every morning and every night. They don't leave you."

Your soul is starving. He hadn't realized how deep this cut her.

She moved to sit on the bed with him. "If I am going to marry you, live with you, and love you the rest of my life, I cannot have the unknowable in our marriage. Do not hide the truth from me, Marc. Can you appreciate that?"

Her words grabbed him by the throat. Charlotte understood about stepping through the darkness more than he had realized. She needed solid ground; she needed the door half open. "Yes, I can appreciate that. And I will explain the realms when the time is safe. I promise. I think you are remarkable, Charlotte."

Wolf Magick

At 2:45 PM, Marc accelerated the gas pedal in his Volvo up the ramp onto the Merritt Parkway toward New York City. Traffic was clogged, but he'd allowed himself plenty of time to be at Van Cleeves Gallery by four o'clock. Cars weaved in and out as he struggled to keep his mind on the road ahead.

How would he maintain a relationship with Charlotte when a vital part of himself *was* the wretched unknowable? All his efforts to obscure and misdirect to keep the boundaries of his history hidden suddenly felt breached. His mom knew only what her husband permitted her to know about the Sexton magick. How in hell did Da maintain that kind of silence and still make a good marriage?

Would Charlotte's love be strong enough to weather his history? And what about their children? What if their son or daughter inherited the Sexton gift? How would Charlotte accept it?

Do not hide the truth from me, she'd said. Half his life was hiding the truth.

After parking the car at a nearby garage, he hustled the streets to Van Cleeves on West 55th Street and pressed his way through the glass double doors. Surprised at the crowd already mixing about, he mingled in, searching for Charlotte. Several of her landscape sketches hung on the walls along with Rilke's illustrated poems in bright silver frames.

Her signature illustration, *Child in Red* was featured center stage, the ghostly red swing and surreal crescent moon attracting everyone to it. He noticed a throng of women, champagne glasses in hand, conspiring remarks—most of which were a bit too esoteric for his appreciation. *Woman in Love* held his eye for a long time—a broken window, darkened and mute, with a candle flame that was disappearing into a frothy rain. After reading the poem, he considered the image again. Does love make a woman disappear like that candle flame is fading out? A loss of presence? He had to disagree with Rilke on that one.

A waiter approached with a tray of champagne flutes, which he didn't want, but obliged rather than be the only one without a glass. Still no sign of Charlotte.

No one was viewing *The Panther* so he stood before it—reading the poem describing a captured panther behind bars—and sipped a surprisingly high-quality champagne.

"Caging the untamable, right?" a man behind him said. "Impossible to take the wild out of beasts."

Marc turned. "Probably," he agreed to be polite.

"Cages should remain empty," the man grumbled.

As Marc strolled the gallery, he hadn't expected Van Cleeves to be so sprawling. A crowd huddled before an alcove at the far end, and he weaved his way there, thinking he might find Charlotte.

Angling into the alcove, he overheard a woman speaking to her companion as they walked out. "Too weird. I think I hate it." When the group broke apart, a large illustration in heavy black ink hung shoulder height.

A Private Sky. Charlotte Knight.

"More concept art than realism," a guy in a denim applejack cap said. "It's got a sold red dot."

Marc wanted to step back from the sketch. A flock of blackbirds swarmed out of a man's head into a darkened skyscape. Seated in a Victorian wicker chair, the man held a rifle on his lap, his calm face straight on the viewer. Was that Sir Duncan? At his left boot lay an aged pumpkin, a basket of apples, and a pearl-handled knife.

The sky projected a spinning effect moving counterclockwise. The whole image might make a person dizzy for a second. Each bird at the forefront hung its sharp beak and cunning eyes over a castle with turrets. The birds' wings extended in ragged shawls. From their heads, sharp points shot up in blurred diamond shapes.

Long straw legs hinted scarecrow effigies. But it was the birds' claws spreading out in tiny white-and-black piano keys that disturbed Marc. Some odd musical omen?

"Are those crows or ravens?" a young black woman asked. She had a mess of black curls, red pouty lips, and copper discs dangling from her ears. She copied the sketch into her pad; when she saw Marc watching her, she snapped her tongue. "I'm an art student. It's legal, you know, to copy anything as long as I don't sell or publish it. So stop gawking at me. I'm not some kind of thief."

"Oh no. I wasn't thinking that. They look like crows to me." Actually, they reminded him of battle crows, omens of the dead.

"Okay, crows. I'm Isabella."

"Good to meet you, Isabella. Marc Sexton." The sketch drew him back. He recognized the castle in the background as Elysium Fields from a photo Sir Duncan had shown him. A rather small decaying fortress.

Isabella slashed her pencil across the page, imitating the strokes on Charlotte's sketch. "I love those birds' pointy heads. Awesome. And the single cracked tombstone in the corner. What's the meaning of that, do you think?"

"Oh yeah. I didn't see that."

"A sepulcher. Some kind of abode of death? Where is the artist?

I'm dying to meet her." She craned her neck to the front of the gallery. "Have you seen her sketch, Rilke's 'On the Edge of Night,' poem in the other room by the bar table? Knight does Rilke's *'violin-bodies'* in modern V-shapes. Love it. I'm so amped."

"I'm here for Charlotte Knight too. When I find her, I'll bring her over to you."

"Cool. Thanks." Isabella went back to her drawing. "Those tumbling clouds are weird. Noisy and overflowing. How did she do that?"

Marc focused on the skyscape. In the shading, he couldn't make out much.

"Do you think the crows are calling us?" Isabella turned her ear to the wall, listening.

"Not crows, they're rooks." Charlotte came up from behind Marc, hooking her hand on his arm. "Sorry, Marc, I've been practically kidnapped in the other room. Geoffrey wanted to do a live recording."

"Oh! Hi, I'm Isabella Jones. Your surrealist portrait is epic. I've been doing a study. They're not crows?" She dug into her satchel shoulder bag and pulled out her phone. "I'm a shameless photo bug. Do you mind, Charlotte? May I call you Charlotte?" She clicked a photo. "Why did you choose rooks?"

Marc couldn't get a word in for five minutes and stepped back while Isabella latched on to Charlotte. She had everyone's attention in her dark-silvery long dress and red, vintage-laced ankle boots. Absolutely shimmering.

He decided to browse the various exhibits while she attended to her guests. Upstairs he found Philip John's exhibit. Modern seascapes with exotic blood-red waves and fire dragons. Overpowering was all he got; he knew he had a lot to learn about appreciating art. By 6:30, Marc descended the steps as the guard at the door escorted the last guests out. Charlotte waved him down, standing at the reception table with the gallery owner Geoffrey Brink, a jazzy guy in a white tee shirt, jeans, and tuxedo jacket. He gave Marc a stiff handshake as they exchanged polite banter.

Geoffrey cheered Charlotte. "You made all the right moves tonight," he told her. "I'll update the sales with you next week."

Marc moved in, placing his hand on Charlotte's waist and pulling her close. She had a miraculous tiny waist, and he loved scooping his hand around it.

A loud banging at the front doors made everyone turn. The guard signaled to the man at the door. "We're closed."

The man continued to slam his fist on the door.

"Wait." Charlotte moved toward the entrance. "Geoffrey, let him in. That's Sir Duncan."

Geoffrey gave a signal to the guard, and Sir Duncan Hawkinge burst in, face flushed.

"I'm so sorry to be late. I came as soon as we landed. Charlotte!" He threw his arms around her. The panic on his face alarmed Marc—especially knowing that Duncan was supposed to be on business in London for three weeks. Why the sudden return?

"Geoffrey," Marc said, "this is Sir Duncan Hawkinge, Earl of Elysium Fields."

Geoffrey extended his hand. "A pleasure, Sir Duncan."

"Good evening. Splendid to meet you, Geoffrey," he said as their hands met. "Charlotte." He turned. "As soon as I saw your photo of the portrait, I booked a flight back."

"Why? What's happened?"

"I need to see the portrait. I want to purchase it tonight." Sir Duncan shot his words at Geoffrey and Marc.

"It's sold," Geoffrey said. "What's going on, chap?"

"My apologies. Sorry to intrude. May I contact the buyer? I need to make an offer."

"We don't give that information out. I'm happy to let them know you're interested."

"Yes, please. May I see the portrait for two minutes? Only two minutes."

"Of course. Come with me." Charlotte pulled him toward the alcove.

Marc followed Geoffrey, who was clearly annoyed. "Is this guy a tad wacky?"

"He's as stable as they come. Usually."

At the entrance to the alcove, Sir Duncan stopped abruptly before *A Private Sky*. He thrust his hand over his chest. "Your photo wasn't clear enough to see the sky. Charlotte . . . Charlotte," he said in a begging tone. "There it is."

"There what is?" Marc asked.

"Those wretched storm clouds. That God-awful mess."

Geoffrey stepped up to Sir Duncan. "See here, this illustration is one of Charlotte's best. Distinctive. Persuasive. I wouldn't have it in my gallery if it failed quality."

"Sir Duncan, why are you so upset?" Charlotte asked. "When I sent you the portrait photo on Friday, you didn't respond. I assumed you were okay with it and—"

Sir Duncan put his hand up to stop her running on. He raised his chin, brow furrowed. "When I arrived at the estate on Tuesday, the rooks were on fire in the trees."

"On fire?"

"Every one of them burning, perched on the branches, on the castle roof, shooting flames out of their heads. Hundreds of them."

Charlotte swayed back on her heels.

"The damnable birds kept on burning. Even as they were flying, they blazed the very air." He pulled his phone out and showed a video. Flocks of flaming rooks spiraled up, jagging the sky with streaks, and then one by one they zoomed into the clouds, burning them orange.

Charlotte gasped. Marc and Geoffrey watched over her shoulder. "I don't know what to say," she murmured.

"Is this for real?" Geoffrey asked.

"Absolutely. They burned for hours. Without consumption."

Without consumption? Marc noticed the points on the rooks' heads were not diamonds as he previously thought. Each point resembled the eye of a flame in guttering flashes.

"Those bloody bastards," Sir Duncan cried out. "You'd think they'd be burned into ashes, wouldn't you? Not these rooks. They're still cawing over Elysium Fields, screeching from the cloud sack you drew." He pointed. "Still burning from their own fuel or oxygen or God knows what inside those clouds. My dear, dear girl. Rooks on fire! What have you done?"

Charlotte moved closer to Marc, slipping her hand into his, terror in her face. "Sir Duncan, you can't possibly think I set fire to your rooks in Kent, England?"

"I don't know what I think. They burned precisely as you have illustrated. Flames shooting out of their heads and wheeling everywhere. How could you know this?"

"I didn't know."

"Bloody hell, they haven't stopped raging for three days. Listen." He played another video. Jaunty wails echoed down from a darkened sunset on Elysium Fields.

Marc held Charlotte's hand, returned his focus on the portrait, on the earl's hypnotic face, the cloud-bundled mass, and the burning birds cleaving to the sky. *Rooks on fire*. What had she manifested?

Inside the hatched lines, he found a windy thrust. Jaa Morland had lived her wind magick on Draakensky in windy thrusts. Jaa had engaged many wind beings with obscure, streaming faces. Fortunately, she had Frau Holle as a guide. He recalled Jaa describing the vaporous Frau Holle rolling through dark hollows and blowing sonorous gales through the windmill's blades.

Examining the windy thrusts again and points of fire in *A Private Sky*, Marc resisted the urge to raise his hand to touch the painting, knowing the risk for him to physically engage it.

Charlotte's magick is taking a dimensional leap.

Chapter Fifteen

Darkness Drops Again

"I feel like a gloomy monk plunged into the dark ages," Charlotte muttered behind her menu at their corner table in the Monk's Court. She regretted her critical tone. The rustic 18th-century Benedictine monastery had everyone speaking in quiet voices as if the walls lined with vintage books had ears. After such a dreadful ending to her first solo art show, the quivering shadows from the candlelight and strained whispers did not cheer her.

Carved oak rafters made for a low ceiling, the color of old ash. Dark alcoves filled with oversized coppery tomes huddled into murky pockets from stone archways that dripped with candlelight wall sconces. These flickering darklings reminded her of long-forgotten chants from ghost-monks. *Rooks on fire. Rooks on fire. Rooks on fire.*

A monastery bell rang softly; the *ting* made Charlotte turn her head. Marc turned as well. Waiters stepped lightly, dressed in their white tunics. Blanched ships navigating a calm sea—that's how she would draw this scene. "And the creaking of ropes and masts," slipped out beneath her breath.

"What was that?" Marc asked, topping off her wine glass.

"Nothing."

"You want to talk about what happened today?"

"You mean this horror for Sir Duncan? Please change the subject."

"Of course. Shall we start with the white cheese and berries?" Marc loosened his necktie.

"Whatever."

Minutes passed without a single word, only the wine between them. She knew Marc was thinking the same thing. *Rooks on fire.*

"This place is rated three Michelin stars," he perked up. "I'd kill to get one Michelin star for The Grackle."

They ordered with Brother Hugo, who had an elegant French accent. The lamb and sausage cassoulet arrived golden and juicy, succulent on Charlotte's palate. Thick bread slices drizzled with warm cream performed exquisitely—surely one of the best meals Charlotte had ever eaten.

Rooks on fire. What have you done, Charlotte?

"Charlotte, your silence is killing me. We need to talk about this."

She sipped her wine. "Why, do you have something you want to say to me? Like this is all my fault? My bizarre artistic talents? My narrative calamity? Or is it my incompetent magick that caused this disaster at Elysium Fields?" She fanned her face with the cloth napkin. "I'm sorry. I don't mean to snap at you."

"I know how to handle snapping." He brightened, then went dead serious. "And I wasn't thinking any such thing. I'm thinking we need to be extra cautious here. Magick can sometimes feel as if it's a . . . threatening process."

"Yes, yes, you have warned me about all that. I didn't intend for rooks to burst into flames on Elysium Fields. I was drawing cloud chambers. Ridiculous. Georgia O'Keeffe can paint them, but mine were completely overdone. What a disaster I've created."

"This event is deep elemental magick," he offered gently, "energies that have broken free, possibly into a higher level." He said it with such kind measure that she wanted to scream.

"Elemental magick breaking free? Oh, that's a good one. Fine. Subject closed. I'm thinking about dessert. What should we order?"

At a nearby table, a waiter served crêpes Suzette with orange slices, performing a flambé spectacle of red-hot fire to a theatrical applause from the patrons.

What sinister flames. Charlotte slapped the dessert menu down. "Don't you dare order anything flambé."

At the finish of dessert—chocolate-dipped meringue and Café au lait—she asked the waiter what kind of flowers centered their table. The drama of the pale lavender kept calling her.

"Bleu foxglove, Mademoiselle. You are welcome to take them home with you. Our compliments." Brother Hugo exited with a slight bow.

"Mademoiselle," Marc said, imitating the French inflection. "Sounds lovely. Although, Madame is much finer. Would you like to talk about a wedding date? Or maybe we should run off. Get married in Paris? Let's elope!"

She puffed a sigh. "Say it, Marc. *Rooks on fire.* You want to say it, don't you? The words are practically written on your forehead."

He wore a deadpan expression. Was he stumped on how to respond? Not Marc. He knew way too much about magick to be puzzled. "Say it, Marc. *Rooks on fire.*"

"Rooks on fire." He placed his napkin on the table, flattening it with his palm, the expression on his face so intense that she leaned back. "Charlotte, say what's on your mind."

She tossed her napkin on the table. "How did my rooks, in *A Private Sky* here in New York, manifest fire at Elysium Fields in Kent, England?"

"I don't know the mechanism. Magick can be a labyrinth with irregular networks and passages that exceed the limits. One observation is clear. You are executing the first principle of magick: the inherent interconnectedness of all living things within the universe. And beyond."

Fear driving her hands to tremble, wanting to ask, dreading the answer, Charlotte curled her tongue, scraping her teeth. Maybe she could scrape away the entire day and night. "Interconnectedness? With what exactly?"

Marc's sharp blues were dead center on her. "It's possible . . . you have connected to fire magick."

Fire magick? She immediately remembered an old painting of the goddess Minerva in a Roman graveyard scene. Minerva, her mother's namesake, stood with three white skulls at her feet, the bony heads shooting out forks of orange fire as her body disintegrated in a twisting of hot pink flames. *Fire magick.* Those two words nearly burned her cheeks, sending her sliding right to the edge. Hanging on, biting her tongue, tightening her lips, she leaned forward. "No. I most certainly have not connected to fire magick!"

Chapter Sixteen

Broom, Meadowsweet, and Lilac

Tuesday morning, Charlotte dragged herself out of bed, bleary-eyed from successive bad dreams she could not recall. Leftover jitters and sweat dripped down her back. On the nightstand, the Monk's Court bleu foxglove blooms greeted her.

She swung her feet on the floor. Something cracked. Old floorboards saying good morning. "Shut up." A bitter taste erupted from yesterday's caffeine-dazed indulgence still holding her stomach hostage.

Sunday and Monday had moved painstakingly slow, intensifying her anxieties, *rooks on fire* becoming a hammering mantra. Fire magick? Like a driver losing control of a car, should she brace for a crash? Or let go of the wheel and cover her face?

She had wasted away Sunday with old movies, naps on the sofa, and black-cherry ice cream. More exhausted than she realized, Monday beat out a nervous rhythm, keeping her in her nightgown all day. She commended herself on baking a peasant bread, soothed by the aroma of yeast, the kneading and pounding and flour dust swimming the air.

During the rising and baking time, she began reading the novel *The Mists of Avalon*, which Marc had recommended. King Arthur's kingdom, Lancelot, Merlin, Morgaine, and Lady Vivienne all came to life in an enchanted magickal saga about the women behind the throne of King Arthur. Listeners of the woods, gazers of stars, and the holy isle of Avalon entertained her for hours.

Dinner was apples, bread and butter, and a third pot of coffee. Didn't it feel good not to have to work in the studio or speak to anyone and just live inside this cozy pocket? Not really. Drawing had always been her stabilizer and now after the disaster of *A Private Sky,* she couldn't put pencil to paper or find the courage to even climb the spiral steps to the studio. She rationalized that she had drawn Sir Duncan's portrait from real life. A man sitting in her studio chair. What a horrific narrative she had created. Ghastly.

Sir Duncan had called three times and texted her twice. She had no words. She responded to Marc's inquiring texts with *I'll come by on Wednesday, maybe.*

Charlotte fondled the bleu foxglove bell-shaped blossoms on the nightstand. Aunt Loretta used to wear a similar pale lavender floral-print dress. "That's it." She jumped up, tossing the bed covers. "I'm going to fill the windmill with flowers today." Surrounding herself with blooms would get her out of this malaise. Monet insisted on having flowers every day. *So shall I. Slay the fears.*

Ten minutes later, she strode out the door as a misty fog massaged the air. No sun today. Sunrises and sunsets had become addictive; Charlotte didn't want to miss a single one. She headed toward Heida's boardwalk to the river.

Stop calling it Heida's boardwalk. The boardwalk will do. On the way, she filled her arms with yellow broom flower branches, white meadowsweet, and fallen oak twigs. Late blooming lilacs too, dripping wet from the drizzle. She wrapped them in a towel from the shed, left them on an obliging rock, and walked the boardwalk to the river.

With her rain slicker hood up, she strolled along, the trees watching, listening to her sneakers slap the wet wood. Trees had their own secret lives, hiding their roots, keeping their seeds tight inside. As she passed the horse chestnut with its limbs arching, it chanted *my power is trust*. The old copper beech fluttered its leaves with a whistle, *I greet you today*. This was not just a philosophical question for Charlotte, but a spiritual certainty.

At the gazebo overlooking the river, she sat down. This was the place where Jaa had died, her yellow scarf flat on her chest, her right-hand fingers spread as if reaching out to someone. How beautifully Jaa had connected to this landscape, honoring the wind, especially Frau Holle, as if the land itself drew breath every day. Was Draakensky a breathing entity?

A flock of wild geese flew the widened air above river waves rolling high. The falls thundered in deep descents. Clinging to a rocky shelf, narrow waves spilled into hypnotic rhythms. A rocking lullaby.

Rain fell heavier now, curving around her head like heartbeats. Across the river, a prick of light flashed on Yew Crag. Something flamed in the fog there, within the wooded groves. She wanted to trace the odd form as it moved through the trees. She lifted her finger to draw the image in the air.

Before she could finish, her phone dinged in her pocket. She pulled it out.

KELSEY SEXTON.

Instinctively, she thought to ignore the call. Then she'd have to call Kelsey back. This was Marc's mother. No point in putting up fences before she even got to know his family. Sheila probably gave her the phone number.

"Good morning, Kelsey," Charlotte answered cheerfully.

"Hello, Charlotte. Am I calling at a bad time?"

"Not at all."

A weird pause.

"Forgive my abruptness. Are you doing anything for lunch today? I would love for you to come to my house that I share with Cousin Diana in Sleepy Hollow. I'm dying for us to get to know each other. And I know it would please Marc. I'm leaving for Dublin soon, and I'm unsure when we can meet again. I'll make an Irish tea. Would one o'clock be suitable? Please say yes. May I text you the address and directions?"

She felt inclined to make an excuse. Had Marc told her they were engaged? "Of course I'll come. An Irish tea? I'd like that. Thank you. One o'clock. See you then, Kelsey."

She speed-dialed Marc's cell and left a message. "Hi. Your mom called and invited me to lunch today in Sleepy Hollow. Does she know we're engaged? You told her, right? I'm going there at one o'clock."

Charlotte hurried down the boardwalk. Inside the windmill, she arranged vases of flowers in the living room, kitchen, and bedroom. Maybe she'd bring a bunch of lilacs to Kelsey. Picturing artist Mary Cassatt's *Lilacs in a Window* painting, Charlotte arranged a bunch in Jaa's clay pot, making the stems a haphazard design of dark purple and white blooms, similar to the painting. Cassatt preferred to present her floral scenes without narratives, just as a moment. Degas painted fleeting moments too. Maybe she should try that technique. If nothing else, the lilacs would provide a conversation piece if the visit became awkward.

After showering, taking forever to choose an appropriate outfit, she texted Marc again and drove through the descending fog. Exactly at 1:20, the GPS lady announced, “You have arrived.”

Charlotte pulled over and quickly dialed Marc again. “Hey Marc, where are you? I’m in Sleepy Hollow. Text me, please.”

She pulled into the driveway and noticed her cell service had shot down to a single bar. Perfect, a dead zone.

Kelsey opened the door to a Victorian-styled house before Charlotte was even at the front steps of the pillared front porch. After a stiff greeting in the foyer, Kelsey performed a bright smile and gave Charlotte a hand-on-the-shoulder gesture, but one that too felt stiff. Kelsey took the lilacs. “I can smell the rain on them. So pretty. Thank you.”

“I’m sorry I’m late. The fog slowed me down.”

“I figured as much. Come into the sunporch.” Her aqua silk blouse swung over jeans as she led the way to the back of the house.

The sunporch fanned open from double doors. Charlotte admired its white wicker furniture, floral chaise lounges, plush cushions in plum, and glass tables. Stacks of decorating books arranged in hammered steel bins sat beneath a white bookcase of family photos. In a silver frame, a photo of Marc and his dad, a suave blond and beefy man, showed both elegantly dressed in white shirts and red ties. Matthew’s arm curled around the teenaged Marc, their faces so similar, even down to their cleft chins.

On a top shelf perched a giant photo of Sheila Sexton, the arborist in Concord, shovel in hand, next to an evergreen. Red-headed, like her mom, Marc had described his sister as a born-again vegan, tree-hugging, eco-nut.

On the adjacent wall hung an oil painting of William—the academic, as Marc affectionately defined him—a Ph.D. psychologist in his graduation cap and gown (Princeton, no less), now living in the sunny veneer of Los Angeles, a professor with a thriving private practice. What a family Charlotte was marrying into. Would she be equal to the task? One thing for sure: she would not apologize for not having a family.

Outside the French-paned windows, the fog had grown thick, blocking the view. Charlotte glanced into the adjoining kitchen, where beige stone countertops featured an ornately carved vintage tea kettle emitting steam on the enameled stove. The spout extended similar to the curve of a swan's neck. Wouldn't she love to draw that in a still-life? So much safer to draw objects instead of hares or rooks or British earls.

From the hallway, a woman entered the room. Rubenesque was Charlotte's immediate impression. Her gray-streaked black hair waved over her shoulders and well-endowed chest. A thin red scarf tied in a knot beneath her ear held the curly mess. No choker pearls at the throat, but she carried Ruben's Baroque inspiration.

"You must be Diana." Charlotte reached out for a handshake.

"Diana is working today," Kelsey said. "This is Cousin Niagra. We drove down together from Boston."

"I'm thrilled to meet you, Charlotte." Niagra shook her hand.

From the broad planes of her face, Charlotte guessed Niagra's age to be close to fifty. Her eyes were clear brown, the lashes fringed without a hint of mascara. The no-makeup sisterhood—natural, real-world women, a movement that Charlotte had rejected, preferring color and eyeshadow to design her face.

"Heavens, what gorgeous lilacs. Let's place them on the table." Niagra spoke breathy and slow. "Mmmm," she inhaled.

Niagra wore tight jeans and a blousy black top with lantern sleeves so long they covered half her hands. Charlotte felt slightly overdressed in her sleeveless navy pencil-striped sheath, her go-to for any occasion.

Kelsey appeared from the kitchen with a three-tiered tray of tiny sandwiches and sweets. Charlotte noted the table set for four. "Is Marc joining us?" Her hopeful tone was far too obvious.

"Only us girls," Kelsey chimed.

"Oh. Who is the fourth?"

Kelsey fussed over a drooping lilac stem.

Niagra placed a hand on Charlotte's. "We often set a place for one of the recent dead. Or the former dead in the family." Her voice dropped an octave. "Old Sexton tradition."

"I see. And who might that be?"

"I've invited Auntie Bran," Niagra said. "Marc's grandmother. Mamó."

"Yes, Marc has told me about Mamó. Sings her praises all the time."

"I think he prefers Mamó more than he does me sometimes." Kelsey gave a toss of her hair. "Shall we sit down?"

Niagra sat and patted the chair for Charlotte. "How perfect that you brought us lilacs, Charlotte. When Auntie Bran died, Marc filled her coffin with lilacs. The purple haze over her chest was magnificent." She cupped her hand around her mouth. "We recognize that lilacs whisper the intentions of the dead. Ohh, my ears are stirring this second just by telling you."

Chapter Seventeen

Irish Tea on the Sunporch

At a white-iron, curly, antique glass table, the women gathered, a self-conscious threesome, discussing springtime temperatures while Kelsey ceremoniously poured bubbling hot tea into each cup. She presented the treats graciously, Niagra contributing spotty punctuations about the meal—"tasty," "delicious"—in what became a series of long pauses between Kelsey's offerings: "Cream cheese and cucumber?" "Cream puff?" "You must try the fairy cakes." "I prefer the spiced loaf with nuts and raisins."

The lilacs centered on the table were indeed emitting sibilant notes, or maybe it was the blood rushing in Charlotte's ears. She quelled her nerves and raised her left hand to dab the napkin at her mouth, wishing Marc would call, wishing her heart would stop throbbing.

"Whoa." Niagra reached for Charlotte's hand and held it. "That ring is an eye-stopper. A sapphire. Now that is not your typical engagement ring, is it?" She blinked cheerfully at Charlotte.

Kelsey leaned in, her expression critical. "Stunning, Charlotte. Of course, Marc never does anything typical, does he?"

"Hardly ever," Charlotte tried to sound casual, wanting to pull her hand from Niagra. Her fleshy palm radiated unusual heat.

When she finished examining the stone, Niagra lifted her head. "Look at that, Kelsey, an emerald cut. Marc chose that cut?"

"He did," Charlotte answered, half tempted to ask why that was significant but decided to let it go.

"Congratulations!" Niagra patted Charlotte's left hand. "Kelsey, we must have a toast. Get The Sexton."

"Get The Sexton," Kelsey muttered and rose to fetch the whiskey bottle on the sideboard.

Charlotte's phone showed no bars at all now; she tossed it into her handbag.

Niagra lifted a book from her bag on the floor. "Charlotte, I'm the narrative historian in the family. That is since Auntie Bran passed last year. She was the Sexton Lore Keeper. Now it's my job."

"Oh? Sounds serious."

"An honor. I lived with Auntie Bran for a year in Ireland. We spent hours sitting by her pond while Auntie told me all the family stories. I loved it. I must jot down Marc's engagement in my journal. Auntie Bran would insist on me keeping accurate family events. She was the eleventh Lore Keeper. I am the twelfth."

Mamó's place setting and empty chair sat directly across from Charlotte. Beyond, heavy-laden fog swarmed the French-glassed windows and doors, the outside world gone blind. Normally she enjoyed foggy days, but today the grayness felt suffocating.

"Fog is so enchanting, isn't it? Celts think of mist as a curtain. Auntie Bran used to see little feet and hands in it."

"Little feet and hands? You mean she saw ghosts?"

Niagra shrugged extravagantly. "Sometimes Mamó did, but

these were fairies. Hey, I know, let's go into the mist!" Niagra rose. "Kelsey, shall we bring our whiskey outside to the patio?"

Kelsey placed The Sexton bottle with four glasses on the table. "I don't think so, Niagra. The humidity will mess up Charlotte's beautiful hair."

"I don't mind," she answered as politely as she could.

"Too damp out there." Kelsey poured the first whiskey into the short-stemmed glasses and placed it at the empty place setting for Mamó. Niagra took a bite of her tea sandwich while jotting notes in her ledger.

Kelsey poured three more glasses. At the same time, Charlotte felt her hair oddly move at the back of her neck—as if someone was standing behind her, gathering the strands and running a hand over her head. She stiffened, fearing the hand might yank her head back.

Twisting her shoulders uncomfortably, she shivered as fingers slid through strands of her hair, caressing lightly. The sensation grew oddly affectionate; it was a frequent endearing gesture of Marc's to caress her hair. Charlotte flicked a glance at the empty chair, now dappled in shadows from the goose-neck table lamp. She stretched up; the hand fell away. *Where is Marc? Why hasn't he texted?*

"The mist is heavenly out there. Come on, Kel, we could step outside and make our toast to Marc and Charlotte. Auntie Bran would love that. Shall we?"

Kelsey pursed her lips. "I'd rather not. Let me refill the teapot." Her voice switched to a more forceful register. She turned and quickly stepped into the kitchen.

Niagra sighed. "Charlotte, I have something to show you, if you don't mind." She perked up and lifted another book from her bag.

"This is the Sexton family album. We're dying to show you, now that you'll be a member of the family."

Niagra opened the photo album to pages of black-and-white photographs—monochromatic, and several daguerreotypes—with cracked, faded surfaces and murky tints from 1900s Ireland.

"This is Mary Sexton. The tenth Lore Keeper." Niagra pointed to a worn photo of a young woman with a tiny turned nose, hair swept back in a loose bun at the nape of her neck, a striking profile pose in a lace shawl that tempted Charlotte to touch the image.

"Mary was the seer in the Sexton family. Born in 1890. A real anchor for the Sextons. Over a hundred when she died. Slender as a stick but a strong physicality, according to Auntie Bran. Mary lived with Auntie Bran for a few years during the 1950s."

"So Bran was a Sexton, not an in-law?"

"None truer. Auntie Bran refused to give up her Sexton name when she married. Scandalous at the time not to take your husband's name. A bit of a revolutionary, Auntie Bran was. She made sure her only son, Matthew, had the Sexton name on his birth certificate. Auntie was a repository of knowledge for the Sexton clan. Now, I'm thrilled to be following in her footsteps."

Kelsey returned with the steaming kettle and poured hot water into a simple green china teapot.

"Was that Bran's tea kettle?" Charlotte had a sense it was. Scrolls and curling clover etched across the steel.

"From her mother, yes. Marc and I brought over trunks of family china and glassware." She lifted the whiskey glass, her strawberry blond wisps framing intense features, chin up. "May love and laughter light your days together. To Marc and Charlotte." She shot the liquid straight down in one gulp. "Welcome to the Sexton clan, Charlotte Knight."

"Sláinte! Health and blessings to you both." Niagra knocked it back.

"Slan-cha," Charlotte repeated the pronunciation. Charlotte drank hers in three swallows. "I wish Marc were here. Thank you for welcoming me. The Sexton family sounds amazing." She tried to make her voice warm, but it had an edge that even she noticed.

Kelsey sat down and took the album from Niagra. She paged to the inside cover. "Charlotte, here is the family coat of arms." She exposed an image of a green and white shield with a Celtic cross. "Most Irish family crests have harps or lions, heavy scrolls. Ours is quite simple. Mary designed the coat of arms. As Lore Keeper, she earned that privilege."

At the top of the crest, a banner heralded the name SEXTON with slashing swords and a Celtic knot. The centerpiece sported the face of a gray and white wolf.

"The original is on parchment at the Irish Whiskey Museum in Dublin," Niagra told her. "Isn't it captivating?"

"A wolf. On the family crest. Captivating, yes." And not surprising, Charlotte thought.

Niagra raised her brows proudly. "There was some family disagreement about choosing a wolf because wolves are extinct in Ireland. Have been since around the late 1790s. They agreed because the wolf represents fierce warriors and loyalty to the pack. Just like loyalty to a family."

"This wolf's face is so calm. Almost graceful. Hardly the image of a fierce warrior."

"She's a gentle beauty," Kelsey added. "Fierce? Without a doubt. Wolves are relentless protectors."

"She? A female wolf? Does she have a name?"

"Mary Sexton named her Finnwolf."

Kelsey lifted the teapot. "More tea?"

Chapter Eighteen

Image Forth Your Wolf

In White Plains, at the Westchester County Courthouse, Marc strode out into the haze. Drizzle made him hurry to the parking lot. He got in his car and switched on his cell phone to check his calls. Dozens flashed into the scroll, but before he could scan them, the device rang. SHEILA SEXTON.

"Hi, Sheila."

"Where have you been?" she screamed. "My God, I've been calling all morning! I thought you were dead or something."

His sister hadn't earned the nickname *Shrieking Sheila* for nothing. "Hardly. I had to surrender my cell. I'm at the country courthouse on a jury summons."

"Oh hell, you're not on a jury, are you?"

"Just the first day. Last-minute notice, but they settled the case right as the trial began. They let us out now."

"Listen, Mom didn't go to L.A. to visit William. She left at five o'clock this morning to drive back to Sleepy Hollow."

He turned on the engine to defog the windshield. "When is she flying back to Dublin?"

"She's not. That's why I called you six times like a maniac. She's invited Charlotte for lunch at the house. An Irish tea."

Marc tensed up. "When is this?"

"Today! Right now. And guess who she's brought with her? Niagra."

"Niagra," he practically growled the name. "Please don't tell me that."

"She did! My guess is either Mom wants Niagra to do her dirty work and tell Charlotte all the foul crimes of our wicked family history, or she wants Niagra to do a psychic reading on your betrothed. You'd better get over there! Poor Charlotte. She's in an ambush with those two. This is my fault. I'm such a dope telling Mom about your engagement plans. I'm so sorry I blew it. None of this would be happening if I hadn't blabbed. But you know how prickly Mom can be, always maneuvering the conversation."

"Yes, I know. I'll take care of it. On my way. Talk to you later." Of all days to be out of contact. Of all people, Niagra. Her father, Norman Sexton, did right by naming her after the Falls—Niagra's dramatics were famous for bursting in racing currents. A woman whose passion for the theatre's spotlights never gelled, she moved on to becoming a successful audiobook narrator with her masterful voice.

Fog pressed the windows; he'd have to crawl to Sleepy Hollow. He pulled out and drove straight into a bottleneck of cars. While sitting in the stalled traffic, he listened to the umpteen voice messages and read the texts, then dashed off a text to Charlotte: SO SORRY. I WAS CALLED FOR JURY SERVICE THIS MORNING. ON MY WAY TO YOU NOW. NO WORRIES. WE'VE GOT THIS.

Did he have this under control? His mother had an agenda—what a sneaky little luncheon on a Tuesday afternoon. And Niagra, the Sexton Lore Keeper, what was her mission today? All Sexton Lore Keepers took an oath to protect and preserve the lore, especially the Celtic magickal traditions. Niagra was bound not to reveal the occult knowledge handed down by the ancestors. Not without legitimate cause. *Damn.*

Traffic opened up on Route 287, although it still moved slowly. Visibility grew worse when he drove on Route 9 through Tarrytown—fogging an Etch A Sketch screen across his windshield. He blinked repeatedly to clear the gray blindness, taking the curves slowly.

The fog thickened. Dark vapors streamed like whales swimming through the air. A strange odor of mud filled the car. Burning heat gripped him. Sweat beaded his forehead.

On the front hood, a wolf face zoomed straight at him. Marc slammed the brakes. He hit the emergency flashers and swerved over. The monstrous wolf, mouth open for a sharp bite, pressed the windshield.

He recognized the furry head, black pointed ears, and white blazes on the sides of the head. Fangs. The Ripper.

A scream clogged Marc's throat. *No, no. no.* Struggling to take a breath, he saw images of loose rocks on a barren slope materialize as if on a screen.

Stinging words pulsed his mind. *Image Forth Your Wolf.*

Marc jolted, hands flying off the steering wheel. He crossed his arms, fists over his heart, desperate to escape the assault.

Image Forth Your Wolf.

Resisting the summons, breaking the mind state of wolf, and chanting his star incantations, he heightened his will, swallowed the howl bursting up his throat, and grabbed his silver wolf pendant.

Image Forth Your Wolf.

He squeezed the wolf head and shield into his fleshy fingers. "I will *not* image forth my wolf. This hunt has ceased! Be gone. By my stars, be gone. Be gone!"

Chapter Nineteen
Skeletons at Sleepy Hollow

Kelsey shot a wide-eyed nod for Niagra to proceed while Charlotte held her attention on the Finnwolf coat of arms. The girl appeared fascinated, running her finger over the wolf's face. "Are you tracing Finnwolf?" Kelsey asked, forcing softness into her tone.

"Oh, I'm sorry," Charlotte pulled her hand away. "Sometimes I need to touch an image. Many artists are tactile. This wolf is quite alluring. Finnwolf, huh?"

"Would you like to hear the story of Finnwolf?" Kelsey prompted, a signal to Niagra that the girl was truly interested in learning more.

"Finnwolf is a real wolf?"

"I'm not permitted to reveal the lore. Only Niagra has authority, as Lore Keeper." Kelsey sat back, hands folded on her lap, giving an exaggerated exhale to Niagra. "The Finnwolf narrative is Mary Sexton's story. Isn't that right, Niagra?"

"That's true. I must remain obedient to my pledge and the lore as told to me by Auntie Bran. She received the lore directly from Mary. So, I have to ask: Kelsey, do you think Charlotte has a *valid* need to know the lore?"

"I do. If Charlotte is to fully know the Sexton family, I think she'll find our history important to her marriage to Marc. We can trust her discretion." She shot a covert blink to Niagra.

Niagra appeared to give that some thought. "I suppose that is valid reason, for the good of Marc. Auntie would approve. Let me see. Ahhh, to fully understand the Finnwolf narrative, and Mary, I need to begin at Shehy Mountain, the O'Leary sisters and—"

"Oh don't. We can't bore Charlotte with all that," Kelsey cut in.

"It's an essential foundation to the accuracy of the lore," Niagra insisted and paged through the photo album. "Here, we have a photo of Shehy Mountain." She flipped the pages. "Right there. Four summits. It all begins on Shehy Mountain when the O'Leary sisters cast a malicious spell, bringing down the sun."

That made Charlotte turn her head closer to Niagra. "Sorcerers?"

"Indeed. Sometime around the late 1730s or later—we're not precisely certain of the timeline—the O'Leary sisters moved to County Cork, in the south of Ireland. They were gifted a cottage at the foot of Shehy Mountain, a mud cabin with a thatched straw roof. Dirt poor, no real livestock, only a few hens."

"Potato diggers, they were," Kelsey added, popping a cookie into her mouth.

"You like to jeer, Kel, but the sisters were sophisticated conjurers. We're not talking about kitchen witches here. The O'Leary's sorcery was nothing to scoff at."

"They came from nothing," Kelsey pointedly told Charlotte. "Young women selling herring in the Dublin streets. The townsfolk ran them out of Dublin as soon as they suspected witchcraft."

"That's true," Niagra agreed. "In County Cork, the Sexton clan knew the reputation of their dark powers, spread the word of their sorcery, and everyone shunned them as witches."

"Fat bratty monsters. They hated the Sexton clan."

"Kelsey, please let me tell it as Auntie Bran would." Niagra cleared her throat. "The Sextons were powerful leaders in the villages at the time. They owned sheep, cattle, and horses. When the Sextons put a black mark on you, everyone followed suit. Auntie Bran said there must have been well over a hundred Sexton cousins spread out from Brandon to southwest Limerick."

"Over a hundred cousins?"

Kelsey shrugged, raising a palm. "Not unusual for Irish families to have six or eight children back in those days, and then their children would have a brood. Matthew's third cousins are spread out across the whole island."

"Very fertile, the Sextons," Niagra quipped. "So as not to bore you, I'll make this a snippet, as Auntie would say. One Sunday morning, at sunrise, one of the Sexton men tending his sheep saw the O'Leary sisters at the foot of Shehy Mountain, chanting. The four of them tied each other up in colorful yarns in a circle, conjuring down the sun."

"Why? To channel the sun's energy?" Charlotte asked.

"To strengthen their sorcery. Their incantations brought down little fireballs and flung them over the summits, setting fires to the trees. But sun magick wasn't all they were skilled in. Within weeks, a pack of wolves descended the mountain."

"Black wolves," Kelsey put in.

"While there were some black wolves in Russia and Scotland, none were ever reported in Ireland. The black wolves attacked sheep on the Sexton farms. The Sexton clan lost half their livestock. A bloody atrocity, Auntie called it."

"Some wolves attacked the horses," Kelsey added.

"Draught horses. Sexton losses were devastating." Niagra

dropped her voice to a whisper. "The O'Leary sisters fulfilled their vengeance against the Sexton clan for ostracizing them."

"That stupid Rosaleen, the eldest sister, blind in one eye, envy in the other," Kelsey remarked. "Rosaleen possessed the highest powers. Mamó described her as having a ghosted heart, spilling her outrage onto her sisters. They hated the Sextons because of their wealth and power in the community."

Charlotte sat back, shock on her face.

Niagra lifted her stemmed glass. "Let's have another, shall we?"

Kelsey poured a second round of The Sexton.

"At the time, many of the wolves in Ireland had been exterminated," Niagra continued, "although there were a few gray wolves in the south. Bounty hunters were still scouting the countryside for wolves into the late 1700s. England and Scotland had long exterminated their wolf populations."

Kelsey wondered what was going on in Charlotte's head. Was the girl getting all this? "It's horrible to say," Kelsey said with a quick gulp of her whiskey, "but in the end, the sisters got what they deserved. Forgive me for speaking out, Niagra," she snipped.

Kelsey knew the lore was protected knowledge, but even Mamó had sometimes agreed that the past was a veil that sometimes needed to be lifted. *I'm protecting the future of my family, and Marc. And the legacy. Right, Mamó?* The empty chair offered no sign to her.

Niagra released a *tsk*. "Heck, yes, they did deserve it. They fooled with dark magick. Brought down fireballs from the sun. Conjured a pack of wild black wolves to Shehy Mountain and drove them to attack the Sexton livestock. And attack their horses. The sisters were asking for trouble."

"I've never heard of wolves attacking horses," Charlotte said.

"The O'Leary sisters' magick had complete power over the wolves. *Kill-spells,* Auntie called them, kill-spells that drove the wolves to attack relentlessly."

"My God," Charlotte sighed.

Kelsey smoothed the tablecloth, sweeping a few crumbs away. "The Sexton men tried to counter their magick but failed. So, they did what they had to. This was their land invaded, their livelihood destroyed."

"I'm afraid to ask." Charlotte sipped her whiskey. "Did they go on a rampage and shoot the sisters in their beds?"

"Not quite. The O'Leary sisters—Rosaleen, Dervla, Hester, and Una—*were* found dead in their beds, though, you got that right." Niagra finished off her tea. "The Sexton men went to battle. They poisoned the O'Leary's well."

Her face aghast, Charlotte blurted out, "Poison? Murder? The Sexton men killed all four? Sister James once told me that a murderer carries the last breath of his victim inside his own lungs to forever haunt him."

Kelsey fought off a shudder. "We need another pot of tea," she said, and hurried to the kitchen.

Chapter Twenty
Secrets of the Old Bones

Kelsey poured another brew of Irish tea. Steam wafted up from the teacup to circle Charlotte's appalled face. This girl couldn't possibly appreciate the Sexton history or the struggles of the ancestors. Between reality and meaning resides the power of blood. Celtic honor. Survival. Brotherhood.

With Charlotte's scant and disjointed family, without real parents or siblings, and her vague ancestry, the girl lacked the foundation Marc needed for his wife, for his gift. What could she possibly know about the bonds of familial love? Commitment to the bloodline? Service to the heritage? This sweet thing would never be able to truly support Marc and his Celtic legacy to the Sextons or Finnwolf.

And that sapphire engagement ring. Emerald cut. That ring was a duplicate of Mamó's ring. Marc desired his wife to image his grandmother. Kelsey felt a scream kick in her gut.

Fog clung to the French windowpanes, lurking shapes and oppressive silhouettes stretching into the sunporch; she decided to close the blinds, making a beeline toward the windows.

"I wouldn't do that," Niagra advised Kelsey.

Her tone was sharp. With Niagra's telepathy in high gear, Kelsey knew to follow the lead. She sat down. "Charlotte, no one can justify cold-blooded murder. Times were different and quite desperate then." She splashed tea into her teacup.

"But poison? All of them? What a dreadful death."

"Probably arsenic," Niagra offered in a gentle tone. "We can't know for sure. When the O'Leary mother arrived from Dublin to bury her daughters, she—"

"The mother witch," Kelsey interrupted, noting a frown from Niagra.

"Yes. The mother witch," Niagra snapped. "The mother dressed her daughters' graves with bright red roses. Within hours the petals turned completely black. That's how Auntie Bran tells it. Black roses, by power from the Otherworld, to display the sisters' high powers of sorcery."

Kelsey offered a plate to Charlotte. "Chocolate-covered cherry? We can't have a proper Irish tea without chocolate and cherries."

Charlotte accepted one.

"Take three, please. We need sweetness at the moment. My mother never had an Irish tea without cherries."

Charlotte placed three on her plate. "Did the Sexton men get away with murdering the sisters?"

"They did," Kelsey answered. "Word went round that the well had become contaminated. Not uncommon in those days with livestock and manure. The witches were dead. No one said another word about it."

"And what happened to the black wolves?"

Kelsey gave a stiff upper lip to Niagra. "Well, the O'Leary's witchcraft was still active, even after their death."

"You mean the wolves still attacked the livestock?" Charlotte frowned.

Niagra jumped in. “The sisters’ kill-spells had grown stronger in the Otherworld. Those wolves were even more vicious. They broke through fences and feasted on the sheep, ripping them to shreds, leaving pens and fields a bloody battlefield. The Sexton men recognized it as the O’Leary Death Magick.”

“Death Magick. From the Otherworld,” Kelsey confirmed.

Charlotte mouthed the words, clearly afraid to speak them aloud.

“The Sexton men had to stop the black wolves or lose everything,” Kelsey added. “You see that, don’t you, Charlotte? These wolves were beasts raping the land, performing the vengeance of the sisters.”

“ ‘Let there be hell,’ the Sexton clan said.” Niagra downed another gulp of whiskey. “The men went on night raids with their rifles to the wolf caves and dens. The Sextons lost a young cousin during a raid. Seamus had reached into a den of pups, and the alpha wolf of the pack ripped half his arm off. Seamus died of blood loss. They shot the she-wolf dead and fire-bombed the den to kill her pups.”

“God no.” Charlotte’s shoulders twitched. “They burned the babies?”

“The alpha male went into a rage. Attacked a bounty hunter, tearing open the flesh clean down to the thigh bone. The alpha got away and later killed two more Sextons. They named the wolf ‘the Ripper,’ ” Niagra said.

Charlotte’s face went aghast.

“Auntie Bran said the farm wives wrote in their diaries that they could hear the Ripper’s angry shrills from Shehy Mountain. The baying laments went on day and night for his she-mate.”

Charlotte teared up. “So the Ripper was the last of the black wolves? He lost his she-mate, his pups, his den. And his pack. All alone? Belonging to no one?"

Kelsey rose and opened the glass door. "Stuffy in here. Let's get some air." The Sexton world had a darkness that could be suffocating. The air streamed in and she recalled Matthew quoting Yeats, *There is another world, but it's in this one. We all live inside these two states in our world—this living among the dead.*

"Eventually," Niagra continued, "they hunted down the Ripper. Shot him up brutally. Burned his body on a barren slope, in a pit, on Shehy Mountain."

"And that was the end of it?" Charlotte's voice lifted, full of hope.

"Not quite. There were wolf hauntings. Severe. A kind of feral madness came upon a number of the cousins. Melancholy. Convulsions. So the Sexton men performed a ritual of their own magick. The men aimed their magick at the Ripper and his pack."

"What kind of magick?"

"Blood magick."

Chapter Twenty-One

Empty Chair at the Table

Kelsey lit three candles on the table, a prompt for Niagra to proceed into the lore.

As each candle flamed, Niagra straightened her posture, her expression taking on the solemnity required. "Blood magick is extremely powerful."

With a quiet reverence, she placed her right hand upon her left. "In order to protect the Otherworld realms and the Sexton family from the vicious hauntings of the Ripper pack, they made a blood covenant. They banished the Ripper pack from the Otherworld. By their spilled blood, the Sexton men cursed the black wolf souls into a lost realm for all eternity."

Niagra anchored herself face to face with Charlotte. "What I'm about to tell you is the unfolding truth in the Sexton family. When we listen to Mary Sexton's lore, we absorb it. We enter into its powers." Each word she weighted with calm and measured clarity. Not for the listeners, Kelsey knew, but for the honor of the lore being spoken aloud.

Kelsey braced herself. Her silence was required whenever sacred lore was revealed—a lesson she had learned from Matthew, especially in his warnings that, *sometimes, we borrow from death way too much.* Kelsey felt sure that Matthew would approve of what she and Niagra were revealing, for the good of the Sexton legacy, the Silver Brotherhood and Sisterhood, for Marc, and for his heirs.

Niagra breathed rhythmically exactly as Mamó had trained her to prepare for the transition about to materialize.

"Mary Sexton knew of the brutal wolf killings and the Sexton curse to banish the wolf souls. In 1911, even by her tender age of twenty-one, she fully understood the magnitude. She had a unique gift, a connection to the wolf lore that went deeper than anyone else's."

Charlotte's eyes moved to Mary's photograph in the family album still open on the table.

"Mary's gifts went far beyond being a seer." Niagra paused appropriately for Charlotte to slip across the threshold with her. "When we speak lore aloud, we are engaging Mary in all her powers, because Mary's presence lives on in the Otherworld. Do you understand, Charlotte?"

Charlotte turned the sapphire ring around her finger. Maybe it was more shock than fear that the girl struggled with, Kelsey thought. Hiding her feelings took strength. The girl kept her dignity—Kelsey gave her that much. How odd that Charlotte suddenly folded her hands, right palm over left palm on the table, exactly like Niagra. The girl was already within the gravity of the moment.

"Charlotte, we are in the dark in this lore." Niagra's voice played out in full drama. "On the night of Samhain, October 31, 1911, Mary Sexton blazed a new path." Niagra's words penetrated, a mesmerizing pendulum, pitch-perfect volume, soft diction, and punctuated pauses.

"This is how Mamó told it to me. And it's Mamó who is inviting you into our magickal lore."

"Long, long ago, during Samhain when the veil between our world and the Otherworld is thinnest, on a clear day, wolf howls came down off Shehy Mountain.

"While the hearth fires blazed in Mary's bedroom, with every brush stroke of her hair at the looking glass, she heard the wolves' songs breaking, brutal and without pause. Full of hunger.

"A chorus of little pups yelped begging howls, shooting their pain into Mary's heart. Tears streaming her face, she rushed to the window. Shehy Mountain. The peaks, clefts, and summits, broad green highlands, and the fading glory of the leaves summoned her.

"She gathered her cousins together: Albert, Donnell, and Cormac. These Old Fathers had heard the wolves' songs. It could only be the ghosts of the Ripper's black wolf pack. Dead wolves' songs, almost two-hundred years later.

"Mary knew these wolves by her heart and by her wisdom. The four Sextons ascended the mountain, Albert the eldest, a shaman, following Mary at the lead. Air swirled around Mary, a silver rope pulling her up the terrain. Mary led the Old Fathers to a barren meadow, near a thorn tree, to the Ripper's grave.

"There, Mary found the phantoms of hatred, rage-driven, rage-tormented black wolves of Shehy Mountain. Mary called up brazen white ravens to flock the skies, and in all her Celtic wisdom, she summoned Finnwolf."

"Knock! Knock!" Marc's voice bounded from the foyer. "Anybody home?"

Kelsey leaped from her chair. "It's Marc."

Charlotte jumped up, hurrying into the foyer.

"Talk about riptide timing," Niagra said, fingers fanning her face.

"I can't believe it. You were almost there, Niagra. Why did he arrive at this second!"

"Don't fight the current, Kel. Auntie Bran would say *journey wisely*."

"Haa," she muttered.

Niagra rushed to the foyer to greet her cousin, leaving Kelsey standing with her arms drooping at her sides.

At Mamó's place setting, plate, teacup, and a full glass of Sexton whiskey, Kelsey couldn't resist. She lifted the glass and knocked it back, her chest heaving. The deep fog at the windows burned off instantly.

Harsh sunlight lashed across the empty chair at the table.

Chapter Twenty-Two

Through the Seer's Eye

In the foyer, Marc kissed Charlotte, noticing her response was oddly rigid. Niagra threw her arms around him, gushing her hellos, gabbing about how long it had been, and how marvelous he looked, and did he have trouble driving in the fog, and did he want something to eat, and *a thousand congratulations* as she ushered him into the sunporch.

His mother offered him every treat on the table, but he couldn't stomach a single crumb. He noticed the open family album. They chatted for an hour, much to Marc's impatience—Niagra lobbing questions about The Grackle and the latest news of Bedford, his work with the Homestead Foundation, and *when is the wedding? Did you pick a date?*—while Charlotte sat quietly next to him. From her silence and distraught expression, he sensed the conversation over tea had disturbed her.

At five o'clock they said their goodbyes, and Charlotte followed Marc's jeep back to Bedford on the 45-minute drive to his house. In the kitchen, Charlotte sat at the table, absorbed in answering her phone texts.

He offered her a stemmed glass of cabernet.

She lifted her head. “No thanks. I’m driving.”

“You don’t need to drive back to Draakensky tonight. Stay.”

She tapped her keyboard. “Can’t. Don’t they need you at the bar tonight?”

“Not this week. I loaded up the staff for day-and-night shifts in case I got on a jury for the week. I’ll make an omelet and salad for dinner?”

Still tapping the keyboard, she muttered a yes.

He grabbed eggs, lettuce and spinach, cheese, and celery out of the fridge. “Sir Duncan called me yesterday. We had a long conversation.”

Charlotte placed the phone down. “Did he? I suppose I should apologize for everything.”

“He doesn’t expect an apology. I think he just wants to clear the air.”

“What am I supposed to say? I cannot explain my elemental magick breaking free, now can I?”

He began ripping pieces of lettuce. “We never explain magick. Tell him what you told me. About your narrative imagination. Your creative process is true.” He hoped he could allay her fears. Becoming afraid of one’s magick had its risks.

Charlotte wore a sulky expression.

“Besides,” he added, “there is surely a level of occult provocation at Elysium Fields. And part of the event might have been from Sir Duncan himself. Ancestral guilt is quite powerful in the bloodline. DNA and all that.”

“Ancestral guilt,” she murmured.

“Generational transgressions are carried in the body or the mind. Trespasses from our predecessors can demand recognition. Or revenge.”

"Revenge? Do you think Sir Duncan is in danger?"

"I wouldn't speculate."

With a sigh, she raked her hair back and moved to the counter. "What can I do to help?"

"Scramble four eggs? Set the table?"

She cracked eggs into a bowl while he greased a baking dish. Her scrambling became excessive beating. "That's enough. Can you finely chop some celery?"

"Yes, I can finely chop celery," she imitated his inflection.

He poured the egg mixture into a round baking dish, ground in salt and pepper, and added dollops of ricotta cheese. "So, did my mother stuff you with chocolate-covered cherries?"

"She did." *Chop-chop* went the knife on the board, bits of celery flying. "Your family album is epic. Gosh, over a hundred cousins?"

"I hardly know them. Would you reach around to the pantry and grab the jar of dried cranberries? And the apples."

She entered the pantry and returned, though she'd forgotten the apples. "Got it," she said with eyes lowered and quickly resumed chopping.

He tore spinach leaves into the egg mixture, ready to open the subject. "What did you three chat about during the tea?"

"Oh, this and that," she said flatly.

"My family can be overwhelming. Was it awfully tedious?"

"How much celery do you need?"

"A cup. That's plenty. Hand me the shredded cheese."

She lifted her face to him, mouth clenched. "Who is Finnwolf?"

He scooped out a handful of cheese. "You mean the wolf on the Sexton coat of arms?"

"Isn't there a real Finnwolf?"

A real Finnwolf. How far did their conversation go? "I need the apples."

She went back into the pantry.

He spread the shredded cheese on top of the spinach-egg mixture and placed it into the oven. "That'll be done in ten minutes."

She stood before him, holding two red apples, her head poised like an owl's—straight and steady. Had she been gifted with night vision, she'd be staring right through him. He reminded himself to keep everything in a calm balance.

"So, tell me about Finnwolf."

At the sink he rinsed his hands, searching for a simple answer. "Finnwolf is a realm walker in the Otherworld. You sure you don't want half a glass of wine?"

"What does that mean, a realm walker?"

"A traveler who knows the Otherworld's portals and gateways. We think of Finnwolf as *Mac Tíre,* son of the land."

"Son of the land. What else?"

He began peeling the apples. "The ancient Celts revered earthly wolves as guides. Mostly because their howls here could communicate with the Otherworld."

"Is Finnwolf an earthly wolf?" A tremor distorted her voice.

He chose his words carefully. "Finnwolf's mission is to transport souls of wolves into their wolf realm in the Otherworld." Spearing an apple slice, he offered it to her.

She popped it in her mouth, chewing slowly. "You mean a psychopomp?"

"Right. Psychopomps can take different forms of animals or ancestors. A rather dangerous occupation though. Psychopomps are sometimes captured by opposing powers. We recognize

Manannán mac Lir, son of the sea, as a psychopomp. He's known to use his magickal steed to transport souls over the seas in the Otherworld. Manannán carries a sword that never misses its target. He is a spectacular guardian of the Otherworld. Mamó said the steed is known as Énbarr, as 'swift as he is strong.' Énbarr has a dappled blond mane fringed over wild black eyes."

Her expression went slack.

He could see she was distressed. He tickled her chin and winked. "When I go, I want to ride with Manannán on Énbarr over the sea froth and foam to victory. How thrilling, right?"

Charlotte sucked in a breath, unamused. "I'll set the table." After taking two plates out of the cupboard, she held them to her chest. "Shall I set a place at the empty chair in front of the window?"

The knife twisted from his hand and fell on the board. "What?"

"Niagra had a place setting on the tea table for Mamó. She said she invited her to be with us. You don't keep the Sexton tradition?"

"No, I don't."

She grabbed two forks and two knives from the drawer and turned. "Why not? Unusual that you, of all people, wouldn't hold to the Sexton tradition."

"I don't need to do that with Mamó. She communicates easily enough with me."

"How does she do that? Are your napkins in the pantry?"

"Top drawer on the right. Mamó sends me signs. A familiar object will turn up in my field of vision. Or I'll hear her voice. A single word or two emerges in my head. Most of the time, she comes to me in dreams. I told you about my dream where she invited you into her house in County Cork, through the red door?"

Charlotte set the plates on the table, placing each fork and knife down slowly, positioning them with care as if she were performing a difficult task. "I remember." She turned abruptly. "Have you ever seen Mamó? Like when you saw Heida appear in the bar after she died?"

He added the chopped apples into the salad bowl, tossed in pecans, blue cheese crumble, and cranberries. "I did. It was about three weeks after Mamó's funeral, and I had just returned from Ireland. Early morning, at sunrise, something tapped at my bedroom window. I saw Mamó walking in the tree grove. She touched the trunks and branches, almost dancing between the trees. A moment I savored, knowing she had come home with me."

Charlotte fussed with the napkins, folding them into neat triangles. "Only once?"

"Only once."

"Did Mamó ever touch you?"

"No. She's never come quite that close."

"Hmmm. Cousin Niagra is a charmer. I liked her immediately. She boasted about your cousin Mary Sexton. I take it Mary was the star of the family. A Lore Keeper and seer like Mamó."

"She was. A beauty, refusing three marriage proposals. When she did marry, she had two sons. They're dead now."

"Did you know Mary?" She poured water into her glass.

"She died when I was a child, about eight years old, in 1991. I remember her, though, from my summers in Ireland with Mamó. Soft-spoken and tender as a lamb. She taught me Checkers. No one was sweeter than Mary. Her eyes had a way of crinkling up all sparkly. Mary was the only one who called me Marcus. She called me her little pup and pet my head."

Charlotte pivoted, her shoulders raised. "Mary pet your head? How? Show me how she pet your head."

Her startled tone caught him. He dried off his hands and stroked her head, running his fingers over her hair. He had to kiss her if only to melt the angst on her face. "Stay with me tonight," he said, pressing his head to hers.

"Can't. I have work in the studio." She moved to the kitchen window and lifted the pot of rosemary from the windowsill. "Mmm, I love the aroma of rosemary. This is practically a shrub; it's so big. Shall I put this on the table with us? And the thyme and sage too?"

"Sure."

While he tossed the salad and dressed it, he kept an eye on her as she arranged the three herb pots in a row and fiddled with the fairy figurines in them, making a border of greenery along the backside of the table. Adding the water pitcher, wine bottle, and breadboard, she staged it as a still-life scene.

He could see she was deep in thought. One of the things he adored about Charlotte was her talent to create pretty tableaus, everything allied and ambient.

Out the window, the sun lowered on the tree grove. Maybe Mamó was present, listening, pleased that such a gifted woman was soon to be added to the Sexton family.

"Very pretty, Charlotte. I may leave the pots there instead of on the windowsill."

"Oh, I forgot the salt and pepper grinders." She reentered the pantry and returned to the table, keeping her back to him as she spoke, fussing over arranging the plates. Then she abruptly excused herself to the bathroom.

When she finally came out, after an unusually long time, he took the omelet out of the oven and placed it on the table.

She squirmed in her chair and kept shifting her weight as she ate. "You know, Marc," she said between bites, "you shouldn't have quit the Culinary Institute. You have the makings of a spectacular chef."

"My chef days are long over, but I'm glad you like it." He paused. "Are you okay? You seem . . . uncomfortable."

"I'm fine."

"Niagra didn't overwhelm you with her dramatics?"

"She's fascinating. All that enthusiasm." She devoured her last piece of omelet. "Your family history is shocking, I'll say that. The Sexton clan brutally killing wolves. And how savagely they went after the black wolves on the mountain."

"Appalling, I know. Exterminating wolves was common in Europe at the time. Especially after Oliver Cromwell set it in motion with his wolf wars." He helped himself to more salad. "My Sexton ancestry carries barrels of guilt."

"Hm. Killing and banishing wolves is bad enough, but murder? Poisoning the O'Leary sisters? My God, what a horrendous crime."

Niagra had revealed the O'Leary sisters? He wanted to shrink away. "My family saga is horrific, I know. Let's change the subject."

She bit off a piece of bread and twisted her shoulders as if in pain. "Have you ever taken off your wolf pendant?"

Startled, he took a minute to get a grip. "Sure, I take it off. The silver requires polishing."

"And what happens when you don't wear it?"

He sat back and sipped his wine. "Nothing happens. I clean it and put it back on."

She pursed her mouth thoughtfully. "When you consider its source, from the Lupus star constellation, I would guess that your wolf pendant possesses powerful magick. Maybe some secret knowledge you embody when you wear it?"

He finished off his salad. He should have known to expect this. With his mother's meddling and Niagra feeding her the Sexton history, she had moved from curiosity to suspicion.

"Take the pendant off, Marc," she ordered in a voice he almost didn't recognize.

"What?"

"Take the wolf off and lay it on the table."

He lifted the chain over his head and placed it on the table in front of the rosemary pot. Letting the moment slide, he said, "What, did you expect I might disappear?"

The color of her grays sharpened hard on him. "How does the wolf pendant protect you? You said it was a guardian."

"It keeps my magick safe."

"Safe from what?"

He struggled to think of an appropriate answer. "From other magick. Do you want dessert?"

"And what happens if you don't wear the pendant for a day or two? Or a week or a month?"

"I don't know. I wear it every day."

"Would you lose your magick if you stopped wearing it?"

"I *am* my magick, Charlotte. Body. Mind. Soul. But my magick might change."

"Change how?"

"Become something less. Or something else. I have yogurt with honey and fresh raspberries for dessert."

"What if I wore it?"

His heart thumped. "I don't think so, Charlotte."

"Why not?" she asked, stretching her left shoulder and rubbing it excessively.

"Because it doesn't belong to you," he said gently.

"Belong? That word actually isn't about ownership, is it?" She bit her lip. "*Belong* means for a person to *be longing*, *be yearning*. We're all so hungry to belong to something—family, spouse, career, a home. So, it's true . . . the wolf pendant be-*longs* to you and you be-*long* to the wolf."

He couldn't deny it. He wouldn't admit it either. In his hesitation to answer, she leaned forward. "Is Finnwolf your silver wolf pendant?"

"No."

"Is Sky Wolf your silver wolf pendant?"

"Sky Wolf is not a symbol. Sky Wolf is a flesh and blood reality, begotten through magick, but nonetheless an earthly, fully alive wolf. I see you're troubled by this. What did Niagra tell you about Finnwolf?" He poured more wine into his glass.

Charlotte rose, her mouth firm. "Not enough, Marc. Not nearly enough." She grabbed her purse and entered the foyer. "Nice dinner. I'll call you tomorrow. Goodnight."

"Charlotte, wait. Please don't leave."

She was out the door, practically running away from him.

"Charlotte!" He followed her outside.

Inside her car in seconds, she pulled away, just as his cell phone rang.

JACKSON.

The yellow Fiat sped down the driveway. *Not nearly enough?* For God's sake, what did that mean? Exactly what secrets had Niagra told her?

Chapter Twenty-Three

The Burn

Marc answered the call—"What is it, Jackson?"—his voice cutting low.

"Don't panic," Jackson said. "We've had a kitchen fire, but we're okay."

His stomach lurched. "What happened?"

"Two pans on the rear burners shot up flames. Something must have failed with the automatic range hood sprayers. Flames burned up pretty high, spewing black smoke. Charlie got there in time to hit the manual Fire Knight, and the sprayers smothered it."

"Did you evacuate?"

"Didn't need to. Charlie got the fire arrested fast. Dining room and bar were clear the whole time. I called 9-1-1 anyway though."

"Anybody hurt?"

"No, we're fine. We've got chaos here. Liz tripped on the stockroom step and sprained her ankle. It's swollen from here to kingdom come. Her sister drove her to the ER. Jean-Pierre had an emergency with his wife and had to leave. The bar has been slammed all night."

"I'm on my way. Jackson, is the line moving?"

"Brigadier Petrovna is in full command. We're managing."

He scooped up his car keys from the foyer table and rushed out. Jackson's words, *We're fine*, repeated in his head. Kitchen fires. He had had his share of those for a lifetime.

When he arrived, two fire trucks were flashing lights on the side street. Inside the kitchen, the line appeared to be performing its balancing act producing dishes at breakneck speed, Petrovna yelling "four broco, two sliders, two lamb," while others were mopping up water, and servers were ferrying dishes out. He was surprised the kitchen wasn't in total bedlam, although smoke still hovered even with the fans going and windows open. "Where's Charlie?" he asked Jackson.

"Freaking out. In the walk-in. Swearing in Italian like you've never heard. I think a few Chinese profanities mixed in too."

The walk-in. The soundproof cooler, a sanctuary for Chef-scream-therapy. Marc had been there several times himself over the years. He threw open the door and found Charlie pacing the cabbage aisle.

"I'm sorry, Marc," Charlie shouted, breathless and flushed. "I'm sorry. My fault. All my fault. We were in the weeds. I don't know what the hell happened. We had a VIP, some senator who wanted his burger charred. I turned away to flash it on the grill because Ryan had his hands full. I fucked up!" His high cheekbones were red from the thirty-five-degree temp, his slanted eyes wide as black golf balls. Singed black hairs poked out near his temples.

"Any burns?"

Charlie spread his fingers and palms up. "Don't think so. Honest to God, this never happened to me. The flames were shooting up fucking footballs. They spun out across the ceiling!"

"Take it easy. I've set pans on fire. Sent the fryolator into flames at least twice." He showed him a burn scar on the side of his wrist. "Go warm up, please, before you fall over." He gave him a pat on the back as he exited. "Everyone is okay. You saved the day. Thank you, Charlie."

Fire Chief Werner met him in the hallway and assured him all was secured, although he needed to have the Knight fire-suppression sensors inspected. "Odd the flame detectors malfunctioned. Probably grease buildup. Take it easy, Marc."

Marc surveyed his customers. In the dining room, a party of ten at the far end, every table occupied, booster chairs with three kids, standing room only in the bar. *Holy hell, this could have turned into a disaster.*

He did a walk-through, announcing to his customers that they had put out a small kitchen fire and reassured them there was no danger, not to be alarmed by the fire trucks outside—only a precaution. At the bar, he jumped in taking orders, refills, tallying the tabs, and even found a moment to text Liz at the ER to check her condition.

By closing time at 10:30, after the last of the customers strolled out, he went back into the kitchen and called an impromptu meeting to praise the staff for their impressive teamwork. "My heartfelt thanks to every one of you for working together so successfully. You are my champions. Special thanks to Chef Charlie's fast acting—our official fire-dragon slayer." Everyone applauded, Charlie tipping his chef's cap to the staff.

In his office, Marc flopped into his chair, turned on the desk lamp, and composed a quick email to his insurance agent. Grease buildup on the range hood fire sensors? He'd had the hoods inspected, cleaned, and tested last month. Couldn't have been more than three weeks ago. He had to get that in writing because Chief Werner would probably be filing a report soon.

On his desk, Mamó's vintage brass clock with its exposed mechanisms chimed eleven o'clock.

Feeling sweaty and parched, he went into the restroom. In the mirror, he caught a glimpse of himself, cheeks flushed, mouth grim. A burning sensation made him splash water on his face. He stretched up and dried his face. The mirror reflected his open white sports shirt, exposing his bare neck and chest—no silver-link chain.

My wolf pendant!

Chapter Twenty-Four

Wolves Are Howling on Draakensky

As Marc pulled the jeep into his driveway, ripe stars came rolling out above the house. In the backyard, the night air roiled in a spasm over the tree grove. He knew night spasms from another time, in another realm, when wolves marched forward, their grizzled chops snapping like grinding bones. No way was he going back to that.

Pushing the images away, he burst through the door, anxious to find his wolf pendant, and rushed to the kitchen table, expecting to see the chain near the rosemary plant.

No chain. Not near the sage or thyme. With a step back, he scrutinized the table. It had to be there. He lifted his plate and put it in the sink, then Charlotte's plate, salad bowl, and omelet dish, checking the counter surface. He removed the breadboard, wine bottle, and water pitcher. No pendant on the table. He ruffled the rosemary stems, sage, and thyme, expecting the chain to drop out.

He checked his chair and Charlotte's chair. With a broom, he swept the floor, thinking he was just not seeing it. Nothing.

Had Charlotte taken it? All those questions about him not

wearing it and its secret magick. They were talking, making eye contact. Surely he would have seen her pick up the chain.

Sitting down, he felt certain Charlotte would never do such a thing. She was a bit off, though. She had run out so fast—was that guilt? Once more, he scanned the table, chairs, and floor. *Charlotte must have taken it. She's testing me. Testing my magick.*

He grabbed his cell and called her. 12:10 AM. No answer; he left a message. "Charlotte, I've misplaced my wolf pendant. Did you see where I left it? Please call me."

In that moment, even though he stood straight, feet solid on the floor, he had the odd sensation of not feeling the ground beneath him. Like the earth had shifted. *Shifted.*

With no time to lose, he called Charlotte again. No answer; he texted: I'M COMING OVER. BE THERE IN TEN MINUTES.

He sped out.

When he pulled up Draakensky's driveway, the houses and grounds were dark. His car's headlights shone enough for him to see the windmill's sails turning. He banged the door knocker and yelled for Charlotte. Eventually, he saw lights in the windows and heard footsteps. She greeted him in boy shorts, a red tee shirt, and her hair tied in a tail under her ear.

"Marc, it's after midnight. What's going on?"

He pushed through the doorway. "I can't find my wolf pendant. I placed it on the kitchen table. You saw me put it near the rosemary plant, right?"

"Yes." She tilted back from his volume.

"Well it's not there. Not anywhere in the kitchen." He moved into the living room, which was a chaos of drawing pads, discarded sheets, dusty charcoals, pastels, and an easel crippled on the floor as if she had flung it.

She meandered the room, turning on the table lamps.

He hated to ask. "Did you take it, Charlotte?"

She swung her head around. "Don't be absurd. I'd never take your wolf pendant."

"A few hours ago, I would have thought the same. But right now, as I'm standing here, unable to locate it, I have my doubts."

Lifting a pillow, she batted a charcoal dust stain on the corner. "Marc, you can't possibly believe I would *steal* your jewelry," she said with an expression not so much hurt as guarded.

"No, I don't think you stole it. But with your questions and telling me to take the chain off . . . are you testing me? Well, you made your point. I admit I need the wolf's protection. Why? Because without that protection, I'm vulnerable to a more powerful kind of magick. Does that answer your question? Now hand over the pendant before I explode."

She gave up trying to pound the stain out of the pillow and plopped down onto the sofa. "You know what?" She rubbed her arms as if cold. "In moments like this. . ." Her voice went timid. "I wish I had a piece of chocolate cake, because I need a guilty pleasure."

"Christ almighty, Charlotte. Don't fool with me." An urge to snap, snarl, and swipe at her, claws extended, seized him. *Stop it!*

She raised her head. "I did not take your pendant. I would never do that."

He half believed her—she said it so genuinely. "Charlotte, if you didn't take it off the table, who did?"

Toying with an eraser in hand, she rubbed it over her thumb, back and forth. "Well, I . . . I'm afraid to say that's another issue."

Afraid to say? He tossed the sketchbooks aside, knocking two off the sofa, and sat next to her. "What does that mean?"

She tightened her shoulders, and he saw her brace herself. "I may have done something tonight that . . . caused . . . that maybe I shouldn't have done."

Her guilty expression struck him. "I need the pendant back. Damn it, Charlotte, tell me."

She tossed the eraser on the coffee table, eyes riveted to her knees.

"Why can't you look at me? You know where the pendant is!"

"I think I do." Her eyes cast down on the floor now.

"Where?"

"A place where you probably cannot retrieve it." Those eyes squeezed shut.

"Last call, Charlotte," he shouted. "What have you done?"

She leaped from the sofa, wringing her hands. "Marc, you know the chair by the window at your kitchen table? Well, I . . . I put a teacup and saucer place setting there, from your pantry. You didn't see the setting because I hid it behind the herb pots."

"At the empty chair?"

"And I invited the dead."

Relieved, he leaned back. "You invited Mamó to my table? There's no harm in that. She's long been my guardian."

Mamó's synchronicities had come often and without call. This night, though, with Charlotte's invitation to his table, what was Mamó's communication? If Mamó had manipulated the wolf pendant, why? Of all people, she knew how critical it was to his safety. This was not Mamó's usual hide-and-seek tap on the shoulder to wake him up to a secret logic.

Charlotte paced before the fireplace, a panther in a cage anxious to be let out. "I didn't invite Mamó."

His chest caved. "What?"

She stopped pacing. "I invited Mary Sexton. I'm sorry! I let it happen. In fact, I wanted it to happen."

"Let *what* happen?"

"During the tea luncheon today. Someone fondled my hair. Pet my head."

"Mamó touched you?"

She shook her head. "I thought it was Mamó, but after you showed me tonight how Mary petted your head, I realized it wasn't Mamó who came to the tea table." She braced her hand on the armchair. "It was Mary Sexton who petted my head."

Marc had had no contact from Mary in the Otherworld. And now, Mary had come to Charlotte at their tea?

"When I set the place setting for the dead at your table tonight, I invited Mary."

"Why would you do that?"

"I wanted to see if she'd come to me. During dinner, I began to feel a presence. Something circled my head. Someone stood right next to me. I was so uncomfortable."

"Did you summon Mary when you were in the bathroom?"

"I did. I set the place setting at the table. Then I set the intention. It was more than a presence. She was there. At one point, I thought Mary was leaning on me. She was so heavy, I had to get away. As soon as I got home, I started drawing."

She lifted her sketch pad and paged to the back. In a sprawling image, in charcoal and black ink, a mountain spread in the background, a woman at the front.

"That's Shehy Mountain, Marc. *Cnoic na Síofra*. Did I pronounce it right?"

He could hardly believe she knew the Irish name for Shehy Mountain.

On the page, he saw a score of black wolf faces, some baring their teeth, others as floating heads hovering on the edge of the summit. No bodies, just wraith-like figures come up from a netherworld, miasmic and shrouded. Shadow wolves, ten or more.

"You drew this tonight? Black Wolf Realm. On Shehy Mountain. You saw this?"

"All I could see was that image."

Scattered across the mountain's flat bald ridge, three gray wolves poised at the forefront: one standing with paws splayed, ready to leap, one crouching preparing to attack, one running fiercely up a hill.

At the center stood a woman, drawn as a profile, her upper body angled, head tilted, crinkled eyes gazing back. With a crown on her head, she wore a robe, fur-trimmed collar, and the robe's train spread down the mountain's terrain.

"Why is the woman wearing a robe?" he asked.

"Oh no you don't," Charlotte said. "You don't get to ask the questions. That woman is your cousin Mary Sexton, and you know it. This is October 31, 1911, Samhain. I saw Mary Sexton. On Shehy Mountain. Mary is answering the wolf howls. The summons." Charlotte sat down next to him on the edge of the sofa. "This time, I get to ask the questions. Because Mary isn't telling me everything. Which one of these gray wolves is Finnwolf?"

Marc's whole body went limp. Niagra had revealed the Shehy Mountain lore.

"Is Finnwolf the wolf standing at Mary's side in the forefront?" she asked.

He couldn't answer.

"Is it? Or the one crouching beneath the thorn tree?" She pointed, waiting for his response. "Then it must be the one charging up the hill."

Marc wanted to scream. He could hardly fathom he was observing an image of Mary Sexton on Shehy Mountain with three gray wolves.

"Which one, Marc? Which one is Finnwolf? Tell me!"

He didn't have it in him to speak the words. When falling, maybe it was best to just dive. Marc pointed to the gray wolf at Mary's side, then pointed to the one crouching under the thorn tree—and to the wolf running, his tail flared straight out.

"All three wolves . . . are Finnwolf?"

"All three."

Dumbstruck, she dropped back against the sofa. "And Mary's three cousins? Albert, Donnell, and Cormac, who went with her up the mountain on Samhain?" She pressed her fist to her mouth.

He had spent most of his life building a wall around this truth, and now Charlotte had severed it like a rope fence.

She pushed the drawing pad into his lap. "These cousins—these three men—are shapeshifters?"

His chest hurt. All he could see was a pack of black wolves' faces. Black wolves with hungry jaws, swollen shadows hanging on the mountain's edge with their fiery eyes. And the three gray wolves . . . defenders on the battlefield.

He fought off the numb feeling and refocused on Mary's robe and crown. Not really a robe, now that he saw it again. Mary wore a tufted gown that billowed out into elegant plumed tails, furry and wide. And not a crown on her head. He recognized two high-pointed ears and shining tufts of hair framing the face.

"What do you think of Mary in this illustration?" Charlotte asked.

He had never felt so humbled in his life. "Mary is . . . exactly as you have her imaged forth."

"As wolf queen? That's right?"

Hearing Charlotte speak the words *wolf queen* made him clutch his stomach.

"Tell me about Mary's magick. Mary wants you to tell me. She may be dead, but she is still your cousin. Do you want to honor that or not?"

He laced his fingers in Charlotte's hand, trying to map what energy realm she had accessed to have seen Mary and this event in 1911. What could he read inside Charlotte? All he got was a sense of flowers. Sweet scents, soft petals, the aroma of a clean green leaf. It wasn't until that moment he noticed the room had vases of lilacs. The room held an air of Jaa's flower obsession.

She waited patiently, with eager expectation, and holding her breath—as he was.

"Marc," she said softly, "I drew Mary bold and powerful because that's how she came to me. She has a luminous dust across her face. Do you see it? Something meaningful is happening there. What is it?"

In a flash, he realized Charlotte was putting her faith in him—to honor Mary, to honor truth. "I think, maybe, lost times." A distant voice echoed in his head: *My little pup, brave Marcus. For all your mischief and magick to come.* When had Mary said those words to him? Over a Checkers game? Or during one of their walks around Mamó's lake?

Marc studied Mary on the page, her palm raised to Black Wolf Realm emerging over the mountain's edge, holding back the wolves from descending upon the summit, protecting all as wolf queen; her beautiful hand, delicate as a flower, like the lilacs on the tables, and yet showing a depth of strength to bar Black Wolf Realm.

"Have I shocked you?" Charlotte reached for his hand.

"Yes," he admitted.

"You believe in my magick, don't you, Marc?"

"Of course I do. But this . . . goes too far."

"Why, because it's tearing down your walls?"

"Charlotte, you said the pendant was in a place I could not retrieve it. You know where it is. Tell me."

She paged the pad to a final illustration.

He riveted on a portrait of Mary, her face melancholy, hands on her lap, fingers entwined on a link chain, loosely holding his wolf pendant.

"No. No. Can't be." He chucked the pad on the floor. "Tell me you didn't do this, Charlotte! Tell me you didn't give my wolf pendant to Mary."

"I did not. Mary is telling you. She lifted your wolf pendant."

He shook his head. "Mary would never do that. She wouldn't leave me vulnerable. Why would Mary snatch away my protection? Put me at risk to Black Wolf Realm? Put you at risk?"

"I don't know. But that is the image that came to me. And I was compelled to draw it. Messing up sometimes, but she drove me to illustrate that scene. My head was bursting. I'm exhausted."

What did Mary want? Was she driving a wedge between him and Charlotte? Or was this the work of the Old Fathers? Albert, Donnell, and Cormac driving Charlotte away, rejecting the marriage, protecting their Finnwolf legacy and heirs? Of course Mary would lead the effort with the Old Fathers to protect the legacy.

My little pup, brave Marcus. For all your mischief and magick to come.

Mary had never been his adversary. Until now. The gifted seer, wolf queen, a woman skilled in Finnwolf magick, soul magick, and clairvoyance.

He bolted from the sofa. A chorus of wolf voices shot through him. He wanted to throw his head to the sky and howl with them. Needing air, he ran to the door and threw it open. Conscious breathing would serve as his anchor to stop his body from filling up. He breathed in, both hands braced on the doorframe, holding on.

That chorus of wolf howls broke into him. Not just in his mind this time. Not just surfacing from fear. These howls soared from Draakensky, from the earth and trees and river.

"Did you hear that?" Charlotte came rushing to the door. "Wolf howls."

Wolf voices pulsed in hard calls, severing the air. If their rusty calls could murder, he'd be dead on the doorstep. Beyond the windmill's flood lights, darkness thickened. Bog holes rotated. Mangy swirls came down. The moon peeled itself into white whips.

"Night spasms," Marc uttered. A cold fear choked him.

Nerves vibrating, his spine began to twist. Drums beat into his gut. A hot twang filled his ears and head. Any second the triple spiral would emerge to capture him.

"Black wolves are on Draakensky. Get inside, Charlotte." He smelled bitter snow in the air despite the warm night. "And don't open the door. No matter what you hear." He hurried off the front step.

"You're not going out there," she called after him. "Should I call Jimmy Cruz? Do we need help? Please, Marc, what should I do?"

"Do nothing. Stay inside. Call no one. Do nothing, Charlotte!"

His muscles charging, feet swelling, eyes spinning—summoned—Marc plunged into the darkness.

End of Book I

Book II

"I believe in the practice and philosophy of what we have agreed to call magic, in what I must call the evocation of spirits . . . and I believe in three doctrines that have been the foundations of nearly all magical practices:

—That the borders of our minds are ever shifting and that many minds can flow into one another, as it were, and create or reveal a single mind, a single energy;

—That the borders of our memories are as shifting and that our memories are a part of one great memory, the memory of Nature herself;

—That this great mind and great memory can be evoked by symbols."

W.B. Yeats, *Magic, Ideas of Good and Evil,* 1903.

Chapter Twenty-Five

Beyond Midnight

Black wolves on *Draakensky. Black Wolf Realm.* Charlotte stood in the doorway, tempted to dash after Marc. Running rampant in the treacherous woods, even with a flashlight, could prove trouble. Was Marc running to the river? The falls? Yew Crag?

Do nothing, he had said. *Call no one.* At two o'clock in the morning, who could she call, except Jimmy? She switched on the boardwalk lights to the back acre. She could manage the boardwalk, but what good would that do if Marc was downriver or beyond the falls near the steep ridges?

In the bedroom, she hurriedly changed into jeans, a sweater, and yanked on her hiking boots. The wind dragged up loud wolf howls, harsh notes crashing like rockslides off a mountain. How close were these wolves? What kind of magick was happening?

Do nothing, he'd said. *No matter what you hear. Stay inside.*

Before heading to the boardwalk, she decided to wait. Charlotte sat down in the chair directly in front of the hatched window with a view of the woods. After five minutes, she grew impatient and went out the front door. The wolves' voices had grown distant now, echoing across the sky, but still persistent.

"Marc?" She screamed out. A cold throbbing thickness circled the air. She sensed snow in the air as the windmill sails spun. "Marc!"

Putting her faith in him, she committed to waiting a few minutes before she'd try the boardwalk. Back inside, she lit a candle and put it in the kitchen window just as Aunt Loretta used to do. *Place a candle in the window and let it call everything home to you.* Chilled to the bone suddenly, she wrapped herself up in a knitted afghan, sitting at the kitchen table. Waiting for Marc.

Time halted when waiting. Each minute a forever. Her pulse slowed; the wolves howled wildly. "Mary, why did you take his wolf pendant? I thought you loved Marc. I'm sorry I summoned you!"

The *swish, swish, swish* of the windmill blades spun counterclockwise. Through the window, the sycamore tree swayed under the floodlights, wind directing its movement, hissing, speaking . . . something.

Jaa had had Frau Holle to guide her. Charlotte now had the Lady of the Wind, her companion on Draakensky. Was she near? Wind beings were so elusive. The sycamore dipped and pulled, rock-rock-rocking her. She fought to stay awake. A sense of being buried—heavy and limp—made her head drop, eyelids dipping, then closing. It was not only the day's exhaustion, not only the stampede of wolves breaking across Draakensky, but the blink of a mystic eye surrounding her that pressed her eyelids.

A secret hand stroked her hair as Charlotte slipped hauntingly into sleep.

Interlude II

Draakensky

The wolves of Shehy Mountain are howling on my Yew Crag. Their voices dive fast into my river and at the same time soar the treetops. My sky is quaking with their calls. These Shehy wolves race through my groves, their pulsing shadow bodies hard as black granite. What phantom souls they have become, waiting beneath the white moony disc above, hauling their Black Wolf Realm with them on the hunt. But wait. Hush. I see a man running my paths.

Is it a man? His feet are bare and massive with claws. He is heading toward Yew Crag; over the bridge now, he runs to the yew tree grove. He howls a wild song.

His head elongates. Fangs break out. His hands contort. Muscles are rippling his body like lightning rods. Limbs are twisting. Skin bursts into monstrous hide and hair, all black. He is on the ground now, trembling, perhaps to calm the force of violence—man becoming wolf on my forest floor.

This force has the sky convulsing. My trees are hunched and shivering. The stars, though, they have their wisdom and remain as steady light.

Up from the darkness, the wolf warriors gather in a small clearing in my yew grove. I sense their relentless craving. I can smell it on their breath. Ravenous. Incited to kill by a band of sorcerers who tether them from afar.

These sorcerers are spitting sparks, creating an umbilical cord, provoking these wolves to ambush the prey.

Each wolf—I count fourteen—prowling the man in his fur and flesh. And yet this is no man. His humanity lost, this is wolf.

The stalking begins. A savage delight on their wolf snouts, they show their gross teeth. The lone wolf on the forest floor is surrounded but smart enough not to risk a leap and run, lest the pack attack at once.

My moon friend is shedding her light. I see the weave of a dragon wing downriver. Who has summoned the river dragon to Draakensky? She arrives from the constellation Aquarius, the star water-bearer, by power of Beta Aquarii, the brightest Aquarian star. What task does this sparkling dragon have here on this night?

The lone black wolf on my forest floor rises on all fours. Hackles up, defensive, shooting warning growls to the pack that is slowly closing in.

From the rear, another black wolf comes forward, its head broken, ebony cones for ears, bony eye sockets ablaze, daggers for fangs. The alpha male, a withered, mangy soul. He stomps the ground. Like a lash has scourged his hide, he springs up on tremendous legs and lands within striking range of the lone wolf.

In this standoff, I see no way out for the lone wolf surrounded by so many who claw up the earth to display their slashing skills. What will he do, this humbled wolf with kind eyes and a gentle snout? Surely they will tear this wolf to pieces as he clings to my forest floor.

Nine wolves circle tightly around the lone wolf. The other five make a backup regiment. The alpha takes charge in front.

This lone wolf hunkers pitifully to the ground, surrendered, head pressing the dirt between his front paws, tail curled in trembling fear. What despair he endures.

The wolves advance a margin.

The sorcerers send their spell, a magnetized black and purple rod, to the pack's feral appetite. Fifteen mouths are drooling with hunger to kill.

The alpha male growl-barks. Yet, I detect a note of hesitation in the quality. Another growl-bark, this one a direct order; his pack holds in abeyance. What lull is this? A false pause, no doubt.

I ask, what trick are they perpetrating? A cunning wolf pack outsmarting the prey to take him whole? Or, a clever momentary sacrifice for a greater desire? A calculated risk, but to what purpose? What desire do these Shehy wolves have stuck in their claws? Feast? Revenge? Thrill-killing? Or, my wisdom advises: something else. I suspect a pawn in the desire for a more advantageous win. What win are they seeking, these feral beasts?

In the river, at the deep falls, our star dragon floats up. She is the harbinger in bright marigold, scales curly, her golden wings invoking celestial wisdom that I am denied.

The alpha male approaches the lone black wolf. Nose to nose, they are. The lone wolf's eyes are pools of terror locked into the alpha's bony sockets of reddish fire. A mesmerizing gaze from one to the other swells between them.

The sorcerers rear up, whipping the air into hot discharges. Shouting, they chant Gaelic demands, voices sizzling.

The alpha male acknowledges our star dragon with a snort. Dragon light kicks up the river waves, her tail creating a signal I do not recognize. Yet the alpha male does and releases a high-strung howl.

Answering to his name, the lone wolf rises on wobbly legs.

Fifteen wolves, propelled with desire now, charge him with open jaws—commanding their authority, crushing his body into theirs, converging their flanks into one fearsome mass of black wolf. Captured, caged, conjoined into their pack, he advances with them, victim to their masterful power, surrendered to a greater mystery.

Tumultuous paws beat thunder as sixteen wolves race through Draakensky's woods, vanishing from sight.

Our star dragon sails downriver to her rest and returns to Beta Aquarii.

Chapter Twenty-Six

Into the Deep Heart

As the sun journeyed up on Wednesday morning, Charlotte sprang awake. Bolting from the chair, she fixated out the window. Leaves rustled and tree branches cracked. Thumping. Someone ran the river path. She hustled outside.

"Marc?" The sky hung low and swollen; blue jays squawked.

A black wolf appeared from behind a copper beech. He pawed his way to the opening of the path. Gray hairs mixed in around the face, but the wolf's coat spread black as pitch.

Charlotte clung to a tree trunk, frightened to call attention to herself. Muzzle low, sniffing the ground, the black wolf raised his nose to sample the breeze near a squirrel lodged up in a tree. His stealthy body weaved forward among the trees; his jaws parted. The terrified creature scampered higher on the branches. Then the wolf set his desire on another squirrel hopping rocks. The wolf darted, leaped, and grabbed it, sinking its teeth into its neck.

As it devoured the furry thing, Charlotte turned away, stomach roiling, hiding her face behind the tree. When she poked her head out, the wolf arched his head up, sniffing, ears pricked high. His yellow eyes met hers.

She veered back. The wolf did not. Immobilized, panting, his eyes flared into a golden color, molten hot. She could paint those eyes. And then, something else looked back at her from the yellow stripes within. Those eyes belonged to a man, not beast.

Seconds passed before he backed up, his black fur ruffling, blood on his jaws. A string of drool dangled from his tongue. Shifting on his paws, faltering as if in a panic, he shot left, vaulted the air, hit the path hard, and raced off, leaving a trail of swaying branches behind him.

The reverberations from the rumbling earth sent Charlotte into the windmill for cover. She paced the floor. A black wolf! What was this? Don't panic, do something. *Do nothing, Charlotte.*

Do nothing, and nothing happens. She was done with doing nothing. She sprinted to the shed and found the old baseball bat in a bucket of rakes. The second her boots met the river path, she was sure she would find Marc.

Slamming her feet into the soil, she ran hard, sending twigs and stones flying. Charlotte reached the river's edge at the falls, ragged breaths tasting peppery on her tongue. White-capped waves thrashed over rocks, noisy as hell. "Marc! Marc!"

Clouds pressed, threatening rain. She sprinted downriver as far as the vacant cabin in its foreboding barrier of the thick pines. She called out to Marc again, knowing the deserted terrain would not answer back.

At a point near the bend, the river idled between weeping willows, gray and green and whistling. Whistling a safe alert? Or whistling a warning trill?

Onward through two more trails, she approached the cross-paths and took the longer path that led back to the windmill, shouting *Marc* repeatedly between gulps of air. Finally, the path narrowed to the finish behind Heida's cottage, swerving to the carport driveway.

Leaning on the carport post for a breather, Charlotte heard footsteps on the driveway gravel. She sprang forward.

Marc huddled near the garden stone wall, hand on his jeep door, feet bare, his clothes ripped at the seams, shirt shredded, trousers torn. His hair stood up as if in a white fright, face ashen as if dead. *Dear God.*

He sensed her presence and put his hand up to stop her approach. He wavered there for a moment. "Don't. Please." His voice was horribly brittle.

Wanting to run to him, she halted, her foot in midair. She had never seen him so dazed. His whole body trembled.

Struggling, he flung the car door wide and raised a stiff leg, wincing, gripping the door for support. His entire spine appeared hunched, with vertebrae poking up. One arm turned outward, both his hands were swollen red. Once inside, he started the engine, one hand hiding his face.

"Marc?" she cried out. "Please, let me—"

He raised his hand again to stop her, then jerked the car into reverse and sped out.

At the opening of the river path, among the weeds, she spotted Marc's black shoes scattered near a tree. The leather appeared to have exploded, the sides ruptured into chunks and the top into flaps. Inside, the insoles were split open.

She turned both shoes over. The outside soles had erupted too. Breaks and fractures, lumps and slits made a shocking pattern. Two paw prints with curved claw markings.

Crushing the shoes to her chest, knees collapsing to the ground, Charlotte shrank. Her tears came in torrents.

Chapter Twenty-Seven

Dust in the Attic

Rain splattered the windshield as Charlotte sat in her yellow Fiat, motor running, clenching her hands on the steering wheel, ready to drive to Marc's house. The lurking fear of it all played hard despite her efforts to calm and gather herself. Tree-muffled thunder grew from Yew Crag. The timber groves there screamed at her, a rattle of echoes. *The forbidden secrets of the crag*, Jaa had warned her, *where the wind is long. Even the twigs do not sleep there.* Yew Crag was where ghosts chose to gather on Draakensky.

Shivering, brooding, rationalizing until she couldn't bear it another minute, she slammed the gear into drive and headed out of Draakensky. In her rearview mirror, she glimpsed Camaroon perched on the windmill roof. He rotated his head as owls do. Wings opening, he flew down and swerved alongside the driver's side window.

"What do you know, Camaroon?" The raptor trailed her to Marc's house.

In the driveway, his white jeep had been parked askew. Slanted rain hit the pond, making her mind skid. She got out of her car and slowly approached the house. At the entrance, her hand poised over the door knocker. Would he answer? Or even let her in?

She hit the door knocker. All quiet. Across the back lawn, pond side, near the weeping willows, shadows lurked. Shadows in the rain? *We only see shadows from the presence of light.*

Furry black figures swayed with humped backs, tails high. Ten of them, an army, skulked around the pond, fiery eyes straight on her. *Black Wolf Realm.* Two wolves darted back and forth. One settled down at the front as if on guard, panting, tongue lolling. Others patrolled the pond's edge. Their positions were oddly placed, yet she could see they had formed a stronghold.

She quickly pushed the front door open, closing it behind her. "Marc, are you here?" The house sank in shadows, damp as a winter's day, no lamps on, the kitchen dark too. A wooden end table lay in a broken mess near the trash cabinet. A kitchen chair had toppled over. At the sink, the throw rug lay bunched up.

Please be all right, Marc. She climbed the staircase to the second floor. "Marc?" The bedroom was dark, the bathroom vacant, except for lingering steam. At the end of the hallway, hanging from the ceiling, a white globe fixture shed light over the attic steps.

Marc always kept the attic door locked. *Storage for my dad's things from his cabin,* he had told her. The wooden door had slats and black iron fixtures. She moved up the stairwell. Another few steps. An erratic tapping broke above her head—nails scraping on a wood floor.

She held her place on the fifth step, eyeing the bookcase on the landing. The door was open a sliver. The scraping taps grew louder.

Horror seized her, urging a retreat. *I'm here to make sure Marc is safe. To hear his voice. To look into his sparkling blues and know that he's okay.* "Marc? Marc, are you here?"

The tapping stopped. She took another step. A thump came from above.

"I'm coming up." She hustled up the remaining steps and pushed the attic door open.

Black iron wall sconces shed low light against the horizontal brown timbers that lined the attic walls. Ceiling spotlights from the rafters produced only patchy light. Marc stood at the far window, back to her, wearing jeans and a navy pullover. An iron black-bellied stove burned wood behind a grate. The scent of sweet ash soothed her. "I came to see if you're all right."

She stepped into the room. On the right, a tall wooden chair, carved with wolf heads on both arms and the top, stood on a circular carpet, the design of which she could not make out. Baskets full of white tree branches and dried sage surrounded the circle, creating a centerpiece, barring entrance, reminding her of St. Sophia's church altar protected by the white marble communion rail.

Across the room, tattered storage trunks and copper pots filled with logs staged an eerie scene. Candles, crystals, drums, and flutes decorated the shelves. Near the window, an animal skull hung on the wall. A horse skull? Above, like floating stags, several sets of antlers, white and brown, adorned the rafters.

She counted eleven mirrors perched randomly on the floor, a few framed in tarnished silver.

"I'm here," she said.

Marc turned. "So you are." His voice sounded normal, the tone grateful in how he emphasized the word *you*. Darkness hid his face.

From behind, nail taps startled her. She pivoted. Sky Wolf came forward. She sniffed the air, paused, and with a satisfied trot, she settled down before the wood stove, the firelight polishing her white fur into a pearly coat.

"Sky Wolf? Inside the house?" she said to open the conversation.

"A temporary visit. I'll have to let her out soon, or she'll start tearing the place apart. She's already chewed up two throw pillows. And then crashed into an end table. Wolves need wide open spaces."

"I saw the broken table. What a mess. She seems bigger than when I've seen her outdoors."

"Yeah, she's small though, thigh-height. Not skilled at climbing a flight of steps. I had to practically carry her up. She doesn't weigh more than about sixty pounds. Sky Wolf, *stay*."

"Have you taken to feeding her now?"

"No. She snatched a rabbit earlier. Rabbits are fast, but she stalked it with perfect patience. Her strike was breathtaking."

Charlotte tightened her shoulders at the thought of the poor rabbit being captured and eaten. "Marc, are you okay?"

"I'm fine now."

From what she could see of him in the shadows, he appeared normal, standing straight, head up. "Was Sky Wolf with you last night?"

"She was."

Charlotte felt drawn to the wolf chair, the high back topped with an exquisite wolf staring down on her.

"And the black wolves? On Yew Crag?"

"A pack of fifteen."

Walking closer to the wolf chair, she stifled an urge to touch it. She could smell the wood. Cedar. "Does this chair belong to your father?"

"Most everything in this room is his."

"Do you sit in his chair?"

"Never."

She nearly blurted out, *Why not?* but held her tongue, feeling vulnerable asking so many questions. He had all the answers. And some were likely to determine her future. The antlers above kept plucking at her with their pointed curves and white bones. They wanted to fly, she thought. She could almost hear the stags grunting *urps*.

From the spotlights, the wolf chair wore a wavy appearance. Each wolf's face on the arms displayed gently carved eyes, slightly upward. Reassuring, at least, that these two wolves were not peering directly at her.

She walked around the carpet, wanting to run her fingertips along the chair's grooves. In its position, she could touch the backside without violating the circle. She meandered behind the chair. The spotlight shed enough light for her to see soft ridges. Unable to resist, she ran one finger down the back.

"What are these engravings on the back?" She crouched down to see clearly. "Oh, I see. It's inscribed. Names? . . . Albert. Donnell. Cormac. The Old Fathers?"

"Uh-huh."

"All Finnwolf," she said and read the list of names beneath the top three: "Keane. Carbry. Lucan. Raghnell. Anna-Kerry. A woman?"

"First female Finnwolf. Anna-Kerry attended stillborn wolf pups. Carried them to the star wolf realms." He moved closer and leaned on a whiskey-barrel table with an iron lamp, which he did not turn on.

Charlotte continued reading the back of the chair, "Timotheus. Onney. Callum." Here, she paused. "Matthew. Marcus."

Standing up, she kept an eye on Sky Wolf, who was calmly grooming herself.

"Did Mary Sexton carve your name into this chair?"

"Da carved it."

"And where are these people now?"

"All passed on."

"Except for you. Why isn't Mary's name carved there?"

"Mary is not Finnwolf."

"No? Why not?"

He took his time answering. "Finnwolf requires three gifts. Mary did not possess the three gifts. She became a witness in the Sisterhood. As Lore Keeper, as wolf queen, which you have aptly identified. Mary guarded the Finnwolf bloodline."

"Three gifts. What are they?"

He kept his head down. He hadn't looked directly at her, and in the low light, in his position at the barrel table, most of his face remained hidden.

"Tell me."

He gave her a crisp nod and raised his left palm. "Holding strength on the left." He closed his fist. "Holding Finnwolf powers on the right." Another fist up. "And a deep wolf heart at the center." He crossed both fists over his chest.

"And why didn't Mary possess these gifts?"

"Mary's gifts did not include Finnwolf metamorphosis powers. Wolf magick is selective. Although Mary did carry the DNA in her bloodline to shift. Her son Lucan inherited it."

"I see. And you? You have all three gifts. You're the thirteenth Finnwolf? Same as your father, performing as a psychopomp?" She had to swallow hard to get those words off her tongue.

"That's not who I am. No."

"Aren't you?"

He moved closer, near the spotlight, his face clearer now, blond wavy hair framing his face, but eyes cast down. "I don't like saying this aloud because words . . . names . . . carry energy. When spoken, the breath and intention energize them. But you're right. I owe you. And if I have to speak them to anyone, it should be to the woman I am going to marry." He positioned himself directly under the spotlight.

She stepped nearer to meet him on equal spacing, an arm's length away. This was the man she loved, but not just a man. He was something else now. "Marc, will you please look at me?"

Slowly he lifted his eyes to her.

She went rigid. "Your eyes!" The gorgeous blues she expected had altered into yellowish stripes, the irises iridescent with darkened gold, haunting and beastly.

"The color will fade. It's a reflective layer that grows for night vision during the physical transformation."

"Marc!"

"Da had the same breakthrough in his eyes after he returned from a journey. I promise it will fade."

"What journey? What happened to you last night?"

He turned away. "What happened? I was summoned. I couldn't find enough power to resist it." He faced her again. "Charlotte . . . Charlotte, this is not how I wanted to do this. I needed the right time. The right opportunity to—"

"And so it has come," she cut in. "I saw you! All black fur. On four legs. Stalking the river path. An animal, hunting. Hunting a squirrel, and, and—" She couldn't go on.

"If it's any consolation, I vomited it up."

She dropped her head. *Dear God, how will I ever find any of this bearable?*

Gently, he touched her chin with one finger and raised it as if she were the most precious woman alive. He smelled of pine and salt.

"You cannot be this, Marc! You cannot!"

"I am not Finnwolf."

"I found your shoes! Busted open." Tempted to beat his chest, she screamed, "Your name is on that chair!"

"I do not travel the wolf realms. I do not transport wolf souls to the Otherworld. I don't even know the cosmic geography. I may very well be the son of Finnwolf, but I do not practice the Finnwolf quest." He shook his head, a grim expression.

"If not, then what are you? Tell me. Everything."

"There is no *telling* everything. The words will distort the reality, cut you, and leave you wounded."

"Stop protecting me. I have a right to know. I'm here, aren't I?"

He didn't blink. Was he thinking she wasn't strong enough?

"Charlotte, this is not a report of events. It's not this happened first or that happened next. This is an experience. The knowledge requires you to engage it. You get on the charging horse and ride, no matter the danger."

She pushed her shoulders back, a stab trembling in her gut, and asked, "And if I ride that charging horse?"

"This knowledge, it will belong to you. You own it. There's no riding that horse back home to the comfort of the barn."

His words fired through her. "You think I should choose to live in the dark? Not know? My God, Marc, how could you even *ask* me to marry you, and not tell me about Finnwolf?" The words stumbled out between gulps. "Because this is not only about Finnwolf. This is about Black Wolf Realm. Our life together. Our future."

He took a step back. "You're right. I have no excuse. If you want to walk out on this, no one would blame you. I hid this because I couldn't bear the thought of losing you. I would have preferred to be the romanticized Merlin who shapeshifts into a thrilling owl soaring the sky, but I wasn't given that gift of metamorphosis. I was given something else. The blame is mine." His voice lowered. "It's just that . . . when you saw me on the river path . . . stalking the squirrel . . . I wanted to die."

She ached for him, recalling the black fur, the toothy jaw, thick paws, and the bloody squirrel he'd devoured.

Did she truly want to know everything about his wolf magick? In the mirrors on the floor, she caught scattered reflections of herself as if in a chiaroscuro painting—light and shadows playing hide-and-seek, her face dwarfed and dappled. One cracked mirror distorted her features into broken gray slits, reflecting her face slashed into a deformed monster. Mirror magick. Matthew Sexton practiced mirror magick. Of course he did.

On her left finger, she turned the sapphire ring round and round. How could she have a life with this man? A family, children . . .

She could call it quits this minute. Walk out. Don't look back. *I'm skilled at running away. I know the drill. Start over again. I'll be fine. I know how to make it.*

She wanted to know everything. But maybe not knowing would be an easier darkness. Knowing everything had its risks. What dangers were here? How could she choose this for her life? For her future? What if Marc brought her to the farthest corner of the universe with his truth? *There's no riding that horse back home.*

Bright yellow caution flashed everywhere. Wolf magick. Finnwolf. Shapeshifting. What kind of madness was this? The yellow stripes in his irises shone harshly. She caught the gleam of a wolf there. Fierce, primal, something wild surviving inside him.

The sapphire ring's brilliance illuminated under the spotlight. She turned it around her finger, twisting, pushing, slipping it over her knuckles until finally she held it between her fingertips.

Conflicted, battling her heart, battling her mind, her fears jangled and surged. Slowly, she let the ring drop on the table.

Marc slammed his eyes shut.

Instant regret seized her. Crushed, fighting tears, she forced herself to the attic doorway. One hand loosely on the door jam, the despair tightened her throat. Her legs stiffened in a panic. One foot on the first stair down. The other foot wavering over the next step, she tottered there, unable to descend the long, plunging flight down.

A *tap-tap* of Sky Wolf's paws on the wood floor trilled.

At her side, Sky Wolf's amber eyes gleamed up. The pearlescence of her white fur invited a stroke. She sat on her hind legs and raised her face valiantly. A treasure, this wolf, so strong, standing alone, her gentle snout begging for a caress. Charlotte stretched out a shaky hand and lightly petted the side of Sky Wolf's back.

The wolf threw her head back and sang a delicate, soul-wrenching note.

We are wolf.

Broken, unable to direct her foot to the next step, she released her fingers from the wall and slid down, hands covering her face, unable to press back her aching sobs.

Marc's arms suddenly embraced her. His head pressing hers, cheek to cheek, he hushed into her ear. "Please don't leave like this. Give me a chance? Please?" She sensed the grief in his body, his chest hitching, his heart pierced, hers bleeding.

Sky Wolf whined and stomped the floor.

"I need to let her out," Marc said impatiently, then directed Sky Wolf, her legs splaying as she made a ruckus down the steps. "Wait here. Please, wait."

Charlotte sat alone on the top step. The blaze in the black stove flicked light against the walls. It made a pretty pattern, even soothing, at such a dread-filled moment. What could she say to Marc now? He knew she'd failed to walk out. She'd have to give him a chance and accept his wolf magick. And whatever else existed.

On the wall opposite, a gray wolf cape hung with white pelts and leather-trimmed bindings fastened to silver buckles. Above it sat a painted wolf mask—hard and hideous, wicked blue eyes, red nose, smeared red lips, rows of teeth protruding from a wide, sinister grin. A blood monster. Was this what she was choosing?

When Marc returned, he guided her up from the top step. His embrace warmed her, his arms so reassuring. A white tower, he was, and she clung to it.

"Let's go downstairs," he said.

"Not yet. What is that wolf cape? On the wall."

He turned. "That's Da's cape, although I don't recall ever seeing him wear it. Vikings wore similar wolf skins to merge with wolf intelligence."

"And that mask?"

"Also Da's. The Mask of the Red Mouth. The borders around the wolf's face are blue crystals. Blue celestite connects to wolf peace as ethereal guardians."

"There's nothing peaceful about that wolf face. It's monstrous."

"That it is."

"What's behind the mask?"

"Another mask."

"And behind that?

"An obscurity. I don't know enough about it to say."

"Why not?"

"The magick contained there is 'powerful and dangerous,' in Da's words. He had promised to instruct me— 'train you to understand it,' was how he put it. But he died. It sometimes clicks, which Da insisted was normal. I suspect the mask holds some kind of dimensional magick, some of it harmful. A portal, maybe. Certainly far too potent for me to gamble with."

A lingering silence made her squirm.

"Stop looking at it. When you engage the Mask of the Red Mouth for too long, it's possible to draw it to you."

Next to the mask, on the wall shelf, she noticed a glass bottle filled with silver, *Maid O' Clover* printed in green on the glass. She had seen that same bottle in Marc's pantry. "What's in that milk bottle?"

"Da's sixpence coins. Embossed with an Irish harp. Flipside is a wolfhound. 1928. Mary gave them to Da. Forty-one coins. I loved playing with them as a kid."

Sky Wolf's howls outside broke from the distance. Her call had an unsettling vibration. "Will Sky Wolf be safe out there? I saw black realm wolves by the pond when I arrived."

"I know where they are. The pack is sniffing out a front line. They're still under the kill-spell. Sky Wolf knows how to be safe. Were the wolves shoulder to shoulder?"

"Not really, kind of random around the pond."

"They're waiting. Waiting for my next transformation."

"Next transformation?" She failed to keep the panic from her voice. "How many times does this happen to you?"

He leaned on the door frame, dread in his expression. "It happened only one other time."

"When was that?"

He seemed to like that question and moved toward the carpet. "To know that, you need to come with me. Will you come into the circle? You can experience everything there. I promise the path is safe."

She sucked in a breath. "What path?"

"Into my magick."

"Into your magick. To where?"

"To Shehy Mountain."

He pushed a basket of sage aside, opening a threshold to the center of the circle. Under the spotlight, woven into the carpet fibers, a triple white spiral illuminated. He entered, turned, and extended his arm. The yellow stripes faded from his eyes like a breeze had swept his face, calling her into his sky-blue orbs.

"Take my hand." His palm opened.

Marc's hands had always been little miracles for her—his delightful squeezes on her waist, his fingertips caressing her chin or skimming her lips, the pleasures of his lovemaking. Holding his hand, it was like he carried her very soul.

This was the truest man she'd ever known. A man who held the mysteries of the universe inside him. Wasn't that one of the reasons she fell so deeply in love with him? Only a few months ago, he had held her hand and asked her to *live the magick* with him. *Be the magick.*

Under the spotlights, he stretched his palm nearer to her. "Be brave, my lovely."

Chapter Twenty-Eight

The Magickian's Circle

Marc drew Charlotte into his circle. She tucked her right hand inside his with surprising faith. They lowered themselves, cross-legged on the carpet center, their knees touching. Marc sat with his back to the wolf chair; Charlotte faced the three wolf heads.

"This is your father's circle?" she said, a quiver on her lips.

"I've made this circle my magick." Marc could see her temples visibly throbbing. *She's frightened and yet determined. Wandering between dread and curiosity is unsettling.* He appreciated the fragile nature of what was about to happen and admired her faith in him and her courage. Charlotte possessed an abundance that he vowed never to lose, no matter what. That sapphire ring might be off her finger, but her hand rested in his.

"Feels odd. What happens here?" She stiffened.

"We let the present vanish. Let it disappear, like a ripple on water behind a duck as it swims away. Only here, we float in a circle."

"And where does the circle bring us?"

"To the past. We allow past time to unwind into an open coil," he said with a gentleness he knew she needed. "We observe the past." Fear on her face shone like wet plaster. "Relax, for God's sake, we're not going to blast through the roof." He dared her with a quirky smile.

She jerked away, pulling her hands out of his. He yanked them back and held them firmly so she couldn't get free.

"Marc!"

"Do not let go of my hands, Charlotte. Not even for a second."

"Why are we going to Shehy Mountain?"

"To observe the night of October 31, 1911. Listen to my words. Drift inside them with me. I'll tell you when we are going to move outside of the circle of present time."

A reluctant twinge on her face, she asked, "Is this like a daydream?"

"If you want." He gave her a wink.

"So, not a daydream? Then what is it?"

"A daydream works fine. Follow me. The words will carry you. Keep your vision on this blue crystal geode." He placed a spherical rock between them that had been sliced down the center, exposing rings of blue crystals with a tiny vacant center.

"Come with me, Charlotte, through the blue crystal. Stay tight inside my hands at all times. We are in my childhood home, an old farmhouse huddled inside eight acres of Lewisboro's forest. I'm ten years old. It's Friday afternoon, about five o'clock, the end of summer in August, and so hot the air is steaming with humidity. I come home from playing ball at the park. Da's in the kitchen, rummaging through the drawers searching for a screwdriver. He can't find anything without my mom, and she's away in Dublin visiting her sisters.

"Da says to me, 'I need you to work in the kitchen tomorrow.'

He's frustrated as all hell, dumping wrenches and hammers on the counter. I *hate* working in the restaurant, scrubbing pots and pans for hours. I tell him no, that I'm pitching in the baseball game, and walk out of the room.

"He yells at me, 'Get back in here. I swear by my stars, you are working in the kitchen tomorrow!' Now, my dad was the calmest, most soft-spoken, peaceful man. Never laid a hand on us. So when he yells, I know something is off. But I'm a defiant, smart-ass kid, and I'm not missing out on pitching the game. I slam my bedroom door. In my room, I have a screen door that leads out to the back porch. He kicks open the bedroom door, belt in his hand. He comes after me. Well, I'm not having any of that. I take off like a racehorse, out the screen door, down the steps to the back acres.

"At the farthest acre is a rock wall formation with a stack of boulders at one end that has a cubby space. My secret hideout. I crawl in, thinking I'll wait it out till he cools off.

"I hear his feet pounding as he comes through the woods, yelling for me to come out. It's hot as hell beneath this rock. I can hardly breathe. Sweat is pouring out of my body in buckets. His footsteps approach the rock cave. He stands there, my father, three times my size, ready to strike the second I emerge."

Marc felt Charlotte squeeze his hands, a grimace on her face. She kept her awareness fastened to the blue crystal.

"Panic is a strange power. It has the force to trigger at the most vulnerable moment. And it triggers me. I'm burning with salt and fire, drying up with thirst, practically suffocating. My skin bursts. Every hair follicle explodes. I can't catch my breath. My jaw breaks apart; teeth shoot out in excruciating pain. My tongue is swelling until it fills my mouth. Every muscle twists into spasms. Cramps everywhere. Bones buckling and unbuckling, hands and feet distorting into paws, toenails hooking out. My head, my eyes, and my ears are scorching! And all I want is to howl."

Charlotte shivered. She was with him, feeling the sensations.

"With one hand, Da yanks me out of the cubby. He holds my head and kisses me between the eyes. And then he does the most astonishing thing. Da shapeshifts into Finnwolf."

Marc paused, suddenly thirsty, the memory so alive, draining his fluids much like that intensely hot day.

"Da draws up his power and becomes a huge gray wolf. His coat is magnificent, streaks of silver, practically glowing. And now, we are the same gray colors, and I'm feeling so proud. I'm only a pup, juvenile size, and falling all over myself, unable to even stand. Da begins to howl. I match his howl. Da sings from his heart a deep song. And I sing with him." Here, Marc choked up. "And you know what, Charlotte? Da sings for me."

Charlotte broke from the crystal, tears streaming her cheeks.

"Place your eyes back on the crystal," he instructed gently.

"As Finnwolf, Da teaches me how to run, how to gallop, high-leap the stone walls and the skill of dipping into the landing smoothly. We run through field after field. When a wolf races, he is elevated into pure glory. I practically fly between the trees. I would have followed Da anywhere."

Marc paused for a clean breath, desiring to see his father again. The caress of his soft hand on his head, the man's face that never failed to make him feel safe.

"Da leads me through the woods, across meadows and streams, stampeding into Bedford. We run Yew Crag. I learn how to maneuver between the winds and dive over the chasms. I'm chasing the sky and winning. Nothing—absolutely nothing—beats the euphoria of a wolf's speed and strength.

"Now, close your eyes. Here's where we fly back. This level of magick only manifests if you keep your eyes closed, safely inside the lids. Stay inside my energy field. Do *not* let go of my hands. No matter what you think you see, stay with me. Roger that?"

"Roger that," she returned in kind, this beautiful, courageous woman that Da would have dearly loved.

"Every Finnwolf has access to the time-lapse portal of October 31, 1911, on Shehy: the mountain that Mary Sexton climbed with the three cousins in search of the Ripper and his pack. Each Finnwolf journeys to the mount to be an observer of the original Oath Takers, because each Finnwolf takes the same oath and spills their blood covenant to the quest."

Charlotte opened her eyes. "Blood covenant? Witchcraft?"

"Close your eyes or you'll sever the force. The Finnwolf covenant is not evil witchcraft. Quite the opposite. We are going to Shehy Mountain for one purpose: to observe the observers."

She inhaled, blowing air out slowly in an attempt to remain calm. "And who are we observing?"

"The twelfth Finnwolf, Matthew Sexton. And his little pup, Marcus. I don't recall exactly how Da did this, but that summer day of my first metamorphosis, in 1993, after galloping through the forests, I was suddenly riding Da's furry back. Loons flew at our sides, leading the way. Time merged and looped, practically disappearing. We rocketed into an outer darkness and landed on the first summit of Shehy Mountain. Here's where we time-slip into the field. Da is a master of time-slips."

She followed his instruction, holding tight inside his hands, pressing her knees harder against his. He loved her commitment; he loved her resilience. "Watch for the edges of twilight behind your lids. I'm going to amplify my pulse. You'll feel it. You'll hear my heart drumming *baaa-bam, baaa-bam.* Follow the rhythm. Ride it with me."

He reset his highest energy, and he called up Da's power words from Yeats's poem:

"Come Away. Come Away. To the waters and the wild.
"The dim grey sands with light,
"Weaving olden dances,
"Mingling hands and mingling glances,
"Till the moon has taken flight,
"Come Away. Come Away."

Chapter Twenty-Nine

Old Bones and Oath Takers

Come Away . . . *Come Away* . . . into the soul of Shehy Mountain, deep with rustling air. Swift wings of birds, peat bogs and tussocks of white grass. Skeins of water and old red sandstone. On this night, the mountain inhales all creatures.

The twelfth Finnwolf arrives. He brings his son, little pup, as observer—the youngest this mountain has ever seen—as a witness to the Oath Takers. The Old Fathers are pleased to know another Finnwolf is preparing to join the Silver Brotherhood.

Behind a rubble of rock, their observation post, Finnwolf surveys the landscape, keeping silent while little pup breathes hard next to him on the slope. The pup's muscles quiver with his whimpers, and his gray paws curl in, so frightened that he huddles at his papa's belly. His pup is far too young for this witnessing journey, but Shehy Mountain knows there is no denying the wolf summons when it demands to *image forth*.

Scents of fox, rabbit, and deer grow heady. Little pup blinks; his snout rises to get every fragrant note. This amuses Finnwolf, the innocence and delight of youth. This is his first *imaging forth*, and already he's becoming a witness on Shehy Mountain. This pup is destined for high conquests.

Beyond the thorn tree, there lies a pitted grave. The Ripper's flesh and bones had burned to ashes and were buried long ago. The Ripper's last breath, a horrific sharp cry that shook trees and sky, had sent birds and stags fleeing.

The Old Fathers stand with their wolf queen in all her beauty. A conference of voices emerges as they fire up conifer logs, bilberry, and heather branches near the pitted grave.

Flocks of white ravens swoop down at the wolf queen's bid, her secret keepers. Constellations pour silent bravos as the wolf queen directs the Brotherhood and Sisterhood vows, bound by silver cords.

The Old Fathers gather together. Albert at the lead, drumming a cosmic rhythm to the stars. Donnell and Cormac pouring water from the River Lee into the soil. When the ground is sufficiently drenched, they take three steps back in synchronized precision, each slitting a thumb, each dripping their blood drops into Shehy Mountain soil. They proclaim their quest:

We are kindred creatures in this land,
Wolf blood dripping from ancestral hands,
Man and wolf, we are brothers brave,
We wash old deeds, come away, come away.
We pledge to ferry, to protect, to guide,
Save wolf souls in eternity, we abide,
We declare our wolf magick against shadow wolf might,
We are Finnwolf Legacy, we carry sacred light.

Drumbeats fade. At the summons, each man shifts his human heart to wolf heart. Shifting old bones to wolf bones, restructuring and reshaping the flesh, hair to gray fur, breaking all known earthly laws, these three men *image forth* their wolf magick.

Firelight burns down. The moon glosses then retreats behind a stray cloud as a howling flows over Shehy. The song is hot with growls. A pack of shadow wolves, jaws open, eyes flaring, charges up Shehy Mountain slopes.

The wolf queen enchants her three gray wolves with her powers. Together, they broadcast a hypnotic yellow haze across the mountain. Each Finnwolf shoots Celtic ogham patterns, a magick net of whistling arrows upon the pack, the Silver Brotherhood in full power. They chant, *Return to the roots of your souls.*

Wolves spin off, a chaos of soul shadows, bundled and snared. Starlight draws them up, returning them to their destiny, lost in Black Wolf Realm.

Silver Brotherhood and Sisterhood descend the mount.

Inside the foaming darkness, Finnwolf and pup emerge from their observation post, the witnessing complete. Safe on the summit, little pup is free to run beneath the friendly stars, bask beneath the moon, and feel the soft earth against his tender paws. Finnwolf trots off to inspect the perimeter to ensure all is well while his pup learns to dash over boulders and swerve the cliffs. Proud of little pup, Finnwolf is pleased how quickly this one has learned the skill of the *shake-off* and performed the stiff-legged jump, rearing up and landing his rigid front legs. He will become a mighty Finnwolf. Perhaps a lord.

Attracted by the scent of the ashes, little pup halts to sniff near the pitted grave. The moon peels off its light in a loud buzzing. Mangy swirls hump the terrain, erupting the soil, making his small paws tremble. Bog holes are rotating toward him. Little pup huddles down, whimpering.

A singular black shadow, high as a tree, swarms the mount in a convulsive pocket over little pup. Helpless, he is pulsing with terror.

Ripper breaks the air with a searing howl, a flying blackened monster. Hair matted in thickets, crooked fangs snapping, red and black flames shooting from wide bony sockets.

Little pup cries out. Ripper leaps. His massive jaws sink into little pup's belly, thrashing him in a fierce violence as the night spasms suck them up.

Charlotte shrieked, legs bolting, hands tearing out of Marc's. He shot backward from her horrific kicks slamming into his gut. The attic walls shook, air zinging. Marc ricocheted in a roll, crashing his shoulder into the wolf chair. Baskets tumbled. Sage branches spun.

From the rafters, a pair of antlers hurtled to the floor. Marc's heartbeats hopscotched so severely his pulse might have fled clear out of his body. Doubling over, he gasped for air and grabbed a chair leg for support. "Get out of the circle. Go, Charlotte!"

She lay on the carpet, sobbing, cold wind whipping her hair. He crawled to her and, hooking his arm around her waist, dragged her beyond the circle's perimeter. The wind fishtailed through the attic, raining down more antlers until the gusts dropped down hard as dead bodies.

"You broke the trance," he said through his panting, pain searing his chest.

"Ripper captured you! My God," she wailed, hands over her head as another antler crashed to the floor. "Ripper had you inside his jaws!"

Marc stretched out flat on the floor to settle his breathing. His thoughts swam, remembering the images when Ripper came at him, the bruising flips, the hard jaws clamping down, the teeth crushing into his belly.

"Ripper didn't capture me," he slurred the words. With a hand on his chest, he inhaled slow breaths as his pulse subsided. In some ways, he had thought it was God's mercy that had delivered him out of Ripper's jaws. Certainly some benevolent power had saved him on that mountain.

"I can't stand the thought of this! How did you get away?"

"Da attacked Ripper. I remember almost nothing."

Charlotte reached toward him, her terror a white pall on her face. "I'm sorry! I panicked. I'm sorry I let go." Her voice trailed off. "Are you okay?"

"Not yet," he managed. After several minutes, he sat up. "You're trembling."

"It's freezing in here."

"The stove fire went out." Marc stumbled up as his foot crunched on a broken antler. "Ugh, no." Almost all the antlers had come down, a wreckage across the floor.

Charlotte picked up several white shards.

"Leave it. Come downstairs. We need to rest."

Chapter Thirty

The Thirteenth Finnwolf

In front of a blazing fire in the living room, Charlotte and Marc stretched out on the floor with pillows and an afghan. In the glow of the flames, Marc had a dreadful sense of loss. Maybe it was the stress that lingered after such a powerful trance. Maybe it was seeing Finnwolf again and remembering his first wolf experience with Da. What he wouldn't give to hear the man's voice once more.

"Marc, your body is so hot."

"I'm okay. Da gave me instructions about trance journeys. It fades fast. But you're still cold." Odd that she reacted with chills. The most common bodily reaction after a trance was heat exhaustion.

She sat up, rubbing her temples. "I'm fizzing all over. It's electric!"

He handed her a nearby box of chocolates. "Your body is struggling to find balance. You need to restore glucose to the brain."

Charlotte popped a chocolate into her mouth. The fire kicked up. Wide-eyed, she bit down on her lower lip, fidgeting with the afghan, restlessly moving her legs up and down. Her heightened conscious awareness was in full swing.

"Okay. I have to ask," she blurted out. "I'm clear about the Old Fathers, but explain Black Wolf Realm."

"In their cursed and banished state, the wolf spirit suffocates. The wolves are not only deprived of the Otherworld peace but also denied a path to reincarnation. That kind of complete isolation degrades their souls. They enter Black Wolf Realm, reduced into shadows, doomed to slowly perish from eternal life.

"Lost souls?"

"Lost and starving. But driven to survive nonetheless. Mary saw these shadow wolves in her visions. She discovered the wolves breaking out of the sealed realm. They hunted other wolf souls. And eventually, the shadow wolves became soul-eaters of dead wolves. They absorbed wolf blood to infuse their own soul energy. All this Mary knew to be true."

"Soul-eaters?" Charlotte tried to cover up her shock.

"Da said the soul-eating was a backlash that the ancestors hadn't foreseen in their greed for power and punishment. Da attempted to counter the Sexton curse with his own magick but failed repeatedly. There was nothing he wanted more than to reverse the ancestors' curse."

Beads of sweat burst from her forehead. A tear rolled down her cheek. Her body heat was rising to burn off the trance energy. He wanted to kiss her. Instead, he said, "What's going on in that pretty head of yours?"

"You are the thirteenth Finnwolf. Did you take the oath?"

"At eighteen years old, I declined the quest. I rejected the oath and blood pledge." He felt his voice go weak. "I disappointed Da something fierce. And then he died a year later. I was incredibly stupid, Charlotte. I should have told him I wasn't ready, but I knew I didn't want the quest and could never live up to it. And now that decision is a broken bone that won't mend."

Charlotte tightened her hands on his, unable to swipe the tear loose on her cheek.

"This is my grief, not yours. Matthew Sexton is still my hero and is still Lord of the Wolf. He carried me home from Shehy Mountain. I might have died there."

"How did Da get you back here?"

Da. She called his father Da. Marc loved that—the warmth of her voice on that single syllable cheered him. Her affection for him was already present. Without a doubt, if Da had met Charlotte, he would believe in her completely.

"I don't know what magick Da used to make the return. He had skills unfathomable to me. Da was an arch-shapeshifter. He experimented with magickal time-slips and reality dimensions. Magickal reinventions became his obsession."

His chest swelled, wishing the man were still here, living in his cabin, calling Marc on the phone, his smooth bass voice—*Hey there, my boy, what's shakin'? I swear by the stars, I need to see you. Come home.*

"Do you remember returning from Shehy Mountain?" Charlotte asked.

"Not much. I lost consciousness. I woke up in my bed, fighting a raging fever, a ten-year-old kid with a brutal belly ache, bruised all over, and completely bald."

"Bald? What happened to your hair?"

"Da shaved it off. He didn't want my mother to come home and see me with black hair. I'm happy to say it grew back blond." He tapped her cute nose.

She wiggled up, bent her knees, and hugged them at her chin. "Black hair?" She jutted out her lip. "Wait, you were a gray wolf, same as Da. Little pup was gray, right?"

How could he explain this? He had to stop *being* his secret. At the very least, he had to stop being it with Charlotte.

She tilted her head. "Why did your hair turn black?"

Hiding nowhere, because there was nowhere to hide, he searched for the gentlest words. "When Ripper seized me, when he held me there inside his jaws, he left his mark on me."

"What mark? That can't be right. I don't believe it."

"When you saw me on the river path this morning, you didn't see a gray wolf, son of Finnwolf, did you?"

The fall here would kill him. If she was going to be his wife, deserving of the truth, knowing all, they would have to carry this together.

Charlotte's face flushed. "I saw—a black wolf." Fireplace flames shot up. A log fell, zinging sparks. "But you are the son of Finnwolf. The thirteenth. A gray wolf." Both her hands fisted up tightly as if that could stifle the rest of the thought that she was too terrified to speak.

The devastation on her face cut him. There was no turning back now. How would she take this? Dare he confess the reality? The absolute truth moved up from his belly, an overwhelming desire to unburden himself. The words formed in his mind, words he had never spoken aloud.

"Charlotte . . . Ripper branded me . . . his black wolf. He claimed me, the son of Black Wolf Realm."

Chapter Thirty-One
Sounds of Breaking

For two solid days, torrential rains struck the green barn, tree grove, and the pond that overflowed into pocked wells, flooding the lawn, guts of mud everywhere. Fifteen black wolves stalked the property, their dank breath leaking black streaks through the wet air, spreading their Black Wolf Realm, inching closer to the house by the hour. Hissing wolf chants broke from the hedgerows.

So smart, these wolves. Artful in their patience. Appearing to be far away and yet near. Appearing to subdue their opponent by appearing inactive.

Marc knew better. All warfare was based on deception. When the enemy was at ease, when the timing was right, the ambush would hit violently.

Wicked storm gusts battered Marc's house to the point that he felt just as battered. His tree grove hung down. Every branch drooped into withered arms, their green majesty weakened and ragged.

These two days jumbled together. Charlotte had stayed with him at the house—half-resisting, half-yielding. *Son of Black Wolf*

Realm—the horror loomed silently on her lips. *Son of Black Wolf Realm*—the words a dagger drawing fear into her face, slicing her voice into threads of dread, holding her hostage. The doomed destiny of it all remained a weary solitude between them.

Marc managed The Grackle from home, a muscle inside his jaw constantly ticking the whole time—through their polite conversations, through their troubled silences, through the unseen sapphire engagement ring left upstairs on the barrel table. Everything now was a humbling presence of doubt, time spent creating distractions, watching old movies, cooking, working out on the treadmill, all in an effort to bury the reality. *Son of Black Wolf Realm.*

Left to her own silences, Charlotte baked loaves of peasant bread—her mental therapy that brought calm. Marc watched from the doorway of his office as she kneaded the dough, her peripheral vision forever near the kitchen window, her *black wolf watch.*

He had caught her muttering about them—"vile . . . grisly"—as she sat by the fogged dining room windows, drawing pages and pages of wind-shook rain. She refused to draw the wolves, of course, and instead copied images of Merlin and Vivienne as lovers from the book *In the Forest of Broceliande*. That pleased him.

At night, Marc and Charlotte were distant shores. No lovemaking. He missed connecting with her body, missed how she would wrap herself around him, missed her sexy, slow burn as he prowled every inch of her, and the delight of her pleasure. Even when they lay back to back, drifting off to sleep, he could feel her passion leaking into his flesh.

She lay the same way now, curling away from him into her dreams. Her rhythmic breathing told him that somewhere in all this, she found peaceful sleep.

He had not. Jumpy and distracted, hungry, he stalked the house, finding himself sitting in Mamó's wicker rocking chair in the attic, whiskey in hand, listening to the rain pound the roof as if it might pound through his head.

On Friday night, Marc attempted a tender moment as they lay on their separate pillows in bed. "Please, can we talk about this? We're universes apart here. What are you thinking, Charlotte?"

Reluctantly, she propped herself up on one arm, hand cupping her chin. At first, she said nothing, going blank on him, then she grew deadly serious. "On Tuesday night, when you . . . shifted. Tell me what happened on Yew Crag."

Not the question he expected, he faced her squarely. It would be a thorny confession. "The pack surrounded me. Fourteen wolves and Ripper. They closed in, ready to kill. No way could I have fought off the pack. Even Da would have had a hell of a time, and I didn't have half his strength or anywhere near his wolf magick."

"What did you do?"

"I sensed they wanted their revenge against the Sexton curse, and they wanted the thirteenth Finnwolf to pay it. That would end the Finnwolf legacy forever. I drew myself down, placed my head on the ground." He searched for the right words. "Sometimes, surrender can melt the highest aggressions."

She sat up, her expression pained. "What do you mean? You surrendered to the pack?"

"It was surrender to their will or lose everything. They forced me to follow them. We ran north. I kept to the back. On the run, the smell of raccoons distracted me. Rabbits and deer, the scents drove me wild. I wanted to hunt on my own, but I didn't dare try to escape.

"We ran west, dew on the grass, and the sky full of ravens

following the pack. I wanted one. I wanted to jump up and snatch those spicy wings with my jaw. That's when Sky Wolf came up from behind me. You can't know how relieved I was to have her there. The pack didn't seem to mind her intrusion. I figured they knew her if they permitted her to run with us."

"A white wolf, among a pack of black wolves?"

"Sky Wolf stayed at my side, protecting me the whole time. We circled down, ran south, mud and dry weeds everywhere. The pack knew there were wild turkeys there, and we chased them across a field. The delicious smell of their flesh overwhelmed me. Sky Wolf and I slaughtered two of them in seconds. We raced off to the east at full throttle—you can't imagine the marathon, the absolute joy of the speed." He took a second to catch his breath. "As the sun rose, we found our way back to Draakensky."

He threw back the bed covers, a deep rumbling from his gut, recalling the taste of blood in his teeth. "There were coyotes, but Sky Wolf and I couldn't get them. A bobcat too. What an intoxicating chase that cat was. He got away, though. That night, running with Sky Wolf, head-to-head with the black wolves, galloping together, we were one wolf, one body. I breathed the whole planet, from the roots and bones, the moonlight, green conifers, and the bloody flesh of the earth. I was soaring! Soaring! No limits! Nothing beats the velocity of being wolf. Nothing!" Panting, gripping the sheets, shaking, he saw the alarm on Charlotte's face.

Horrified, her jaw dropped, eyes bulging into dark gray bullets coming at him. "You *are* Black Wolf Realm," she shuddered the words out through trembling lips.

What had he done, erupting like this, sinking her into the abyss? He snapped himself out of it. "I'm sorry. Wait. Charlotte.

Wait. Feel my heart." He brought her hand to his chest. "This is the heartbeat of a man. Man, not wolf. I know who I am. I know what I am not."

She might have burst, but she didn't. She held herself there. That stiff terror in her face, the unblinking terror of *wolf* that she now saw living inside him. *Son of Black Wolf Realm.*

Charlotte pulled the covers up, curled away, arms hugging herself.

Fraught with tension, worry, disappointment, he couldn't drift off. He lay there, admiring her sleep, utterly grateful she at least remained at his side.

Outside, wolf howls circled the pond. Inside, the Ripper circled his mind.

Chapter Thirty-Two

Ragged Woods

On Saturday morning at ten AM, Charlotte sipped coffee at the kitchen window. The rain had stopped, leaving the lawn ravaged with potholes. Mud streaked the patio flagstone. Wind furrowed the sky. The sun worked hard to break clouds while a dozen blackbirds circled above the tree grove. Wolves were not in view, but she suspected they were not far. Behind the hedgerows? Marc's words surfaced in her head: *Man, not wolf. I know who I am, Charlotte. I know what I am not.*

When Marc entered, she turned.

"Good morning, my lovely." He was freshly shaved and showered, face bright in rapt attention on her. Actually, she thought, bright *for her* in his desire to mend their troubles. The tension in his forehead, the brows pulling together, deepening the crease, told her that he was struggling. Standing tall, shoulders bracing, he was the image of a gentle warrior in that moment.

He poured himself coffee. "You're quite charming in that jeans skirt and lacy cotton sweater. All in blue. And look at that: the sun is out."

"I am feeling refreshed today. I don't see the wolves out there this morning. Did they retreat?"

"Probably not. A pack maneuver, I'm sure. I got a text from my mother. She sends you her goodbyes. She's on her way to the airport for Dublin." He paused at the window. "Awful lot of crows out there."

"Weather predicts 70 degrees." Her chest rose and fell as she tried to keep steady. His intense blues lulled her. Impulse urged her to wrap her arms around him and rest her head on his chest. They hadn't kissed in days. Even so, doubt held her feet to the floor tiles. And in that rooted position, she said, "That downpour was so loud last night. I woke up around two AM. You weren't in bed."

"I was in the bathroom." He sloshed milk into his coffee.

"You were not in the bathroom." She picked dried leaves off the pot of sage on the table. "Not the master bath. Not the hallway bath."

"Sometimes when I can't sleep, I go to the attic."

"I didn't hear you up there." With her fingernail, she snipped a dead stem off the rosemary herb, then sat down at the table. "I heard you up there moving around on Wednesday night. And Thursday night too. That rocker creaks. But I didn't hear you there last night." *Stop fishing. Come out and ask him.*

He must have gotten the hint and sat down opposite her. "I needed to get outside. I sat on the patio for a bit. The air cleared my head."

She gave him a sharp don't-go-pulling-any-punches-with-me expression. "On the patio? In the cold? In the torrential rain? With the wolves patrolling the house? You sat on the patio for, what, two hours?"

"Half hour. And I wasn't sitting in the rain. I was beneath the patio roof. You know, I love these herb pots on the table instead of the window bench. The thyme, rosemary, and sage make an attractive setting."

She paused to gather her words. "I don't recall your coming back to bed."

He lifted his hand apologetically. "You were resting so peacefully. I didn't want to disturb you. I slept on the sofa."

He seemed genuine. He was trying to be straight with her. She saw that. "I need to ask you something."

"Anything," he said.

Happy to hear that, she dove in. "A few days ago when I asked you about Tuesday night on Yew Crag, you said that you were *summoned.* And you said that you didn't have enough power to resist it. What summoned you?"

"The summons is something we don't fully understand. Possibly a higher magick. Could be ethereal guardians, or angels, God. Who knows what creates the summons to shapeshift? It just is."

"God? You think God summons men to shapeshift into Finnwolf?"

"No, I don't think God sets that mechanism into action. There might be a higher good though. Might be the wilderness is protecting the wilderness."

"What did Da think was the source?"

"The wilderness protecting the wilderness."

"Where did Da learn his magick?"

"Inherent. And Sexton DNA. Mamó gave him most of his guidance. But if he were sitting here and you asked him, Da would say he learned his magickal powers from the sacredness of Mother Earth."

She chewed on that for a minute.

"What do you want to do today, Charlotte? Let's get out. You want to take a stroll through the Japanese Gardens at the Hammond Museum? Quite peaceful there. Let's do it."

"Tempting, but I have to go back to Draakensky. Jung May texted me this morning. She sent me the deadlines for the encyclopedia illustrations. It's time I start the preliminary sketches on the goddesses."

"That's good news," he said enthusiastically. "Who is the first lady of choice?"

"Hekate. I have a Zoom meeting late this afternoon with Jung and the anthropologist Eugenie Nye. The second on the list is Ceridwen, goddess of transformation."

"Oh. Who is Hekate?"

"Greco-Roman goddess of magick and the underworld. William Blake has a famous illustration of Hekate. *The Night of Enitharmon's Joy* in pen and ink, and watercolor. I'm excited to get started. I need to work, Marc."

"I know you do. I've been away from the bar too long myself. Jackson has a banjo jazz duo playing tonight. I almost regret giving him free rein to hire entertainment. Banjo jazz." He cringed. "I'm working the bar at five. Come sit on my line?"

"I don't know." She failed to hide the desire in her tone. Being with people, a few drinks, and banjo jazz sounded lively. She missed their social life with Alice Eve and The Grackle bar family. She missed their lovemaking, their chats about art and Etta James music, Avalon and Vivienne, fairies and the folksy Celtic lore he always had on the tip of his tongue. *One step at a time will get you there or make you turn,* Sister James would be saying to her.

He took her hand. "Please, Charlotte," he said, his voice breaking. "I promise. You are safe with me."

Was her heart safe with this man, despite the uncertainties? Despite the dangers? There was no pretending; she loved Marc. And she would love him till she died. And maybe after that too. Feeling her face flush, she said, "I might stop by."

"I love that smile. Let's make this a good day." He turned toward the window, face lighting up. "Well, look who's here."

Beyond the patio, a gray hare hopped across the wet grass. Charlotte couldn't mistake the gray ears, black paw, and that sweetheart face straight on them. *Jilly!*

Marc opened the back door and gave her a whistle. "Hey little girly. I see you." Jilly wiggled her bottom and scurried away. He turned to Charlotte. "Did you sketch her again?"

"I didn't." But she had desired for Jilly to return. For Marc. For Beltaine.

"Your magick has residual powers," he whispered. "You are part of my secret mysteries now."

The rattle of gravel on the driveway intruded. Marc went to the foyer. "What is this now? Jimmy is here."

"Jimmy Cruz?" She moved to the side window near the drive. Jimmy hurried past the hedges. Why would the Chief of Police drop in on a Saturday morning?

Marc opened the door.

"Got a minute?" Jimmy said, a little breathless.

"Sure. Want a cuppa?"

"We don't have time." Jim walked in at a cop's brisk pace, tossed off his cap, and gave a polite hello to Charlotte.

"Good to see you, Jim." She noted him scrutinizing the backyard.

"What's going on? You look like you're about to pull your gun on me," Marc said.

Jimmy's brows snapped together. "Sorry, nothing here is directed at you. We have a report that a dead horse was found on your back acre."

Marc swayed back a step. "What?"

"Near Castleback Road. A mare from Rackman Stables."

"One of Luther Rackman's horses?"

"Apparently, the gray mare got spooked and broke out of the stall. The latch-hinge was busted. We found her about forty feet from your rock wall. An early morning runner spotted the body and called it in. It's a bloody nightmare."

"How did it die?"

"Something attacked her. One hind quarter was ripped open. Belly slashed. Luther's on your property right now. He's ignoring your No Trespassing sign."

"Oh Christ. Luther Rackman. He's insufferable."

"Yeah, the old fucker. Pardon my French." Jimmy glanced at Charlotte, then his phone.

Charlotte placed her coffee down. "What attacked the horse?"

"A bear is the only animal in these parts that could take down a horse that size. We get bear sightings regularly. None lately, though. Marc, we need permission to access your back acres and do a search. I called Wildlife Control, and Rackman has a team coming to remove the carcass. The press is already on the scene, itching to take photos."

"The press?" Charlotte asked.

"Any kind of horse incident is newsworthy in this town. Can we walk the property, Marc?"

"Of course. Anything you need. No photography, though."

"I'll text Oliver that we have your approval."

"Which horse was it?" Marc asked.

"I think Luther said her name was Gramarra."

A moan escaped him. "Gramarra's a champion jumper."

"You ever ride her?"

"No, but I've seen the videos of her. Sleek as satin. Luther must be sick over this."

"He's more than sick. He's raging mad. Damn, look at the time. You want to walk with me?" he said hurriedly.

"Sure. I've got ten acres. What are we searching for?"

"Bear prints, maybe. Primarily, any evidence of foul play." He headed to the back door.

Marc wore a panicked expression.

"I'll come with you." Charlotte linked her arm to his, which she found surprisingly limp.

Chapter Thirty-Three

Gramarra

Cloaks and hoods. That was all Charlotte could think as they trudged through Marc's back acres, avoiding muddy trenches between hundreds of trees and coarse shrubs. The dense evergreens were top-heavy, forming a canopy that shrouded out the sunlight. Pockets of marshes and decay made for dank and gamy odors. Several old trees had been uprooted by storms, flung down with their arms and leafy hands sinking into the earth to rot.

At least there was birdsong. A flock of geese flew overhead, honking brilliantly. She found an odd turning in the air. Breathy. *Hushhh.* Then the sound of something passing. *Whoosh.* Was her Lady of the Wind present? Was she weaving patterns in the air?

Up ahead, Marc suddenly paused. Had he heard it too?

Jimmy didn't speak, too busy skimming the terrain, placing each footing carefully as he led them on. They rounded bend after bend, forged through sticky pine boughs, thorny bracken and bushes, and stumbled over roots and timbers.

The chief halted. He held his hand up. Muted voices swept in from the far right. "This way. Castleback Road diverges up here, right, Marc? At the dead end?"

Marc paused, hands on his hips, taking in the direction. "Yeah, I think you can get to Castleback going east at this point."

Within minutes, they approached a rock wall, the boulders spotted with white and gray lichen. Voices grew louder as they pushed their way through the massive hemlocks to a group of men in a clearing. About a hundred feet beyond them, vans and red police lights flashed on the dead-end road, a local WP-NBC News van too.

"Luther." Marc made a rush toward a thick-bodied man in shabby brown trousers and a faded hunting jacket. "I'm so sorry. What a tragedy." They shook hands. "This is Charlotte."

She reached her hand out. "Nice to meet you."

"There's nothing nice about today, sweetie. Not a damn thing," Luther Rackman huffed. Ruddy-faced, suspicious and gruff, gray stubble lining his low-hanging chin, he flicked his dark, beady orbs beneath wrinkled eyelids. The handshake held clumsy and brief as he turned a hawkish face on Marc. "Look at her. My Gramarra!"

Behind him lay the gray horse, covered by a quilted horse blanket. Dark rivulets of blood streaked out.

"Oh my God. I'm so sorry this happened. What do you need? What can I do?"

Charlotte noticed Marc avoided looking too long at the dead horse. She averted her eyes as well. Thankfully, the head was covered. Dark gray legs splayed out, one twisted up, poking the air. Behind the horse, an enormous humped rock shone like a leaden submarine that had emerged dripping from the sea. Blood splatter on the rock suggested the horse had been trapped against it by the predator.

Luther jabbed Marc's chest. "What can you do? Not a fucking thing now, Sexton! She's an Irish Draught Sport Horse, a

Thoroughbred crossbreed. Top-caliber athlete from Shirley Fields in California. My Gaelic charger. Destroyed!" He limped over to Jimmy. "This was no bear attack, Chief. You got that one wrong."

Jimmy rubbed his chin. "We didn't find any bear tracks on our walk-through. Where's Cullen from Wildlife?"

"Over there," Luther pointed to a guy in a dark green jumpsuit. "He's measuring wolf tracks. Fucking wolf tracks!"

Charlotte's hand flew to her mouth. Marc blanched.

"No fucking bear!" Luther yelled. "A wolf chased her out of the stable, must have pursued her here, and jumped her. Attacked her from behind, seized her thigh, and ripped her belly and neck. My beautiful Gramarra. That savage got her on your land, Sexton!"

"Luther, I can't imagine the loss. I can't even say how sorry I am this happened. She was a breathtaking beauty."

Luther put his face right up to Marc's. "You can't say," he imitated Marc's tone. "You knew a wolf was stalking these parts, didn't you? Didn't you!"

Marc took a step back.

"Officer Oliver here tells me the Chief reported a white wolf on your property. In March. Near your shed!"

Marc and Jimmy exchanged glances.

"And a white wolf on that stupid windmill estate, that stinky old broad Jaa Morland. A white wolf in Bedford? Sexton, you should have warned me we had a wolf prowling the woods. Horses get spooked by wolves." He raised a fist to Marc's face.

Jimmy darted. "Take it down, Luther."

Marc held his ground. "Yeah, I'd appreciate you backing off."

Luther eyed the Chief.

The wildlife ranger near the horse gave a shout. "We've got more tracks here."

They merged around a wide hump of exposed mud some twenty feet from where the horse had died. Cullen pointed to several paw prints, well-defined pad marks, and blunt claw markings. And beyond, a sloppy mess of prints in the surrounding mossy patches soaked with rain.

"He's a big son-of-a-bitch, this one," Cullen said, adjusting his cap. "I'd bet a seventy-five pounder. This print is over five inches. More prints near the elm tree. See there in the sandy ground cover? Hard to distinguish the different sizes. I'd make a guess . . . this was more than one wolf. Possibly a pack, but unlikely."

"How many?" Luther asked.

"With so many obscure prints, it's impossible to know. Maybe an alpha and his alpha female mate, or an alpha and his beta. One wolf uses its bite to hang on to the prey while the other brings it down. Or if this was a pack, they all brought her down."

Marc crouched down and touched one of the prints. "I can tell you these prints are not from the white wolf. She's small. I've seen her prints in the snow, and they're not more than three inches. And I've not seen her running with a pack. She's a lone wolf."

Cullen had suspicion all over him. "We've only had three wolves spotted in the state in the last twenty years. And in March this year, we've had six reports of a stray white wolf. Lewisboro, North Salem, and Peekskill. Go figure. Probably came down from Canada. Not sure why, because there's a hell of a lot more elk and caribou to eat up there than here."

"You're thinking a pair of wolves, Cullen?" Jimmy asked.

"It would take at least two wolves to bring down a horse this size. In December, a coyote hunter killed an eighty-five-pound gray wolf near Cooperstown in Otsego County. His paws were over five inches."

Luther growled. Shoving his hands into his pockets, he turned away.

"What is unmistakably odd," Cullen said in almost an angry tone, "is that there's not a lot of bloodshed for the deep wounds. I would have expected pools of blood. The vet will have some explanation, no doubt."

A van arrived on Castleback Road. Two men got out, unloading ropes, padding, and glides to remove the horse.

"I can't watch this," Marc confided to Charlotte and moved toward Luther. "These prints are far too big to be the small white wolf I saw by the shed. Again, I'm so sorry about all this. If there is anything you need, Luther, let me know."

"When's the last time you saw that white wolf?" Luther asked, a rattle of phlegm from his throat. Charlotte noticed the man had to practically unclench his teeth to get the words out.

"I don't recall," Marc answered dismissively. "I do know she couldn't have possibly taken down Gramarra."

"You don't know shit, Sexton. I guess I'll have to go wolf hunting."

Charlotte was sure she felt Marc's stomach recoil in time with hers.

"Wolves are protected under the Endangered Species Act by the DEC," Jimmy said, his hand resting on his weapon. "You got that straight, Luther? No wolf hunting."

"Yeah, Chief, I got that straight. Straight as an arrow." He mimed holding a bowstring and shooting an arrow directly at Marc.

"Jim? I want my No Trespassing sign enforced. Only Luther's team has permission to remove the carcass. Everybody else stays off my land. Absolutely no photography." He turned to Luther. "Anything you need, Luther. I'm happy to help."

Marc made fast tracks through the woods, Charlotte hurrying to keep up as he thrust tree limbs out of his path. A woman came running after them, huddling through the trees.

"Marc, can I have an interview for the Bedford Review?"

"No interview," he yelled back. "No photos."

He grabbed Charlotte's hand, and they trekked on, the muddy terrain slippery beneath their boots.

"Jeez, that man is bombastic," Charlotte said, avoiding a downed timber. "He seemed angry with you before you even arrived."

"Luther is perpetually angry. When I purchased the land, we had a property line dispute. I won the case, and he's been a sore loser ever since."

"He's a hunter?"

"Rackman is a predator. You should see his rifle cabinet."

They maneuvered across the ten acres, Charlotte's thoughts reeling. *Possibly a pack, but unlikely,* Cullen had said. Was Marc really in the attic for two hours last night?

When they approached the pond area, Charlotte veered off to the ogham tree grove where she spotted muddy tracks. The air over the pond gave off a loamy scent in the sunlight. Near the pond's edge, she hunched down and touched the wet soil. "These are the same wolf prints as the back acre, aren't they?"

Marc moved in to examine the prints. "Definitely not Sky Wolf's. These tracks are from the Ripper pack."

Frogs croaked in the pond, the waves holding rippling sunlight. But it wasn't yellow sunlight; it wore a tarnished glare. Charlotte straightened up, a sick feeling bearing down on her. Across the pond, by the rowan tree, four black hares in hooded capes inched forward on their scrawny paws. Their ugly, hairy toes spread out. "Marc?"

"I see them. The one in front, she's got a droopy eye," he muttered. "Christ almighty."

"But we buried the witch-hares' images. We buried my sketches. Marc, is this my residual magick? Is it?" She felt panic rising.

"I don't know. In magick, we kick the ball down the slope, and it lands at the bottom. Unless something kicks it back. Rebound effect. These witch-hares' powers are stronger than I thought."

"Hideous creatures. Scraggly and hunchbacked." The words stung her tongue. Why had she decorated them with yellow gemstones trimmed on the capes? How absurd and gaudy it appeared now.

The four hares were much larger than she remembered. Were they expanding before her very eyes? Shifting into giant hares now? Over four feet, she estimated. Charlotte slowly walked the curve of the pond toward them, testing to see if they would scamper away at her approach.

The witch-hares remained stock-still for a full minute in the standoff. One of them twitched her warty nose. Another rotated her paws up, boxing the air. The four huddled together, draped stoutly in their hooded capes, juddering with energy.

The one at the front, with thickened whiskers hanging as long as a beard, crone-like with her withered fur, hobbled forward holding something smoldering in her paws. The fat one, a bit shaky, leered behind and chewed on a tree branch.

They formed a small circle with the other two hares. Each of the shadows behind them spread into twisted knots that didn't frame their true shapes. Charlotte couldn't get over how these hares had altered from her first impressions. Were they revealing their true nature or creating impostors?

The tallest of the four moved straight toward Charlotte. With thatched eyes, she broke from the circle, showing off her muscular figure. Behind her trailed a small white sheet that the other three hares had woven in mere seconds. From their paws, each shot out threads, sticks, and stubs.

Charlotte sensed a great stirring as if she were inside a deep pot of air. The white sheet rolled on its own force across the grass and landed directly at Charlotte's feet.

She lifted the papery substance. The sheet illuminated in her hands—a drawing of the four witch-hares in their black hoods on Draakensky's river path.

Her drawing. Restored.

"Marc! This is my witch-hare sketch." As soon as the words left her mouth, the sheet twisted out of her hands and flew up.

More white sheets fell over the pond. They merged into a blazing column of fire that shot up into a red-hot tower atop the water. The tower spread out with intense heat, sending smoke that caught in Charlotte's throat.

Instantly, the fiery cylinder expanded with a *whoosh*—toward the tree grove.

"No, you don't!" Marc shouted, huddling back from the red inferno swirling across his pond and the flames spreading toward him. Firebrands scattered, forming rings, threatening to burn the weeping willow.

Lifting his open palms to the sun, Marc murmured a chant that Charlotte could not understand. He grabbed the sparking air above his head, cupped it in both his hands, and flung it over the pond.

A blazing stellated dome came down.

With both arms up in triumph, he sent his magick forward as if he had pulled down a hundred stars from the galaxy. Of course, he had. The starry dome captured the burning tower, sent it wobbling and sputtering, smothering it into a thin reed.

Her cheeks burning, Charlotte wiped the sweat from her face. The reed collapsed inch by inch into the water, leaving a trail of steam.

She looked at him, aghast. “What was that?”

“That was knowing what kind of star fire to send their magick off my land.” The act left him unsteady on his feet. He chanted again, spreading his fingers wide like wings as if beckoning the air to gather.

The sky clapped. Twenty or thirty great owls swooped across the lawn, their horny beaks zooming toward the witch-hares, claws flexing, wings flapping a ruckus—an avian platoon on the attack, the audacious and proud Camaroon leading the ambush.

Four black shapes jittered away into the forest, necks twisting around, hare-lips baring teeth, uttering bodeful cries. By the time they zigzagged away, their bodies had magnified to almost five feet before they transformed themselves into dissipating smoke.

The great owls settled into the ogham tree grove, making the air solemn with floating feathers.

Chapter Thirty-Four

Horses and Wolves

On Saturday, late afternoon at JFK airport, Kelsey Sexton strolled the Aer Lingus lounge for the third time, worried about her delayed flight. She sent a text to her sister about the delay, which would add to Bree's anxiety. Niagra and Diana had absorbed all her time, leaving no opportunity to visit William, and she had failed to wedge a separation between Marc and Charlotte.

In August, her sixty-seventh birthday visit might provide a more fruitful opportunity. Then again, maybe Niagra was right: *leave it to the Old Fathers to protect their legacy.* But that might prove dangerous. As much as she disliked Charlotte for her son, she didn't want anything to harm the girl.

Kelsey purchased a tea, sat down in an empty row of seats, and opened her laptop to catch some news. A gray-haired man sitting opposite gave a flirtatious wave. Something about him reminded her of Yeats in his late years—the poised mouth, the shock of hair on the left of the forehead. Of all the photographs she'd seen of the dead poet, she couldn't recall a single one of Yeats smiling. If Yeats could smile at her, this gentleman would certainly be warming her heart with a Yeats smile.

Returning to the news briefs, she scrolled down to local Sleepy Hollow news. *Live Breaking News* flashed a headline from the White Plains—NBC affiliate station reporting a horse killed in Bedford. She clicked, and reporter Ashley Smith spoke before a No Trespassing sign surrounded by trees.

"I'm in Bedford today, the mecca of equine stables in Westchester County. Here on Castleback Road, a horse from the Rackman Stables was found dead this morning on the private property of Mr. Marc Sexton. Authorities are investigating what appears to be a wolf attack. That's right, Ross, you heard that correctly."

Kelsey nearly dropped her tea on the floor.

"Authorities are claiming a wolf, or possibly a wolf pack, killed a prize Irish Draught Sport crossbreed mare named Gramarra, owned by Luther Rackman. We are not allowed on the property, and Mr. Sexton has no comment at this time about how or why this killing occurred on his land, but as you can see behind me, local police and equine officials are scouting the area in search of these wolves they believe attacked and killed the horse. While there have been reports of a white wolf seen in the region over the past few months, wolves in Westchester County are extremely rare. We will be updating you with the latest. Back to you, Ross."

"Oh my God, no," Kelsey said. *Wolves? A dead horse? On Marc's land?—If horses were wishes,* Matthew's voice slammed into her head.

Horses and wolves. Marc is in danger.

The boarding screen flashed updates. Her flight would be delayed until 2:20 AM. She'd go half-mad in the wait. She dialed for a car service while the gray-haired man tossed her another Yeats smile, the ghost of the poet never far from her. Ignoring the man, she hurried toward the exit to catch a ride to Bedford.

Chapter Thirty-Five
Hour of the Wolf

At *The Grackle*, Marc had no idea that Jackson had turned the private dining room into a modified Speakeasy, styled with loveseats, coffee tables, and tufted chairs. The Kelsey Room had never been so packed, with barely enough standing room for Saturday's *Banjo Jazz Night.*

This is what happens when the cat's away from the bar for a week, he admonished himself.

At first, the loud "12th Street Rag" had his nerves jangled, even from his distance at the bar. "When You're Smiling" and "Sweet Georgia Brown" weren't too bad. He scanned his line of customers, which was sparse since most were overflowing into the Kelsey Room.

Expecting Charlotte—she was late—he worried that she might not show. She knew by the witch-hares' haughty display of regenerating her sketch and turning it into their own weaponry that this was personal. She hadn't said much when she left. He could use a slosh of The Sexton, but he never drank while tending bar. Maybe a break would do. As he was about to give Liz a breakaway signal, a young man strolled through the front door. He had dark brown hair and wore a white shirt and navy tie. Marc knew right away the kid wasn't twenty-one.

"Hi there," the kid said, quickly scanning the room. He grabbed a stool and sat. "Are you the Marc Sexton on the door plaque permittee?"

"That would be me."

The kid wore a sweet expression, perfect teeth, baby-face complexion with dimples, and a trendy French crop of brown hair slick at the sides. "A Guinness would do me," he said deeply, imitating some kind of cliché military commander.

"Sure thing," Marc replied, stifling his amusement. "You got ID?"

"Sure thing," he added a flattering imitation of Marc's tone and pulled out a driver's license.

Marc gave it a scan and handed it back to him. "This is the worst fake ID I've ever seen. Come back when you're legal." He tossed a wink.

The kid slumped, his penny-eyes losing their shine. "Okay, okay. I'm from *Wildlife Journal*. Joey Tate. I write a column. I would love to interview you about the wolf attack on your property. I want to—"

"Stop right there," Marc said politely. The kid was endearing as all hell, but out of his league. "I've had phone calls all day from the press and denied them all. *Wildlife Journal* won't win an interview over them."

"I'm not the press, not really. Just a resourceful guy who writes about nature."

"Well, you've got two choices, Joey. You can have dinner in the dining room, or I can permit you to have something here from the bar menu, with a soft drink, but if you're here for a story, that's not going to happen."

Joey went deadpan. "I'll have a Diet Coke, please. And fries."

Marc filled the glass, the banjos playing "Old Man," which was thankfully less boisterous.

"Neil Young, right?" Joey said. "Not my era, but my mom loves his music. You live in Bedford a long time?"

Marc placed the Coke down. "Ten years. I grew up in Lewisboro. Where are you from, Joey?"

"Katonah. I'm off to college in September."

"Good move. What are you going to study?"

"Wildlife Biology at Washington State, Seattle. That's why I want to talk to you, Mr. Sexton. Because I've seen that white wolf everybody is talking about." He pulled out his phone and flashed an image. Sky Wolf sat poised on a boulder, paws aligned, in the back acre, staring straight into the camera.

"Where did you take this?"

"On the backside of your property this morning. I'm the runner who discovered the horse. I called it in."

"Who else has seen this?"

"Only my editor."

"May I?" Marc pulled out his cell phone and snapped a close-up of Joey's phone image. "What other photos did you take?"

"Not of Gramarra, if that's what you're asking. Too gruesome." He shuddered. "A real heartbreaker. I think she had bloody tears over her blaze-face, even though equines don't cry."

The idea of blood on Gramarra's stunning gray face with the white blaze unsettled Marc. That whale-shaped boulder in the photo jumped out at him. "You didn't take this shot from Castleback Road. You were on my property, weren't you?"

He crunched his shoulders up. "Yeah, I broke the No Trespassing to get the shot. Big yikes." He raised his eyebrows.

"Sorry. I was zooming in on a black-and-white Peregrine falcon in a hemlock beyond the rock wall. They're endangered, you know. That's when I saw the downed horse. And a white wolf sitting on the rock nearby. Man, I can't imagine that sweetheart of a wolf taking down a twelve-hundred-pound Irish Draught crossbreed, can you?"

"She didn't kill that horse."

"That thought has been living rent-free in my head all day. But the news reports, they're boasting the white wolf is the killer. What spooked me was the report from the vet who examined the horse. He told me that the killer wolf, or wolves, didn't eat the horse."

"What vet told you that?"

"Dr. Harry Temple. He agreed to an interview. The attack wasn't a food kill. Puzzling, right? If the attack wasn't hunting for food, or territorial defense, which is unlikely, or a mating conflict, again unlikely, then what triggered the wolf to attack the horse?"

"Don't know," Marc replied emphatically.

But he did know. He knew Ripper and his pack were on an aggressive hunt for what they needed most. Not food for physical energy. Blood for soul energy.

"I'm waiting for Luther Rackman to call me back. Meantime, I thought I'd get your take on it. Did you know Rackman announced a reward to anyone who gives him a lead on the location and capture of the killer wolf?"

"Capture!"

"Didn't you see his interview on NBC a couple of hours ago? He had his rifle slung on his shoulder."

"Didn't see it. Excuse me, Joey." Panic surging, he gestured a break sign to Liz. In the kitchen, he popped his head in the doorway. Petrovna gave him a thumbs up, even though he could see they were still jammed at the service station and grill.

He hurried down the hallway and pushed his office door open, anxious to find a moment of relief, when he halted. On his sofa sat his mother in a summery silk blouse and slacks, her face uncharacteristically flushed.

"Mom? What are you doing here? What happened to your flight to Dublin?"

"Delayed twice." She rose and gave him a kiss and a tighter hug than usual. "I came because I had to see if you're all right." She rested her hand over his chest. "Are you?"

"Of course. Why shouldn't I be?"

"A wolf killed a horse on your property? I caught the breaking news. What's going on?"

Marc needed to get off his feet; he dropped into his chair. The Sexton on the side table tempted him. "I can't go into it all now. The kitchen's been slammed all night. Charlie's been in the weeds for hours. I've got a Speakeasy in the Kelsey Room. I've had to put a guard at the front door to keep the press out because of this wolf business. Sorry, I'm overwhelmed." He fixated on the desk clock, an attempt to quell his impatience.

"Is that music loud enough?" she said. "What is that . . . banjos?"

"Don't ask. It's not as bad as I thought. Customers love it."

"I've never seen you so tired. You're not losing your strength, are you?"

He poured water for himself from the pitcher on his desk and chugged. "No. Why would you ask me that?"

"I'm worried. I couldn't sit in the airport lounge another minute. A dead horse. 'If wishes were horses.' Remember your father used to say that?"

"Not really."

"What did Da tell you about tumultuous horses?"

"I don't have time for this, Mom. I'm okay. What time is your flight?"

"Two-twenty."

"In the morning?"

"I'll sleep the whole trip."

She fussed with her scarf and tugged at her sleeves. "Horses and wolves. Horses and wolves," she murmured.

Ignoring her, Marc picked up his phone. *Charlotte should be here by now.* Scanning his texts, he found none from her, but a plethora of news outlets asking for his time. He couldn't delete them fast enough. Rackman must have given them his phone number.

"Marc, what did your father say about horses?"

"I don't remember," he answered, tracking the scroll.

"Yes, you do."

"I don't know," he snapped. "Harbingers of strength."

"I see you have your hands full, but must you be so flippant?"

"Sorry. Can I get you something?" he asked.

"No, I don't want anything," Kelsey said.

Head down, he deleted texts until he found Charlotte's message buried in the mess: ON MY WAY. Relieved, he switched screens to a search engine and typed in *Wildlife Journal,* found the website, and pulled up the editorial staff. The e-zine was a small one; no local names that he recognized, but there was Joey Tate's dinky column with loads of photography credits.

"What about 'I hear the shadowy horses,' " Kelsey persisted. "Remember that? Remember Da talking about that?"

He lifted his head. "Sorry, what?"

"Your father. 'I hear the shadowy horses.' "

"I don't know."

"I think you need to visit your father's grave," she said, her glare like green traffic lights on him.

Visit my father's grave? He could have counted his heartbeats—they were that loud. "We've been through this. Da is not in that cemetery."

"Maybe so. I've been talking to Niagra. Our chats about the Otherworld have brought everything back. Marc, I need to know your father is at peace in the Otherworld. And if he's not in the Otherworld then . . ." Her voice faded out.

A dollop of patience might serve, but he couldn't find it. "Maybe not everyone enters the Otherworld," he tossed out, and went back to his cell phone.

"You mean other possibilities?"

She wanted to hear him say the list again? He couldn't do the *he's in heaven, or reincarnated, or resides on the Welsh Isle of the Dead* routine. He grabbed The Sexton and poured. *Just one ounce.* The sound of the liquid hitting the glass immediately quelled him. "May I pour you one?"

"My stomach is too upset for whiskey now."

Marc's whiskey went down silky and smooth; immediately, his focus settled from the subterranean madness of the day.

She stood up, wringing her hands. "The news report mentioned a wolf pack. A wolf pack kills an Irish Draught horse on Sexton land, and you don't think this is significant? What would your father say? What kind of danger is this?" she nearly shouted.

Mamó's desk clock struck the half hour. "Nine-thirty, Mom. How are you getting back to the airport?"

"I have a car on call. I need to leave by eleven. I could do with a pot of tea." She began pacing in the small space between the file cabinet and the window. "There is something on my mind. It's about Matthew. I think he's—" A knock at the door made her gasp.

"Yes?" Marc called out. "Calm down," he told his mother.

Charlotte shyly poked her head in. "Hi." She pushed open the door. "Since when do you have a guard screening customers at the front door? What's going on? Ohh. Kelsey. Hello."

Her face immediately cheered him. "Hi. I'm keeping the press out. Come in."

"Charlotte, how nice to see you." Kelsey made a resolute lean-in and squeezed her hand affectionately. Oddly genuine. "I was just telling Marc I could use a pot of tea before I leave for JFK. Will you join me?"

"Sounds good," she replied warmly. "This place is jam-packed. Bar is certainly jumping."

Behind Charlotte, Petrovna waved frantically to Marc. "We've got a crush at the bar."

"I'm coming." As he exited the room, he gave Charlotte a squeeze on her waist. "Catch you later, Miss Knight."

Chapter Thirty-Six

A Kind of Darkness

Marc darted to the bar, the banjo jazz practically rattling the rafters, and got the crush under control. Between shaking up cocktails and the backlog of tabs at the register, he got a spare minute to stream the NBC Rackman interview of Luther spouting his bravado and snatch a glimpse of Kelsey and Charlotte at a window table. Charlotte was completely engrossed with Kelsey chattering away about God knows what.

He made his way back to Joey, who was tapping his fingers on the Coke glass, finishing off his fries.

Marc leaned on the bar top and spoke softly. “Are you aware, Joey, that violating a No Trespassing sign is a criminal offense? A misdemeanor. Punishable by a year in jail.”

The kid’s jaw went slack. “Well, no.”

“Here’s the deal. I don’t press charges against you, and you destroy that photo. Nobody, and I mean nobody, sees it. You don’t sell it. You don’t loan it. You don’t duplicate it anywhere. And that goes for your editor.”

“Yeah, yeah, I get it. Scout’s honor.” He raised his hand. “But can I have a quick Q&A?”

Marc almost laughed. He had to admire the kid's plucky ambition. "You give me one question, and I'll give you one answer. And no questions about the horse."

The kid put his head down. "Ahhh, great, give me a sec." He drained the rest of the Coke. "Okay. Tell me about the first time you saw the white wolf." He pulled out his notepad.

"First time?" He took his time to compose his answer. "At night. I heard this howling. Her voice was full of sweeps and graceful pitches. I ran outside. She stood beneath the stars, a majestic wolf queen all sleek and shining. And peaceful as a prayer. If anything could teach us how to embrace wildlife, it would be this white wolf."

The kid scribbled madly.

"Print that, Joey Tate."

At ten o'clock, the Kelsey Room cleared out. By 10:30, the bar had reduced to two men finishing off their beers, Liz cleaning up, and two staffers clearing the dining room. He sat down at the front table with Charlotte while Kelsey busied herself with a phone text. He noted two wine glasses and empty teacups, and his mom's calmer expression. Charlotte's elusive turn of the lips told him nothing. She could blank out on him at times, but he knew by now that this was her way of taking time to sort out her emotions.

"My driver is on his way now," Kelsey told Marc.

He reached for Charlotte's hand beneath the table—a risk he almost didn't take because if she had pulled it away, he would have flinched with regret. She squeezed it back.

"Your mom and I were chatting about your farmhouse in Lewisboro and Matthew's cabin near the brook," she advised with a lilt in her voice as if to clue him in.

"That old stuff? Not exactly thrilling childhood history," he remarked, trying to read his mother.

Kelsey finished off her wine.

"Feeling better, Mom?"

"Thanks to Charlotte, yes."

He perked up. "Oh? Why is that?"

"Charlotte remembers the poem. Yeats's poem. The line I told you."

"I do know it. '*I hear the Shadowy Horses, their long manes a-shake.*' It's not one of Yeats's most famous, but I remember that line."

"I don't recall. Da knew a good deal of Yeats. Not my bailiwick."

"For heaven's sake, Marc," Kelsey said. "The lines are engraved on his headstone. When was the last time you visited his grave?"

"Been a while."

"Maybe we can visit tomorrow?" Charlotte offered.

Marc knew perfectly well that Charlotte had zero fondness for strolling around cemeteries. This was his mother's idea.

Kelsey fiddled with her bracelet. The limp posture, a sullen mouth, dread hung all over her. She caught Marc observing her, and she immediately straightened, the steely Kelsey Sexton called to attention. "Your father talked about horses many times, and the magick they possessed," she told him, her words thick.

"Okay."

"This is important. Your father had recurring dreams of horses."

"I know he did."

"Red horses. Fire horses. Shadow horses."

He turned to Charlotte. "Mamó knew red horses to be harbingers of death. Mom, Gramarra was dark gray."

"Matthew believed," Kelsey addressed Charlotte, "that memories exist within all of Nature. Past and present events.

Surely, Marc, you recall his horsehead wand. Don't you recall that conversation?"

The horse-wand. He flashed back to his teen days when he had sat cross-legged on the spiral-print carpet in the timber cabin, his father in the wolf chair, the brook swishing outside the open window, all those antlers dripping from the ceiling, the oak horsehead wand as tall as a cane propped against the brick fireplace. Their chats, about the elements of circular magick, time dilation, and the power of time-travel fuses came back in a rush.

Da's face, peace-filled, his words flowing easy and gentle. *Our ever-shifting minds . . . the ever-shifting memories . . . part of Nature . . . part of the one great memory . . . past, present, and future.* Those sittings carried great felicity from father to son every Saturday morning.

"I do recall a discussion of Yeats about memory and Nature. *'Shadowy Horses,'* sounds familiar."

"With eyes . . ." Kelsey struggled to remember the poem. "*'With eyes glimmering white.'* " *Ding* went her phone. "My driver is here. Double-parked at the front."

They rose. Marc reached out for a goodbye embrace.

She held him tight again, clinging, and rubbed his left arm. "There's not an ounce of color in your face. You remember, your father lost his strength three days before he died. He could hardly make a fist. I couldn't bear to lose you too," she said, a tear breaking loose.

"Mom, I'm thirty-nine. I'm not going to have a heart attack. Besides, Charlotte keeps me strong."

Kelsey appeared to hold her breath at his words. She quickly turned to Charlotte and embraced her. "It was helpful to spend time with you. Thank you. For everything. I mean it."

"Pleasure is all mine. Goodbye, Kelsey," she said. "Safe travels to Dublin."

Charlotte stood at the window, her small hand raised in a wave as Kelsey departed.

When she sat down, Marc poured wine into her glass. She declined, so he drank it. "That was a sweet goodbye. Did you charm my mother, or did she charm you?" he said, quite pleased.

"At first, a little of both, then not so charming."

"What did you two talk about?"

"Oh you know, this and that."

"What . . . this and that?"

"After the tea, we ordered a bottle of wine, and she asked me what birth control I use. It was thumbs down after that."

"I'm sorry. She can be unbearably blunt."

"She's quite skilled at it. She proceeded to tell me that I didn't know everything about you and that I need to rethink our marriage because there were secrets that you would never reveal."

"She said that?"

"Her exact words: 'Marc will never press the play button for you.' Savvy, huh?"

Marc stretched back into the chair. "I suspect you did a heroic job of correcting her?"

"I told her I read the names carved into the wolf chair. That surprised her—my presence in the attic. Two more glasses of wine loosened her up. She described the day she found your father dead in the cabin. What a horrible shock to find him sitting in the wolf chair, gripping the horse-wand. She's still crushed by it, Marc. Then she carried on about the horse-wand. What is that about?"

"Da had carved a horse head into an oak branch as a conduit.

A walking stick, actually. He charged it for protection and during his last months, he slept with it."

"That's chilling. You weren't home the day he died?"

"I was away at college. He had called me that morning. We spoke a long time."

"About what?"

Marc sipped the wine. "The presence of Black Wolf Realm."

"How much does Kelsey know about it?"

"Not much. Da educated her selectively about his magick and his journeys to the Otherworld."

"Selectively. You mean half-truths? That sounds so misleading. Kind of like half-lies, you think?"

"Half-truths, yes. Half-lies? I wouldn't go that far."

"Your mother is a mess, Marc. She's terrified that the horse's death has triggered some fatal event and that your life will be suddenly snatched away. She's struggling with questions about your father's death, confused and frightened. Kelsey called his magick dangerous. Was it?"

"Da explored dimensional magick. Time-slips. Magickal loops and death wheels. Yeah, those realms *are* dangerous. He protected me from the details and would never reveal the dangers to his wife."

"Well, Matthew didn't do Kelsey any favors by keeping her blind to his realities. What a cold chain she has been bound up in all these years. Her ignorance has only enlarged her fears. She feels powerless." Charlotte folded her arms. "Liz is signaling you at the bar."

He stood up. "Close the bar, Liz," he called out and sat down, grateful the dining room had emptied out, leaving the two of them alone.

Charlotte folded the paper cocktail napkin, unfolded it, and toyed with the ragged corners. They sat in silence. He waited for her to speak because he knew she was about to metaphorically hit him.

She snatched a sip from his wine glass. "What did Da tell you about Black Wolf Realm the day he died?"

There it was. Charlotte, ready to seize the moment with her voracious desire to take a bite of forbidden fruit.

"Da warned me. 'Beware of black wolf shadowing.' He had been obsessed with Black Wolf Realm. He hated—I mean, utterly detested—the fact that the ancestors had used their blood magick to curse the wolves into exile and perish them from eternity. Da tried his own blood magick to counter their curse, but he failed again and again. And then he died."

Charlotte placed her hand on his. She had such a shy touch sometimes.

"He never gave up the crusade. That day he died, he made a trance journey. That's all I know. Da wouldn't reveal the details. And my mother knows none of this."

"Marc, you know I could never live in her kind of darkness, not knowing the reality of your life. I'm more inclined to walk out on a lie than the truth. You know that, right?"

"Loud and clear."

"Kelsey wants you to visit Da's grave."

"I hate going to his grave."

"Do you? I promised your mother we'd go tomorrow."

"You did what?"

"She was adamant that you needed to visit the gravesite. I promised we'd go. I'll pick you up at noon and we'll drive to North Salem. Forest Green Cemetery, right?"

"Charlotte—"

"The bar doesn't open until three on Sunday. You'll have plenty of time."

Marc knew he would need all his fortitude and artful savvy to command a *No, we are not going.* He also knew that at the moment, he lacked the strength to master it. "Tomorrow? With everything else going on? Did you see Rackman on NBC?"

"I did. He sounded maniacal, spouting his vendetta against an animal for payback. Offering a reward of $10,000? Disgusting."

"Rackman's old Bedford money. I'm appalled that he's making an appeal to the DEC for a permit to kill Sky Wolf." The idea of Sky Wolf's death made his gut ball up. He wondered about Sky Wolf's soul truth. Would Sky Wolf return to Lupus? Or was there some other earthly destiny?

"Where is Sky Wolf? Is she safe?" Charlotte said, her voice desperate.

"I don't know. She takes off for weeks sometimes before I see her again. She goes north where there's better hunting. I expect she'll return to me at some point. She usually does."

"If she returns to you at the house, Rackman will be on the hunt for her on his land and yours, won't he?"

"The law prohibits hunting on private property, but that won't stop Luther." He turned the stemmed wine glass round and round on the table. "Sky Wolf has a keen sense of danger. She knows."

"Knows she's being hunted by Rackman?"

"Sometimes I think Sky Wolf knows everything." He pulled out his phone and showed her. "That's Sky Wolf, sitting on a rock in my back acre this morning. Joey Tate, the runner who called the police, took the photo. I'll tell you about him later."

"Ohhh, Sky Wolf is so sad. She's mourning Gramarra's death,

like a human." She handed the phone back, her brows tightening into a worried furrow. "Listen, Kelsey thinks you are in danger. And I sense danger here too. The Ripper pack is stalking your property. You don't have your wolf pendant. Sky Wolf can't guard you if she's gone north. Kelsey thinks you should sleep with Da's horse-wand. She insists you need your father's protection. Will you?"

He finished the last of the wine. Charlotte wanted reality, but reality wore slow-walking shoes, leaving faint prints in the mud, keeping its weight hidden.

"Will you?" she repeated. "Sleep with the horse-wand for protection?"

The horse-wand! "Please, Charlotte. I don't know. I need to check the kitchen and the Kelsey Room, tally the receipts, and close up." He stood, unsteady, a bit woozy, his own weight suddenly too heavy for his legs. He needed air. He needed to run. Run a race through trees, under moonlight, up mountain slopes, and sleep with his belly warmed by the good earth beneath the stars. He turned to go.

Charlotte rose. "Wait."

His ribcage ached in his turn back to her, this woman standing with him, her head tilting forward, her bronze hair in the low lights like a warm sunset. How could he free himself from this black wolf madness and be with the woman he loved? For the first time in his life, he had found someone who truly made his world exquisite. He put his hand out to her. She took it. "You know I loved you first, right?" His voice shattered a little when he said it.

She drew him to her mouth, the kiss capturing a new passion he hadn't felt before. In the embrace, she rested her head against his chest.

His heart throbbed loudly. Was she listening? Even though Black Wolf Realm existed among them now, did Charlotte know that his heart was *not* the son of Black Wolf Realm?

She kissed him again. "Come back to Draakensky. You are safe with me."

If only her kisses could keep him safe.

Interlude III

The Old Magick

Beneath my darkened sky, Draakensky's fragrant pines exhale their swaying aromas into my wind. Ahhh, the old magick is here. In the heart of this night is the ultimate terrain for lovemaking.

River waves smack. We have balmy spring breezes. Waterfalls burst. Above, victorious Orion glitters around my yews, although hidden as he shifts westward in the season's passage. Still, a lacy dome of starlight persists, creating sky lanterns.

I see the man here. I see the daughter. They walk across the lawn, past the flower garden of white snapdragons. The daughter pulls the man's hand toward the windmill. Quiet laughter. Playful calls. She teases him. He thinks she is leading him inside for a romp, no doubt, but she detours the front door.

On the south side of the windmill, where my breezes are tepid, she hurries him to a space below a hatched window. Bracing herself against the windmill's structure like it's a bulwark, the daughter turns away wisely, enhancing the seduction of his roving hands. Dropping her eyelids, she fiercely kisses him. He whispers between gentle bites of her ear.

I shall not eavesdrop. Being voyeur is fine enough.

Draakensky's four sails are whirling, the blades spread wide above their heads, kicking up wind with muted roars, shifting yellow hues into multicolor. Tints of hot pinks strike up circles into spiraling rainbows. The old magick, ahhh, yes. Blue and silver and honey-colored rays are flying as these two are painting the sky.

The man is creating enigmatic green flushes from his body, his feet planted firmly on the grass. He smooths her hair with kisses. She runs her hands down his chest, making promises as they prepare for passion—unbuttoning, unzipping—every moment burning urgent.

He's handling her aggressions magnificently. She is a river of glossy hair. No daring fantasies here; this is a hot reality. Their lips are made for each other—her sighs begging, his voice tender.

I am not spying, not really. I am curiously amused how these two lovers could live on lust alone. She is most definitely his. Moon and mouth. Stars and fingertips. Rippling breaths. Their bodies clasp. The daughter wraps him like she has wings. Nothing can tear them asunder.

She draws him deeper. This woman is summoning a kingdom.

He lifts her. Thrusts. Converging on and on, they are, in raptures of kisses. Oh! Look how beautifully they break into each other.

With the midnight hour skating by, they stream themselves beneath the spray of the wild blue north, into the south's yellow, and cross the easterly and westerly green plunges. They become a whirling couplet of magickal colors illuminating all of Draakensky, to the river, to Yew Crag, and beyond.

Owl feathers drift down. Proof of this daughter's prowess and might. I am proud how she unlocks the secret boughs of my air—this old magick.

Chapter Thirty-Seven

Valley of the Dead

Sunday morning broke. Charlotte woke early, hoping to get in a few hours' sketching time of the goddess Hekate. She planned to do three rough studies. "Hekate," she read aloud as if she could conjure the crone deity, "a secret sorcerer." Queen of Ghosts. Queen of Witches. Reputed to be evil, but discovered to be a goddess.

She closed her notes. "Let's see who you are, Hekate, on my page."

Her cell phone dinged a text notice. KELSEY SEXTON.

HAVE YOU FOUND MATTHEW'S HORSEHEAD WAND? I'M SURE MARC HAS IT IN THE ATTIC. PLEASE, FIND IT AND SLIP IT BENEATH MARC'S BED TONIGHT. I NEED YOU TO DO THIS FOR ME, CHARLOTTE. MARC MUST NOT LOSE HIS STRENGTH. WE SEXTONS, WE PROTECT EACH OTHER. EVER GRATEFUL, KELSEY.

Charlotte replied. I WILL SEE TO IT. HIS SAFETY IS CRITICAL. I AGREE. CHARLOTTE.

While Marc slept late, she drafted Hekate in a flowing nightgown as mother, maiden, and crone. Charlotte decided to present the goddess as three fully developed women unified as one, each facing out as past, present, and future. After two hours, she finished off one illustration with ghost figures unraveling at the right and left borders.

Pssssst, sailed behind her.

She turned. “Ohhhh, man of my bliss,” she said to Marc as he popped up from the spiral staircase into her studio.

In pajama bottoms and tee-shirt, he climbed the top steps, the expression on his face betraying how much he thoroughly enjoyed her compliment. “Thank you for being so amazing last night,” he quipped. “Are you some kind of ballerina with that high-leg wrap?”

“Yeah, that’s me, Anna Pavlova. I was on a mission.”

“For incredibly hot, straight-up sex in the garden? We may have defied gravity last night.”

“Mmm, we were flying, weren’t we? Did you see those colors from the sails spinning above us? Greens and blues. Practically a kaleidoscope.”

“Didn’t see a thing. I was occupied with other sensations.”

She blinked flirtatiously and covered her sketch. “We’d better hurry if we want to get to the cemetery by noon. Coffee is hot on the stove.”

“You really want to do this cemetery thing?” he moaned.

“I do. I’ll pack us a light lunch.”

“Lunch? You want to picnic in the cemetery?”

“The Victorians did it. Women carried parasols and baskets of bread and fruit, and lunched sitting on top of the graves.”

“Who told you that ridiculous story?”

“Anthropologist Eugenie Nye. She would know. Let’s hustle.”

On the car ride to North Salem, Marc munched a piece of toast, unwilling or uncomfortable speaking. Once at Forest Green Cemetery, hand-in-hand, they walked the paths through borders of small rocks and colorful wildflower patches, angel statuary, and neat rows of boulder headstones.

"I've never been to an eco-friendly *green* cemetery before," Charlotte said.

"Uh-huh."

"I once saw a sign at a cemetery entrance that said *Come In.* Kind of funny, huh?"

"Yeah. Funny."

"The air smells good here."

"I guess."

"A clean cottony scent."

"Is it? Da was buried in a cotton shroud. Most here are buried in wicker coffins."

"Oh."

"The body completely decomposes into the soil. Da wanted white cotton," he repeated.

After walking up a few hills, they reached a plateau perched above the rest of the graves. One lonely headstone with a Celtic cross engraved into the rock sat on the grassy crest, surrounded by blue lupine flowers that must have been over three feet tall.

They sat on a stone bench.

Matthew Liam Sexton, 1955 – 2002. Beloved Husband and Father.

"They had green cemeteries as early as 2002?"

"A few states began green burials around 2000. My father wanted his interment to be a natural return to the earth. He was the first to be buried here when it was private land. He donated money to get Forest Green Cemetery established."

"Why don't you like coming here? The air is full of halcyon moments."

"There's nothing of Da's physical life here. He's completely decomposed by now. After twenty years, even the bones are gone. Wherever his soul lives, it's not here."

No bones. Her mother had been dead and buried for over thirty years. Her father's body had sunk somewhere to the bottom of the Atlantic Ocean—the arduous searches never recovered his remains. His bones were long gone too.

The gray boulder headstone was taller than Charlotte had expected. A mitt-like hump protruded on the left corner. Charlotte wanted one of the blue lupine spires and slipped off the bench to snip one between her fingernails as a flock of crows squawked from a distant tree.

She sat down, holding the flower, reading Yeats's poem titled "He Bids His Beloved Be at Peace," which had been exquisitely carved on the rock's face. With her phone, she snapped a photo close enough to read the inscription.

Her left knee touched Marc's; she rested her head on his shoulder. "Do you remember the poem?" Charlotte asked, if only to break the silence bearing down. "Is there a line that resonates for you?"

She read the words aloud:

"I hear the Shadowy Horses, their long manes a-shake,
"Their hoofs heavy with tumult, their eyes glimmering white;
"The North unfolds above them clinging, creeping night,
"The East her hidden joy before the morning break,
"The West weeps in pale dew and sighs passing away,
"The South is pouring down roses of crimson fire:
"O vanity of Sleep, Hope, Dream, endless Desire,
"The Horses of Disaster plunge in the heavy clay:"

Here Charlotte paused, feeling the death images in the words. She wondered if Marc was feeling the same. He remained fixed on the giant boulder headstone.

"Beloved, let your eyes half close, and your heart beat,
"Over my heart, and your hair fall over my breast,
"Drowning love's lonely hour in deep twilight of rest,
"And hiding their tossing manes and their tumultuous feet."

"Marc, did your father choose this poem because of its mysticism? Because it casts a spell?"

"I don't know, does it? There is something in the words that . . . strike."

"Yeats is famous for his words creating a kind of mesmerism. Similar to entering a realm. He studied the occult. Sister James thought Yeats had magickal gifts. She called him a trance-poet."

"What did Sister James think of this poem?"

"She interpreted the shadowy horses as reflecting an apocalyptic vision. Four directions. Four horsemen. War, conquest, famine, death. It's a worthy interpretation." Charlotte began kicking her leg. "But I'm not sure I agree. Even if it's not apocalyptic, the poem has a horrific, dark element that is unfathomably deep."

"I'm somewhat dense about poetry, but I see this one has impending doom."

"Hmm . . . *'hiding tumultuous feet. Eyes half closed. Hidden joy.'* It does remind me of the Sexton family secrets . . . hiding tumultuous truths."

"That far meadow is inviting, a perfect green. Are we done here? We can walk back through the meadow," he said hurriedly.

She stopped kicking and placed both feet on the ground. "Not yet. What tumultuous truths are you hiding from me, Marc?" After their lovemaking beneath the windmill, she was sure their level of trust had made a leap. If there were a single energy that flowed between them now, it moved in a synchronized heartbeat. "I need to know."

"Ask me anything you want," he shot back matter-of-factly.

"On Friday night, during that rainstorm, did you shift and run with the pack again? Were you the other wolf with Ripper that attacked Gramarra?"

"No. A thousand times, no. I did not shift."

"Then where were you? If you were in the attic before you went to sit outside, why didn't I hear you moving around?"

"Because I was seated on the carpet inside the circle. I thought I might get some counsel from Mamó."

The relief in her breath was palpable. "And did Mamó answer?"

"I'm not sure. Someone did. A voice came forward in my head. *Do draíocht.* Gaelic for *your magick.*"

"Dree-ukt," she pronounced the word as he had. "Your magick?"

"Mamó knew a bit of Gaelic, but it wasn't her usual voice, unless she was deliberately making it sound deeper. For an instant, I thought it might be Da. I hoped it was. I mean, I was sitting in his circle. He knew Gaelic too. Unlikely though, since he's not made contact with me in all these years. I can't figure if the voice was redirecting me or admonishing me. A warning maybe? And if not Mamó, *who* dropped that thought into my head?"

The edge in his voice, the disappointed note on the word *who* urged her. For his sake, she wished it had been Da's voice. Another question slid quickly off her tongue, a notion that had been pressing her. "I've been thinking. You weren't surprised that Ripper killed Gramarra, were you?"

He jerked his shoulder. "It makes sense, doesn't it? Horses are strength. Speed. Victors. Mamó often spoke of the magickal 'horse of the heavens, Echdae'—the sun. The Celts recognize the horse as the power that draws the chariot of the sun across the sky." His attention moved again to that far meadow.

She gave him a moment, then asked, "So, you *knew* the Ripper pack attacked Gramarra?"

"Not at first. But I understood after the fact. If Ripper is going to survive and lead his pack to victory, he has to be at full strength and speed. Full soul strength. His withered soul can't do it. Ripper must be triumphant. The entire pack must be triumphant. Ripper pack killed Gramarra, not for food, not out of defense, but for bloodthirst. They killed Gramarra and drank in her strength, for their souls to be victorious."

"Victorious at what?"

His eyes found hers. Blue stars, slashing hot. "For their battle ahead."

She shook her head, not understanding and yet fearing the worst.

"The Ripper pack desires to be wild again. To hunt, race through forests, and feast on elk. To sleep under the stars and know the warm earth on their bellies. To be wolf family with pups." He braced his arms across his gut, holding himself tight.

Of course Marc would have sharp instincts about being a wolf. And about Black Wolf Realm. He believed in wolves. Understood them. He believed in the Finnwolf quest. Even though he possessed the Finnwolf power, he chose not to practice it. She wondered if it was truly Kelsey who had wanted Marc to visit the grave. Or was it Da working through her, calling his son here?

"This is who they are, Charlotte. *We are wolf.* With every leap and howl: *we are wolf.* That's why the pack didn't attack me on Tuesday night. I've been puzzled why they didn't take their revenge against the Sexton clan and slaughter me on the spot when they had an easy advantage. Instead, they forced me to run with them. Clever, right? *Howl with us. Image forth your wolf. Become wolf.* What a strategic maneuver to lull me into a sense of safety, coercing me to join the pack."

Charlotte quelled a shaking fear rising from her belly. "If they don't want to kill you for revenge, why coerce you into the pack?"

"These black wolves, they desire something more, far more than revenge. I know that now."

"More than revenge? What exactly?"

"They want to return to life here, as feral wolves . . . as earthly wolves."

Charlotte dropped her jaw. "Earthly wolves?"

"In order to do that, they need to transform out of shadow wolf."

"Is that even possible?"

"A few months ago I would have said it's not possible, but now, today . . . I see that kind of metamorphosis would require a powerful magick. The highest magick. Magick that shadow wolves don't possess."

Her fears surging, she asked, "What kind of high magick?" The words caught dry on her tongue. "Your magick?"

"*Do draíocht,* the voice told me—*your magick!*"

"Marc, you don't mean—"

He lunged to his feet. "I'm son of Finnwolf. Born with ancestral Finnwolf magick in my blood. And that same blood carries the crimes of my ancestors. I ran with Ripper pack! Sky Wolf at my side. I know the pack's deepest desires now."

Charlotte clenched her stomach. She needed to keep clear and steady and not let fear dominate.

Marc stood before the headstone, his chest aligned with the Celtic cross. He lifted his head as if waking up. "Charlotte, Ripper and his wolves are demanding that I surrender my magick to them for the metamorphosis."

She hung on his words. "But you can't do that—surrender your magick—can you?"

"I am my magick. Body, breath, and soul. *Anam*, life's vigor. Not only Finnwolf magick, but Alpha Lupi star magick generates my life now. This is who I am, my life vowed to the stars. The day I surrender my magick, the day I breathe my magick into their wolf souls is the day my body dies."

Dies. The shock of that word broke her.

"Charlotte, if I give my magick to Ripper pack while I am alive and breathing, it possesses far greater power for them. If they kill me first, only the weakened remnants of my magick are left to devour. Fifteen wolves. They want—they need—all of my living magick. That's the debt they want me to pay."

She jumped up, grabbing his shoulders, eye to eye with him. "And if you don't surrender your magick to them? Ripper pack cannot just seize your magick. Do they have the power to steal your magick?"

"That would incite quite a battle. Me against fifteen wolves."

The warm breezes turned cold on her face, lifting Charlotte's hair off her shoulders, tossing the locks back, making her feel naked. "And if . . . if they won that battle?"

He reached for her hand and clenched it. "Even Da could not win that one. Without my magick, like Gramarra, I die."

Chapter Thirty-Eight
Front Door of Midnight

Marc couldn't pull himself away from the name *Matthew Liam Sexton* carved on the headstone. If stone could speak, these words would be shouting. He calmed himself, suddenly recalling the words, *a wolf devouring the sun*—a childhood bedtime story from Da. *Once upon a time, there was a clever wolf who became the sun.*

Charlotte spread out a thin blanket before the headstone, her mouth tight, hands trembling. They sat side by side on the surface of Da's grave. Tears welled, but she didn't let them drop. Marc admired her steadfastness as she poured two glasses of wine, the splashes making the only sound between them. Peasant herb bread, Irish cheddar, black olives, bright red apples. He'd nearly forgotten her Victorian-esque picnic.

They ate without a word. Nuthatches flitted the trees—the boulder headstones around them creating a bald audience.

"You know," Marc said, wanting to ease her fears and his own, "my father used to make up bedtime stories. Adventures of wolves and witches. Kings who laid down their swords. Fantastical kingdoms with warriors who were shape-changers. Bubbling volcanoes and sea dragons with long green eyelashes. Their tails could capture a giant. The queens, though, they were the exalted ones. Queens would charm the beasts into submission with enchanted arrows."

"You had an exceptional father."

"He was. Ancient Celts believed death is never the conqueror. That's why we cling to the Otherworld spirits so desperately. I remember a story Da told me about a poet's curse. A Celtic poet was murdered, and as he lay dying, he uttered a curse upon the murderers. Within days, the killers died of rotting flesh. Now you know why I'm not keen on poetry."

That made her laugh.

Marc leaned back, locking on Yeats's words. *The north unfolds . . . the east hides . . . the west weeps . . . the south is pouring.* It was beautiful and terrible. An apocalypse? No. Something else. Too many paths ahead. Which direction to go?

"Did Da practice star magick?" Charlotte asked.

"I'm sure he did."

"Was the Ripper pack after Da for his magick?"

"He never said. If they were, they didn't get it, or they wouldn't be hunting me. I could fill a book with everything that my father never said."

"And the horse-wand, would that have protected Da against the Ripper pack stealing his magick?"

"Probably. Unless a higher magick countered it. It's always been a question in my mind if Da's sudden death was caused by a slow loss of his magick. The body weakness, the isolation, the covert journeys. I knew that Da had endured a dark secret during his last year, especially in the final weeks."

He moved closer to the headstone and ran his fingertips along each line of the words carved into the granite.

"Marc, what is it? Your face is flushed."

"Yeats's line '*The south is pouring down.*' I recall Da saying that in the Otherworld, there is a southern portal into the underworld realms." He touched the upper lines again. " '*I hear the Shadowy Horses . . . hiding their tossing manes.*' Why were those lines so meaningful to Da?"

"Yeats's poems are heavy with symbolism. '*Tossing manes*' reminds me of arrogant women. Yeats exercised tremendous psychic power in his work."

Slowly he turned to face her, gazing at Charlotte's brave brow and the dauntless mouth, and that insight she had just laid upon him. "Yeats was psychic? Of course. I didn't fully realize that until now. Da was psychic as well."

A calming presence came over him. A nearby cherry tree shed dappled light over Charlotte in an unusual canopy. Sunlight passed between the leaves, drenching her in a glow. She could be his anchor, the queen in his sanctuary, charming the beast into defeat.

" '*Shadowy Horses.*' " She was studying the inscription again. "Was Da especially fond of horses?"

"Warrior horses are a theme in Celtic heroism. There are chants for riding equine energy for protection. I don't know a single one of them."

"I need to ask. Is Da's horse-wand in the attic?"

Waiting for his reply, she batted an eye at him. "Marc, your mother is determined that you have protection. I agree, now, more than ever. She says the wand is in the attic and wants me to place it beneath your bed."

He turned away, shaking his head.

"For God's sake! This is you against fifteen vicious wolves on the hunt to steal your magick and let you die. Fifteen wolves eager to kill you for it. You need protection. Please." Her voice broke, and a tear dropped to her cheek. "Where is it?"

Where is it? The wand had been charged with Da's powers and his sacred knowledge. The wand could clear blockages and dispel negative forces. Da had invoked spiritual figures with that wand. On one of their Saturday morning training sessions, Marc had witnessed Da bring forth a field of opposites via the horse-wand. Figures materialized against the wall, malevolent spirits and creatures free-roaming from the in-between realms. This potent tool had to be kept in a sacred place.

"I don't have it," Marc said.

"Can you get it?"

"Not possible."

"Why not?"

"Because I placed it beneath the *front door of midnight*. That's where Da instructed me to secure the wand. Exactly as he instructed Yeats's poem to be carved on his headstone and instructed that his body be buried in white cotton."

She made an impatient grumble. "And where in hell is the front door of midnight, whatever that is?"

He pinched his lips, regretting having to say the words. "We're sitting on it."

The drive home made Marc edgy, as if he weren't unnerved enough. He could practically hear Charlotte's mind clicking away. He might have explained the idiom about the front door of midnight, but wasn't it obvious?

"What shall I tell Kelsey when she asks me about the horse-wand?" she said, practically reading his mind.

"Tell her . . . it's not in the attic."

"Oh Marc. She's going to want more than that. How is it possible that Kelsey doesn't know you buried the horse-wand in Da's grave with him? She's his wife. Shouldn't she know?"

"Da wanted it with him, that's all I knew at the time. Maybe I've been infinitely stupid about this, but I trusted Da knew what he was doing. And I kept my pledge not to tell. Can we close the subject now?" He opened his cell phone and scrolled the breaking news headlines. "Christ, no, this can't be." He tapped the screen. "They found two dead horses in Putnam County this morning . . . suspected wolf attack . . . unusual draining of blood from the carcasses . . . two reported sightings of a white wolf in the area." He shoved the phone into his pocket.

"Sky Wolf is in danger in the north now?"

"She's tracking Ripper pack." He opened the window. "I'm burning up here." He wiped his brow. "Gramarra, and now two dead horses. The pack is building their potency fast. I cannot stay in this lull for long, or I'll weaken like Da."

If only Da had kept notes about his magickal operations. What principles was he exploring in those final weeks? With these wolves on the hunt now, Marc would need armor, guidance, weaponry. Something began to buzz inside his head. He recognized that buzz as his magickal energies surging forth. Battle-ready was all he could think.

"Take the next left. Drop me at the bar. Can you come back at eight and drive us back to my house? Will you stay tonight?"

"I will. But what are we doing? Your face is red hot. Oh Marc!"

We, she said. He reached over and placed his hand on her thigh. "If I am going to survive this, I need you to help me."

"What are you going to do?"

"The only thing I can do. Create war magick."

Chapter Thirty-Nine

Ancestral Guilt

At *The Grackle*, Marc hustled through the back door at three o'clock. Only three customers at the bar and two in the dining room spurred a momentary relief that he had time to pull himself together. The kitchen staff operated at a normal speed.

In his office, he grabbed a fresh shirt and tie from the closet, struggling to recall Da's description of the Otherworld. *The architecture is a vertical position. The earth at the center as core. Celestial realms to the north. Underworld realms have a southern portal.* He remembered his father's promise: *Someday, you will learn to be a horizon walker and discover the safest paths. When you're ready, I will illustrate the teleportation spirals in the east.*

Those days never came. Marc's refusals to learn the horizon paths in the Otherworld came fast off his tongue in his youth. Da accepted that his son wasn't ready and that time would heal Marc's doubts. Time performed no such miracle.

Marc headed to the bar, holding the worries at the back of his mind. *Stay sharp. Work on the task at hand.*

The bar crowd grew busy by seven o'clock. His face still hot, his stomach roiling, he used all his discipline to be attentive and cheerful for his clientele. He switched the news on the TV monitor to the cheerful greens of the PGA Sunday Golf Classic and piped in piano music. Steady, locked, and loaded, Marc eagerly shook up cocktails and tended the register tabs, shooting an eye to the front door.

Much to his surprise, Sir Duncan Hawkinge strolled in. The earl took a quick seat, his square, brawny face somber.

"Good evening, Sir Duncan," Marc shot a welcome. "Good to see you. How's your Irish tonight?"

"If I ever needed a Sexton and soda, this is the time. How are you, Marc?"

That was a loaded question. "Good enough."

"And where is your splendid fiancé?"

"I expect her soon. Something on your mind?"

"I need The Sexton first." He wore a grim expression.

"That sounds ominous. Got troubles?"

He bowed his head. "Elysium Fields has crashed to a halt."

Marc straightened. Their previous conversation about *A Private Sky* and the horrific rooks-on-fire incident had left much unresolved. He was aware that Charlotte had sent a note of apology, but the result was a gulf of embarrassment between the earl and Charlotte. And the earl hadn't responded to his last phone text, a clue things weren't going well.

Marc poured the whiskey and set it down. "A halt? What does that mean?"

Sir Duncan took a deep swallow, then turned down the corners of his mouth, expressing a clear *no*. Another deep swallow of The Sexton. "I need to explain this with Charlotte here. So when's the wedding? Am I invited?"

Caught off guard by the abrupt change of subject, Marc blinked. "Of course you're invited. If we indeed have a wedding."

"Don't say it. Are things getting chopsy? Hit me again." He pushed his glass forward.

"I wouldn't say that. Between you and me, I've been thinking about sweeping her away." Marc poured a quick refill. "Catch a plane to Rome or Paris, take our vows in a Catholic church in the countryside. And the big finish, honeymoon on the Italian Riviera, maybe Portofino."

"A nuptial escapade? How snazzy of you, Marc. Will Charlotte consent to this romantic abduction?"

He nearly laughed. "You think I should kidnap her? Maybe Verona will entice her."

"What, you don't want a fancy Irish wedding?"

"That's the last thing I want."

"What's the last thing you want?" Charlotte appeared at the bar, dressed in a white leather jacket that reflected her bright gray eyes. He loved her gray orbs—loved how the color flowed from slate to steel to silvery as they did at the moment.

"And there she is," Marc said, puckering his lips at her. "How long have you been standing there?"

She returned the kissy gesture. "Only a sec. Sir Duncan, hello." She lifted her chin, cheeks flushing. Marc noted the waver in her voice.

Sir Duncan gave a gentlemanly bow. "A pleasure to see you, Charlotte. Lush as always."

"I don't know, is it a pleasure to see me?" Charlotte confessed and shyly slipped onto a stool.

"Indeed, it is. I came here specifically with you in mind. Your artistic passion for Elysium Fields might have been rather loud and imperious, but I certainly admire its veracity. And there was no need for your gracious apology. You are true to your art."

"You're wonderfully kind, Sir Duncan." She turned to Marc. "I'll join the earl with a Sexton and soda."

"Jolly good."

Marc poured a light one for her.

"Take a gander," Sir Duncan said, offering his phone. "We carry on. Elysium Fields, no more."

Marc stretched over the bar to get a peek. "Christ almighty, what did you do?" Elysium Fields stretched out in rubble and smoke as the video camera spanned the estate, the stone castle in heaps of broken stone, brick, and cement cinders.

"Oh, Sir Duncan," Charlotte said, her mortification clear.

"I was tempted to dance in the wreckage. That is, after the wrecking ball completed its task. The demolition approvals came through from Town and Country Planning. Right or wrong, it is quite rewarding to destroy something."

"But Elysium Fields is your ancestral home. Surely you—"

"Save it, my dear. My ancestors are imprinted into the soil and stone, infested by their crimes. As I live and breathe, the Hawkinge past is now torn asunder. We are left with the dusty hope for better days." He scrolled down to another image. "The rooks on fire have relocated into the timberland, near the wetlands."

In the photo, Marc observed a legion of blackbirds, grounded, but standing upright in rows, an army ready for action. "What are they doing?"

"Immovable. On guard, they are. Day after day after day. I am no fool. No one can call me a wally. The rooks are waiting for me to act." He downed the second Sexton.

"To do what?" Charlotte asked.

"That's what I wanted to speak to you about. I owe you this much, Charlotte. Fortunately, I was able to purchase *A Private Sky* from the original buyer. I'm bringing it back with me to Elysium Fields and"—Sir Duncan looked away, then returned to Charlotte—"I plan to set it afire."

Marc thought Charlotte would scream, but she sat frozen, hand caressing the whiskey, her lips parted in shock.

"Wicked elements are lurking in this portrait. It's time to do something."

"And you think burning the image will accomplish what?" she asked.

"After destruction, comes creation. Yes? Out of the duel comes the cleansing."

"Sir Duncan, if you burn the portrait of the rooks on fire, aren't you also burning your image? That's you sitting in the forefront on your land."

"Exactly. Do I not walk in my ancestors' footprints on that land? Have I not inherited their earth, their crimes, these ghastly sins? Do I not carry their guilt in my body? I may not have personally earned this guilt, but the devil of it is stinging my blood every day." He knocked his chest and turned to Marc. "What do you think?"

Ancestral guilt feeds on itself. Marc knew that much from Da. Crimes against nature or any humans are more about the victims than the violators. Da was driven by a similar ancestral guilt from the Sexton forefathers, the wolf killings, the blood magick curse. "Sir Duncan, your family circumstances are layered with unknown and unresolved elements that contain power," he offered. "What are these rooks haunting? Who are these rooks? Are they lost in this world? Or are they Hawkinge pawns?"

"Lost? I don't think so. These are hell-rooks. A murdering, swindling, cheating, hullaballooing clan. Forgive me, I'm getting a bit squiffy from The Sexton." He finished off the last drops in his glass.

Marc handed him a bar menu. "You're not leaving here until you eat something. What do you want?"

"I want"—he turned to Charlotte—"to have your permission to destroy the portrait. To burn *A Private Sky* out of this world."

The pain on Charlotte's face made Marc want to reach out to her. In the mirror behind the bar, in the muted light there, she held her own reflection for a long moment. "Charlotte," he said slowly, "maybe you want some time to think about this?"

"Sir Duncan." Charlotte faced him. "I've been paid for *A Private Sky*. The portrait belongs to you. Monet took a knife to a number of his paintings. If you believe that burning *A Private Sky* will destroy the Hawkinge history for you, I'll agree."

"Sir Duncan," Marc cut in, "you don't want to burn your portrait with this intention of family destruction. Don't fool with ancestral unresolved energy. You might do better to bury it. Give it back to the earth."

Sir Duncan waved him off. "Nonsense. Charlotte sounds sure of herself. She's an intelligent woman, competent to the core." Sir Duncan reached for her hand. "You are a pearl. My deepest gratitude." He squeezed her fingers. "We are all ghosts carrying the dead lifetimes that came before us—ancestors be damned!"

That Sunday night, as Charlotte slipped into her nightgown and into Marc's bed, *A Private Sky* continued to trouble her. The image haunted her mind's eye.

"Sometimes my artistic creativity shoots ahead of the execution on the page. Things can get reckless. I lost control of the portrait, Marc. Regrets are stupid, but here I am." The silky fabric warmed her back as she snuggled down, anxious to relax after such a harrowing day. "Sir Duncan is right. He does carry that wretched ancestral history, and I envisioned it when I drew the portrait. I made it real in this world. Rooks on fire."

Marc curled his arms around her. "Your portrait is a true rendering of the Earl of Elysium Fields. Some purpose is fueling it. Regrets are an appalling waste of energy."

A purpose? "Do you think there's a risk if he burns the portrait?"

"There's always a risk when we choose destruction. Especially the pathways of the ancestral dead. If he's burning his image out of malice, that energy can ignite spiritual forces to react and produce a backlash."

She shot up. "A backlash? Directed at me? Because I'm the creator of the portrait?"

"Doubtful. Sir Duncan needs to bury the portrait. The earth has redemptive powers. But it's not my decision or yours. It's decided now. Besides, I'm not convinced about those rooks. They exhibited traits of battle crows, especially aligned in formation, waiting in the timberland."

"You're right. It's decided. And I'm exhausted." She flopped down on the pillow. "What are battle crows?"

"Battle crows have power to weave death, war, or resolutions. They perform their own mission. Mamó believed they bring truth."

"Charming."

"Will you stay with me tomorrow? Bar is closed. I need you to help me with my war magick."

"Marc." She ran her fingers along his jaw. "I don't know a single thing about war magick."

"You're a daughter of Avalon. A sister to the goddess Vivienne. When you put pen to paper, you are a seer. You have powers I lack. I need your magick, Charlotte."

His expectation dug a hole straight into the pit of her stomach.

Chapter Forty
Wolf Guardians

Sunday night grew warm. Windows open, calm air, no sound, not even a whisper of wind; in Charlotte's mind, hungry for the wind-swept Draakensky, she returned to the soft-sighing trees, to the fragrant green hollows of Yew Crag, the river and surging falls, the giant hemlocks guarding the sky. She drifted on images of sunrays warming her face, thinking how badly she needed flowers—clusters of mountain laurel bursting pink blooms. She would pick an armful and fill the windmill. A visual of great white lilies curving out of a glass bowl eased her slumber.

Whang! Gunfire bolted her awake.

She shot up, dawn breaking with dull light at the bedroom window. The opposite side of the bed lay cool with the quilt thrown back. A look-see at the bathroom—dark—then the hallway—dark—urged her to rise. Maybe it wasn't gunfire. Maybe a dream. Was Marc out on a sunrise run? Was he out searching for Ripper pack?

She padded to the doorway. At the far end, lights from the attic stairwell shone on the hardwood floor. Stepping up the attic stairs, her nightgown hem dragged behind. "Marc?"

The attic lights shone on the wicker rocker and wolf chair. She halted at the rim of Marc's circle, cool air tingling her shoulders. On the carpet lay an open book. She read the page, Yeats's poem, titled "He Bids His Beloved Be at Peace." Taking one step in, she snatched up the book. On the page were small hand-written abbreviations—not Marc's hand—in the margin. After placing the book down exactly as she found it, Charlotte turned to leave.

Hollow clicking emerged from where the wolf cape hung. The Mask of the Red Mouth perched above it, those smeared red lips and protruding teeth. The wolf's hard blue eyes stared straight out. Magick that was *far too potent to gamble with,* Marc had said.

What kind of mask was behind the Mask of the Red Mouth? What harm would a quick peek do? *Stop looking at it,* Marc had told her. She recalled when Aunt Loretta had told her not to look at the car accident when they had driven past a two-car collision, surrounded by police cars' whirling red lights. She couldn't resist the desire to see the drama, the fear of looking, but the need to see it nonetheless—and then the shock of people bloodied and mangled in steel, a child crying in the back seat.

The mask stopped clicking. Moving closer, she stretched her fingertips to the mask's sides to lift the face off the wall.

Bang!

Her hands flew back. That *was* a gunshot. From the tree grove.

Bang!

Luther Rackman. Dear God! She ran to the window. In the half-light, Marc came running out of the back woods, his hoodie running suit blending into the rising dawn, Sky Wolf trotting at his side. Throwing open the window, she yelled, "Marc!"

He raised a hand and pointed to the garage. She dashed down the attic steps, holding up her nightgown to avoid tripping in her haste. By the time she reached the garage, Marc was already inside, crouched on the floor, calmly rubbing Sky Wolf's belly.

"How bad is she hurt?" she asked, seeing blood on Sky Wolf's rear leg. "Was that Luther's gunfire?"

"The bastard grazed her. I think she's okay, though. You're good, right, girl?" He dabbed the leg with the hem of his sweatshirt. "It's just a nick. Not much blood. She ran on it fine."

"Thank God she's okay. That stupid Luther. We should report him to the police."

"I called Jimmy as soon as I heard the first gunshot. Right now, though, I've got to get Sky Wolf to safer ground, away from here, in case Luther comes hunting for her. And I can't confine her inside the garage for long."

"We can bring her to Draakensky. Luther can't hunt her there, and she knows Yew Crag. I have the shed. Plenty of space for her. Can we drive her in the jeep?"

His jaw dropped in an incredulous expression. "Drive a wild wolf in a small moving vehicle? She'll go berserk. But . . . maybe she'll tolerate the van if I sit with her. I've got to unload the liquor cases first."

"Go on. I'll stay with her. She's licking her wound already." Charlotte petted her head with long streaming motions. Her fur—absolute silk. That face could belong to an angel, amber light shining from her eyes. Sketching her would never do justice to her radiance. Sky Wolf made a little whine and lifted her head. Fierce. Bold. But something bewildered there. She had probably never heard gunfire before, let alone been nicked in the leg.

"Sky Wolf, why did you come back here?" she said, sinking deep into her amber-light gaze. "Don't you know it's not safe here for you?"

"She always returns to me. No matter the distance. Sometimes I think we're never apart." Marc heaved case after case of liquor from the van. Without stopping, he stacked twenty cases on the garage floor.

"Will she stay on Draakensky if you stay there with me?"

Marc paused, head down, hand bracing the van door for support. He swayed, taking in shallow breaths.

"Marc?"

Face pasty white, he slid down the side of the van, legs splayed out.

"Oh my God. Stay there. I'll get you some water." She dashed out across the back lawn to the patio kitchen door, scanning the yard as the sun rose. No sign of Luther, but on the far side of the pond, she spotted three wolves—hulking black, mangy fur spiking their backs. She burst into the kitchen and grabbed her handbag, two bottles of water from the fridge, and the bagged peasant bread from the counter basket, then banged open the back door, ready to dash.

She stopped short on the patio. Fifteen wolves surrounded the backyard. Ripper's bony face beckoned from the rear. A weird sound *chirred* in the sky. Black-plumed birds smothered the treetops, a hundred or so, grim and ghastly, wings spread, their *caw-caw-caws* like rusty thorns screeching on metal. They threw off rank odors, pungent and musty. The smell of carrion. In their prowess, the birds swarmed together, their black bodies showing off warrior strength in tight formation.

Ripper wolves leaped with excitement at the flying cavalry. Some wolves raced, their black paws making circles between the trees. Others tossed their heads in bellowing howls, humping their backs in fighting postures.

The crows answered them with raucous squawks. Seconds later, they merged with the wolves' howling. What a horrific chorus blasting to the treetops. The pond churned up dagger-fingered waves as if shivering in the cacophony.

Ripper stomped the lawn, his elephant-like paws a savage threat of what he could crush with one leap. Releasing a blaring howl, he furiously exclaimed:

We are wolf.

Ripper advanced slowly, fangs shining, toward her.

She stepped sideways. The garage was some forty feet away. No, she would not race out, for that surely would invite the pursuit. She had no confidence that she could get inside the garage ahead of Ripper's speed.

We are wolf.

Charlotte conceded, whispering, *Yes, you are wolf*, with hand over heart, at the same time side-stepping away. She placed each foot firmly on the grass, her pulse throbbing, while the pack of black wolves stood by, anxious for Ripper to signal attack.

Despite their surveillance, she kept moving. At one point she stopped, Ripper acting as an obstacle by his hulking presence, his dingy fur clumped and matted at the chest, his face vicious, ready to strike despite a weakened, melancholy stance.

The troop of crows swooped over her head. Their black wings descended like fast-flying capes. More side-stepping. She reached the garage door, leaping inside and slamming the door behind her. One crow slapped the glass window, making a loud crack—a warning swipe.

No sigh of relief was deep enough.

On the garage floor, Sky Wolf sat against Marc's body, her fur a white blanket around him, one paw resting on his chest. She made whimpers, nestling her nose at his face, tenderly licking his chin and cheeks. This secret kiss was more precious than Charlotte had ever witnessed. *Of course Sky Wolf returns to Marc. This wolf would follow him across the universe.*

"Marc." She knelt, thinking she'd better call an ambulance, but then he opened his eyes. "Drink this." She lifted his head. Sky Wolf kept licking his neck.

Marc gulped down half the bottle. With a wobble, he sat up. "Hey girl." He patted Sky Wolf.

"You look better already. We need to get out of here. Ripper pack is in the grove. Get in the van with Sky Wolf. I'll drive."

The army of blackbirds zoomed by the garage windows. "Battle crows," he announced.

"They're allies with Ripper pack now. We need to go. Can you stand?"

He managed and within minutes, Marc and Sky Wolf huddled in the back of the van. Charlotte sped out of the driveway, leaving wolves and battle crows to be free tenants of land and sky.

"You feeling better?" she asked, seeing the sky clear into a safe blue behind her.

Sky Wolf sprawled halfway on his lap, Marc filling up on bread and water. "I could use a dab of butter."

"Ha!" She wanted to throw herself at him with kisses. "I do love you, Marc Sexton. Tell me something, why did you go out at dawn?"

"I saw Sky Wolf in the woods. And there's no need to speed. Slow it down, please, before Sky Wolf gets crazy. Open the windows. She needs more air."

After opening every window, wind whipping in, she took a second to calm herself. Charlotte steadied the gas pedal. "What exactly are the wolves doing, Marc, surrounding us like that?"

"Claiming territory. The alpha wolf's first task to the pack is to invoke aid to their cause. Ripper's made a call to action. Battle crows joined up. Together, they will isolate the prey before they ambush."

"And so must you, Marc."

As soon as they reached Draakensky, Marc walked Sky Wolf to the shed and, once inside, sat with her a few minutes so she could connect his smell to the new place. Within seconds, she darted out the door, an arrow sprung from the bow. She surged past the sugar maples with a joyful howl that went on for a full minute, echoing among the trees.

"That's quite a love song," Charlotte said, keeping an eye out for any flying crows, at the same time scanning the woodland for Ripper pack. Was that a rabbit scampering beyond the rock wall? A hare?

As they made their way to the windmill, Marc still unsteady on his feet, she asked, "How do you kill shadow wolves?"

"You can't."

He limped to the garden. They sat on the white bench beneath the dogwood tree. Camaroon perched on the windmill roof, his body reflecting the sun. "There he is," Marc said, "Merlin's companion. I wish I had his owl wings."

"Can you annihilate shadow wolves?"

"If that were possible, it would have been done."

"What war magick are you creating to stop them?"

"I don't have a lot of time to fool with here. I have to do this today."

"What do you want me to do?"

"What you do best, Charlotte."

"What's that?"

"Manifest the dead."

Chapter Forty-One

Be My Anchor

Inside the windmill, Charlotte cooked breakfast while Marc rested on the sofa, catching up with phone messages. She carried in a tray with steak, toast, eggs, and a pitcher of orange juice.

"Of course he denies everything," he murmured, tapping the text.

"Who denies everything?"

"Rackman. Jimmy texted me. Luther's boasting a pack of denials and excuses. They'll keep a patrol on him and update me later." He sat up, horribly pale now.

"Luther denies firing at Sky Wolf? But you saw him, didn't you?"

"I didn't see him fire. I can't file a charge as an eyewitness, but the shots came from the direction of his property, without a doubt."

"Jimmy will handle it." She sat down on the ottoman as he ate. "What did you mean, *manifest the dead*? You're only saying that because my sketch manifested the thirty-nine owls into your ogham tree grove in March after they died from Heida's spells. That doesn't mean I can—"

"And your premonition of Camaroon flying onto my arm before it happened. And rooks on fire. And Jilly," he said firmly.

"Rooks on fire was a mistake. A terrible, stupid mistake. I was dabbling where I shouldn't have."

"No mistake," he said through a mouthful of steak. "None of it was a mistake. Not even the witch-hares. With magick, all things are interconnected."

"Marc, I did not consciously intend any of those events or any of those manifestations."

"Exactly. At some level, you are receiving knowledge. You've got a mirror inside your subconscious mind, and when you put pen to paper, you see it and create a deeper reality in our world. Can you imagine the power of your magick if you put conscious intention behind it?" He crunched the toast. "I needed this breakfast. Thank you."

"My pleasure." She rose.

He grabbed her hand. "Where are you going?"

"I need a shower." She brushed off her nightgown. "I've got wolf hair all over me."

"Me too. Wolf hair becomes us." He gulped down the orange juice. "Don't go."

Charlotte sat: a bit of a standoff, him eating, her watching him, the windmill sails spinning at the windows. Counterclockwise. "Southeast wind today. Moving pretty darn fast too. It's shocking how the wind speaks. Since I've been living on Draakensky, I've learned the difference between listening to the wind and hearing it."

"You're right. Southeast wind is speaking, telling us, right now is the time to act."

"You're not fit to act on anything right now."

"My physical strength may be diminishing, but not my will. I know you're frightened. So am I."

She shifted her head away for a second.

"Charlotte, you have a double power. And I need it. Charlotte, please."

She snitched a slice of steak off his plate and popped it into her mouth, chewing slowly. "What is it you want me to do?"

"My only chance of success over Ripper pack is to go beyond my elemental magick. I need an anchor and a threshold guardian. Be my anchor, Charlotte."

"How do I do that?"

"First, I need you to establish the structure. The same as when you sketched Rilke's poems into images in our world. I want you to sketch Yeats's poem into a visual here on Draakensky."

She shook her head. "That poem portends death. It's too dangerous."

"Maybe. Maybe not."

"There is no *maybe not*. Yeats wrote from his entanglements in the shadow world, lured by all its mystery. '*Horses of Disaster. Vanity of endless desire.*' The apocalyptic symbolism carries hopeless death in that poem. You said yourself it has impending doom."

"Isn't that where I am right now?"

"Marc," she begged, "please." Everything told her that the death in that poem possessed a hidden realm. "There's magickal power in Yeats's words. It's way too ominous for me to go poking around into his narratives, recreating his words into images on paper. Look at what happened to Elysium Fields! That portrait caused serious destruction. Sir Duncan will never be the same. No, Marc, I'm not going to do it."

"I'm losing my strength here by the hour. That collapse in the garage today—"

" '*South pouring down fire,*' " she shouted. " '*Eyes glimmering white.*' Do you honestly want me to bring the meaning of that image, that pathway, here into our lives?"

"Da is buried beneath those words, written in stone. Da was on a trance journey when he died. Yeats's poem creates a trance, does it not?"

"A trance that might be deadly for you."

"Twenty years ago, I laid that horse-wand on Da's chest and folded his hands around it. I scattered soil over his body. I did that! I read Yeats's words aloud and shed tears. Twenty years of no contact with him from the Otherworld. Because he's not in the Otherworld. There's been no twilight of rest for Da."

Twilight of rest. Marc was quoting from the poem: *Drowning love's lonely hour in deep twilight of rest.* She paced the room, wringing her hands, each step hard on the floor. Could she deny Marc this? Would he lose all his strength, lose his magick to Ripper pack, and follow Da's lost destiny, whatever that was?

"Charlotte, didn't you once tell me there are realms in literature and art?"

She halted. "Did I?"

"Yes. Wasn't Yeats a poet who wrote from an alternate realm?"

She had spoken of the artistic and creative realms, of Rilke who had explored creative realms. Yeats knew about Otherworld realms. A sudden fear gripped her.

"Charlotte?"

"You'll have to spell it out for me. What are you saying?"

"Yesterday at the gravesite, something opened for me. I didn't know until this morning. In the darkness before the sun rose, Yeats's lines began running through my head. Like a recording."

"Which lines?"

"All of them. I could almost hear Da's voice announcing each word. Or maybe it was my voice; I can't be sure. But, if there *is* a magickal realm within art, within Yeats's poem, then maybe . . ."

Clenching her hands together, she stood at the far window. Sky Wolf howled somewhere in the distance. Camaroon perched on a tree branch in the garden, holding his guard, hooting a cracking rhythm. The speeding southeast wind made every tree bend. And the river waves crashed over the falls in rhythmic chants—*Draakensky, Draakensky, Draakensky*—as if she were inhaling all of it into motion.

She turned to him. "You want me to sketch Yeats's poem . . . make it a visible reality. Here, on Draakensky. In fact, you are telling me to manifest Matthew Sexton."

"If there ever was a saving grace, you are it." He rose from the sofa and embraced her. She lifted her face to him, a staggering terror seizing her.

"Charlotte, there is only one way to go here. I need you to summon Da's Finnwolf."

Chapter Forty-Two

Wrapped in Yielding Air

The afternoon passed with Marc slipping into a much-needed sleep on the sofa. Charlotte lit a candle on the coffee table, the flame licking shadows over his bleached jeans, his blonde hair wet from the shower. An arm hung limp, palm open. With the gun-metal gray pullover, he seemed a gallant silvered knight offering a hand to her.

Charlotte climbed the spiral steps to her tower above the thrashing river and crag. A light rain tapped the studio windows.

Ready with pencil to paper, she hesitated, recalling Sister James's picture of Yeats's gravestone, inscribed with *Cast a cold eye, on life, on death. Horseman, pass by!* She would be entering the words of a dead poet, going down into the dungeons of Yeats's mind, his dreams, prophecy, and his occult kingdom.

" *'He Bids His Beloved Be At Peace.'* " Always begin with the title. She entered.

In space, in time, free images moving, old images quietly charging, she drew lines of yellow dusky winds for background.

" *'I hear the Shadowy Horses.'* "

With heavy shading, she constructed the north to unfold night for contrast.

Clinging lute-strings insisted on hovering at the eastern border, so she flicked them in. From the west, she blocked wide borders of ivory, taupe, and white as each color claimed the passing light.

Old sad air dominated the center point with lots of contour hatching. Dark waves of hair appeared—long, wind-caught, flying high from every slash of her pencil. Gales came galloping on the foreground, becoming stippling fast strokes.

Charlotte sat back. Something breathed on the page. The exhale grew hot on her hand. Ears electric hot, a fever burned inside her head.

"Matthew, please, are you here? Where are you?" Her hand cramped with tension, the pencil overheating between her fingers.

In space, in time, at the south she slashed hot yellow that poured down over a distant mountain. She cross-hatched crimson fire for secret eyes, which appeared to her utter surprise.

A tumult of black roses began falling from the sky, loose blossoms, which she shaded purple. Coming off the far mountain, four stallions, in reddish hues, descended with flaring nostrils and tails so wild, they flew off the page. *Shadowy Horses.*

Riding the steeds in an accursed darkness of charcoal smudges, four figures in black dresses buttoned up to the neck arrived on the page. Their hair streamed out of black hooded capes, trimmed in jewels. Charlotte saw bare feet dangling against the horses' sides—hairy toes spread out as she sketched them into ugly black paws.

She nearly cried out, her hand unable to stop sweeping her pencil in curves and shapes across the paper, rendering four husky women on four blistering-red stallions.

"Ohhhhhhhh." A strange voice floated from the page. "Sisters, ohhhh my sisters, we have won!"

Charlotte lurched. *Sisters! Four sisters. Four shapeshifting witch-hare sisters*. Reeling back with a wail, she toppled, her chair flipping to the floor, tossing her sideways.

"Marc! Marc!" She scrambled up, breathless and panicked, feet stumbling down the spiral staircase. Each stair felt a mile long until she reached the living room. "Marc, it's not Da inside the poem's realm! Marc!"

The sofa abandoned, the candle snuffed out, a pervasive silence chilled the room. Bedroom, bath, and kitchen were vacant.

Fearful, she opened the windmill front door. Rain swayed across Draakensky in a cruel sting. In the garden lay Marc's jeans and gun-metal gray pullover trashed beneath the white dogwood tree. A single wolf howl echoed, dissolving instantly.

Interlude IV
Daughter on Draakensky

The daughter is running my green wet hills. She wears a white sweater, long at her ankles, against the late-day coolness, knitted hood up, dragging the hem behind like a bridal gown's train. Above the riot of crows chattering, I hear her heart knocking.

Rain is subsiding now. A sky hand is whisking it away. Ripper pack is scattered across Draakensky with good cause. Steamy pockets are lifting through the leaves. I see smoke. Little fires are burning.

The daughter travels the paths with voice-cracking calls for her beloved. She has discovered the secret of the witch-hares.

She crosses the footbridge over the river to follow Yew Crag trails.

Patience, little heart. Keep on the path.

She listens carefully to my wind, urging her forward.

Follow the trapped mist to the gorge. Do not divert.

Her footsteps turn in that direction. She stumbles on the dark ruts and hollows underfoot.

Cut to the north at the junipers. You only have a chink of time.

She is running now. Her stride pounds a determined rhythm. My oaks and elms, even the maples, are proudly bowing to offer clearance.

You will find a water meadow, misty and frail as death. Hurry.

She has a fair chance of making it with the wind at her back. My wind, smart and steady, is creating a warm touch as she circles across rocky terrain. I hear a melody in the tufted gusts sweeping the daughter onward. Well, well, if it isn't our Lady of the Wind. Welcome!

Hurry, my dear daughter. Jaws are snapping on Yew Crag. And I fear, fires that bite.

Chapter Forty-Three

The Siege

Baseball bat in hand, Charlotte studied the weak sunlight breaking across the sky. A pattern spread out like a leopard's skin, goldish with obscure spots of blackened clouds. The image stitched itself to the air in a canopy.

"Marc!" she called out, trotting as the swish of her sweater's hem gathered wet leaves off the ground. Wind stirred them up into circles. *Lady of the Wind. Are you here to be Marc's threshold guardian?*

The footpaths became a chaos of ferns, bracken, and smashed weeds. Fear of losing her way slowed her down. Outcroppings and ledges arrived without warning. She tripped over tree roots, practically anaconda in size. Venturing deeper into Yew Crag, she took notice of odd tree shapes and boulders as markings on her self-made trail.

This deep into the crag, the woods thinned. Barren trees loomed. Withered branches hooked down. Trunks stood mangled with decay. Their heady brows hung completely bald of leaves, silent and forsaken, not a single birdsong in the air. Something had ripped a huge bite into this crag and sucked out all the green. What a jagged forest of gray ghosts. She half expected a moldering stone castle of broken battlements cloaked in vapors to appear on a far summit—Castle Dracula haunting the sky.

Marc, where are you?

From behind, a sharp crackling halted her steps. Jaa had said there were bears on Yew Crag, and bobcats too. She tightened her fist on the baseball bat.

Moving ahead again, she took the short bend uphill toward a water meadow and past pools of pondweeds. A coin of mist materialized in the distance. The moisture warmed her cheeks but stung her eyes. Clearing her vision, she spied the horseshoe ravine that Jaa had mentioned. *If you hike to the horseshoe ravine, turn back immediately, for you have entered the crag at its most dangerous backside.*

The semicircle of land was a perfect omega figure in the middle of the woods. The U-shape, upside down from Charlotte's position, sported boulders on each end like footings, opening to the south. Both curving sides—east and west—held rock sheers, slabs, and broken ledges forming a dark gulch.

At the center of the horseshoe ravine, a giant platform sat. A floating island of sorts. The platform sprouted half-dead greenery, whitened trees, scrubby bracken, and shriveled, grayed moss on the rock formations. A cavernous, deadly site.

All here had been reduced to an aristocracy of rock, vast stony clusters, stabbing cliffs, and monstrous blackened boulders. High bulwarks and dungeon clefts made the mind stagger on the brink.

Charlotte moved carefully toward the overhanging cliff at point south, the western daylight dulling the air. In the distance, smoke swam over the crag as a tumult of hoofs broke through the trees.

Black Wolf Realm?

So strong was the pounding, the earth shook her legs, causing her to sway off balance. Nearly tumbling forward, she snapped back, both hands flying up, grasping the air. The baseball bat flew, whirled over the cliff's edge, and was sucked down by the frightfully dark gulch. Not a second to even scream, she lifted her head to see a pack of horses plunge into the crag.

Four steeds with burnt reddish hides, heads oversized and covered in red-hot angry masks, sped like beasts out of hell. The most unlovely monsters Charlotte had ever seen. Riding them bareback were four fearsome women, their hard faces full of woe and gall, stampeding straight at Charlotte. Skirts ablaze with fireflies, hair flaring out lusty and thick, they breathed salty, bitter fumes into the air.

Charlotte knew them immediately. No longer disguised as witch-hares, they revealed themselves. The O'Leary sisters of Shehy Mountain.

Rosaleen. Dervla. Hester. Una.

The sisters circled the ravine, sweeping up dust, making rapid-fire loops into a magickal spinning circle. A wave of dizziness pressed down on her; Charlotte fought it off by digging in her heels and tightening her belly for clean breaths.

A woman suddenly appeared only six feet away. Not scrawny or parched with age, she displayed an odd beauty, her skin rosy, lips heart-shaped, auburn hair kinked into wide, highly-polished chains down her back. Her brass-buttoned dress, the color of burnt rust, hung down to her bare feet. The left eye drooped with a heavy lid.

Rosaleen, the eldest half-blind sister. Only now did Charlotte realize one of the four horses had no rider, galloping in formation with the others.

"Are you searching for *him*? The thirteenth Finnwolf?" Rosaleen spoke, her voice weighted in a thick Irish brogue. With her riding stick, she pointed to the horseshoe ravine plateau.

The center platform was covered in shaggy mounds, a mess of bramble and thickets and fallen timbers with dead branches poking up. A blackish hump blurred at the forefront. Furry. Leggy. A tail streamed out. *Black wolf.*

"Marc!" Charlotte doubled over in an agonizing scream. She clutched her hands to her chest at the horror of his wolf body like a felled tree in the middle of the ravine. Darting forward, she stopped abruptly.

The southern opening of the horseshoe was far too steep for her to descend, the darkened gulch far too wide to leap over. Screaming for Marc to respond, she knelt near the edge, hands out in a hopeless effort to reach him.

"There lies the son. The last Finnwolf. Dead in his splendid youth," Rosaleen shouted.

"He's not dead!" Charlotte swerved up, her feet unsteady on the rocky soil.

"You're hoping he's alive? Hope is for fools." She smacked her lips.

The three other sisters rode the ravine, roiling their Gaelic chants. At the lead, the first one swiped the air yellow from her torch as the horse rounded a bend. Her head covered in a bonnet of black roses, lips crimson red, arms raised, she yelled, "I am Dervla the Fireblade."

The second witch drove her steed hard, hands gripping fire wheels, big as tambourines with burning spikes that she spun in a hood around her. "Harken to me, Hester, carrier of death wheels."

Charlotte veered back as the third sister galloped past her.

"Unnnaaaaa," she screeched with a snap of her fire claws, leaving a trail of orange to streak the ground.

Witch-hares . . . and fire witches.

They circled the ravine, gleeful in their equine speed, casting their chants; Charlotte's stomach quaked beneath their voices.

"They are the power of three," Rosaleen boasted. "As I will it, so it must be. We have knocked the Sexton clan to their knees." Her tongue sparked thin flames. "We have flung the last Finnwolf with a scorched heart."

"I don't believe you," Charlotte shouted back.

Rosaleen instantly formed a fireball in her hands. She directed it to the rocky rim, where it obediently perched on a boulder, barely seven feet away. Burning high, the fireball peeled its layers off, revealing a clear, giant sphere.

Charlotte watched shapes form inside the crystal ball as if she were peering through a glassy periscope.

Draakensky Windmill materialized.

The churning river. Gushing waterfalls.

Monstrous fir trees.

A black wolf raced the paths.

Behind the wolf, Ripper pack wolves sped in tight pursuit.

The chase went on for only seconds when fireballs dropped through the trees, some spaced apart, others like cluster bombs.

The wolves panicked into skids and tumbles, cascading out of control, hurdling rocks, and

scattering into a crisscrossing frenzy in all
directions.
The black wolf on the path skirted trees,
cowered at turns,
dodging flames at every turn, charging
wildly to escape.
He leaped across the bridge to Yew Crag.
He surged over the terrain, stumbling,
tail flying,
fireballs and fire blades falling
left and right.
At the horseshoe ravine, he came to an
abrupt stop, legs primed to leap, half
darting, half starting, confused by the cliffs
and gulches.
His ears rammed forward.
He pounced, searching for a path out.
A fireball shot down. It transformed into a
flaming dagger.
The cruel, hot shaft pierced his chest.
His body twisted and flipped into the air,
slamming him onto the platform in the
middle of the horseshoe ravine. Isolated.
Abandoned. Forsaken.

Charlotte shrieked, her hands fisted to her mouth. She crumpled to the ground, a wounded animal, legs folding, heart stuttering.

Rosaleen leaned in, brownish lips alarmingly close. "There will be no magick for Ripper wolf pack! None, ever! No magick surrendered, seized, or otherwise. It is forbidden by my sisters. Ripper pack belongs to our magick only."

Charlotte struggled to breathe, unable to rise, but kept an eye on the three sisters carving their magickal circles around the ravine, their chants swarming her head.

Rosaleen studied her coldly. "You are Draakensky's little sorceress, aren't you? You should appreciate *our* magickal powers. We appreciate your fine sketch magick." She flipped back her shiny braids. "How we adored your illustration. The black capes are divine. So fashionable. Una especially loved the sparkling jeweled trim. How kind of you to adorn Beltaine hares. We carry vigorous sorcery, never to be underestimated."

"I know who you are, Rosaleen."

"Pleased to hear it. We know all the witches. You, certainly, and even the lunar witch Heida Mead from Draakensky. Heida broke through the seals of Black Wolf Realm to escape. A masterly feat. We brought Heida into the Realm of Duinn with us. We take care of our own. And we will take care of you too. Such a pretty enchantress and so resourceful in your art. How are you at sketching fire bells? Hester has a longing for ringing fire bells."

Charlotte rose to face the witch, planting her feet hard on the soil. "You know nothing about me. Get away!"

With her riding stick, Rosaleen pressed the point into Charlotte's chest. The wooden head had twin ragged points at the top that snagged her sweater. On both sides of the flattened plane, eye sockets, two deep holes in a grooved muzzle with teeth . . . an elongated head.

A carved horse head wand.

"The O'Leary sisters are as powerful as any man's sword. Our bloodline exceeds Sexton magickians. I'll tell you our secret. We struck down the mighty Matthew Sexton."

Charlotte looked her straight in the right eye, cloudy brown, a mosaic of mud.

"The Wolf Lord! The highest Finnwolf. The great mage who thought he could make time disappear. Lofty ambitions, he had. The arrogance! As if any Sexton could wield more powerful magick than the O'Leary sisters. We cheered his failures."

Charlotte veered away from her haughty face.

"We scorched Matthew Sexton's heart on the horizon gateway to the Realm of Duinn. His trance shielded him against Dervla's fire blades but not for long. Hester's fire wheels did the deed when he thought he was safe. Sexton magick reigns no more." She waved the horse-wand in a circle, one eye glowing with her proud admission.

Charlotte seized the horse-wand with both hands. A shock of energy surged into her palms, knocking Rosaleen back.

"Mine. I won that battle. Mine!" Rosaleen darted forward, her swipe nearly whacking Charlotte's face.

The two punched and jabbed, backs arching, arms wrestling, heads butting, faces nearly touching, the stench of witch-smell like burnt salty fish.

Rosaleen struck a ferocious kick, sending Charlotte sprawling to the ground. "You dare to test *our* magick?" She waved the wand at her. "We command Shehy black wolves, *our* kill-spells upon them. Finnwolf power is annihilated. The Sexton Silver Brotherhood, all of them dead."

Finding another surge of energy, Charlotte scrambled up and plowed into Rosaleen with the strength of a bull. The horse-wand stung her flesh, but Charlotte managed to twist and loosen it, at the same time raising her knee in a powerful thrust to the witch's belly.

Rosaleen went down, careening to the cliff's edge, her witch body a twisted roll, plowing to a halt when her nose smashed into the rocky lip.

Charlotte pointed the horse-wand at Rosaleen's head, hoping its power would pin the witch to the ledge. With no knowledge about magickal wands, she held both hands on it tightly, commanding *Be still, be still, be still.*

Rosaleen lifted her head, that greedy rusty mouth in a snarl. "You fail, little sorceress." She struggled to rise, stumbling to the edge as a gale broke over them.

The cool underwind hit Charlotte's face. A gentle slap. This was her Lady of the Wind. The gust lifted her arms to reposition the wand straight across her chest.

The squalls blew hard, extending the wand's power surge. Charlotte recognized the message the Lady of the Wind had brought.

Reach out.

Charlotte immediately made an invocation to summon the water goddess. "Goddess Vivienne, a daughter of Avalon seeks your help urgently," she called, her voice steady, her blistering will on each word. "By the power of the Lady of the Lake, you, Rosaleen O'Leary, shall be still. By the Goddess Vivienne, by the power of the Daughters of Avalon, you shall be still. Upon this rifted rock, Rosaleen, *you shall be still.*"

The fire witch gripped the rim of the gulch, disabled inside the mantric chant that Charlotte continued to intone: "You shall be still, you shall be still, you shall be still . . ."

At the far side of the horseshoe, Dervla, Hester, and Una drove their steeds, spewing fire from their weapons that licked the air. Their faces raged as the horses snorted and tossed their manes, speeding toward Charlotte. Dervla held her fire blade highest. Hester rotated her fire wheels out like cannons. Una extended her burning claws in gigantic pitchforks. Their brute power would trample her in seconds. Stepping back, fighting off the smoke clogging her throat and heat singeing her cheeks, she turned, searching for a path, knowing she'd fail to outrun the steeds.

From the crag, ear-splitting howls broke across Draakensky. A massive wave of black, fangs, and tails blasted in like raiders. Ripper and his fourteen black wolves ambushed the terrain, jaws clacking.

Above, a hundred battle crows swooped down. A fleet of attack aircraft. Their wings blackened the sky, carrion fowl sending boisterous *caw-caws* thundering.

Shrieking, the three sisters summoned their magick, shooting their orange flames into the sky to burn the crows. More battle crows advanced from the north, diving at the steeds. The four horses reared up, front legs rotating madly, heads lurching; they staggered and bucked in the chaos.

Spires of old trees smashed to the ground from the roar. The gulch vibrated—even the boulders along the cliffs quaked in their place. On the platform with the very earth giving way, Marc's wolf body tumbled into a shivering crevasse.

Charlotte cried out, hoping he would somehow survive.

The wolves raced toward the witches, an army of land warriors. Charlotte huddled at the center's south between the two opposing forces: fire witches on their bucking horses at the east, fifteen wolves in a battalion of snapping jaws at the west.

Their standoff made a strong battle line beneath blood-orange smoke and fiery shafts. Charlotte would be crushed any second if the two charged each other. With nowhere to flee, she lifted the horse-wand and cried out for herself and Marc.

Out of Draakensky's hills, speeding in like lightning, eyes raging white, Sky Wolf broke through in a triumphant starburst.

Chapter Forty-Four

Wolves Devour the Sun

Trailing streaks of white light, hauling a cape of shooting stars on her back, Sky Wolf skidded in proud and brave to the front of the pack. Ears pointed high, she threw her head back and bellowed out a ferocious howl. *We are wolf.* From her head, she shed stellated shapes that rose to the sky. Battle crows gathered into a tight regiment over the ravine, their caws answering Sky Wolf with noisy turbulence.

With Rosaleen still dazed on the cliff's edge, and the three sisters' magick interrupted, the horses vaulted back from the battle crows. Dervla and Hester fought to rein in their stallions. Una, shrinking with terror, struggled with her bucking steed, completely out of control.

Charlotte withdrew, horse-wand in hand, maintaining its position at her chest.

Dervla charged up to wield her fire blade. Her horse speeding now, the witch shot the burning blade in a javelin throw, directing the fire at the wolf pack some fifty yards away. A torpedo of yellow-ocher flames arched up that would surely come down to explode the pack of wolves.

Caaaww! Caaaww! Caaaww! Battle crows dove on the fire blade.

With ear-splitting shrills, the crows imploded it with a wicked energy force. A thousand shards flashed. In seconds they were snuffed out. Charlotte had never seen such magnificent avian magick.

Ripper swung up on his hind legs in a savage fury at the witches. His ferocious howls reached a velocity that made Charlotte's eyes shake. What unbridled rage. His pack joined in, every one of their notes creating a blaring cacophony at the witch-horses.

Dervla's horse spun in a frenzy and collapsed, a calamity of spiraling legs and flying mane, hurling the witch into a pit.

From the rear Hester charged, her high-pitched voice wailing as rows of her fire wheels spun up, rolling toward the wolf pack—a flaming array of cogs, spindles, and rims spitting hot crimson.

At the front, Sky Wolf countered by expanding her body into a hulking white icy mass. Her size tripled, discharging a bristling wind from her spine. Thick icy mists spread in a wave, taking out the air.

Charlotte felt her skin glaze over: legs shivering, teeth chattering, fingers and toes going numb in the sudden deep freeze. She knew air was active; air was a kingdom; and Sky Wolf, the ice queen.

Ripper pack inhaled Sky Wolf's frozen weaponry. They drank in her polar windscreen. Every black wolf swelled up, dripping sharp icicles off their hides, releasing ropey ice pellets that spewed from their jaws.

We are wolf.

They sprang in a manic surge, fangs shining and sheathed.

Each wolf exhaled a roar that could have matched any lion's, their bellows shifting into a whizzing, gigantic hailstorm. Even the sky howled ice.

The wolves—the fury, the vengeance, the wrath.

Fearless of the storm, they were the storm.

In one thrust, they blasted their frigid whirlwind upon the witches. Horses toppled, their screeching *neighs* clanging everywhere.

Dervla rose from her pit as ice daggers and pellets split her into heaps that resembled broken limestone statues left in ruin and rubble.

Una's steed clamored on all fours, dumping her on the lip of the ravine where she made a cowardly retreat, scrambling to a rocky cove. Hail stormed down. Sheets of ice descended. The witch sank into a grizzled slab of black snow. Only her smothered fire claws remained exposed in mangled tentacles, giving off a discordant hum.

Charlotte averted her eyes at the monstrous sight.

Fearless, Hester drove her heftiest fire wheels in a frenzied attack at the wolves, reaching them within an arm's length. Sky Wolf's ice nooses captured each wheel and spun them into soot and ash. Hester prepared to fire again when the wolves barreled ice rollers at her witch form. She went down with her fire wheels into a flattened, brittle shard that smoked purple.

Could the wolves' ice weaponry destroy all this wicked power?

Rosaleen was the last of them, still clinging to the crest. In a fury, the wolves leaped on her. Sixty paws stomping, claws tearing, their ice-breaths stabbing her energy force. Her witch form disintegrated into an obscure mess of shadows, a skull-like shape on the cliff's edge. Ripper wolves hacked the remnants until only gray corpse-threads remained.

Never had Charlotte witnessed such vile destruction, a literal mutilation of witch power—the O'Leary sisters ruthlessly torn asunder.

Stars. Wind. Ice. Sky Wolf—the master.

If Charlotte were to draw it on paper, she'd strike heavy, obtuse blots of charcoal gray captured inside black ice monuments, rick-rack fringe outlining spherical globes fading into a threadbare and wrinkled universe.

What kind of thorny soul-scapes are these? the viewer might ask.

In a distant tree dripping with ice, Charlotte caught a figure moving—a broken shadow. The scent of ash hit her. Heida Mead. Heida present on the crag?

Charlotte swung the horse-wand in a wide circle, over and over. "Be gone, Heida, you have no power here." Each rotation spun forward her will. "Return to the Realm of Duinn. Return!"

The vapory figure dissolved, quavering like a crooked finger.

As the air settled, as Sky Wolf shook off her star dust, Charlotte scanned the ravine, spotting the four shadowy horses. Riderless, they fled into the vapor from whence they came—erased from the scene entirely. What would become of the wicked sisters' souls now, after this fall? Would they return to the Realm of Duinn? Or be exiled?

Stretched across the horseshoe ravine, a silhouette emerged, shapely and tall. Charlotte recognized the water goddess, Vivienne, Lady of the Lake. Her graceful figure drifted the sky in a twilight calm.

What passage happens now for these sisters? Charlotte asked.

Vivienne offered both her hands up. *Because the four sisters chose to become sun elements in life, so shall they become in the afterlife. In the sun's setting rays, their souls may enter and burn off the wrath of old. The sisters shall remain outside of the Otherworld, illuminated in their own presence as ghost-fires in the astral realm.*

Ghost-fires. How unfathomable, Charlotte thought, to exist as a flaming entity.

On the horizon, beyond the precipice, a blaze of burnt orange dropped from a quarter sun. It simmered there, boiling. Rosaleen. Dervla. Hester. Una. Their fringes plunged into the bloody crimson slit of the lowering sun.

Chapter Forty-Five

A Scorched Heart

The horizon left a ghostly hue on Yew Crag's horseshoe ravine before the onset of darkness. Marc's wolf body lay nearly invisible on the platform crest.

He can't be dead. A scorched heart. I can't bear it. Charlotte wanted to scream.

Ripper pack huddled together, rubbing each other's heads and licking faces. Sky Wolf pawed the soil and whined a lament. The Ripper, his mangy head down, joined her. Within seconds, all the wolves followed the action, front and back legs spewing up the earth, announcing their authority.

Satisfied with the display of comradeship, Sky Wolf trotted to the south edge of the ravine. Nose to the sky, she released a stunning call. Her notes swept up in a high timbre and sailed through the air. Ripper wolves joined her crescendos as the north wind swept in. What an anthem they performed. Southeasterly gusts unfolded. Westerly air swooped down.

Their chorus of voices shook the winds into a fine, warm mist.

The wolves continued their singing, their voices transforming the mist into wide balls drifting in the air. The hazy globes tumbled.

Charlotte listened to the melodies as the wolves' howls directed the globes to merge into one mass. It twirled then rotated out. A vaporous sphere appeared. Shrinking and then expanding, it reshaped into an astonishing hollow tunnel.

Circulating currents elongated a clear channel—a passageway that floated over the gulch and slid to the center platform of the horseshoe.

What wolf magick was this? Charlotte approached the passageway. "Sky Wolf, may I—?"

Ripper wolves howled guttural calls, forcing her retreat.

The watery tunnel opened wider, and Sky Wolf darted in. Ripper and the pack followed one by one. They hurried across, reaching the platform and gathering around Marc's wolf body, sniffing, braying, their tails down.

Four wolves pressed their bodies together, forming a tight pallet of sorts. Lowering themselves flat to the ground, the other wolves rolled Marc's wolf body onto the backs of the four bearers. Rising carefully, they carried him in a slow procession through the tunnel and back to safe terrain. The pack followed closely; they appeared nearly entwined. Once on the rocky surface, the four paused, heads bowed, legs proudly bracing the burden on their backs.

Sky Wolf and Ripper at the lead, the remaining ten wolves surrounded the pallet, pushing Charlotte back, their authority a barricade of black bodies. She was not a participant. Only a witness to their ritual.

As they moved ahead, she followed at the back, horse-wand in hand, the tunnel dissipating into thin air.

They allowed for no stopping, paws marching in a coordinated pace through the wooded course, over hills, and down the trails to

Draakensky. One black wolf with a white chip on his ear sang throaty, fluid notes. Others joined in making eerie music.

For the first time, Charlotte understood these wolves. The wolf was the pack, the pack was the wolf. For the first time, wolves were singing in harmony on Draakensky. Darkness set softly. Silver shimmered on the river waves.

Once they reached the windmill, rounding to the shed, Charlotte opened the door, and they moved into the wooden enclosure, windows opened, the dirt floor warm. The four bearers moved to a corner and tenderly rolled the body onto a heap of grass clippings that the gardener had stored.

With little room for Charlotte, the sixteen wolves packed the shed wall to wall. Charlotte pressed herself against the doorframe, stretching forward, eyes acting like a camera lens zooming in on Marc's wolf belly as it shuddered with uneven breaths. *Alive. Saved. Will he make it?*

The wolves surrounded him, several hugging his back to warm him. One of them stroked his paw on Marc's paw like a brother holding a dying hand. Other wolves let out little cries.

Ripper sat at Marc's head and sang out, a kind of ballad that caressed Marc's body as his belly rose and fell. His eyes opened slightly.

Ripper tilted his head close to Marc. Their eyes met—sad eyes drooping in Ripper's bony sockets, fearful light in Marc's. Each wolf took a turn to gently lick his bloody wounds on legs, belly, and chest.

Ripper was the last to taste Marc's blood.

At the door, Sky Wolf butted her head against Charlotte's thigh. She resisted the nudge. Sky Wolf prodded again, this time so hard that she had no choice but to move outside the door. When she attempted to move back inside, Sky Wolf growled.

Charlotte pushed in. “Sky Wolf, he needs me. Let me—”

Sky Wolf pushed her again with a force that might have knocked her down.

“What is this now? Let me in!”

She wanted to touch Marc, sit with him, speak to him, even if she had to do it with every wolf breathing down her neck. She forced her foot inside. “Let me in.”

Sky Wolf snapped. And snapped again. Two more wolves lunged, growling.

Charlotte withdrew. The pack owned Marc now; she knew not to challenge them. She remained outside the doorframe, arms folded, huffing loudly.

The three wolves moved closer now, Sky Wolf's jaws in a guttural rasp. She gave another growl, then a final snap, butting her head at the door, shutting Charlotte out with a *thwack*.

How dare they exclude her? How dare they! Charlotte was ready to blow apart. She moved to the shed's window. The pack sang their songs over Marc, Ripper's voice sweetest of all as if he were healing every heart in his pack—love notes between shadow and soul.

With the sun set, time drew down the minutes—or was it hours? Charlotte's legs grew weak from standing watch, her body ready to drop from exhaustion. With no moonlight, all she could see were wolf eyes glowing through the darkness.

She returned to the windmill.

Would Marc be strong enough to shift back? Would he have enough magick to perform the transformation? Would his heart sustain the metamorphosis? Maybe by morning, he would return. He'd come dashing into the windmill, give her a warm hug, kisses all over her face, and say her name in his tender baritone.

"Marc. Marc. Marc. Shift back, please." Charlotte created her own summoning.

Her sketch pad on the dining table lay open, pen and colored pencils aligned.

The first principle of magick is that all things are interconnected.

She lifted the pen and sketched his face, his body, a full portrait of Marc Sexton standing at the door of Draakensky Windmill. Another portrait of him at the bar, leaning on folded arms with a bottle of The Sexton in the foreground. A third image at the ogham tree grove, and even one with Camaroon perched on his arm by the willow tree. Rough drawings at best, but hard reality in black and white. Pen in hand, she dropped off to sleep.

Light at the window awakened Charlotte. Draakensky had awakened too, all garland and green. Outside, Camaroon hooted from the windmill roof. Sails turned clockwise. Northwest wind. Jaa had claimed the north wind was a gateway to the spirit—courage to face challenges. The west, a gateway to the body—harvest and health.

With Draakensky's winds on her side, she made her way past the carport to the shed inside a cubby of trees. As she approached the clearing, the tangy smell of blood filled her nostrils; in the distance, she saw a bloody deer carcass.

Three wolves, ears perked and tails high, bounced playfully with each other. Their fur gleamed thick as black velour in the morning sun. More of Ripper's wolves rested between bushes, their coats svelte, faces calm. Counting them, all fourteen present, she ran to the shed. Even with the windows open, the pungent wolf smell overwhelmed her. All she found were hanging tools, buckets, and dried grass cuttings heaped in the corner.

Panic rising, she turned. Ripper stood outside the doorway, tall, muscular, his head and body covered in sleek, healthy fur, his tail thick with reddish streaks. Eyes no longer in cracked bony sockets, Ripper's vision streamed out of almond-shaped black opals in an unblinking stare on her.

A wolf can take your stare and turn it back on you, so you see yourself. Marc knew that. Now she did.

With quick steps, she walked back to the windmill, scanning for Marc. Ripper followed at her heels, his pack behind—no longer ravaged shadow beasts haunting the land.

As she approached the windmill, from the corner of her eye, a shadow lurked in the garden. She closed her eyes, her breath gone shallow. It hurt too much to look, to breathe, to think what she might see in the garden.

Near the garden's white bench, a black wolf sat, shoulders high, face tilted—healthy, serene, almost luminescent, from paws to furry backside to mesmerizing amber eyes staring out.

Marc's Finnwolf.

Charlotte moved slowly, each step closer, and sat on the bench. All her fears realized, all her desires dashed, with both hands she caressed his head. The wild in him came forward from his breath as it warmed her fingertips. This Finnwolf revealed such beauty, his stealth, fur soft as mink, face glistening with clear light. Something released from his face, straight at her. The deep secrets present within him she would never know.

"What is it in your heart that makes you shine?" she whispered.

Ripper howled, making her jump. He tossed his head in a command to his pack. They gathered around him. Sky Wolf leaped to the front next to Ripper. Unity was their strength now. Ripper and Sky Wolf howled together, synchronizing their calls.

Heeding the summons, Finnwolf joined the pack at the back. He aligned his paws, puffed out his chest, and gave a stout call. She wanted to leap up and snatch him away. Would this be the last howl Charlotte would hear?

"Marc?"

He turned, crinkled his snout, his face shimmering, holding her in a momentary trance.

Ripper howled once more. His pack stampeded toward the river, departing Draakensky, charging northwest, full-blooded earthly wolves, Finnwolf following. They were, Charlotte had to admit, beautiful champions of liberty.

They plunged into the woods before she could blink back the tears.

Left alone between garden and windmill in the spring air, Charlotte might have drowned in the despair. This was no illusion. She knew wolf magick to be absolutely real.

Gripping the edge of the bench, feet hard on the ground, rocking herself, a startling truth came home. Marc's entire life had led up to this moment. His destiny remained bound with the destinies of Da, the Silver Brotherhood, Sky Wolf, and Black Wolf Realm. Charlotte dug the soles of her feet into the soil, the wound of such a destiny burning pure and piercing.

"You gave all your star magick to the pack? All, Marc? Nothing left to save yourself?" She burst out her own howl.

Chapter Forty-Six

Mask of the Red Mouth

Charlotte's footsteps echoed loudly up and down the spiral staircase. She packed the car, the windmill sails wailing unbearably, and departed Draakensky without a look back. She arrived at the green barn exactly at nightfall.

The absolute stillness of the pond drew everything into sharp corners. Windows darkened, no shine. An expanse of green lawn, not a single flower in bloom. The house had no one walking about.

She keyed the front door lock and pushed in. The rooms appeared unusually narrow as if someone had compressed the walls and ceilings.

In her left hand, she carried Da's horse-wand. At the inglenook fireplace, she placed it against the gray and white stone, next to Da's milk cans filled with apple tree branches. "This doesn't belong there, does it, Marc?" The wand deserved to reside in the attic with Da's possessions. She owed Marc's magick that much.

Charlotte climbed the first flight of steps to the bedrooms. No, she would not sleep in Marc's bed without him. After another flight of steps to the attic, she flooded the room with light and placed

Da's horse-wand by the black iron stove. Satisfied, she tossed kindling and a log into the grate. Fire burst forth.

Sitting in Mamó's wicker rocking chair, she found a peaceful moment—the fan-shaped windows, the roof's steep pitch like a church. In the corner, the yellow table with candles and crystals throbbed in the flickering firelight. On the barrel table, her engagement ring rested inside a brandy snifter glass. Marc had stored the ring exactly where she had left it. *Be the magick,* he had said. *Will you be my wife?*

Getting up, she felt herself surge with delight and slipped the sapphire ring on her finger. "I'm here, Marc. Here, among all that you are. I am the magick with you. Do you believe me?"

At the black iron stove, she grabbed the horse-wand and walked straight into the magickian's circle. The Sexton Finnwolf chair towered over her, its gentle wolf faces summoning. What would these three wolves want with her now? Her skin grew prickly at the thought.

Securing the horse-wand into a side groove against the wolf chair, she drew a clean breath and sat down in Da's seat. In the same spot where he had died. She sniffed the room: scents of sage filled her nostrils. An acerbic odor caught her. Deer in the woods?

The crack of a tree branch made her ears perk up. A stag in the tree grove? She recognized a gamy scent.

A sharp clicking sound made her heart skip. Da's Mask of the Red Mouth on the opposite wall.

Rising from the wolf chair, she positioned herself directly in its path and made slow steps forward. "What is so great and powerful about you?"

Charlotte counted forty-two teeth on the mask, all the same size, no wolf fangs. The nose and nostrils protruded above the smeared red, gaudy lips. Eyebrows extended like brown-painted worms to the sides of the head.

Another two steps. Its eyes altered from blue to clear. The blue crystals around the mask's border blurred up. Those bloody jaws shimmied in a ghastly chatter.

Clickety-click, clickety-click, clickety-click.

"Mask of the Red Mouth. Are you here to scare me away? What magick are you protecting?" With both hands, she placed her fingers around the sides. Feeling its rough wood, splinters tacky against her fingertips, she lifted the mask from the wall—something watching her, she was certain.

A cloudy puff smoked at her face. She turned away, placing the mask on the floor. As the puff dissipated, she saw the second mask built into the wall: concave, white, oval, with hollowed out cheeks, nose, chin, mouth, and forehead. Rimmed in silver, large eye slits revealed an inky darkness beyond. The temptation to slip her face into the concave mask drew her head forward.

Keeping her face from touching the silver rims, knowing to engage it might prove risky, she remained a safe distance back, close enough to peer through the two silver eye slits.

Sparkling blips flowed horizontally, left to right. Other blips flowed right to left.

Nearly transfixed by the blips, her hands tingled. Cold sensations pricked her ankles. A sudden force tugged her body backward.

She fought it but failed. Icy hands lifted each ankle and placed it down in footfalls behind her. Toe to heel, the force directed her feet across the floor and into the magickian's circle.

Instantly, Charlotte found herself sitting in Da's wolf chair by no power of her own.

The Mask of the Red Mouth zoomed across the attic floor with a loud clatter. She knew this action was to frighten her. It did. Landing at her feet, the red mask pressed her with its invisible force as if she were tied there by heavy chains.

It possessed such mysteries. “What is your secret? What wolf magick do you know? I want it!”

The red mask rose through the air, its vacant eyes and bloody mouth looming. It landed in her lap. With her arms and legs pinned down, body weighted into the seat, Charlotte squirmed helplessly. Her shoulders braced back; her ribcage tightened with every struggling breath.

Trying to scream failed as her mouth and tongue dried up. Everything went blurry. Feeling a tightness in her chest, she feared she might stop breathing entirely.

Charlotte’s hands grew cold. Fingertips stiffening, she flexed them. Her palms suddenly forced open, an icy drop fell into her right hand. The force squeezed both hands into fists so tight that she nearly cried out.

Something moved around her, a large hulking shape. Her heart beat wildly. An odd beat skipped in—flicking—like the cracking of bones.

Clickety-click, clickety-click, clickety-click.

Unable to shift in her seat, she fought to remain alert as the mask slowly crawled over her belly, slithered up her chest, and pressed her throat.

Her fear erupting, no voice or breath to scream, the Mask of the Red Mouth attached its face to Charlotte’s in a feverish drone.

Interlude V

Draakensky Magick

I see them, sixteen black wolves, plus one white, a stream of glorious warriors trotting north through the forests to where the eagles soar. My trusty wind sends Ripper pack wolves out to the kindness of the earth.

A mountain is not far, with crests and clear ponds. The scent of deer and beaver will provoke a hunt for Ripper pack. Night descends. Stars emerge.

Healthy and strong, the vibrancy of the pack will not cease. At sunrise, they will travel farther north, find their home where they will feast on elk, soak in sunbeams, frolic in the rain, and race with the wind.

These feral creatures, you probably know by now, have written their signatures on our skies. Next time you are out in the cool of the day or a balmy twilight, cast yourself up. See their clever silhouettes float across the blue expanse. Watch them gallop over the moon with tails swaying. Stars are their brightest eyes. Sunshine is their beating hearts. Joy alone permits their wolf magick.

The magick of Draakensky triumphs. Did you doubt it? This

daughter of Avalon, she may never dance with her beloved in his Ireland, but she knows the magickal swan with great wings soaring across the lake. This daughter, she knows the secret mystery—we are all Draakensky.

Chapter Forty-Seven

Champions of Liberty

Sleeping with the wolves, Finnwolf awoke. He quietly rolled up and trotted down the embankment near the stream to drink. If there was a farewell gesture for the Ripper pack, he didn't know it. When they had seen him dying, stranded in the ravine, they carried him home, bathed him in kind touches, howled their healing songs. Each one of their souls had dipped their loyalty into his soul. He owed them his life.

As they had licked his bloodshed on Draakensky, the wolf within called. Finnwolf heightened his will. Not a surrender—a choice to release his Alpha Lupi starlight to flow into their wolf souls, just as it had flowed into his soul on the beach in Australia. Each wolf breathed in his star magick with grateful bows. Ripper, the last to transform, had glowed like a black pearl, eyes full of grace.

Ripper honored Finnwolf to live as a member of his pack. To run and hunt with them, to play and protect, to be bonded into their wolf dreams. *Spirit of wolf never dies.* There was no final howl as long as star magick shined.

When Ripper pack awakened to find him gone, they would

know this Finnwolf had chosen his own song to sing. *I am wolf. Another calls me home. Ripper pack, forever may you be free.*

The life of a lone wolf would be a dangerous one without a pack to protect, without their affection and their community. Would Sky Wolf at least join him on the journey home?

At his side, Sky Wolf brushed against his rump. The two lapped water together. When finished, Finnwolf trotted south toward the pathless woods. He stopped at the edge, turning to Sky Wolf, sending his desire by pawing the earth. *Will you come?*

Sky Wolf joined him without hesitation. Of course she did. She knew their bond was unbreakable. Sky Wolf led the way home through open tracks where they raced around valleys, alongside streams, through pastures for safe travel. At a lake full of cattails, they paused to rest, drinking together, side by side, paws nearly touching.

They crossed the lake. In the deep water, Finnwolf held on to Sky Wolf's tail with his mouth as she guided them home, swimming together as one wolf crossing the divide, paddling their paws the long distance to the shore. When they reached the sandy mound, Sky Wolf nestled her nose in Finnwolf's neck. The affection drew Finnwolf to play. They jaw-wrestled and mouthed each other's muzzles, rolling in the gritty sand, a rowdy farewell to the northern hills. Onward south. The vaulted night sky moved with them southeast, stardust on their noses and tails, the stars cheering them on.

Once they reached Bedford's woods, at the green barn and tree grove, Finnwolf lunged toward the pond. Sweet dew on the grass. Scent of squirrel. Owls overhead hooting their welcome songs. He looked back to Sky Wolf. Where was she*? Don't abandon me now, please.* He gave a short howl.

Trotting into the grove, at the yew tree, he paused, waiting for Sky Wolf to come bounding around the bend. Instead, a figure approached him. Petite. Shapely. A woman in a long robe. Plumed tails, furry and wide, flowed behind her as she walked around the pond. Shining tufts of hair with silvery specks streamed around pointed ears. The wolf queen.

"Our brave Marcus. My little pup. Look at you."

He recognized her tender voice.

"We bear witness to your compassion, this task you have endured, this choice you have made. Your wolf heart has unspeakable beauty. You have made every Finnwolf proud." She fondled his head, rubbing his ears.

He snuggled his nose into her open palms.

"Rest easy. The O'Leary sisters may have risen in darkness to abuse their sun magick, yet now all four sleep within the solar sunset, as was the source of their power, and their choice. A destiny your Lady of the Lake has sanctioned. Vivienne has collapsed Black Wolf Realm. The daughter of Avalon, your Charlotte, has a wise understanding of these mysteries."

Finnwolf eased his body down, paws straight out to her.

"The knowledge of the events at the horseshoe ravine will surface inside you in fragments in due time. Its wisdom will come, I promise. Now, my little pup, be still." Holding up his silver wolf pendant, with her hand cupping his jaw, she looped the chain over his head and positioned it around his neck.

"*Do draíocht.*" Her tone soft and deep.

He felt the warmth of the silver against his black fur.

She placed a lingering kiss on his head. A bolt shot through him. A triple spiral burst into view, calling up a drumming enchantment. His body triggered, her magick flowing.

Front legs swelled and cracked into arms. Hind legs reshaped into calves and thighs. His jaw shrank, teeth sliding, gums shivering. Shoulders and chest elevated to jack up the ribcage at the same time his spine realigned. Finally head and neck rotated upright. The last to shift, black fur shed into the grass as a spontaneous wind turned his wolf hair into tumbleweeds.

Naked, feeling the predawn air cooling his burning skin, he found his faded blue jeans and gray pullover on the grass. His body restored, he slipped them on and limped over the lawn. With each step, he found a new balance. The May spring air provided a soothing tonic. An urge to run seized him. Even with his failing night vision, he ran the pond's perimeter, lap after lap, the overflowing dark sky making him as strong as the stars.

Marc slowed to a trot and paused by the yew tree, scanning the pond and trees for her—the one he knew as Mary; the one he knew as the wolf queen. Searching for her loveliness, wanting the caress of her hand once more, he knew his wolf queen had vanished.

And nowhere could he find Sky Wolf.

Sunrise arrived boldly. At the green barn, he burst through the front door and bounded up the steps to the attic. Would he find Da now? Would he finally hear his voice, after all these years of silence?

Da, Black Wolf Realm is collapsed. Ripper pack is alive and free. They have come home to Earth, to be among the living. Finnwolf is no longer. Da? Please answer!

At the open attic doorway, his anticipation plummeted. Charlotte sat stiffly in Da's wolf chair, her face covered in the Mask of the Red Mouth. Panicking, trying to make sense of what she had done, he snatched the mask and swept her up. He carried her down the attic steps to the deck outside his bedroom and placed her on the lounge chair.

Sun bursting, fresh air blowing, he shook her. "Charlotte, Charlotte! What did you do?" Marc ran his hands over her arms and shoulders. He was practically hyperventilating with fear at what she may have released on herself.

Slowly she stirred. Eyes opened, with the tip of her thumb, she touched his chin, running it across his lips. "Is it really you?"

He went weak with relief. "Yes! Were you expecting someone else?"

"It *is* you." Her face brightened.

He kissed her with all the tenderness he had. "Convinced?"

She swooned just a little. "But, how did you—?"

"Seems I have a wolf queen taking care of me."

"You do? Of course you do. Cousin Mary?"

"She's the only wolf queen I know." He couldn't contain his delight. "Are you okay?"

"I think so. Where is Ripper pack?"

He bit the inside of his cheek and it felt so good to do that. "I withdrew from the pack. They're not my home. I traveled back with Sky Wolf. Mary was waiting for me at the pond." He brushed a lock of hair off her cheek. "I had no magick to shift back. Mary knew." He took the silver wolf pendant off, dangling it from his hand. "Mary triggered my shift back."

"I can hardly believe it." She pressed her head against his. "Put the pendant back on."

"No need. The Finnwolf legacy is fulfilled. Ripper wolves will find their home in the north and live peacefully." He sat back. "Charlotte, why did you open the Mask of the Red Mouth?"

"I thought . . . maybe it possessed some secret magick to bring you back."

"Did you access the second mask?" he asked, a bit afraid of her answer.

"I did."

"Did you engage it?"

She shivered. "I'm not sure. I don't remember."

"Charlotte." He took her left hand and immediately flinched. "You're ice cold."

He warmed her hand with his breath and rubbed it, seeing the sapphire ring on her fourth finger. "Ahh!" He burst. "You found it."

"It's mine. I'm never letting you go."

"Those are the most beautiful words I've heard in days." He did more hand rubbing and breath-warming on her right hand. Those fingers were fisted tightly. While he warmed her, he asked, "What happened in that wolf chair? Why did you put the mask on your face?"

"I didn't."

"Who did?"

"I don't know."

"Charlotte, was something released from the red mask?"

"Maybe. I'm not sure." He kept rubbing her right hand and had to pry open her fingers. "What's this?"

A silver coin lay in the center. He lifted it. A sixpence. "This is Da's coin. 1928."

Had Charlotte accessed Da's magick? Or some variation of his magick? Or Da? "Did Da put this coin in your hand? Did you see him? Did he contact you?"

"I barely remember. It's a blank."

"Was he here with you in the circle?

"Everything is so foggy. I only remember being trapped in the wolf chair. I'm sorry." She buried her face in his chest, hanging on to him.

He pulled her up, face to face. “What did you see when you sat in that wolf chair? When you looked through the mask?”

She struggled to recall. “A wolf. With a red mouth.”

Chapter Forty-Eight

The Unknowable

In the shower, stray wolf hairs washed off Marc's body into the drain. He might have to spend the rest of his life wondering about his father, the Mask of the Red Mouth, and its magick. Would he ever know what labyrinths existed there? Was Da still protecting its magick?

He punched the faucet off, robed up, and stepped out, the sixpence coin on the vanity top. After a shave and dressing, he deposited the coin in his trouser pocket and climbed the attic steps. At least the coin was something. A contact. A presence. He'd have to be content with that for the moment.

Before returning the Mask of the Red Mouth to the wall, he stood before the white oval inner mask. He squinted through the silver-rimmed eye slits. A black abyss. White blips raced back and forth; something implicit there, as he breathed inside the oval mask—unexplored cold depths. A chill slithered down his spine.

Tiny sparks moved left and right. Several jumped ahead, others jumped backward. Slow, then fast. What was this jumble of blips at the center? A chaotic energy field, maybe. A threatening darkness waved toward him in a sudden flood. The sensation of falling into the abyss made him veer back.

Without the foundational knowledge, without Da's knowledge, Marc would surely be lost in such a dimensional realm. He hooked the Mask of the Red Mouth back over the white concave mask. Whatever existed there remained a mystery—the many unknowable chambers in his father's life. The damned fucking unknowable! Da's secret mysteries were like being caught in an unceasing spinning trance. And always, always the seeker swallowed whole in its silent lure.

Let it be. He headed downstairs.

In the kitchen, Charlotte sipped a cup of strong Irish breakfast tea. The tree grove boasted lush green in the morning sun as she listened to the wind breathe across the lawn in smooth inhales and exhales. She recalled the mask's clicking, repeating inside her head. Not the actual sounds, but she felt its presence, a veiled, breathy voice over her face. *You've crossed the divide, Charlotte Knight.*

She *had* crossed over. She had tempted fear by stepping into the forbidden magick of the Mask of the Red Mouth. And it had placed Da's silver coin in her hand. Maybe in some Otherworldly way, the magick there ignited a force in Marc's return. If there ever was a daring miracle, this was hers.

Marc came strutting in, his shocking blues full of luster. He had dressed in a white knit pullover and black jeans, which gave her that feeling of solid reality. What was more grounding than black and white?

"Hey there, my lovely, I have an idea. What are you doing next week?" He took her free hand inside his and held her waist, swaying her into an easy dance.

She matched his rhythm perfectly. "Me? I'm sketching studies of Hekate for Jung. Why?"

"I have an invitation, m'lady. Let's fly away. You and me. To Verona."

She laughed. "Verona, Italy?"

"What a kick to hear you laugh again. That's the one."

"What, like Romeo and Juliet? They had rather pathetic endings."

"I know a church there. Sixteenth century. The Sanctuary of Madonna della Corona, near Lake Garda. The church clings to a cliff as if hiding on Mount Baldo. Wisteria everywhere. Marble and statuary. I have an old college buddy there."

"Oh yeah? Who is that?"

"Father Giuseppe Mancino." He pulled her hand into his chest, holding it there like a treasure. "May I kidnap you to Verona and marry you?"

"Ohhhh, that *is* tempting."

He spun her around.

Just then, the pond water rippled under a sudden gust. A white swan stretched flamboyant wings and let out a trumpet call. She was the image of a glass flute filled with white roses in absolute bloom. Rilke's poem in *Les Roses* came through, the words unfolding, *to breathe what drifts about their blooming spirits*. They could both bloom now and invite the future to enter.

Marc swayed her in his arms. She answered with tiny kisses on his chin, a delicate little smack at his sexy cleft.

"Is that a yes? I can kidnap you to Verona?"

She sealed it with a deep kiss.

From somewhere beyond, the veiled voice of the Mask of the Red Mouth broke through. *Clickety-click, clickety-click, clickety-click.*

Epilogue

The Calling Forth of Power

On Sunday afternoon, June 26th, Marc opened the bar at the usual time, three PM. Alice Eve had delivered vases of pink Chinese peonies for the dining room tables; the sun streamed through the potted palms in the bar front windows. He loved the Sunday bar shift from three to nine. Sundays didn't have the usual weekly clamor and clatter. Instead, quiet voices pervaded as if people had come from church and carried the solemnity with them.

Man, it felt good to be back in the U.S. Verona's serene beauty still lingered—the stone-carved birds and Renaissance gables of painted flowers. Tall, leafy orchards and rose-lined palazzi at every turn. Charlotte and Marc had created their own love story on Lake Garda.

The first customer walked in, a guy in a short-sleeve V-neck, showing hefty muscles and a swagger of macho as he sat on a barstool. "Afternoon," he said. "I'm the only stranger here?"

"No strangers at The Grackle. Only friends you've not met yet. How are you doing today?"

"Fabulous. Expecting my wife. I'll have an Old Fashioned while I wait."

Wife. Now that's a perfect word. He tapped the bar top. "You got it." He began mixing the whiskey and bitters.

"Cheers," came a voice from the bar's far corner.

Marc swung around. "Sir Duncan." He strolled over. "And cheers to you. How is the Earl of Kent?"

"Delighted to be here. Where is your beloved betrothed today?"

"I don't know about her, but my wife is on her way over."

Eyebrows shooting up, Sir Duncan gave a hoot. "You devil! You kidnapped her to Verona?"

"Charlotte loved every minute. We made our vows on Mount Baldo at the Sanctuary of Madonna della Corona. The bride wore emerald-green chiffon, apple blossoms, and *Giulietta* glass slippers from Prada in Milan. I think I'm saying that name right."

Sir Duncan burst, "How perfect for the City of Love and Poetry."

"And the big finish: we honeymooned on the Amalfi coast. Sunset sails every night. Moonlit walks in gardens that would put paradise to shame. The Italian cuisine, pasta, seafood, the wine, a knockout. We flew back a few days ago."

"You look like a man still on his honeymoon. Congratulations, chap! Will there be a wedding reception?" he razzed.

"A small one. And yes, you're invited. By the way"—Marc almost didn't want to ask, but did anyway—"how is Elysium Fields?"

Sir Duncan grew serious. "This is why I'm here today. Charlotte needs to hear this. I'll wait for the bride."

"You drinking Irish today?"

"Whiskey wisdom. Is there any other way to drink in this place?"

"No there is not." Marc grabbed The Sexton.

Within the half hour, Charlotte and Alice appeared at the front door.

He scooted around the bar, gave a wink to Alice, and a serious kiss to his wife. He adored the way she still wore her bride's glow in a white summer dress, her hair all topaz luster. Or maybe it was leftover moonlight from their Amalfi passions.

"You're looking spiffy today in that bold red tie," Charlotte crooned, straightening the knot.

He loved when she did that. "Just a little fearless passion of an ordinary husband."

"Nothing about you is ordinary. Oh. Look who's here."

Sir Duncan sauntered up to her with a hug and praises on the nuptials. "Marc's been telling me about Italy."

"Absolutely spectacular. We bought our wedding wardrobe in Milan, married in Verona, and swam in the Tyrrhenian Sea at Amalfi. I'm so happy to see you. Are you well?"

"I am. And I have news."

"Sir Duncan." Alice put her hand out. "We meet again. Do you remember me?"

"Of course. Bedford's most esteemed floriculturist. Sit down, Alice."

Marc noticed that a good twenty minutes had gone by before Sir Duncan brought up the subject of Elysium Fields. Tending his line, he caught fragments of their conversation.

"I had planned to burn the portrait," Sir Duncan explained to Alice. "Those lunatic rooks squawking. Cranky old women. My bloody wretched ancestors! I swear several of them had murderous faces and lethal claws ready to devour me."

Alice flushed at such a statement. "Surely you're speaking metaphorically."

"At the risk of setting propriety at naught, I shall decline to answer. The next day I went for a morning walk. I decided I would do the deed that very hour, burn out the malefic ancestral entities and their blasted history. The sky beat down a horrific, bitter wind on me. The ancestors, they knew I was determined to destroy every last memory of them on my land. Oh bloody hell, I didn't care if the Devil spat on Elysium Fields at that point."

Marc moved closer to listen, keeping an eye on his line.

"I threw *A Private Sky* into the bonfire. Oddly, it caught fire on only one side, burned for only a second, and then the bloody wind yanked it out."

"The wind?" Charlotte said.

"And a rancid odor with it. I chased it down and delivered it back to the flames. The damnable gales yanked it out again. Mother Nature. What was she doing making such a demand over me?"

"Was She?" Charlotte tossed an inquisitive quip to Marc.

"Damn straight. That old cow-mother, she sucked out the fire entirely." Sir Duncan turned to Marc. "That's when I realized I had to take your advice, Marc. It struck me. These ancestors objected to the destruction. They desired a proper burial as you wisely suggested."

Charlotte gasped. "Of course, the sepulcher in the corner of the portrait."

"I didn't understand what the sepulcher meant at first. That cracked tombstone you drew puzzled me. Until I realized that precise corner of the portrait had refused to burn. I dug a grave, placed the portrait in, and covered it with soil. What a bonkers dance I did for myself, stomping the living hell out of it with my boots. And at the end of it, I left my footprints in the soil. And that, my dear Charlotte, is a portrait I will commission you to sketch. I have a photo." He lifted his head in a rowdy laugh.

"That's the spirit," Marc chimed in.

"Can you believe the bastards accepted the interment? We cleared up the demolition rubble, felled half the front woods, and dynamite-blasted a partial of land for a meadow. Elysium Fields is now void of the ancestral ghosts, those wicked rooks no more! My private sky is clear."

Marc gave him a salute. Ancestral bloodlines. They possessed the power to converge. *We all carry inheritable guilt within the forever dark.*

Sir Duncan downed the rest of The Sexton. "One must live everything and make one's way home."

"Come have dinner with us, Sir Duncan." Alice stood up. "What are you going to do with the estate now? Build a new castle?"

"I'm thinking of building a library garden."

"Sounds very British." Charlotte slipped her hand into his arm. "Let's eat. I'm starved."

"Dinner with two of the loveliest ladies in Bedford? I shan't refuse. We bid you adieu, Marc." Sir Duncan escorted the ladies on both arms into the dining room.

Over an hour later, the bar line slowed to only one customer, not unusual since most preferred to be outside on the breezy patio. Marc leaned on a stool for a break, sipping coffee, when an impish young man came strolling in.

"Well, well, Joey Tate." Marc shook his hand. "Are you legal yet? Don't think so."

"Still nineteen."

"You're not going to hassle me about writing a story, are you? Luther Rackman's drama has faded out. I've not heard a word from him."

"No sir. I came to say goodbye, Marc. I'm leaving for Falmouth,

Maine. A volunteer position at the Wolves of Maine Sanctuary before I leave for Seattle State."

"That's great news. What's the job?"

"Photography! But also caretaking and studying wolf behavior."

"You'll be brilliant. All good luck be with you. You want a Diet Coke?"

"Mmmm, I think I need to graduate to club soda."

"Good choice."

Marc did the soda, tallied checks, filled a few drink orders for the patio diners, and when he turned around, Joey wore a charming twinkle and pointed to stacks of coins on the bar top.

What a goofy kid. "Keep your money, Joey. The club soda is on the house."

"Oh no, Marc. The coins are for you."

"What, you want to pay me in quarters? And that's far too many."

"They're not quarters." His voice went deep as he scanned the room. He was the only one sitting at the bar now.

Four stacks. Each about ten coins deep. Marc lifted one. Irish sixpence, embossed wolfhound and harp. He surveyed Joey's face. "Forty sixpence coins?"

"Yep. All 1928. Forty-one to be exact. Including the coin in your pocket."

"Interesting trick, knowing that. What do you think you're doing?"

"No trick." Joey's expression held deadpan. "You've been carrying that coin in your pocket every day for the past month."

Marc tilted back on his heels, a flicker of panic cutting in. "Where'd you get these coins, Joey?"

The kid's brown eyes wore a glint. His jaw appeared bigger now. Dimples disappeared from his cheeks. Cheekbones widened, and he lost that kid-face.

Joey hitched his chin up. "Take the coins, Marc."

"I already have forty-one 1928 Irish sixpence."

"I know you do. In an old milk bottle in your attic." Joey gave him a hard stare. Creases appeared at his mouth, and a faint cleft formed in the chin.

"You're not Joey Tate."

Turning left, then right, checking out the place, Joey refocused. "What if I told you, right now, as we speak, on June 26th, the time is fifteen years ago. Joey Tate is four years old, and he's playing in his sandbox with an orange dump truck in his backyard in Katonah?"

Marc held his breath.

"Joey's mom is sitting nearby, drinking an iced coffee on her patio, listening to Neil Young songs. She's a single mom, pretty lady with auburn hair, works as an accountant. She's on her phone chatting with her sister about her ambitions to be a tax auditor."

"What is this?"

"This is the calling forth of power." His voice suddenly carried a smooth bass tone, the inflections melting off his tongue.

The face suddenly reshaped with intrepid features—skin ruddy, a faint stubble of beard, eye-wrinkles accented vivid blues. Hair turned blond and grayish, receding into a neat hairline and pushing a full, straight brow.

The kid is shifting, literally aging before me.

An expanding barrel chest shifted up into square shoulders that a king could flaunt. He raised a beefy hand to his jaw, rubbing the cleft like a wizened mage.

Marc blinked and blinked again. The man sitting on his bar line was the image of Matthew Sexton.

Holding himself together, Marc consciously felt his feet on the floor, braced his hands on the edge of the bar, and searched for a new breath.

"This summer—that is, in your relative time—Joey Tate falls in love with the Maine wolves. In four years' linear time, he'll graduate from Seattle State with high honors. In Canada, he sleeps with timber wolves on an extraordinary photo shoot. Two years linear time later, in winter, he follows the Icelandic white-tailed eagle on assignment for a wildlife journal. He swims with the seals off the coast of Australia. In Ussuri Russia, Joey tracks Mongolian wolves up Ko Mountain for an acclaimed photo expedition for *National Geographic*. At thirty-one-point-six years of age, he safaris to Africa to capture images of leopards scaling trees in Maasai Mara, which wins him the Wildlife Photographer of the Year Award." He paused. "No need to be alarmed, Marc. Your brave young Joey here granted me an entry realm long enough to access his timeline for me to shift."

Marc's mind reeled. Entry realm? Access to human timelines? Knowing the future in the present—only Da could travel beyond space-time and enter realms of time-slips. And there he was, sitting at the bar, larger than life within an arm's length.

"Da? You're here," Marc murmured.

"Shapeshifting has no boundaries. We both know that. Joey Tate is an obliging volunteer, although the boy will remember none of this. I promise to leave him with a context though."

"All these years, nothing. And now you're here?"

"Didn't you know I would blaze a path back to my family? To you especially. To my sweet baby Sheila, the tree adventurer, growing the planet greener by the day. And William, a scholar! A Ph.D. psychologist. That surprised me."

"And your wife? Mom has searched everywhere for you, a sign, a fragment. She's devastated there's been no contact."

His blue eyes went wet, and his lips trembled. "I know, I know. Believe me, I've tried. It's not as easy as you think to break through the veil and become present enough to be recognized. I *have* imaged myself forth to her. My Kelsey's been looking in the wrong places. Tell her love has not fled. Tell her Yeats said it right. *'When you are old and grey . . . and full of sleep . . . of their shadows deep.'* Tell her that."

"What does that mean?"

"That, my boy, is a secret between my wife and me. When you tell her, my Kelsey will know where to find me. I will be there."

"And what about all the times *I've* called you? Did you hear me?"

Da exhaled a pained expression. "Finding my way to answer you became . . . blocked. In the Out of Time, in my wanderings, there are strong under-shadows. Powerful barriers, impossible to penetrate. Especially when a higher power has been protecting you so fiercely. That magick has been fueling Nature's destiny. I had to step back and let it play out."

"Do you see us?"

"I am privileged to observe. Fragments here and there. I see you have a wife. Charlotte. Ahhh, she pleases me greatly. A daughter of Avalon! Our wise and brave Ladies of the Lake. She's a beauty. Gifted more than you know."

"You've seen Charlotte?"

"She's a stouthearted one. Daring to sit in my wolf chair. Daring to tempt the Mask of the Red Mouth." He gave a wink.

Marc slid his hand into his pocket, to the silver coin. "Do you have any idea how much we've missed you?"

"I am aware, harshly aware, of the shock you all endured. I know my death, in this linear time, hit everyone head-on." He dropped his chin, a gesture of defeat that Marc rarely saw in his father. "I made a mistake, Marc. I was behind the evil, instead of in front of it. I never saw the O'Leary sisters' burn coming at me."

"You went after the O'Learys?"

"What choice did I have? I failed to counter the ancestors' Black Wolf Realm curse. It could *not* be penetrated. The only option was to liberate the wolves from the sisters' witchcraft. Death realm energy is not so different from life energy."

"Were they operating from death wheels?"

"They were. I engaged their fire magick outside the Realm of Duinn. My trance didn't hold. My shields failed to protect me. Those four women possessed a vicious and powerful bloodline of magick that I underestimated: high skills in death force manipulation. In the end, though, the fire witches did not win, did they, my boy?"

"They did not."

"Your Mamó, she knew the Sexton star magick would keep you safe. But Mary, she knew you had a place in the Silver Brotherhood. Clever lady snatching your wolf pendant. Mary set you free!" Da's face was beaming. "*You* freed Ripper pack. You gave them liberty. They live and breathe freely on this precious earth by your gift. And our universe just got a whole lot bigger."

"What do you mean, our universe?"

"I cannot begin to tell you the voyages that exist within light speed. The Otherworld has multiple hidden realms to navigate. The Mask of the Red Mouth." He brought his hands together tightly. "For years I explored the abyss there. Observing the movements and patterns. Testing the powers. Pursuing the meaning." He leaned in and whispered. "Marc, wolves are the keepers of time."

"Keepers of earthly time?"

"Of the time-slips."

Marc could hardly believe the words. Da spoke with such immensity, a frightening *otherness* about him that he had never seen. And yet a strange and beautiful power breathed there, completely alive in him.

Da gave a familiar chuckle. "I unlocked the time-slip through the Mask of the Red Mouth." His eyes went blue-diamond hard, electrifying, like eternity gazing out. "The mask connects to a braiding of the time continuum. It rotates into a magickal loop. I discovered that loop."

Fear flicked Marc's belly. He pressed his weight against the rim of the bar to steady himself. They had spoken about time weaves, loops, and continuums. The multiverse, the cyclical and expanding elements of circular magick. Time travel with arrows of time that could trap a person in endless loops of time-fuses, all a fearsome jumble of dangers in Marc's mind.

Da's face flushed. "Past and future time flow in both directions. Forward and backward. Traveling simultaneously. Right now, every *tomorrow* exists in every today. Every *yesterday* exists in every today. And smack in the center of past and future is the glorious present. We live inside all of it!"

"What field of magick are you talking about?"

"That's my boy. Stay with me. Past and future are not separated by time. They flow within eternal time of the present. From my present, Joey is a kid in the sandbox. From yours, he's a nineteen-year-old sitting at your bar. To some other present, he's scaling the trees in Maasai Mara with the leopards. Everything happens in the *now*. A magickal density! Inside that density is every star. Stars!" Da radiated a million-dollar smile.

Almost afraid to think, unsure of the power Da was calling forth, Marc searched for his breath—which seemed to be decreasing by the second—Da softly sipping it in.

"The highest magick, Marc, is halting time." He stretched his arms out, scattering the coins across the bar top. Each coin floated up into forty starbursts, which he blew into an arch at Marc's head.

Instantly the space in the barroom condensed like a ladder clacking in. Air gave way. The room spread into a masking fog as the walls reshaped into rows of concave pillars that closed around them.

Everything stalled. Like a clock shattering.

With nothing solid beneath Marc's feet, a yawning darkness floated up. The sensation of sinking made him reach for Da's hand.

His fleshy palm felt warm and strong as steel. In sync they were, belonging to each other once more. He voyaged into an evaporating space, seeing Da's face, dauntless, as wide as the ocean.

"What do you see, Marc?"

"I see you, Da. Only you."

"We are part of it now. You and me. Together, within a timeless, spaceless empire. Stars are the doorways."

Stars are the doorways, Marc repeated silently.

"Oh my little pup." Da's face stretched wider. "What are we here for if not to transform life? You are everything I hoped for. Your Finnwolf settled the score. Your Finnwolf healed the past, present, the future. Your visit to Australia and drawing down

Lupus star magick is sacred—we are all stronger with the stars. Ripper wolves now have a future into a bright wave."

Da's voice began fading as Marc's lungs expanded, as he tasted his breath again, as sunlight bathed the bar front windows and potted palms, as Joey—no longer Da—sat at the bar, lips moving silently, his right hand on the club soda, blondish-gray hair shifting back to a straight brown, the cleft in his chin fading into a kid-face. Joey mouthed words, silently chattering on.

Marc could hear only Da's distant voice.

"I am in the stars of eternity . . . within its swinging doors. I circle the cosmos. We can exist inside celestial adventures. Draw down the secret universe! You will find me there."

"Da! Stay, please stay."

"We forever have our stars." Da's voice flickered away, inhaled by the glittering tunnel, words ringing in deep notes . . . vanishing . . .

"My wolf still sings for you, my boy!"

Welling up, feeling the floor beneath his feet again, Marc surged back into what he recognized as forward marching time, clock restored. He ran both hands over the bar top—forty coins gone—except for the one inside his trouser pocket. Instead, now forty stars gathered into a tiny sphere. It spun before him, a dangling eternity. What secrets resided there, tempting him to be discovered? He knew all Da had said to be the absolute truth. He knew it by his heart.

Marc scooped up the sphere of stars onto his chest. Holding it there, he felt the stars burst into him with a hot jolt.

Da's magick of the stars. *Clickety-click, clickety-click, clickety-click.*

Joey slugged the club soda. "Man oh man, it's hot in here." He opened his collar and loosened his tie. "So you agree about the stars, right? Dead stars and their light are still a reality we can see. How cool is that? While I'm in Maine at the wolf sanctuary, I'm planning to camp out on Cadillac Mountain and do some serious stargazing. Do you star gaze?"

Marc heard himself answer, "Yes, I do. All the time." His mind sharpened. The colors and sunlight in the bar grew vibrant, burning bright as never before. "My dad taught me the constellations when I was about six years old. I remember thinking the stars were observing me."

"My dad's not around much. What did your dad do? Restaurant entrepreneur, like you?"

"Matthew Sexton? He was a Celtic adventurer. Always on a quest. He still is."

"Hey, has your white wolf been around lately? Man, I'd love to see that sweetheart again," Joey prompted.

Images flooded in. Sky Wolf drinking with him at the cattail lake, their playful jaws wrestling, teasing each other's muzzles like kids having a last roll in the grass. A wolf's farewell.

"I haven't seen Sky Wolf." Marc's heart ached. If only he could see her one more time, *just once more.*

"You named her?"

"That's who she is. Sky Wolf, from the star constellation Lupus. And ever bright."

"Where do you think she is now?" Joey asked, a kid wanting a happy ending to a fairy tale.

"Maybe Sky Wolf has returned to the north. Maybe she's connected to her pack and on the hunt as we speak. Or, maybe that glorious white beauty has found a way to return to her star by her majestic star magick."

"Yeah, I like that. We have the universe with us forever, right?"

"I swear by the stars, this is true."

"Gotta hop, Mr. Marc Sexton. See ya around." Joey pushed off the stool.

Charlotte strolled in behind the bar, her white dress swinging, pressing her body gently into his, her hand slipping around him. "What stimulating bar chat is happening over here? Talking stars, are you?"

Marc scooped his hand into the dip of her waist, savoring his wife with a lavish squeeze. "Talking stars, I am. And thinking of celestial adventures. Breaking out of time. Breathing in the constellations. Soaring into a new magickal realm."

"How delicious." She sparkled at him. Right there, the loveliness of love. She planted a proper kiss on his cheek. "Is this another of your deep secrets?"

"The deepest ever."

She gave a shy laugh. "I married a man with a hundred secrets. And what is this secret mystery? Is it crying out to be discovered?"

By now, he knew to trust his wife, a daughter of Avalon, a brave magickian in her own right, and possibly on her way to becoming a goddess. He dreamed up images of them as modern-day sorcerers, his own Lady of the Lake beneath the oak leaves and moonlight. Imagine the fantastical magickal realms they might embrace.

He took her in his arms. "I have it on good authority, Charlotte, this mystery is in drawing down the secret universe. Let's explore it like Merlin and Vivienne. Shall we search for the cosmic swinging doors and reach for the stars, my lovely?"

Acknowledgments

If I were to name all the people who have lit the flame within me or nurtured me into the blooming of this story, there would be a hundred names. Gratitude begins for my publisher and staff at Crystal Lake Publishing, especially Joe Mynhardt, who sails his ship of authors through the deep literary seas with a steady hand at the helm.

My editors, ever strong in their insightful skills, urged me to grow my perspectives and reminded me of the pillars of storytelling whenever I broke one. From their direction, I learned another level of literary competency and creative distinction. A million thanks to John Robin of Story Perfect Editing Services for the deep dive and the 'Paula tree' on a snowy hill in Canada. To Stephen Black of Black Thoughts Editorial Services and Richard Thomas of Storyville. All three of these talented editors have built new and exciting discoveries for me during *Wolf Magick's* evolution.

My research and fact-checking for *Wolf Magick* drove me through stacks of over forty books, copious reports and magazine publications, and consultations with professionals and librarians. As in *Draakensky, A Supernatural Tale of Magick and Romance*, where Rainer Maria Rilke's poetry gripped me from the start of that storytelling, in *Wolf Magick,* it was W.B. Yeats's poetry and his *Celtic Twilight* (1893) about mythical beings who stirred my passion that led me to explore magickal realms. Yeats says, "Everything exists, everything is true, and the earth is only a little dust under our feet."

My family, ever-present at arm's reach, sustains me with their affection, support, and trust. My husband Ron, whom I pester endlessly to read my stories; he is my most loyal fan. Gina and Todd, my art advisors. Jon-Paul and Emily, my champions. My grandchildren, who love that I'm a storyteller—Charlie, Scarlet, and Alex, and a joy to have in my heart.

And from the far-flung star realms of the afterlife, my parents, Antoinette and Charlie.

Because reading is a creative and powerful act, I shout out a *thank-you* to all my readers who have picked up *Draakensky* and *Wolf Magick* and trusted me with your time and imagination. Authors build their audience one by one, and each one of you means the world to me. Writing is magickal. This story would not have been born without the mystical white wolf, Sky Wolf, who soars the mountains to run freely with her pack—may she continue to sing to the stars evermore.

Books by Paula Cappa

The Dazzling Darkness
Night Sea Journey, A Tale of the Supernatural
Greylock
Sky Wolf, a Novelette
Draakensky

About the Author

Paula Cappa is a multiple award-winning novelist and short story author of supernatural mysteries, Gothic thrillers, and dark fantasy. Her novel *Draakensky, A Supernatural Tale of Magick and Romance* (Crystal Lake Publishing) won the Gold Medal in Gothic at BookFest Book Awards. Other novels are *The Dazzling Darkness, Night Sea Journey,* and *Greylock* (Crispin Books), and the novelette *Sky Wolf* (Wolf Singer Publications). Her short fiction has appeared in literary magazines such as *Coffin Bell Literary Journal, SmokeLong Quarterly, Sirens Call Ezine, ParABnormal Magazine, Dark Gothic Resurrected, Every Day Fiction, Fiction365,* and in anthologies *Journals of Horror: Found Fiction,* and many others. She is a member of the Society for the Study of the American Gothic. Visit her Reading Fiction Blog at her website at https://paulacappa.wordpress.com/.

BookFest Book Awards, 2025, *Draakensky*
Readers' Choice Book Awards, 2024, *Draakensky*
Gold Medal, Global Book Awards, 2023, *The Dazzling Darkness*
Gold Medal, Global Book Awards, 2022, *Greylock*
Silver Medal, Global Book Awards, 2021, *Night Sea Journey*
Best Book Awards Finalist, American Book Fest, 2017, *Greylock*
Eric Hoffer Book Award Winner, 2015, *Night Sea Journey*
Chanticleer Book Award Winner, 2015, *Greylock*
Bronze Medal, Readers' Favorite Book Awards, 2014, *The Dazzling Darkness*
Gothic Readers Book Club Choice Award Winner, 2013, *The Dazzling Darkness*

Readers . . .

Thank you for reading *Wolf Magick*. We hope you enjoyed this novel.

If you have a moment, please review *Wolf Magick* at the store where you bought it.

Help other readers by telling them why you enjoyed this book. No need to write an in-depth discussion. Even a single sentence will be greatly appreciated. Reviews go a long way to helping a book sell, and is great for an author's career. It'll also help us to continue publishing quality books.

Thank you again for taking the time to journey with Crystal Lake Publishing.

You will find links to all our social media platforms on our Linktree
https://linktr.ee/CrystalLakePublishing

Follow us on Amazon:

Our Mission Statement:

Since its founding in August 2012, Crystal Lake has quickly become one of the world's leading publishers of Dark Fiction and Horror books. In 2023, Crystal Lake officially transitioned into an entertainment company, joining several other divisions, genres, and imprints, including Torrid Waters, Crystal Lake Comics, Crystal Lake Games, Crystal Lake Kids, and many more.

While we strive to present only the highest quality fiction and entertainment, we also endeavour to support authors along their writing journey. We offer our time and experience in non-fiction projects, as well as author mentoring and services, at competitive prices.

With several Bram Stoker Award wins and many other wins and nominations (including the HWA's Specialty Press Award), Crystal Lake Publishing puts integrity, honor, and respect at the forefront of our publishing operations.

We strive for each book and outreach program we spearhead to not only entertain and touch or comment on issues that affect our readers, but also to strengthen and support the Dark Fiction field and its authors.

Not only do we find and publish authors we believe are destined for greatness, but we strive to work with men and women who endeavour to be decent human beings who care more for others than themselves, while still being hard working, driven, and passionate artists and storytellers.

Crystal Lake Publishing is and will always be a beacon of what passion and dedication, combined with overwhelming teamwork and respect, can accomplish. We endeavour to know each and every one of our readers, while building personal relationships with our authors, reviewers, bloggers, podcasters, bookstores, and libraries.

We will be as trustworthy, forthright, and transparent as any business can be, while also keeping most of the headaches away from our authors, since it's our job to solve the problems so they can stay in a creative mind. Which of course also means paying our authors.

We do not just publish books, we present to you worlds within your world, doors within your mind, from talented authors who sacrifice so much for a moment of your time.

There are some amazing small presses out there, and through collaboration and open forums we will continue to support other presses in the goal of helping authors and showing the world what quality small presses are capable of accomplishing. No one wins when a small press goes down, so we will always be there to support hardworking, legitimate presses and their authors. We don't see Crystal Lake as the best press out there, but we will always strive to be the best, strive to be the most interactive and grateful, and even blessed press around. No matter what happens over time, we will also take our mission very seriously while appreciating where we are and enjoying the journey.

What do we offer our authors that they can't do for themselves through self-publishing?

We are big supporters of self-publishing (especially hybrid publishing), if done with care, patience, and planning. However, not every author has the time or inclination to do market research, advertise, and set up book launch strategies. Although a lot of authors are successful in doing it all, strong small presses will always be there for the authors who just want to do what they do best: write.

What we offer is experience, industry knowledge, contacts and trust built up over years. And due to our strong brand and trusting fanbase, every Crystal Lake Publishing book comes with weight of respect. In time our fans begin to trust our judgment and will try a new author purely based on our support of said author.

With each launch we strive to fine-tune our approach, learn from our mistakes, and increase our reach. We continue to assure our authors that we're here for them and that we'll carry the weight of the launch and dealing with third parties while they focus on their strengths—be it writing, interviews, blogs, signings, etc.

We also offer several mentoring packages to authors that include knowledge and skills they can use in both traditional and self-publishing endeavours.

We look forward to launching many new careers.

This is what we believe in. What we stand for. This will be our legacy.

**Welcome to Crystal Lake Publishing—
Where Stories Come Alive!**

www.ingramcontent.com/pod-product-compliance
Lightning Source LLC
Chambersburg PA
CBHW051506050726
47594CB00010B/3986

* 9 7 8 1 9 6 8 5 3 2 5 7 4 *